UNFORGIVABLE

By

Lindsay Delagair

ACKNOWLEDGMENTS

Jan Ayola – Editing
Dr. Crystal Herold – Guest Editing
L.E. Johnson – Guest Editing
Pat Mullins – Automotive/Firearm Advice

Prologue

I was running away, but I didn't know where I was headed. It was dark and frightening. Everywhere I turned was another dead end. I wanted to scream his name; I wanted to see his face, but I couldn't go back. I had to keep running. I wanted to turn around, but there was a force taking me away, and like a strong current in deep water, I was being pulled further out. The tears were coursing down my cheeks and I knew my life was over; he was gone and I'd never see him again.

I was holding something in my hands, and as I struggled to see what it was, I knew what I had to do with it. The knife was as dark as my surroundings, but the blade was razor sharp and I felt it bite into my palms as I traced the curve of it. It was over; there was no need to go on. What use is a heart that has lost its reason for beating? I gripped the handle and placed the tip of the blade against my chest.

Then I saw his face like a light in the darkness. His beautiful face was filled with love. I watched him come closer, his face changing, growing dimmer and angrier. He was right in front of me, close enough to reach out and touch me, but he wouldn't.

His hands took the place of mine over the dagger's handle and then he looked at me and asked, "Why did you throw my love away?"

I couldn't answer; I could only cry.

I felt rain pouring down on me as thunder and lightning rolled.

Suddenly, fury exploded across his face as he jammed the blade into me. The pain was unlike anything I'd known. It was like ice on fire as it plunged through my dying heart. I collapsed. The rain washed into a river of blood, and the last word I whispered was his name, "Micah."

Chapter One

I jerked upright in bed, choking back a sob. My chest heaved in pain, and beads of sweat rolled down my back. I had to catch my breath as the dream faded from my mind. I was gasping for air and shaking horribly. It was still storming outside as I watched lightening split the pre-dawn sky every few minutes. I glanced at the clock. It was 3:30 in the morning and the dream had been so vivid that I still felt the burn through my chest.

Mom would be worried when she got up and I wasn't there, but I'd leave her a note before I slipped out to see him. I pulled on my clothes quickly and scribbled down a few sentences and tossed it onto my bed. Grabbing my purse and car keys, I went down to the garage. I hadn't brushed my hair or put on makeup, but there wasn't time. The dream had me so rattled that I simply had to see him and make sure that everything was still right in my world.

It had only been five days since he came back into my life, and I was so obsessed with the idea that something would happen to ruin our happiness that I was now repeating this terrifying nightmare. I had it last night, but I kept it together. Not tonight; I needed to be in his arms, knowing he was still here and that he still loved me.

My Aston Martin purred softly to life. The garage door opened and I backed out carefully, headlights off so as not to disturb my mother and sister. My tires rolled silently down the long drive as rain pelted my car. He was at the Hyatt until we could find a house we wanted to buy. Money wasn't the issue; between the two of us, we could have purchased the White House, but it was more a matter of finding the perfect place to begin our new life.

We set the wedding date for September 15ᵗʰ, and that was fewer than three months away. I wanted it the day he proposed. I was ready to go to the courthouse and make it official right then, but he said he wanted me to have the kind of wedding that young girls dream about; a decorated church, flowers and bridesmaids, a man of God to take us through our vows as opposed to a clerk in the courthouse, a reception and dancing, and, of course, a honeymoon some place special. All I could think about was spending that first night in his arms and knowing there would be no reason to stop once we were pledged to each other forever.

I pulled into the Hyatt's parking garage and ran through the lobby to the elevator, pressing the button for the seventh floor. I didn't want to end up banging on his door at this time of the morning; that was a good way to get shot, so I dialed his cell phone as the elevator began its ascent.

Three rings and the elevator door was opening into the quiet interior hallway,

"Leese?" came the sleepy voice on the other end of the line, "What's the matter? Are you okay?"

"Hey, can you come to your door? I'm right outside. I need to see you." My emotions were rising with just the sound of his voice. I could feel the tears and the fright from my dream returning, making the need to see him urgent. The phone went silent, but within seconds the door to his room opened.

He was wearing only his boxers, standing there looking like a Greek god with his powerful physique. I know my panicked call scared him as he ushered me in and closed and locked the door. I was in his arms, my cheek against his chest and the tears were coming faster.

"Baby," he crooned, "what's wrong? Did something happen?"

"Oh, Micah, I had the most horrible dream and I had to come see you," I said, trying to stop shaking so hard.

"A dream?" he said softly with a hint of mirth to his voice. "Do you want to sit up and talk about it?"

"Can we just lie together in your bed?"

I could hear the smile form on his face in the darkness, his mouth finding mine for a warm, slow kiss and then moving down my neck. "Baby, we're never going to make it to our wedding night if we get in that bed."

3

"Please, Micah. I've got to be with you. We've managed this before—I need to be in your arms."

He scooped me off the floor and proceeded to the bed, never breaking the kisses he was placing on my neck. He was right. I wasn't making it easy for us to save something for the wedding night, but I knew he could be a gentleman, he had proven that even when I wasn't in my right mind, or my clothes.

He laid me down and I rolled away from him onto my side to give him room to slip in behind me. I felt his muscled arm reach around my waist and draw me against his firm body.

He sighed as he placed a final kiss on my neck, "What was the dream about?" he whispered.

My crying had started to subside and I found myself yawning deeply. The only place I could truly relax was in his embrace.

"Did you tell your mom you were coming over here to see me?

I yawned again, "No, I just left a note on my bed."

"You're really tired, aren't you?"

"I can't sleep anymore unless I have you with me—it's like something is missing."

He yawned and then nuzzled into my hair, "I know what you mean. I couldn't sleep either. What about your dream?"

"How about we discuss it when we wake up?" Now that I was here, and secure in his hold, I didn't want to tell him about the dream. I didn't want to tell him that he ended my life with a blade to my heart. We were out from under the curse of his obligation to kill me. The hit was over when Robert was caught. Micah had spent months arranging his exit from the mafia and we were now free to face forever together.

"All right—in the morning. Goodnight, baby—I love you."

I would never hear those three words enough. In that moment, I wanted to roll over and kiss him; kiss him with all the passion that he had awakened inside me not long after I'd met him. But, I knew if we both went over the edge, our wedding night would become now. I wanted to wait to make it right between us and God, but I was starting to wonder if God was truly concerned about a piece of paper between us or the commitment we had already made to each other?

"I love you, Micah." I fell asleep to the sound of his steady breathing and the warmth of his heart beating against my back.

When daylight came, I knew it was the best rest I had since our last night together at the Inlet Motel months ago. This was the place I knew I belonged, right here wrapped in these glorious arms and pressed to his body. My temperature was starting to rise as I recalled what he was wearing when he opened the door at three-something in the morning. I was so upset when I arrived that my mind wasn't particularly consumed with the idea of sex, but right now was a different story.

His breathing was slow and deep, and his hold on me was soft, so I knew he was enjoying peaceful sleep. I pulled away slowly, trying to slip out of the bed undetected. He was a light sleeper, so getting out of his embrace wouldn't be easy. I heard his breathing shorten just as I escaped, his hand narrowly missing me as my feet found the floor.

"Baby," came his melodic voice, "come back to bed so we can talk."

I laughed as I headed into the bathroom. Talking is not what we'd end up doing if I got back in there with him. I used his comb to get the tangles out of my hair and then used his mouthwash to make sure I didn't have morning breath. I studied his toothbrush for a moment. I knew he wouldn't mind, but I decided against it.

I opened the bathroom door to find him leaning against the door frame, still in his boxers and looking even better than when I saw him in the darkness. "You know that should be illegal, right?"

"What?" he stated innocently, eyebrows rising.

"To look that good," I laughed, still watching his muscles as they flexed and rippled.

He made a deep growling sound, not one of anger, but of need as he pulled me into his arms. His heated mouth gently covered my own, begging my lips to part and let him explore. My hands slid around his thick shoulders and onto his back as I returned the passionate kiss. His granite-like body pressed me against the wall as our moral brakes began smoking against the inability to slow down.

"Are you hungry," I whispered in his ear, hoping we'd find a reason to stop what felt so absolutely marvelous to both of us.

"Mmm—yes, baby, I am," he rumbled his reply. His hips thrust against mine in an apparent showing of exactly what he was hungry for.

5

I inhaled involuntarily and deep as he pushed against me. My left hand turned his face to me as I found his lips. My right hand slid lower, past the hard abdominals, moving down the sleek muscles that were just above the rim of his low-rise boxers.

"Leese, if you go any lower, I'm going to rip every piece of clothing off you right here and right now." His words were quick and forceful, telling me he sincerely meant what he was saying. I had to choose to let this happen, or to wait as we had planned. My hand slid around to his hip and then upward to his waist.

The sound of control returned to his breathing.

"I can't be apart from you, Micah—even if it's just a distance of a few miles from my house to the hotel. I can't really sleep unless you're holding me and—"

"I know," he murmured softly, slowly backing off from pressing me against the wall, "after you got here last night and we went to sleep, it felt like the first time I've slept in months. It's like I was finally—"

"Comfortable," I finished for him.

He pulled away so I could see his face. A soft smile played with the corners of his mouth, "Exactly."

"Maybe we should change the date of the wedding?" I whimpered wanting him to come back to pressing me against the wall, the floor, the bed; I didn't care where as long as he didn't take his body back.

He placed his lips on mine, but it was only a brief kiss as he pulled away, "No, we can wait."

I let my hand return to the place that threatened to put him over his ability to control himself, "Are you sure we can wait?" I teased.

He gripped my hand firmly to prevent me from crossing a dangerous line, "Yes, but—"

"I want you to stay at my house," I blurted. "I can't stay away from you—not now."

"Leese, I don't think your mom is—"

"She already asked me if I wanted you to stay at the house," I quickly added.

His brows rose, "She doesn't think we've..."

I shook my head, "No, but she did—she was certain until I told her what a gentleman you'd been with me."

He smiled. "Good. At least you are helping me get a better reputation. I wondered what she must think about me."

"She thinks you're fantastic, but..."

"But what?" His face getting that concerned look.

"I think she—she thinks you haven't been in the mob very long."

"Is that what you told her?"

"No, I haven't discussed your—your former career with her. I don't think she even realizes how much money you have. Not that she cares about stuff like that, but if she knew I think she might start to wonder." I didn't want to finish by saying that she'd begin to wonder how many people he killed to earn all that money. "I mean she doesn't have all the answers, but neither do I."

"Do you *need* all the answers?"

He tried to tell me many times how horrible he was before he met me, but I didn't want to know then, and I certainly didn't want to know now. I'd seen a glimpse of it when he killed Ricky and Jack right before my eyes, and that was frightening enough for one lifetime. "No. If you want to discuss it someday I'll listen, but you won't change the way I feel about you, Micah."

He was getting ready to rebut me, but I quickly added, "Pack your stuff, please. Come home with me. We don't have to sleep together, but I would just like having you in the house. Please," I added once more for emphasis.

He leaned into me and put a final slow kiss on my mouth, "All right, but if your mom even hints that she's uncomfortable with me being there, I'll be back here at the hotel before you can start begging me not to go."

"Deal." I knew she would welcome him into our home. Mom understood me well enough to know that if I decided Micah was the man for me, there was no need to worry about the rest.

He packed and checked out and then followed me back home.

I never expected Mom to be angry when I walked into the house, and I was afraid Micah would turn tail and run, but he was very patient as Mom let off a little steam.

"All I'm saying, honey, is what if something had happened? You took off from here without telling me that you were going. You didn't call Micah until you got to his hotel. What if something happened between here and there? I would have thought you were with Micah, and Micah would have thought you were home. Who knows how long it might have been before we started looking for you."

"You're absolutely right, Nadia," Micah interjected, as if he was suddenly seeing what she was so upset about. "It could have ended in disaster if something had gone wrong."

I rolled my eyes. Now I was getting scolded on both sides. "But—"

That was as far as Mom would let me go. "I'd rather have Micah stay here at our house, Leese, than for you to go traipsing off in the middle of the night to discuss your bad dreams."

I finally smiled, "Yeah, I think that would be best." I turned to look at him as he forced his smile to stay hidden, "Couldn't you just stay here in one of our spare rooms?"

"Only if Nadia doesn't mind me—"

"Of course not, Micah," she cut him off before he could finish the sentence. "We have five extra bedrooms, besides the apartment down by the pool cabana. I know you two are…" A light blush crossed her cheeks, "…are saving things for your wedding night, but as far as I'm concerned—and God as well I'm sure—you've already made the important commitments to each other—but I do understand the waiting thing," she added to make sure it didn't sound like she was giving a blanket blessing to run upstairs and throw ourselves into bed.

I kissed her cheek, "I love you, Mom."

By late afternoon we were seated on the pool deck watching Kimmy splash around with a friend that had come over to play. Mom was in the house calling a caterer to have dinner brought in tonight. I told her Micah and I could handle the cooking (Mom, unfortunately, was a terrible cook), but she said we'd save that for tomorrow night and let someone else do it tonight. She actually said she was considering hiring a live-in chef since everything was over concerning Robert. She was now living without the constant foreboding fear that everyone that came into our home was suspect. She returned to being the happy person she had been before grandpa died.

"So, are you finally going to tell me about this terrible dream," Micah asked as he let his fingers trail down my arm.

I had almost forgotten about it, "It's—it's not really important now."

"You drive through a downpour and end up in my bed in the wee hours of the morning and now you say it isn't important?"

"I don't even like thinking about it; it was so stupid."

"Stupid-stupid or scary-stupid?"

"Scary stupid," I glanced at his face and then went back to watching the girls.

"Well, then I want to hear it," he stated firmly. "Was I in it?"

My insides went tingly, "Yeah, at the end anyway. It doesn't matter because I'd never—you'd never..." I didn't want to continue. "You want another drink?" I dodged, taking his glass and started to rise from the lounger.

He grabbed my arm and pulled me back down, "Not now." Then he smiled and picked up my glass of iced tea that I had barely touched, "I'll just have some of yours; you're mom makes good sweet tea."

I laughed, "Yeah that is one thing she has down pretty well, boiling water for the tea bags."

"Everyone doesn't have to be a great cook. I'm sure she's wonderful at a lot of different things."

I nodded, "I hope I'm half the mom she is someday."

He rolled onto his side on his lounger and began staring intently at me.

"Your stare can get a little creepy sometimes," I confessed without looking back into the intensity of his gaze.

"You mentioned once about wanting a baby. I was just wondering if you were serious."

I was glad the subject had changed from my dream. At least this subject was about our future together and not my crazy dreams about being torn apart, "Definitely." Then the thought hit me that he might not want children, "how about you? Have you ever thought about having a family?"

"Not until I realized that I'd fallen in love with you. I never thought I'd find someone I'd want to make a commitment to." His smile got broader, "And then you came along and turned my world upside down."

"So," I said, returning the penetrating stare, "do you want to have a baby?"

"I'll let you do that part," he chuckled. "I'm starting to think about several, maybe a half dozen or so, you know Italians like big families."

"I'll meet you in the middle. How about three?"

The stare was becoming smoldering and I had the feeling he was ready to start working on baby number one if I was willing. "What are you thinking?" I finally asked.

"I'm trying to imagine you pregnant."

The look got hotter and I was feeling the need to hit the pool just to cool off before I roasted under his gaze. "I don't know," I blushed, trying to look away from those easily read green eyes, "I can't imagine deserving the look you're giving me if I look like I'm hiding a basketball under my belly button."

"You will, I know it. You'll be incredibly sexy when pregnant, somehow I can tell."

"You're just thinking about all the fun you'll have getting me that way," I quipped.

"Oh, yes, baby, but trust me, I'll make sure you have an equally good time."

"Wow," I said, just discussing this with him was burning me up inside, "I've got to get in the pool and cool off."

He was reaching for me, but I had already dodged his grasp and let out a squeal as I ran for the pool and dove in. I was underneath the water when I heard the sound of his body closing in on me. I was a good swimmer, but he was much more powerful with all those extra muscles; he caught me as I surfaced on the other side.

Kimmy was laughing at us until he kissed me. "I'm telling Mom!" she threatened, but with a teasing edge. The other little girl simply said, "Eew!"

She broke Micah's concentration as I slipped out of his grasp and took off through the water. I swam for all I was worth to reach the ladder, knowing he'd probably grab me before I could exit the pool, but I had squeaked out before he lunged like a great white getting ready to take down its prey. I laughed, snatching up my towel and running inside.

At that moment I heard Kimmy ask Micah to play a game of Marco Polo with them. She evidently liked the idea of a giant shark in the water. I went inside to help Mom set the dinner table, as I heard the girls screaming with delight as Micah chased them around the pool.

"I'm glad he decided to stay," Mom admitted as she handed me the dinner plates.

"Not as glad as I am," I laughed.

She paused, resting her hand on her hip as I put the plates out on the table.

"What?"

"I can't believe my little girl is all grown up and in love. I'm so glad you're happy," she sighed.

I gave her a very damp hug, still wrapped in my towel from the pool. The way she said it reminded me that her once happy life with Robert was over and she found herself suddenly single at 35.
"You're beautiful," I reminded her. "One of these days you're going to find someone that makes you really happy."

Her eyes misted over and she smiled, "I found him, once. I just wish he would have stayed."

I had the feeling this wasn't about Robert, but she never told me very much about my father except that they were both young and made some unwise decisions. "My dad?" I asked.

"Micah reminds me a lot of Lee. He was muscular and handsome, and I was so in love with him."

"So why did he leave?

"Grandpa, my dad, told him he was going to have to make things right by me when I turned up pregnant. Lee wasn't ready, I guess. I wasn't legal age and he was twenty-four. It was marriage, jail or run—he ran. I was so mad at my dad for like two years, until I met Robert and then I felt I had another chance at happiness, so I went for it."

"Did you ever try to find him? I mean to tell him about me?"

"Oh yes, the day I turned eighteen I hired two detectives to find him. I wanted him back in my life so badly, but it was like he had fallen off the edge of the world, completely untraceable. I held out hope that he would try to contact me, but I never heard from him again." Her tears were filling her lower lashes, so I hugged her once more.

The doorbell rang and I knew it was the caterer. Dinner was brought in and placed in the kitchen; she didn't want them to stay and serve. Within an hour everyone was dried and dressed as we sat down to enjoy the meal. Mom was taking Kimmy and her friend to the movies after dinner, and we were invited to join them, but we opted for time alone at home.

When they left, we curled up together on the sofa with the lights down low, a small fire and a little Kenny G. playing in the background. It may not have exactly been the kind of music either one of us was used to, but I had to admit it could set a romantic mood. But, then again, as long as we were in each other's arms, I think we could have had chimpanzees banging on pots and pans and still have been happy just because we were together.

"You know we could use a good bottle of wine about now," he tightened his grip on me.

"I don't drink, Mr. Gavarreen," I reminded him.

"And I don't want you to start drinking, future Mrs. Gavarreen, but I think wine barely counts as long as you aren't a lush that downs the bottle."

"I have a hard enough time keeping my head together with you around. I don't think I could handle even one glass of wine."

"It would make you sleep better," he added.

"I think I'm going to be sleeping just fine to—"

"Leese," he stopped me, "you still haven't told me about your dream."

I groaned reflexively, "I've decided I just want to forget it."

"Did I hurt you? You said I was in the dream and that's the only thing I can—"

"I think I actually hurt you first," I whispered. My eyes were tearing up as the dream came rushing back to me. "I was running away from you, but I didn't know where to go or what to do, except I knew…" How did he get me discussing this? I had determined earlier I was going to find away to avoid telling him the horrid dream and now he had me practically spilling the entire thing out for him to dissect. "Dreams are stupid and they don't mean anything."

"You told me God has a purpose for everything; that would have to include dreams, Leese. Finish telling me: what did you know?"

I sighed, I was certain this dream was going to ruin our romantic evening together. "I knew my life was over. There's no reason to live without you in it." The first tear rolled down my cheek.

"Baby, if I die two minutes from now, you have a lifetime of reasons to live." He kissed my throat, "What happened in the dream?" he urged.

"I put a knife to my chest to end my life."

He was holding perfectly still as if I were a piece of thin glass with too much stress on it. "Did you?"

"No, Micah, you showed up." I wanted to leave it sounding like he was the hero and hopefully he wouldn't ask anymore about the dream.

"Tell me the rest," he pressed.

"You asked me why I threw away your love." My chest heaved as I took a breath to stop myself from sobbing.

"And?"

"Do you have to know everything?" I questioned.

"Finish it, Leese. Tell me the rest." At this point he sounded almost desperate to know how the dream would end, but I knew he would hate me for even imagining that kind of ending.

"You took the handle of the knife in your hands and shoved it through my heart and I died." It sounded so flat without the sound of the pouring rain, and the thunder and lightning from the dream.

He was very still as I wiped my eyes. "That's why I had to come see you. There are no reasons in this world that would ever make me want to run from you. I'd never do anything to destroy what we feel for each other." I heaved another sob, "I'm sorry you had to even hear about it."

He turned my face up to his and brought his mouth softly to mine, "I think it just means you're still a little bit afraid of me. But, trust me Leese, I could never hurt you."

I wrapped my arms around him and held on until I felt my composure return, "I swear to you, Micah, I really do know that; I'm not afraid of you, I'm only afraid that I'm going to wake up and this will just be some dream and I'll still be forbidden to find you."

"What do you mean forbidden?"

"When I went to New Orleans—"

"You came to New Orleans to find me?" he asked, sounding shocked. "When?"

"Right after you sold your house—I still can't believe you sold that house. I loved it there."

13

"*You came to New Orleans*. I didn't know about that and who told you that you were forbidden to find me?"

"Your—your mom."

"Mom! You've got to be kidding. She never told me you were there."

"She said if I kept it up I might be responsible for your death—I couldn't take that chance."

"I was going through hell, but I never knew you were looking for me. I was starting to think you might have changed your mind. I was so nervous the day at the church because I was afraid you wouldn't want to get together with me again."

"Oh, Micah, I hired a lawyer to find out if you were in jail. I left messages for Gwen, and tried to get anyone in your family to call me. I was going crazy before I rented a jet and flew out there."

He kissed me with a new passion, a deep passion of someone who suddenly realized how much he was loved. He laid me back on the couch and placed himself above me.

My heart started to flutter as he covered me with his body and kissed me hungrily. I parted my legs, allowing his body to rest in the cradle of my passion. We hadn't been so intimately positioned since the day I straddled his lap at the motel and then tried to wiggle free. I recalled the heat between us and the desperate way he said, "Don't move like that, baby." I could still feel his grip as he tried to keep me from pulling away.

He rose slightly and looked at me, "I don't have this kind of strength, baby—I wanted to wait, but I've never needed anything so bad in my life."

I didn't get the chance to even open my mouth when the telephone rang. "Crying out loud," I sighed, "Evidently God is trying to tell us to wait because every time, Micah—"

"I know baby, go answer it. It might be your mom."

I picked up the phone by the fourth ring and saw it was R. Faultz on the caller ID. I had almost forgotten about my date tomorrow with Ryan.

"Hello, Ryan."

I watched the look come over Micah's face.

"Thanks. Yeah, it's official, I'm eighteen. No, I haven't forgotten about tomorrow." Nearly, but not quite. "I'm not really sure we should do it now, you see…"

Ryan was asking why I might not be able to keep my promise as Micah was motioning me to hand him the telephone.

"Hold on, I've got someone who wants to talk to you." Oh, how horribly cruel it felt to put the phone in Micah's hand. Ryan was a good friend, and even though Micah told me the day he proposed that I would keep my date, I couldn't see how it could be appropriate now.

"She'll be there," Micah affirmed, "I'll bring her personally." There must have been a long pause. "Ryan? Dude, you still there?" Micah looked at me and smiled.

I know I was cringing.

"Yeah, I'm back. I had to take care of some business, but I couldn't just let you move in and take my girl. Yeah, I know and trust me, I'm not leaving her alone again. Actually, yes I am, but in a separate bedroom. Yes, her mother approved; what kind of guy do you think I am? Never mind, I don't think we have enough time for that answer," Micah laughed once more. "So, where am I taking her, again? Noon, right? Yeah, here she is," he said, passing the phone back to me.

"Hey," I breathed. Ryan only had one big issue—the kind of date he was expecting was two people not three and he asked me to ditch my hit man and come alone. "I can't do that, Ryan—but if you want to back out, I'll understand."

Fat chance. I had a date tomorrow with my very handsome close friend and my fiancé. Ryan still had no clue Micah proposed and that the ring was poised on my finger right now. I put the phone in the charger and came back to the couch. The mood had been extinguished like someone doused us with cold water.

"I could have talked him out of it, you know," I stated.

"You made a promise to give him one date for the use of his car. I'm not going to have you start breaking promises after everything we've been through together. And in three months, you certainly aren't keeping any dates with anyone other than me."

I smiled, as he gave me a quick kiss.

"I'm hitting the shower," he sighed, rising from the couch. "I guess I'll go on to bed unless you want to find a bottle of wine and then—"

"No—I told you I can't control myself now. If you give me a drink, you might as well slip me some Ecstasy because I'm sure I'll end up naked in the pool before it's over."

He burst out with laughter and kissed me again, "Good-night, baby."

I waited for Mom and Kimmy to come home. Relaxing on the couch and watching the fire die out. I dozed until I heard Kimmy's voice. We talked about the movie for a little while and then I went upstairs and went to sleep. Having him in the house worked like a charm because I was able to sleep without the nightmare returning.

Chapter Two

I made it up before anyone else, and went down to the kitchen to put together a little breakfast. I was far from being a gourmet cook, but I could whip up a mean batch of homemade cinnamon pancakes. It didn't take long before the scent brought Kimmy bumbling into the room looking for a bite to eat. Minutes later, Micah appeared. He was wearing shorts and a tank. He hadn't shaved yet, but I kind of liked his rough-around-the-edges look; not quite sure I'd want to kiss those rough edges, but the look suited him.

Kimmy was already digging into a pancake when I placed a stack in front of him.

"Homemade?" he questioned as he poured the syrup over the top.

"Leese makes good pancakes," Kimmy replied.

"And, yes," I responded, "they are homemade." I observed with curiosity as he put the first bite in his mouth and watched the pleased grin take over his face, "Good enough?"

He smiled, "Delicious. So how long will it take to get to this airstrip in Okeechobee?"

"It's about an hour and a half away, maybe a little bit more. You don't have to come. You can trust me to—"

"Leese, I trust you completely, but Ryan? He's the reason I'm coming, baby, not you."

"Who's Ryan?" Kimmy asked, stuffing the last bite of her pancake in her mouth.

"Someone who likes your sister almost as much as I do," Micah replied with a smile.

"Are you going to fight over her?" Kimmy questioned him with no more fanfare than if she had asked if he was going to eat another bite of pancake.

"Absolutely not. Kimberly Margaret Winslett, why would you even think such a silly thing?" I replied before Micah could open his mouth.

"That's what they do in the movies if two boys like the same girl."

"Well, this isn't the movies, and real boys—I mean men, don't have to act like that. Besides I'm the one who decides who I love, not the boys."

"Do you love Ryan?" she asked.

I didn't mean to hesitate. But, I realized Micah was being quiet and staring at the two of us as we discussed the viability of the 'boys' fighting and I was momentarily distracted. "No—not like Micah. Ryan is a friend and, believe it or not, that is different from a boyfriend."

"Oh, I know they're different," she stated matter-of-factly as if issues of love and complicated relationships were things she handled on a daily basis. She looked at Micah and smiled, "Are you gonna beat him up?"

Micah had this really funny grin on his face as he leaned toward her and asked, "Do you think I should?"

I was ready to end this stupid conversation when she simply said, "I think Leese will be mad if you do, so you better not."

I opened my mouth, but at that moment Mom walked in the room.

"Good-morning, everybody. What will Leese be mad about?" she asked, grabbing the plate I was handing her, and then settling in beside Micah.

"If Micah beats up Leese's other boyfriend."

"Ah!" was all I got out.

Mom looked at me like this was not the kind of conversation I should have brought Kimmy into, "Who?"

"I told you Kimmy, Ryan is just a friend," I clarified, my frustration level rising.

"Oh, Ryan," Mom smiled, "he's just a friend, Kimmy. Leese loves Micah, that's why they're getting married. But, she can still have friends that are boys just like Micah can have friends that are girls."

Somehow I didn't like the little addendum she tacked on the end because it wouldn't take any girl long to jump from being Micah's friend to wanting more from him. That was when the whole issue of jealousy rose in my mind. What if Micah started to feel the same way about me having a male friend? What if he got pushed over that emotional edge? I wasn't sure what would happen. I challenged him once on this subject and earned myself a pair of handcuffs and an uncomfortable night.

Micah still wasn't saying anything as he got up from the table taking his plate and Kimmy's to the sink, rinsing them off and then placing them in the dishwasher. "I'm going to go change," he stated as he headed for the stairs without pausing to give me a kiss or a hug or a 'thanks for breakfast.'

I sighed and shook my head as I sat down to eat. I knew this whole business with Ryan was going to turn into a disaster; it had already ruined my morning and I wasn't prepared to handle a jealous Micah for the remainder of the day.

I was in a state of dread by the time 10:30 rolled around. Micah hadn't come out of his room since breakfast, and I was really worried about his mental state when he finally did. I was dressed and waiting, standing outside his bedroom door and just about to tap on it when it opened.

He had a smile on his face as I asked if he was ready. He only nodded. We walked down to the garage, and I opened the door to my car, noticing he wasn't going for the passenger's side. He headed for his Corvette instead.

"You want to take the Vet?" I asked, closing my door and starting toward him.

"We'll take two cars."

I didn't like the way he said it and I was getting the distinct feeling he was up to something. He was being his unemotional self and I hated it when he did that.

"We don't have to."

"Leese, did you want to try out your new car on the strip?"

He knew I was dying to see what it could do, "Yeah, but—"

"Great. I want to see what my car can do, too. Who knows, baby, maybe you'll finally get to race me."

19

I was glad he was at least back to calling me baby, but he was still up to something.

I took the lead as we headed out of Palm Beach up 710 toward Okeechobee. Once out of town, the two lane road stretched before us in one continuous, long, straight sixty-mile line. I had my music playing nearly full bore to take my mind off the pending problem I was sure to be facing in another hour or so. I came up on a little Toyota chugging along at exactly fifty-five miles per hour. Before I could throw on my blinker and go around it, his Corvette blew past us both. All right, buddy, you're challenging the wrong girl.

I had pushed my new twelve cylinders, but only slightly. I pressed the pedal down and let the engine roar. He was giving me a good run as he hadn't let off the gas, and I couldn't over-take him before oncoming traffic met me from the other direction, so I had to be patient and wait for another opportunity. I was on his tail and we were running just over a hundred before he came up on a pickup truck and had to bring it back to the legal limit. As an opening appeared he took it immediately before I could corral him into his lane.

We traveled this way for about twenty minutes before I saw my chance coming. It was going to be close. I would have to make sure my reflexes were timed perfectly as the oncoming semi-truck went by. The stretch would be open, but if Micah wasn't paying attention to my move, this could end with a tremendous car crash. My driving instructor was screaming in the back of my head reminding me the key to any calculated driving experience was safety first. This was definitely calculated, I'd have it down to the inch, but the safety factor all depended on Micah paying attention.

The big rig was now on my left and the very second the back of his trailer passed my rear bumper, I switched into his lane with the pedal all the way to the floor. For an instant, I could tell Micah intended to pull into the lane, but he realized it was too late as I was already beside him and passing.

I laughed as I pulled in front of him, but my laughter was cut short when my cell phone rang; it was Micah and I knew I was getting ready to get yelled at.

"Hey, baby," I gently answered.

"All right, I'm not passing you anymore. You proved your point, and I really do want to spend our wedding night together in a honeymoon suite instead of ICU."

I let up my gas pedal, bringing my car down to about seventy, "I agree. I'll be good—even if you are a lot of fun to race." I was glad that he wasn't angry with me.

He laughed and then told me he loved me and hung up.

Not surprisingly, we made the hour and a half trip in an hour. Ryan wasn't there yet so we parked in the shade not too far from the entrance. I climbed out smiling, but my smile dropped when I saw his face. Maybe he was just a little bit angry about the whole dangerous passing play.

He pushed me against the back of my car, and kissed me, but still didn't smile.

I wrapped my arms around his waist and pulled him to me to soften his anger with a hotter version of the kiss he had given me, "I'm sorry, I shouldn't have tried to take that opening, but you were impossible to—"

He stopped me, placing his hands on either side of my face and giving me the kind of kiss that took my breath away—the kind of kiss that told me just how real the love he felt for me was to him. What I had thought was anger was something else I didn't understand; an emotion I had never encountered with Micah.

When the kiss ended, he suddenly seemed very emotional and some of what I was seeing appeared to be fear. Just what was he thinking? What could make a man who faced death regularly in his previous life fearful?

"Are you okay, baby?" I asked.

"No," came the choked reply.

"Micah, you're worrying me. What's wrong?"

I heard the sound of a classic muscle car coming down the road. I really needed to find out what was wrong with my future husband before Ryan showed up and prevented me from getting to the bottom of this.

"Tell me," I pressed.

Just as Ryan pulled in beside us, he kissed me passionately once more, smiled weakly, and then told me he'd see me at home.

"What!" I couldn't believe it. Now I knew what was going through that mind of his; he had decided to trust Ryan and me alone together, "No—Micah, stay."

But it was too late as he climbed back into the Vet and pulled out, burning the tires as he sped away.

Ryan got out slowly from his car, confusion written all over his face as he watched the Vet pull away. "He's not staying?"

I could only shake my head as he disappeared, my emotions resting on my bottom lashes. Ryan realized I was ready to cry so he approached cautiously as he leaned back on my car, side to side with me and leaving no space between us. He slipped his arm around me.

"Are you okay? You guys didn't have a fight over this, did you?"

"No," my tears starting to fall as I spoke, "he was going to stay, but I think he just decided he's got to learn to trust me and my decisions. I—I just never expected it; it was really hard for him to do."

"Leese," he stopped as a most unusual look hit him. He turned to face me, pulling my arms toward him.

I thought for a second he was going to try to make me embrace him, but it was my left hand he was actually after—the engagement ring.

"Did he... Ah, crap! Did he propose?"

I pulled my hands back from his grasp and wiped the tears away with my fingertips. "Yeah, we're getting married in September."

"Ah, Leese, don't do that. You're too young to be making that decision. Play the field before you buy it."

I couldn't help but laugh, "Wow, I never heard that one. I guess you're my last time in the field then because I've bought it—I love him."

"Does that mean this is a chance to change your mind?"

"No, my mind is made up, and if it wasn't for him wanting to wait, I'd be married to him right now."

"Thank God at least he's got a little bit of sense."

My eyebrows went up, "You're saying I don't have any sense?"

"Not when it comes to him," he answered, sounding exasperated.

I couldn't argue about that. When it came to Micah, I had a very narrow focus, losing my peripheral 'guy' vision. The only other person I noticed was Ryan, but it was because he was—well, he was unique and he had taken a strong interest in me from the first day I met him and never let up. I know he wanted to see what would happen if he and I tried 'us' for a little while, but all I wanted was to keep him as a really good friend.

"You're car looks a little different," I said, changing the subject. "You put an air scoop in the hood?

"Yeah, after some chick in Pensacola beat the crap out of me in a 370Z, I put in a new engine. You won't do that to me again."

"Really? My Aston Martin has 510 horsepower. You might be in trouble."

"Not this time, Leese. I've got Edelbrock carbs, Holley headers, and a new three-quarter cam shaft. You are looking at a supercharged, 454 that puts out over 650 horsepower. I have enough torque to rattle your brain when the pedal hits the floor. My car will eat yours for lunch."

"Hum…this could be interesting, so I get the keys, huh?"

"As long as the doctors say your bullet hole is healed up, you can have the keys."

My hand went instinctively to the scar on my chest, "The lung might tear back open, but if I start turning blue, then just call for a medevac." The look on his face was priceless, but I couldn't keep up that cruelty for long, "I'm kidding—I'm kidding, I'm fine."

The remainder of the afternoon was a blast. He wasn't joking about the car; it was, without a doubt, the most powerful piece of steel I'd ever controlled. I could actually pull the front tires off the ground when I took off. We spun out, skid, slid, and rocketed up and down the airstrip for hours.

Before we said our goodbyes, I challenged him against my car. I knew I was going to lose miserably, but I had to give it a try anyway. I actually beat him off the line simply because my car was lighter and didn't try to eat the asphalt before catapulting into space. But beyond the line, I was a ghost in his rearview.

I thanked him for the date that I originally didn't want to keep, but now was so glad I did. It was a chance to forget everything and just be eighteen and wild for a little while.

"So, you know I'm going to send you an invitation. Do you think you'll be able to come? I know the timing isn't great as far as school is concerned, but…"

Recognition crossed his face. He evidently didn't realize I was talking about the wedding at first. "I—I might be able to make it, no promises, but I'll try. Will I get a chance to kiss the bride?"

"On the cheek," I laughed. "These lips belong to Micah, alone."

He surprised me as he pulled me into his arms without warning, "You could at least enjoy a little freedom, before you say 'I do.' You know just to make sure you're making the right choice."

"Let go of me, Ryan. You are a great friend, but that is all I can offer," I scowled, pushing my way out of his arms. "If you don't want to keep me as a friend, I'll under—"

"Ah, Leese, never, ever think that I don't want to be your friend, but how would I know that you're sure if I didn't ask?"

I grinned and gave him a quick hug, putting a brief kiss on his cheek, "September 15th and you can return that kiss."

He smiled broadly.

"On my cheek," I finished.

With that I left and headed home, wondering the whole time what state Micah would be in when I got there.

I pulled into the drive way at 5:15. Mom's car was missing and I was somewhat relieved because it meant Micah and I would have some private time to discuss my time spent with Ryan, and how he handled allowing me that freedom.

The door from the garage to the house was locked and when I opened it, the alarm gave its shrill warning. I quickly entered the code, realizing I was all alone. Micah's car was in the garage, so he evidently rode with Mom and Kimmy somewhere. I grabbed my cell. Two rings and he answered the phone. They were at one of Mom's favorite restaurants having dinner.

"I half expected Ryan would have asked you to have dinner with him or else I would have waited for you. We only left the house about fifteen minutes ago. Do you want to join us?"

I was actually tired from my adventure and, after all the time I spent driving Ryan's car with the windows rolled down, I felt like half of the air strip was clinging to my skin. There were leftovers in the fridge, so I told him to enjoy himself and I'd see him when they came home.

I showered first and then slipped on a bikini top with a cotton over-shirt and a pair of short-shorts. The last thing I had eaten were pancakes this morning so I was starving by the time I came downstairs and began digging through the fridge. There was plenty of Hawaiian Chicken left over from last night along with Somen salad. I was reaching for a slice of mango bread when I saw the bottle of wine in the fridge. Mom would occasionally have a glass of wine at a restaurant, but she didn't keep it in the house.

This was a bottle of Italian wine and it had been opened. It appeared several glasses had been consumed; I could only pray that Micah didn't buy this in response to having left me in Ryan's hands today. I didn't like the idea of his drinking and I know he knew that. I began to think about what Ryan said to me several times today about the fact that I really didn't know Micah that well and I might be jumping into something I would regret. I couldn't imagine any regrets between Micah and me, but I still didn't want to discover he had a weakness for alcohol.

I was feeling the heat of anger building inside me. I knew it wasn't hard liquor, like the rum he once tried to get me to drink, but why did he need it at all? Wasn't he happy enough to be here with me? Did he really need to have an occasional drink to satisfy something within him? I was starting to boil over. I nibbled a few bites from my dinner, but I lost the need for food. What I needed was an emotional release before my thoughts consumed me. I put the plate back in the fridge and went to the one place in our home where I knew could take my mind off my fears for a little while; my music studio.

Mom had the studio built off the apartment by the pool cabana so when I wanted to really crank up the volume, I wouldn't disturb the whole house, or the neighbors. It was heavily sound proofed, although it could still be heard from outside the studio, but just as a muffled noise that didn't travel far. We had mirrored the room on all four sides and put in the ballet bars for dance practice for both Kimmy and myself, but I didn't do ballet anymore. I just liked to dance and sing when I wanted the world to go away.

I went into the control room and started the computer. Sitting there behind the one way glass, I looked out on the dance floor as I waited for it to boot up. We had put the one way glass in the booth so the dance floor would stay seamless. I found that I danced differently if I thought no one was watching. My dance instructor once told me I needed to learn to dance with an audience because I was very good at impromptu expression dancing, but when I knew I was being watched I was much more subdued. He proved the point by having Mom film me one day from inside the booth when I thought I was alone. The difference was like watching two completely opposite people; even I was impressed when she played the tape back for me.

With the computer up and my favorite playlist starting, I went out to the dance floor and let myself unwind. I had several playlists that went with whatever mood I happened to be in, and right now my mood was mainstream rock and roll; Springsteen, Mellencamp, Loggins, Seger, Golden Earring, ZZ Top—I was ready for a workout.

I slipped off the over-shirt before the first song ended; sweat starting to roll off me as I pushed myself to my physical limit. It was as much fun as Ryan's car had been today. I moved every limb and joint, stretched and flexed each muscle and swung hips and shoulders to the pulsing rhythm; I was having enough fun to forget, temporarily, the bottle of wine in the fridge and the anger that went with it.

'Hurt So Good,' by Jon Mellencamp had just ended and I grabbed my shirt from the ballet bar and wiped the sweat from my face and patiently waited for the next song to begin. My chest was a little uncomfortable, but it wasn't enough to stop me. I knew the next song, from the first note, wasn't from this playlist. It was a killer to dance to and I wondered who had added it to my list, but that was no reason not to enjoy 'Temperature' by Sean Paul. Three and a half minutes later I was dying for a drink of water, but I didn't want to quit. I'd get my drink and cool off before everyone got home, right now was my time to burn up the floor. I wiped my face and listened for the next song.

Okay this was getting weird, another song began that I knew wasn't on this playlist. I had heard it before, but didn't recognize it immediately. The beat was so familiar. I started to move to the pulse, but when the first sounds came out of the singer's mouth I knew right away someone was in my control room. Welcome to the Jungle by Guns N'Roses wasn't one of my songs; it was Micah's.

I stormed to the control room and jerked the door open. Micah was seated there with a smile tearing at the corners of his mouth. "Baby, I never knew you could dance like—like *that*," he said through a smoldering stare.

26

"Ah! You're supposed to be at the restaurant not—not spying on me!"

"We were at the restaurant, but when I told your mom that you were here, she asked them to put our orders in takeout boxes and we brought it back. I was wondering where you were, but your mom figured it out and let me into the control room to—to surprise you, I guess."

"She knows I don't like people watching me dance!" I snapped, my anger getting hotter. I felt as if I could pitch a fit. *"I will discuss this with Mother."*

"Annalisa," he reserved using my whole name for times when he wanted my full attention, and it worked.

I blinked a couple times, letting myself cool down, "What?"

"What made you decide to dance?"

I wanted to yell at him about the bottle of wine. I wanted to know if he drank when he was nervous or upset, but I knew better than to fly off the handle with him.

"I—I just needed to…"

The smile faded from his face as he rose slowly from the control table and turned to walk out of the booth to the pool area.

"Micah," I stopped him, reaching for his arm. He turned and I could see his eyes were filled with hurt and sadness. "What's wrong? You don't like the way I was dancing?" Something was upsetting him and I hoped he didn't think I looked, well let's just say less than innocent on the dance floor. When I danced alone, I didn't feel any reason not to be provocative, but he had told me before that it was my innocence he found so alluring.

Now I could see the tears starting to fill his bottom lashes. I couldn't let him go out the door. I took his face in my palms and softly kissed his lips, "Please, please tell me what's bothering you—I'm sorry if I said you were spying on me."

"Does being with Ryan make you want to dance this way?"

I was too stunned to speak at first, but then I realized he took my pent up anger on the dance floor to mean something else entirely. I kissed him again, slower this time and kept my face only inches from his as I told him no. "You crazy-nut," I whispered, "I was angry. I use dancing for a release when I'm really, really upset."

27

He gave a small sigh of relief, "Then baby, the only thing I've got to know is what are you pissed about? You were dancing your ass off out there."

"Did you buy that bottle of wine after you left me with Ryan?"

His eyebrows went up, "You're angry about a bottle of wine?"

"Do you drink when you're upset? You know how I feel about alcohol."

"Your mom bought it because last night I mentioned about having wine with dinner. She asked if I'd like to have a glass with her when I got home."

"Oh." That put a whole new light on things. "I'm—I'm so sorry, I thought… Forgive me, Micah, I was so angry. I thought maybe you had an issue you didn't want to tell me about."

"I'm afraid a hit man needs sobriety or he doesn't last long. I used to drink casually, just one or two drinks a night on weeks when I didn't have a job to do, but the only time I've been…" He stopped and the 'I-don't-want-to-tell-you,' face appeared.

"We don't have reasons to hide things, do we?"

"The only time I've been absolutely passed out drunk was about three months ago."

"When you went home?"

"I was so sick over leaving you in the hospital, and I didn't know when or if I'd see you again. I think that was one of the reasons why David decided he needed to put a stop to Robert before he found someone else to kill you; he'd never seen me like that."

He tried to pull me into his arms, but I had to push away, "Micah, I'm gross. I'm covered in sweat from head to…"

The argument was moot; he evidently didn't care about the sweat as he pulled me against his clean dress shirt. He smelled so wonderful, he felt fantastic as he wrapped me in those gloriously strong arms and kissed me slow and deep.

"Dance with me, Micah," I whispered.

"I can't dance like you, baby."

"Slow dance with me," I pleaded as I let my mouth trail from his ear to his neck, "please."

"You know I can't say no to you, baby. You pick the song and I'll dance with you."

I went to the computer and noticed that he had gone on Grooveshark to pick his songs. I typed in *'I'll Make Love to You'* and hit the play button, dimmed the studio lights, and took his hand and led him out onto the dance floor. He held me so close and began to gently sway as he pressed me to his body. I inhaled his scintillating scent and felt myself beginning to disappear into his warm chest. His hands slipped low on my hips as I arched my back and allowed my body to swing away from him, pushing my hips against his as I made a slow circle and returned against his chest. He was moaning to the beat of the music as our bodies seemed to become one pulsing rhythm. The song simply wasn't long enough for me to enjoy so much pleasure.

"Oh, Micah," I sighed softly as the song was ending, "I love you."

Our lips met as my arms twined around his neck and my fingers went into those silky waves of brown hair. He was so gorgeous and I simply couldn't believe that he was for me alone. "I've got to be the luckiest girl in the entire world."

He dipped me low and then raised me to his lips.

I kissed him once more and then begged to leave his presence to go hit the shower.

I rinsed off and then slipped on a simple pink, cotton romper that I seldom wore (mainly because I couldn't wear a bra with it), but it was quick and comfortable. When I came back downstairs, Mom was putting things away in the kitchen, Kimmy was swimming in the pool, and Micah was seated out on the deck watching the sunset, still in his dinner clothes.

"We brought you back some food," he said as I sat down by him. "Did you eat?"

"Not yet. I'll get something a little later—I didn't want to miss watching the sunset with you."

He smiled and looked away, "So, I didn't ask earlier, but how was your afternoon with—with Ryan."

I wondered if I should tone down all the fun I had, but trust depends on truth, "I had a great time. He put a new engine in his car and I could actually pull the front tires off the ground."

He laughed softly, still watching the sunset, "Sounds like fun."

"I wish you'd stayed," I added. "You didn't have to do what you did."

"I've got to learn to try things that are uncomfortable for me where you're concerned so I don't end up smothering you. By the way, did he kiss you?"

I was shocked that he threw that question out there like it was an unimportant afterthought.

"No, but..."

He turned to look at me as I struggled to finish what I had to say.

"...I actually kissed him."

I watched Micah's eyes involuntarily grow larger and he swallowed hard.

"He wanted to know if he could kiss the bride, but I told him these lips belong to you alone. I kissed his cheek and said he could return it, on my cheek, after the wedding."

He looked both relieved and upset at the same time.

"I'm sorry if—"

"It's okay, Leese. A kiss on the cheek is infinitely preferable to what I was afraid might happen."

"No," I started to say Ryan wouldn't do that to me, but Mom came out onto the deck with two glasses of wine.

"Micah, would you like another glass of..."

Micah was saying no as I put my hand out for the glass. I could tell she was reluctant to hand it to me, but she did.

"Leese would prefer if I didn't drink, Nadia," he stated without explaining why.

I knew what impression she would come away with and I didn't want her to think he had a weakness for it. "He doesn't have a problem, Mom. I just don't see why it's necessary to use alcohol."

Mom smiled, "Honey, there is nothing wrong with a little wine once in a while."

"I know, Mom, I just don't like it."

"That's because you don't drink it," she added with a light laugh.

I had enough. Micah asked me to try wine and now it appeared Mom was alluding to the same. I put the glass to my lips as Micah reached for my arm, but I leaned away from him and slugged down the terribly flavored liquid. I couldn't help the shiver, followed by an immediate grimace that hit me. It must have been at least twelve ounces.

"Leese!" Mom snapped, taking the glass as I handed it back to her, "you aren't old enough!"

"Now I can say that I have drunk it and I still don't like it. Ah! How do you guys stand that crap—it's awful!" I shivered again.

I noticed Micah was angry, but yet trying not to laugh at my reaction.

Mom turned and headed back into the house, still grumbling about what I'd done.

"You shouldn't have done that," he chided, clearly the anger was winning over the humor. He switched from his lounger to seat himself on mine. "Was that honestly the first time you've ever touched alcohol?"

I swallowed, trying to get use to the odd flavor still remaining in my mouth, "Yeah, but I don't think you have anything to worry about, it's—"

"No matter what anyone says, it's not the taste that draws people in; it's how you feel after you drink it. If you decide you enjoy the buzz then what's to stop you the next time? You said you didn't like me drinking—I won't touch it again, but you've got to promise me to never do something stupid like that again. You pissed off your mother *and* me."

My vision was starting to swim as the tears built on my bottom lashes, "I'm sorry, it's just that you had asked me to try it and it seemed like—"

"When did I ask you to try it?" he responded indignantly.

"Last night," I reminded him, but could see his face was a blank. "It would make you sleep better," I repeated his words.

He sighed and seemed to calm, "I guess I need to pay attention to what I say around you or I'll ruin you."

That was enough to send the tears over the edge. I wanted to run to my room, but he kept me immobile.

"Let me go," I said, trying to push him back.

"No. Why does it upset you if I say I'm ruining you?"

I looked at him, not wanting to say what I was thinking, but I was starting to get an odd feeling. My legs had begun to tingle, like I had danced too long or had suddenly become scared and they were turning to jelly. My stomach was warm and it was gently spreading through my limbs. The fact that my stomach had been empty and I had been thirsty was giving quick access to the wine's effects.

"What happens when you decide I'm ruined, Micah? You won't want me anymore, will you?"

31

"Ah, Leese, don't think that. I can't help myself when it comes to loving you, but if I tear off that beautiful innocence, I'll only have myself to blame."

I was playing with the strings of my romper now, feeling a giddiness that was foreign, especially since I was crying at the same moment. "You're right about the wine," I admitted, taking the cloth strings and wiping away my tears, "my legs feel funny."

"Stop that, baby," he whispered, clamping his hand over mine as I continued to tug nervously at my strings.

I didn't realize at the moment that I had pulled the rim of my romper too low and was exposing excessive cleavage. I pulled it back up and dropped the strings. Kimmy was still swimming and I was hidden by Micah's broad shoulders and chest. He leaned into me and gave me a tantalizing kiss and then grabbed the strings himself. My eyes were wide, but I offered no resistance to stop what he was about to do, and at that moment I wanted nothing more than to let him take control. He began lowering the fabric. He moved closer to me so no one would know what he was doing. His cheek was against mine as his mouth moved to my ear.

"Take it down, Micah," I pleaded. "Don't stop."

"You see what I mean about the alcohol? If I brought that bottle out here right now and asked you to drink with me, would you do it?"

I knew I'd do just about anything he wanted right now. "No," I lied, realizing if he had drank a glass my top wouldn't be teetering on coming down, it would be down and we would be relocating this game of uncovering Leese to a place where I could do the same to him.

"You want me to keep going, don't you?"

"Yes, let's go upstairs, Micah."

"You were right, alcohol is dangerous," he said pulling my top back where it belonged.

"Kiss me, Micah," I begged. The feeling of the wine still traveling through me, and I was ready to forget about the wedding date, the fact that my family was home, none of it mattered. I felt his arms lifting me from the lounger and I was thinking I was going to be carried upstairs and get my wish, but I realized too late he was moving to the pool and before I could tell him no, he threw me in.

Kimmy thought it was hilarious. The shock of the water cleared my head as I moved to the stairs and began climbing out. He was big, but I was contemplating every possible move I had in my black belt arsenal to throw him in the water as well.

Mom heard the commotion and reappeared on the deck as I stood there dripping wet and plotting my revenge.

"Leese!"

I couldn't figure out why she was snapping at me—I didn't throw myself in, but she was grabbing a towel and heading for me. Micah's face had an unmistakable flush to his skin; that was when I looked down at my outfit and discovered how very inappropriate it was when wet. Mom wrapped me in the towel, as Micah stated he'd be back in a while and headed for the garage.

"You'd have been better off to have been in your bathing suit," she criticized, still sounding miffed.

"I didn't jump in. He threw me in!"

"Oh," she said, suddenly understanding what happened.

I went upstairs and changed clothes, still feeling a little odd. I was going to wait up for him to return, but he was absolutely right about the wine and sleeping. I was so exhausted I couldn't keep my eyes open. It was only about 8:45 and I was ready to go to bed.

Chapter Three

I woke the next morning to Mom tapping on my door saying to get up and get ready for church. That was when I felt his presence in my bed. I rolled over and he was staring at me and had apparently slept in my bed all night.

"What are you doing in here?" I whispered.

"I came in to check on you when I got home last night, and I started watching you sleep. I crawled in just to be close to you for a little while and fell asleep myself."

I smiled and snuggled against him, "I'm going to be really glad when we can share a bed permanently."

He kissed my forehead, "Me too, baby."

I could hear Mom down the hallway knocking on Micah's door telling him to get up as well. I laughed, watching the grin spread across his face. "You're really lucky she didn't open my door," I stated. "She would never believe that we can behave ourselves in the same bed."

"Who said anything about behaving myself," he moaned as he began to kiss my neck.

"Come on, Don Juan," I giggled, pulling his arm, trying to right both of us. "You've got to slip out of here before she comes back. We have to get ready for church."

"You need another glass of wine."

I shot him a nasty look, "I don't think so!"

He smiled, "Good girl. But you wouldn't be shoving me out the door if—"

I grabbed a pillow and hit him as hard as possible, "Out!" I shout whispered.

He cracked open my door and peered into the hallway and then he was gone.

Our wedding planner, Linda Doradee, was a member of our church and she had been working this week on finding the perfect location for the wedding. She said we'd get together after church today and she would present it to us to see if we approved. I would have been happy to have it in my church, but she insisted she would find something very special for our day.

We went to the fellowship hall after services ended and she brought out her planning book and began.

"Since you told me Micah's family was French and Italian, I was looking for something with old world charm; I found the ultimate location. Take a look." She opened the book to reveal pictures of a beautiful church that appeared to be very old. "It's Saint Bernard de Clairvaux, a 12th century Spanish monastery that was moved to North Miami in 1925 by William Randolph Hurst."

She was going on about the different areas available for weddings as she flipped through the pictures of the impeccable grounds and buildings. I could see by Micah's face, he was completely enthralled. I would be happy being married anywhere, but I knew how important it was to impress his father and this place would impress the Pope.

"It's perfect," I said, "but I want it all."

Linda looked a little confused.

"Rent the entire building and grounds for the wedding," Micah clarified. He knew exactly what I was saying. Simply renting an area wouldn't do.

"I—I don't know if they—"

"Linda, they may not normally do that, but for the right price, they will," I assured her.

"They already said the 15th was clear," she sighed. "I'll call them tomorrow and ask about using the entire facility. Here is the design you ask for on the wedding invitation. Does it look good to you both?"

We nodded.

"Okay then, if the entire church can be rented I'll give this to my printer. He is local here in town and he said if I give it to him tomorrow, he'll have them done by Wednesday and we can mail them out. Then all we have to do is confirm some dinner menus, music and flowers. Leese, did you find a dress yet?"

"Yes, I ordered a Vera Wang, and it's supposed to be delivered in a few days."

"Perfect! Oh, I almost forgot about the Acqualina."

"What's the Acqualina?" Micah asked before I could form the question.

She flipped to the next page in her planner and the pictures of a high-rise hotel appeared. "I know you two have decided on Maui, but I was thinking you wouldn't want to spend your first married night on a thirteen-hour flight. The Acqualina would be perfect for a few nights of relaxation before you leave for the islands. Your guests can stay here as well. It's a gorgeous facility, they have everything and it isn't far from the monastery."

Micah and I looked at each other. We both wanted that first night to be perfect. I turned the page to view the deluxe oceanfront suite, 1600 square feet of luxury and Atlantic views. I smiled. "It's perfect."

"Sounds good to me, too."

"Excellent," Linda added. "I don't think I've ever had a wedding come together so smoothly. I feel like it could be tomorrow and we'd be ready."

"I'd be ready," I blurted out and then blushed a little, recalling that I was still in church and my thoughts were very unchurch-like at the moment.

We shook Linda's hand and then left for lunch. Kimmy went with a friend for the afternoon and we wouldn't see her again until church this evening. It was nice because it was a chance for the adults to have time to talk. Not everything I wanted to discuss about my pending marriage was suitable for Kimmy's ears. The problem was when we got to the restaurant for lunch, I realized I couldn't bring myself to mention it with Micah at the table either. After we ordered our food, he excused himself to the restroom and I was able to ask my mother what had been bothering me.

"Mom, I've got to talk to you about my first night—you know," I fretted, looking Micah's direction as he walked away. "I don't know much about—about birth control." I could tell Mom wasn't a hundred-percent comfortable with the subject, but she was at least willing for the few minutes of privacy we had before he returned.

She told me I was conceived because that thought never entered her mind when my father swept her off her feet. "But, thank goodness, you are more level headed than I ever was," she stated. "When I met Robert, I wasn't ready for another baby, not right away anyway. I went to my gynecologist and she put me on the pill, but I had a horrible reaction to it."

"What happened?" I asked, hoping she would explain before he returned.

"It gave me vicious migraines. I couldn't even get out of bed. I lost a whole bra size that first month," she glanced down at her chest and frowned. "I never got that back. But the headaches were the worst, and I was apparently forming blood clots. The doctor took me off them, and Robert and I had to rely on condoms. I did try using a diaphragm for a while, but that was really... Well, let's just say I didn't like it."

That was a little more information than I was prepared for—or wanted to hear.

Micah returned as she mentioned I really should discuss it with him.

"Discuss what with me?" he asked, seating himself back at the table.

I rolled my eyes. Who would have thought the one thing I was dying to do with him was a subject I couldn't speak about out loud.

"Birth control," Mom stated as if she was the mother bird and she was shoving me out of the nest to see if I could fly.

"Oookay," he said, his face going red, "I guess I should be more careful when I walk in on ladies' conversations." He looked at me, clearly uncomfortable, "Do you want to—to discuss this *now*?"

I rarely bit my nails, but I became keenly aware of the fact that I was gnawing through my thumbnail.

"I think you should make an appointment with my gynecologist," Mom tossed out. "She'd be able to give you all the options and then you, the two of you, can decide what you want to do—I mean I know what you want to do, but—what I meant to say was—"

"Mom," I said, removing the thumbnail from between my teeth and reaching out and gripping her hand, "It's okay. I get what you're trying to say."

"Great," Micah blushed, clearly hoping we were changing subjects, "Let's just get it on—I mean *get on* with ordering dinner."

We made it through dinner, but it was the quietest meal I'd had in a long time, with the exception of the fact that I couldn't stop laughing as I thought about how tongue-tied we had become.

Monday morning, Mom and Kimmy left early to go shopping, but before leaving she handed me a business card and told me to call for an appointment. When I looked down I saw it was a card for Dr. Kerstin Kannova, OBGYN. Micah was up and enjoying a cup of coffee out on the pool deck, so I took the opportunity to make the call while I had some privacy.

Upon explaining my situation, the receptionist put me through directly to Dr. Kannova. She was very personable and suggested that Micah and I come into her office for a consultation. She said she would go over all the options and see what suited us best.

"Have you ever had a gynecological exam?" she asked.

"Ah, no."

"What birth control methods have you been using?"

"I—I've never—this will be my first time so I don't—"

"Oh," Dr. Kannova replied with a bit of surprise to her voice, "well, you should really have an exam. We can do it the day you come in for the consultation."

"Okay, when do we come in?"

"Hold on, I'm going to transfer you back out to my appointment desk and they'll set it up for you, but I'd like to make it as soon as possible; most methods require some time in advance before they are effective."

I assumed I wouldn't get an appointment for weeks, but to my astonishment they scheduled me for Friday morning. Now the only problem was explaining to Micah what we were doing that morning. I took a cup of coffee and joined him on the deck. He looked up at me and smiled—maybe I'd tell him later, like Thursday night—late Thursday night.

Linda called to let us know, for a substantial price, the monastery was ours for the entire afternoon and evening on the fifteenth. Our invitations would be ready Wednesday after one o'clock, but she wasn't going to be able to pick them up due to a family matter. I told her that was no problem, Micah and I would pick them up.

Tuesday we drove down to St. Bernard's to see the monastery in person. Micah and I were both a little awestruck as we toured the buildings and grounds. The photos certainly didn't do the oldest building in the western hemisphere justice. It left you with a deep feeling of having entered a place that was holy and acceptable to God. We took care of the deposit for the wedding and reception and thanked our guide, and we left to go to the Acqualina.

We didn't say anything for the first five minutes or so in the car; it had simply been too overwhelming, but Micah was the first to break the silence.

"Annalisa, I honestly didn't think I'd care where we said our vows, but I've got to admit I'm glad Linda was looking for something special for us."

"I know what you mean, I just kept thinking: eight-hundred years of history, what a place—"

"To commit our lives to each other," he finished. "I was thinking the exact same thing."

We were all smiles by the time we pulled into the Acqualina. We were taken up to see a deluxe, 1,600 square foot, ocean side one bedroom suite and then shown around the restaurant and grounds, before finishing out our day in the spa. We lay out, side by side and enjoyed an intense massage, four massage therapists and eight hands working every ounce of tension from our bodies. What an incredible ending to a great day.

Wednesday afternoon we drove to the printers for the invitations. All the preparations seemed to be going by so fast and yet the wedding still seemed so far away. Eleven weeks to go was starting to feel like an eternity.

"Hi," I said as we walked into the small print store, "I'm Annalisa Winslett and this is my fiancé, Micah Gavarreen. Linda asked us to stop by and pick up our wedding invitations today."

"Oh yes," the balding man behind the counter said, "I finished boxing them up about two hours ago. Hold on, I'll be right back."

He returned quickly and placed the two boxes on the counter. "Here is one of the invitations so you can make sure it looks good to you."

I was looking at the color and cut and the font, but Micah was looking at something entirely different.

"The date is wrong," he observed as soon as I opened the card.

"What?" the gentleman behind the counter and I said at the same moment.

"August 15th is what Linda had written down," the man stated pulling out her order form.

"No, September 15th is the correct..." I paused and turned to Micah.

"I'll scrap this and start over," the man was saying as he tried to grab the boxes.

"No, don't do that." I prevented him from taking them away. "Micah, do you know what this is?"

"Yeah, the wrong date."

"No—God does everything for a purpose; this is the right date. We've got to move the wedding up!" I was excited to my core. We'd both said we couldn't wait and now it appeared, to me at least, that God was in agreement; we'd marry in six weeks.

"Leese, I'd like to move it up too, but what about the church? They may not have an opening August 15th."

"I'll call right now." I grabbed my cell and dialed information. I motioned Micah to stay where he was as I stepped outside for better reception. When the phone was answered, I explained who I was and that there had been some confusion about our wedding date and we wanted to move it to August 15th. My request was met with a very long pause. "I know that isn't far away, but I was hoping that—"

"I have a feeling," the man on the other end of the line began, "that the Good Lord must be with you on this one because no more than an hour ago, both weddings we had scheduled for that day cancelled—we're available all evening."

I charged back inside and leaped into Micah's surprised grasp, tears rolling down my cheeks. "They had two weddings planned for that day," I cried, still clinging to his neck.

He pulled back enough to see my face, "Had?"

I nodded. "Both weddings cancelled an hour ago—it's ours for the night." I swallowed at the annoying block of emotions in my throat, "Six weeks, baby—only six more weeks."

I don't know how long we stood there holding on to each other trying to understand what had just occurred, but eventually the gentleman behind the counter cleared his throat, "I guess then these are okay?"

Micah planted a soft kiss against my lips, never turning his head to look at the man, "They're perfect," he whispered.

When I finally got in touch with Linda later that afternoon, she flipped.

"But you said everything was coming together, and we were practically ready anyway?" I reminded her.

"I know, but—but six weeks! Okay, look I'll just have to put everything in high gear. Don't worry about it, I'll have it done and it'll be beautiful."

I wanted to tell her I wasn't worried in the least; God moved up the date and He would make sure that it was perfect.

Micah and I spent the majority of Thursday with Linda finalizing every detail from Micah's tux to my bouquet, to what we were serving at the reception, music, songs, lighting, seating, and on and on. I never realized how much work went into a wedding.

We were both exhausted by the time we left her and went to dinner.

"Did you order our plane tickets," Micah asked as the waiter placed our drinks in front of us.

"All done, I did that last night. We board on the evening of the eighteenth and then it's just you and me and Maui for three heart pounding weeks. You'll love our house. It's between Hana and the Haleakala National Park. We can hike to waterfalls or snorkel off the black sand beach."

He reached out and grasped my hand in both of his, his thumbs caressing my skin, and then he lifted it and placed a kiss on the back, "I'm glad the date changed. How about tomorrow we start looking for a house? Our house—I'd like to have one here and another one in Louisiana. We can... Leese, are you okay?"

I know an odd look had come over my face as I remembered about Friday, "Yeah, it's just that we have an—an appointment in the morning."

"For what? I don't remember anything for tomorrow."

"That would be because I sort of forgot to mention it," I cringed.

He picked up on the cringe. "What exactly are we doing in the morning?"

"We're going to see a doctor," I said softly, afraid to give my words any volume, "For a consultation about—about birth control."

His eyebrows went up, "Leese, baby, you didn't have to do that. I can handle the birth control for a little while and then—"

"*You*," I said, clearly surprised.

He lifted his glass and muttered something I couldn't hear.

"What?"

"I'll use condoms," he repeated, barely louder than the first time.

"I don't want anything between us," I stated.

"Trust me, neither do I, but as much as I can't wait to start a family, I don't want you to be a teenage mother."

"This is why were going to see the doctor, she's going to give us some—some options and besides she's said I should have an exam before—"

"An exam? I would think an exam wouldn't be a good idea, or even possible since you've never—"

"I already told her this was my first time and she didn't seem to think it was a problem."

Micah frowned. I could tell he didn't like the idea at all; I was now really glad I didn't give him the whole week to wiggle out of it. The mood for the remainder of the evening was ruined.

The next morning I was nervous, but ready to get this part over with. Micah never came out of his sour mood from when I told him what we were doing. He still thought it was ridiculous to see a doctor over something that was perfectly natural and, as he put it, something people have been doing since God put us on earth. I told him maybe people have been 'doing it' that long, but I haven't and I'd feel better if he give me a little support.

Reluctantly, he agreed and we drove downtown to the doctor's office. It actually became comical when we arrived and I watched Micah's hulking form shrink smaller and smaller as we sat in the waiting room with three expectant mothers who all seemed to want to chat with us as to why we were there; the natural assumption being that we were in the early stages of pregnancy or trying to get pregnant.

I was never so glad to be called back when the nurse opened the door. Micah rose from his chair, but the nurse told him she'd be back to get him when the doctor was finished with me. I could feel his burning stare as I left him among the chatty mothers-to-be. I think he would have rather been facing down another hit man in a dark alley—and to have been out of bullets.

Doctor Kannova appeared to be in her late thirties, blond hair and blue-green eyes. I felt immediately comfortable with her as she spoke with me for a few minutes in the exam room. I told her my fears about the pill and the negative effects that my mother went through with it, but she didn't seem overly concerned.

"So the wedding is in six weeks and this is your first time. Do you have any other methods you are leaning toward? Have you done any research into birth control?"

"Yes, but to be honest what I want seems a little confusing."

"What's that?"

"I'd like to try the rhythm method at first, just at least for our first few nights, but I don't know what we should do beyond that."

"That may not be so easy. The rhythm method requires you to have very good records about your cycle and—"

"I keep a calendar every month. I can show you exactly how my cycles run."

"But are they regular? Most young women—"

"I'm like clockwork, every 28 days on the nose and I don't even vary by a day."

"Well, that certainly helps, but it's such a small window of opportunity and I don't know if that 'window' will be open August 15th. But let's not worry about that right now. I'm going to need you to remove all your clothing and put on this robe, opening in the rear. I'll be back when your changed."

"Doctor Kannova, I do have a question," I asked, stopping her before she could go out the door. I knew this question was the crux of Micah's fears about today. "My fiancé seems to think an exam isn't possible since I'm a virgin. I honestly think he's worried I won't be one after the exam, but he won't tell me that."

She smiled broadly, "Leese, you have a period every month; it flows out of your body. There will be an opening, however small for me to complete the exam. I'm not doing a pap smear or anything like that so you don't need to worry. Most young women by the time they reach your age actually don't have a hymen left to prevent intercourse, but I'm very careful and I promise you I'm not going to ruin anything for either one of you. You'll be fine."

I was comfortable, up until the point where I was sitting on that stupid exam table with the even stupider paper gown that didn't want to stay shut. Now I was having serious regrets about my 'I've got to learn all about birth control,' moment.

She returned to the room with a nurse, "Okay, we're going to start with a breast exam. Lean back on the table for me. Do you do a regular check for lumps or irregularities in your breasts?"

"No, but I know it's something I need to learn."

She opened the gown but stopped immediately when she saw the scar on my chest, "You've had a recent injury?"

"It's a—a gunshot wound," I said quickly.

"I wondered if you were the young woman that had been on the news. I know your mother, but I wasn't sure if you were the person all the stories were about."

"That would be me," I sighed, wondering if she would recognize Micah's name from the news as well. But she went right back to being professional and no more was mentioned.

We went through the exam and she explained how to start at the nipple and work my way out in a small circular pattern to feel for problems. She discussed selecting a time each month for making this a routine for the rest of my life. That wasn't so bad. Maybe this exam business wasn't so tough after all. But, then she went to the other end of the table.

Doctor Kannova smiled as she asked me to relax. The stirrups came out and she placed my heels in them. I couldn't help being nervous by this point.

"You'll have to part your legs, Leese," she stated as her chilly gloved hands touched the outside cheeks on my buttocks, "and I'll need you to scoot down toward me."

Suddenly I had a feeling that a gynecological exam before my wedding night wasn't the best of ideas. Although I was unwilling, I obeyed her request and tried to relax.

Her fingers were probing gently at first and then firmly.

"That's uncomfortable," I managed to say, through my clinched teeth.

"Leese, have you ever tried to do any sexual exploration on your—"

"No," I cut her off.

"I'm going to try to take a measurement on something; it may be uncomfortable."

"It's already uncomfortable, Doc."

"I know, but I need you to lie very still."

Within a few moments she was asking her nurse to bring in her sonogram machine. "I don't know if I can get a shot of this, but it's worth looking at."

I was wondering what she could possibly be discussing. What was so unusual that she needed an internal picture? Now I was going beyond nervous. Was something wrong with me?

It seemed she worked for the longest time trying to get the sonogram angled where she could see whatever it was she was looking at. By this time I was ready to cry. I wanted my wedding night to be perfect; now I was concerned that my body might harbor some type of defect.

"You can sit up now," she said after wiping the gel from my body. "Go ahead and get dressed and I'll meet you and Micah in my office."

"Doctor Kannova, you're scaring me and if this is something bad, I'd rather—"

"No, it's nothing bad. It's just going to make your wedding night a little more painful for you and pleasurable for him."

Okay, there was good and bad in that. I liked the idea of pleasing Micah in every way, but why would there be additional pain for me? Aren't all women the same? I wondered.

When I managed to get dressed and had walked down to her office, Micah was already seated and looking about as comfortable as I was on the exam table. Doctor Kannova wasn't in the room yet, so I whispered to him, "I'm sorry I made you go through this—I didn't know it was going to be so—"

The office door opened and I immediately straightened in my chair. It was an odd feeling, like getting called into the principal's office when you honestly didn't know what you'd done wrong. At least she was smiling.

"Hello, you must be Micah," Doctor Kannova said shaking his hand before seating herself behind the desk. "It's good to meet you."

Micah smiled, but remained silent.

"Leese tells me she'd like to try the rhythm method of birth control, but since you are the other half of this union, I have to ask if you're okay with that, too."

"I—I don't know what the rhythm method is," he stated uncomfortably.

"There are roughly seven days that a woman who has a regular cycle isn't fertile. During this time period unprotected sex is not likely to end in a pregnancy," she began.

Micah nodded as if that made sense to him.

"But," the good doctor continued, "it's far from perfect. Leese expressed to me in the exam room that she doesn't want to try the pill, patch or injection; she wants to keep this as natural as possible."

Micah nodded, "I can understand; I feel the same way."

"Good, because from using your calendar, Leese," she said turning to me, "your wedding falls perfectly in line with your seven days. I actually prefer to only trust this method for about four or five of those days, but that risk is up to you."

"How big is the risk?" Micah asked before I could get the identical question out of my mouth.

"You'll be running about a ten to twenty percent chance that this first union will end in a pregnancy."

We both swallowed audibly.

"I could use a condom," Micah interrupted, his face turning scarlet.

"True and I'd normally prefer something like that in this situation, but after examining her, it might not be a viable solution."

Micah's eyebrows rose and an odd smile pulled at the corners of his mouth, "Why?"

Now I would finally learn what she found so odd about my anatomy.

"You're going to have to forgive me for broaching what I hope is a subject you two have already discussed, but Micah have you ever had sexual relations with a woman before?"

"Yes," he stated bluntly.

"Ever with a virgin?"

"Ah—no," his face was getting red again.

"Good, then I don't have to tell you to forget whatever you learned with that person, because Leese is a little different from most women."

We were both silent, but I was sure everyone in the quiet room could hear my heart slamming against my rib cage.

"Leese, you have a very thick hymen; that's the barrier that partially closes the entrance to the vagina. Usually it is a thin membrane that is, more often than not, broken by a woman herself

46

either by exploration or sports; yours is not thin; it's more than a half inch thick actually."

"What does that mean exactly," Micah asked, curiosity written clearly on his face.

She looked at him and semi-smiled, "You're going to think there is no entrance. She's a bit like Fort Knox."

"But there is an entrance," I said, a little shocked she was telling my future husband that I was similar to an impenetrable government facility.

"Yes, but there is a little bit more. I realized when I was checking you that you have an additional barrier just beyond the hymen. We don't often see it so I ordered the sonogram to make sure I was correct. This is why a condom may not be a viable choice," she said turning to Micah. "You're going to need to be forceful to get past the hymen and you may feel you've met a wall when you get to the next barrier, but I assure you, you can push through it; it's just going to be uncomfortable for Leese, and it might be too much stress on a condom."

We were back to being silent as her words were being ingested.

"I could," she spoke up, "surgically remove most of, or the entire, hymen."

"No!" we responded at the same moment, but I had a feeling for totally different reasons.

"I recommend you take a little tension off an hour or so before you actually have sex," she said, once again looking to Micah. "You under—"

"Yes," he said, red-faced again, but deeper this time.

"I'd prefer to put you on a low-estrogen birth control pill now Leese, so—"

"No—I told you my mother had all kinds of problems with the pill and I don't want to risk it."

"I understand, but you're made from more than just her gene pool; you might not have any problems.

"Just the same, I'd rather our wedding night be as natural as possible."

"I do recommend you switch to condoms after the first few nights. Well," she said standing up and reaching out to shake my hand, "Enjoy your wedding night and take your time. Sex will become more comfortable for you once you two are past the first night, but you are going to be sore." Then she reached out and shook Micah's hand. "You, Micah, are a very lucky man to get to experience this with her."

He finally smiled, "I'm a lucky man even if this wasn't her first time."

Now it was my turn to be red-faced as it seemed the doctor was presenting me as some type of strange prize.

We didn't speak to each other as we left. I handed him my keys and went for the passenger's side.

"You don't want to drive?" he couldn't mask his surprise.

"No," I whispered. I was still rolling everything she had said around and wondering if my first magical night with Micah was going to really be as difficult as the doctor predicted.

He backed out and headed away from the complex, "You're pretty quiet. Are you afraid now?"

"I just didn't expect... I mean, I thought everything would be normal."

He squeezed my hand and then brought it to his lips and kissed the back of it, "You'll be fine, I'm sure it's not going to be quite as difficult as she thinks."

"What if it is? What if I can't take it?" Now I was getting emotional. I craved Micah with every fiber of my being, and I couldn't imagine not being able to consummate a relationship with him.

"Baby," he said, using his deep sexy tone with me, "people get through this all the time. I'll be gentle." I could see the smile was working hard to turn the corners of his lips, though he was obviously attempting to resist it.

I managed a smile as I looked away, "Well, at least it sounds like you're going to have a fantastic night."

His smile could no longer stay down, "I won't lie to you, baby, you're right. It sounds like I'm getting the better end of the wedding night, but I'm going to do everything I can to make it perfect for you."

I brought his hand against my cheek, absorbing the warmth after the doctor's office left me feeling so cold.

He was gently stroking my cheek, but then had to pull away to shift gears. "I love you, Leese; if you tell me to stop, I will. We can come back and have the doctor make this easier for you."

"I can't imagine stopping once we..." I felt a flush of heat fill me, opening the yearning I knew was made for him alone.

"I can stop, if you tell me," he was completely serious.

"Yeah, but I don't think I can," I admitted.

He smiled as we pulled up to the traffic light. He leaned over and kissed me slowly.

"I know I won't want you to stop," I whispered. "You're right, we'll be fine."

Chapter Four

Six weeks were gone in a blur. Linda certainly earned her pay because every single day it seemed she and I were working together to make this wedding flawless. Early on Micah and I discussed the bridesmaids and groomsmen for the wedding. Although we both had plenty of people to choose from, Micah felt it would have been an odd blending of two worlds, Palm Beach socialites walking the aisles with mafia men wouldn't work well. We finally settled on a rather untraditional arrangement. He asked David, to be his best man, and I asked my mother to be my maid of honor. I asked Giorgio if he would mind walking me down the aisle, but when the time came to join the families by the giving away of the bride, my mother would be the one to speak up and give me away. Kimmy would be the flower girl and Mom and David would hold the wedding rings until the moment of exchange.

I invited my Pensacola friends, but the only ones who could make it were Kevin and Carlie. I was disappointed Jewels couldn't make it, but she said her parents wouldn't bring her nor allow her to travel alone. Ryan was still here with his mother in Palm Beach, planning to return to Pensacola a week after the wedding to complete his senior year. He seemed a bit relieved when I told him Jewels wasn't coming down. He said they had basically broken up for the summer, and he wasn't sure if he wanted to see her right now. I didn't like the idea of his being alone, so I offered to fix him up with one of my other friends, just for the wedding of course, but he politely refused.

All seemed to be going well until David and Giorgio flew in the week before the wedding for the rehearsal. We invited them both to stay at the house. But it shocked me when David started to flirt with my mother! And, what was more shocking was Micah didn't seem to think it was a big deal. I stole a few private moments with Micah after dinner that night, pulling him out to the garage and into my car to vent my frustration.

"Baby, David is 29 and your mom is 35, they only have one more year difference between them than we do."

"She's my mother!"

"Well, she is hot."

"Micah!" I couldn't mask my shock, "you never said you thought my mom was hot."

"Leese, I'm crazy in love with you and I think you are the most gorgeous woman I've ever met, but even you said your mom was beautiful."

"Beautiful is beautiful—not hot."

"You're beautiful *and hot.*"

"But—but she's my mother and he—he..."

"Is mafia?" he stated raising his eyebrows at me.

"NO—he drugged me! And, let's not forget, tried to shoot me."

He started to laugh, and then leaned across the leather seat and kissed me, "That was under totally different circumstances, and he does know how to behave when he isn't trying to save my ass or yours for that matter. We both owe him."

"Mom isn't payment," I hissed.

"I'll tell him to cool it and we'll leave the rest up to your mother."

"Ah! Well then that means I have to have a talk with her," I growled, my frustration level rising.

Micah sighed, "Baby, do you really want your mother to know what happened between us *before* I proposed?" I could see a small amount of worry in his eyes.

I calmed. He was right. I couldn't tell Mom what to watch out for with David. And, he was being impossibly polite and charming (a side to David I'd never seen). "Just please do me a favor and let him know Kimmy picks up on things quickly, and I would prefer he didn't make passes at Mom, especially with her around."

"Deal. Besides, I don't think he'll get too forward with Dad here. Now if he were here alone, I think we'd have a problem." He gave me one more quick kiss and suggested we go back inside and stop ignoring our guests.

We walked in to find Giorgio enjoying a card game with Kimmy in the dining room and Mom and David were out by the pool having a glass of wine. Damn wine! I knew I should have thrown it out. But I couldn't deny she was actually having fun. She was smiling and laughing, her eyes sparkling with life and happiness. I remembered her motto about only getting one opportunity to live life. Suddenly, I felt bad for trying to take away a chance for her to feel attractive to someone, even if it was David. I could only hope neither one of them would fall for the other—it could get weird; my step-father-brother-in-law? That was a little creepy.

The next day we drove down to show them the monastery and to rehearse. I brought Mom, Giorgio, and Kimmy in my car; Micah and David followed in the Corvette. When we arrived, Micah had a constant sheepish look on his face as we went through our rehearsal, and I was beginning to wonder exactly what he and David had been discussing on the way down to North Miami. But his face changed when we took everyone on a tour of the grounds and buildings; he was beaming from ear to ear as his father mentioned multiple times that the church was outstanding and beautiful. He had impressed his father and that, I knew, was something very important to him.

We returned home and went out for lunch and then Micah used my car to take them back to the airport.

I wanted to see if Mom was interested in talking about David, but she was off to pick up the shoes she had dyed to match her gown, then she and Kimmy were going to the salon for haircuts and to get their nails done. It sounded like a fun girls-afternoon-out, but I had my day of pampering already scheduled for the day before the wedding, so I stayed at home and waited for Micah to return.

When he came home, I got the distinct feeling he was trying to avoid me.

"I'm going to take a shower," he declared as soon as he realized we were alone.

"Why? You had one last night and I haven't done anything to make you run for it," I teased, wrapping my arms around his waist.

He kissed me quickly and tried to slip from my grip, "I'll be back down in a little while."

"Good," I replied, my suspicions getting stronger, "then we can discuss David—and Mom."

His face lost color as the slight smile he had melted away, "Wh—why? What did your Mom say about him?"

"She's avoiding me, like you're trying to do. What did David say to you on the drive to the church?"

"Leese, do you remember when we were in the Inlet Motel and you thought I'd gone out and done something you didn't want to know about? Do you remember what you said to me when you thought I was getting ready to confess?"

"Yeah, I said... Aaah!"

"Baby, there are some things you really *do* want to remain ignorant about." He was giving me a very sympathetic look, "And besides, we're getting married in six days and I was hoping they would be six happy days."

"*Exactly* what did David tell you?" There was no way he was getting away from me now. I had to know what it was he didn't want me to know.

Micah put his hand on the back of his neck and rolled his head as if he was suddenly stiff, "Well, he used a lot of four letter words."

"What!"

"Yeah, he used like, want, need, and—and love several times. I don't know what the women in this family do to the men in my family, but I'm afraid he is crazy about your mother."

"But all they did was sit out by the pool and talk."

He gave me a strange look.

"That was all they did, right? We were the last ones to go to bed."

For someone very large, he started to get small in a hurry, "Remain ignorant, remember."

"She didn't—they didn't—"

He cringed. "Baby—"

I put my hand over my open mouth, "Did he drug her?!"

"No," he offered quickly, "It was absolutely consensual. *Don't flip out on me, please*. I told him I didn't want to know!" he rolled his eyes toward the ceiling.

I wasn't sure if I wanted to cry or scream. The tears seemed to be winning the emotional battle. Micah was right, ignorance would have been better.

"Do you want to know anymore? I think if you just listen to what he told me, you won't be so upset."

"Would you want to hear about your mother doing something like that?"

"My mother isn't single, and she's 51. Come upstairs with me, baby, and I'll tell you the rest. I don't want your mom to walk in and catch us discussing what happened."

I slumped against his shoulder as he wrapped his arm around me and led me upstairs. He scooped me up as we entered his room. He knew how much I loved it when he picked me up and pulled me in close, placing me on the bed and wrapping his arm around my waist. He kissed my bare neck and began telling me how they had enjoyed each other's company so much they decided to meet downstairs after everyone went to sleep.

"They were both hurting. She got to talk about everything she has gone through with Robert. She didn't know David was the informant that busted Robert until last night. He explained, as much as he could, about the problems he's still facing for doing it. He's been ostracized and it's killing him to be out of the family. She talked to him about your dad and how much she missed him and—and she said how much David reminded her of him."

I was thinking about the fact that she had said the same thing about Micah, but then again David and Micah looked a lot alike.

"David has never said a woman fascinated him, but she did. That's not how he normally views women—they're good for one thing as far as he's concerned."

"Well, he should be happy. He got what he wanted." I said, wiping the last of the tears from my cheeks.

"Baby, he said he didn't want to make a move on Nadia, but she asked if she could kiss him and he said everything just unraveled. He said she seemed so fragile and hurt by everything—he was hurting and he described it as beautiful—my brother who has never used the phrase 'making love' said that was a true first for him; it wasn't just sex. She told him not to expect a relationship, especially since you and I are getting married, but he's in new territory and I know it really messed with his head."

"I could tell," I began, "when I saw them last night out by the pool that she was actually happy. I haven't seen her like that in like forever. I don't want you to think I hate David—it's just weird for me, that's all."

"I understand how you feel about the moral side of this," he empathized, as he stroked my arm. "That's one thing that you and your mom don't share, but—"

"Yeah, if we shared that," I laughed bitterly, "You and I wouldn't be discussing this because I wouldn't exist."

His face descended into the pile of my hair at the back of my neck. I could hear him inhaling deeply as he nuzzled into it, "Then, baby, I'm glad she doesn't because I can't imagine my world without you."

I rolled over and wrapped my arms around his glorious neck as I kissed him slowly and tenderly. He began to moan as his body covered my own. We'd been so well behaved lately that it felt good to forget the rules for a few minutes.

"I guess it proves my point about God having a purpose for everything. I wouldn't have done what she did at seventeen and this wouldn't be happening right now."

"I know I shouldn't ask this and spoil the moment, but your mom told David she was safe, as far as getting pregnant goes. She is, right?"

I finally smiled, "She had her tubes tied after Kimmy was born." But with that said a new worry entered my mind and I had to ask, "What about David? I mean, I know he's been around, a lot evidently, and I hate to think they had unprotected sex, but it sounds like they did. I don't want her life to be cut short because she spent a night with him."

"He's always been careful about that—always. But, he didn't come here for the night and expect to... Well, I'll just say he wasn't prepared. I was actually kind of worried about that because even though Nadia's been with Robert all this time, Robert has been with Sharon and who knows who all she's been with."

"Micah, I've never asked, but have you always been safe?"

He looked at me with those deep green eyes as he tucked a lock of hair behind my ear. I could tell he was getting emotional and I was suddenly afraid of the answer.

"No, not always," he replied with his voice getting husky, "but before I came back and asked you to marry me I went and had myself tested—I couldn't take it if I did anything to hurt you that way. Everything came back fine; we're safe together." Then a broad smile crossed his face, "That is if your rhythm method works. We won't be baby-safe if it doesn't."

"I think we'll leave that one up to God. All I know is in less than one week I'll have everything I've ever wanted. I love you, Micah."

He brushed his lips to mine, "So you're okay about what happened between David and your mom? You aren't going to let her know he told me all of this, are you?"

"No, I'm okay now. I just hope he doesn't end up being my—my step-dad."

Micah busted out with laughter.

"What?" I demanded, pushing at his broad shoulders, trying to wiggle free. He was still laughing, "What's so funny?"

"He was coming up with all those combinations in the car; step-daughter-sister-in-law, son-in-law-brother, and my personal favorite, grandpa-uncle."

Okay, I had to admit it was funny in a stupid way, and I found myself laughing with him.

Chapter Five

The days passed quickly, yet as happy as I was that it had finally arrived, I was scared. The nightmare had returned over the last few nights and I was worried something would go wrong and I'd never have the happy-ever-after I wanted so desperately. I wouldn't feel safe until he was in my arms tonight and we passed the point of no return.

I waited nervously with Giorgio for the wedding march to begin.

He patted my arm and smiled warmly, "I never thought my son would fall in love, but you changed all that Annalisa and I don't think he could have found anyone more perfect."

I smiled with quivering lips. I was afraid to speak and give reason for the waiting tears to roll down my cheeks.

He pressed the back of my hand to his lips, "Be happy together."

The wedding march began and it was time to go. He offered his arm. I laced mine through his and took one long breath and then began to move toward my future, toward my forever, toward the person I loved more than life, Micah.

The chapel was bathed in candlelight, guests filled the room, and waiting for me at the end of the aisle was the most beautiful man in a traditional black and white tux. I kept telling myself not to cry, but with every step I took, I could feel the tears building. I knew there were people present that I should have taken notice of, but I couldn't see anyone besides Micah.

We reached the end of the aisle and Giorgio kissed my cheek through the veil and took his seat with Celeste.

Pastor Anderson from our Palm Beach church began, "Friends and relatives, we have come here this evening to share the joy of the wedding between Micah and Annalisa. Tonight is an outward expression of their love and devotion toward one another. They seek God the Father to unite them in this sacred relationship of marriage and ask you to witness this blessed event. Who here gives this woman to be married to this man?"

My mother stepped up beside me, "I give her to Micah with my blessing," she stated and then took one step to the left.

He turned to us and continued, "The Marriage ceremony is one of the first and oldest ceremonies in all the world, performed in the presence of God, and is a gift that divides our sorrows and doubles our joys in life. This is a joining of hands, a blending of hearts, a uniting of lives not by the strength of the state nor the certificate of marriage, but by the strength and power of the faith and love you have in one another. Please turn and face each other and join hands."

I handed my bridal bouquet to Mom and then turned to Micah and slipped my trembling hands into his warm, steady hands. I suddenly found myself smiling, laughing on the inside. Damn hit man, I thought, always steady under pressure and I'm about to fall apart. He looked at me and returned the smile. I wondered if he could possibly know what I was thinking.

"Micah, please repeat this vow to Annalisa, saying after me: I Micah…"

For me, Pastor Anderson's voiced faded away and all I could hear was Micah.

"I Micah take you, Annalisa, to be my wife, to have and to hold, from this day forward, for better or for worse, for richer or for poorer, in sickness and in health, I promise to love and cherish you forever." Forever wasn't something that Pastor Anderson stated, but I'm glad Micah added it to the vow because he knew all along I wanted forever so badly with him.

And then I repeated my vow to him, my voice remarkably steadier than I felt on the inside. "…I promise to love and cherish you *forever*," I finished.

Pastor Anderson continued, "The Word of God defines for us what true love really is and what it does: Love is patient, love is kind, love is not jealous; love doesn't boast and is not arrogant, it does not act unbecomingly; it does not seek its own, it is not provoked, and it does not take into account a wrong suffered, nor does it rejoice in unrighteousness, but rejoices with the truth; for love bears all things, believes all things, hopes all things, and endures all things, but above all, love never fails. Is this the love you share?" he asked.

"It is," we answered together.

"Then, having committed this kind of love to one another, you have chosen to exchange rings as the sign and seal of the promises you are making today. Micah, do you have the ring for Annalisa? May I have the ring?"

David handed the ring to Micah and Micah placed it in the pastor's open hand.

"Annalisa, do you have the ring for Micah? May I have the ring?"

Mom handed me the ring and I placed it into the waiting hand.

"The rings," he continued, "are a significant token and symbol of this love that you share. They are made of precious metal and stone, reminding us that love is neither cheap nor common; but is in fact a very costly and dear thing. They are made in a continuous circle signifying that we must keep love continuous throughout our whole lives. As you wear these rings, whether you are together or apart, may these rings be a constant reminder of the promises you are making to one another this day.

"Micah will you please take this ring and place it upon the third finger of Annalisa's left hand, and holding her hand in yours, please repeat this promise to her, saying after me:…."

Micah held my hand warmly as he slid the ring onto my finger and stated, "With this ring, I seal my promise to be your faithful and loving husband, as God is my witness."

"Annalisa," Pastor Anderson said, handing me Micah's ring, "Will you please take this ring and place it on the third finger of Micah's left hand, holding his hand in yours, please repeat this promise to him, saying after me:…."

I took Micah's large hand into mine and slipped the ring onto his finger as I stated, "With this ring, I seal my promise to be your faithful and loving wife, as God is my witness."

"Ladies and gentleman, please bow your heads as we offer a blessing for this couple: Now you will feel no rain, for each of you will shelter the other. Now you will feel no cold, for you will be warmth for the other. Now there will be no more loneliness because you are together. The twain has become one and you face one life set before you. Enter into your house together that all the days of your union may be good and beautiful and long upon this earth.

"Micah and Annalisa, you have come before us and God to express your desire to be husband and wife. You have demonstrated your love and affection by joining hands and have made promises of faith and devotion, each to the other, and have sealed these promises by the giving and the exchanging of the rings. Therefore, it is my privilege as a minister and by the state of Florida, I pronounce you *are* husband and wife. Micah, you may kiss your wife."

As Micah lifted my veil, I saw the first tear slip down his cheek. I hadn't realized until that moment my tears had been softly sliding down my face. We looked at each other and, in unison, said, "I love you." I felt his lips envelope mine as he brought me against his chest. My world vanished as he took away my ability to breathe with the most heartfelt, tender, and warm kiss of my life.

"Ladies and gentleman," Pastor Anderson said as he turned us to face the roomful of people, "it is my privilege to introduce to you for the first time, Mr. and Mrs. Micah Gavarreen."

It was so incredible to realize we did it. The door to forever opened before us as we walked out of the chapel as husband and wife.

We exited the chapel as our guest went ahead of us to the reception. The photographer kept us occupied for about another half hour and then we finally joined the celebration. We cut the cake and shared the first slice without smearing it in each other's face, but I could see the smile tearing at the corners of Micah's mouth as he positioned the cake for me to bite into it and the thought popped into his head.

When it came time to share the first drink, I was surprised to find that it was grape juice instead of wine. Micah said wine was traditional, but evidently he changed his mind and decided we would keep our promise to each other to avoid alcohol.

The lights dimmed as the time came for our first dance. The music began and the song we chose, *When God Made You*, by Newsong and Natalie Grant began. I knew I wouldn't be able to stop myself from singing, but I never expected, as he held me tight and slowly spun me across the floor that he would begin to sing quietly to me.

"...but now that I have found you I believe, that a miracle has come when God sends the perfect one. Now gone are all my questions about why, and I've never been so sure of anything in my life... I wonder if He knew everything I would need, because He made all my dreams come true. When God made you, He must have been thinking about me."

He held me so securely that I couldn't pull away to look into his face, but I could tell as he finished those last words he was becoming emotional. Softly, I sang my part back to him.

"I promise that wherever you may go, wherever life may lead you, with all my heart I'll be there too. And from this moment on I want you to know, I'll let nothing come between us... I wonder what God was thinking when He created you, I wonder if He knew everything I would need because He made all my dreams come true. When God made you He must've been thinking about me."

As the song ended and everyone clapped, we held each other for a moment longer and dried each other's tears. From that point on, the dancing was a blur to me. I danced with Giorgio next as Micah took his mother onto the floor. Friends and family began taking their turns dancing with the bride and it didn't take long before someone spun me and I ended up in David's arms.

"Best man's turn," he said with an easy smile.

I wasn't sure how to respond to him simply because, even though I accepted the fact that he was infatuated with my mother, I hadn't spoken to him about what had happened that night. I gave a light smile as he took me across the floor. He was a good dancer, which didn't really surprise me since the ability to move well was one of Micah's traits also. Dancing wasn't how they learned it, but it came from years of fights, struggles and bullet ballets.

"I don't normally like to attend these things," he continued, "and I've never agreed to take part in one, but since you're stealing away my baby brother, I figured, what the hell. Why not?"

"I'm not removing him from the planet, David," I responded.

"Oh, yes you are. You took him out of his world the minute you stole his heart when he was supposed to kill you." His face still wore the smile and no one would be the wiser as to what we were discussing. "We did the majority of our jobs together, but I had a

61

strange feeling when he agreed to your hit that something was getting ready to change, I just never would have expected this. I haven't had a job with him since." He continued to dance me toward the door that led out to the gardens, and I willingly followed his lead as we stepped away from the crowd.

Micah and I didn't discuss his previous victims because when he said I wouldn't want to know how ruthless he was before he met me, I believed him. I assumed he worked alone, and I never imagined he and David partnered on much of what they did. No wonder David disliked me so much at the beginning. With Micah out of the mafia, David was now alone, but it didn't matter at this point since he helped put Robert away. Micah told me after David worked with the police to nail Robert, he hadn't had a job since—no one would touch him. I owed this man quite a bit, but I hoped what I was getting ready to tell him wouldn't be considered payment.

"I know, Micah told me," I said and then changed subjects. "You're sure you can only stay tonight? I booked your room at the Acqualina for two nights, in case you change your mind."

I followed his eyes as he looked over to where my mother was dancing with one of my cousins, "I wish I could stay longer, I just—"

"I trust you are pretty good at being covert, but just to let you know Kimmy is a solid sleeper."

An extremely puzzled look crossed his face.

"The room I booked for you," I continued, "has a guest door to the adjoining room—Nadia's room." I couldn't call her Mom for the moment as I was explaining that he could have access to her, if she were willing. "You will promise me to be discreet and that you'll never ever do anything to hurt her. Agreed?"

I watched his eyes as he studied me.

"He told you?"

I could see the honest surprise.

"He said he didn't want to know because you would make him tell you. I didn't believe him. I've seen people try to beat stuff out of that boy and he's never opened his mouth. *What do you do to him?*"

"You talked with my mother. Did you tell her some things you didn't expect to say?"

The smile on his face grew wider as he began to see my point.

"So you tell me what we do, because I don't know."

"I'm really glad," he confessed as he pulled me tightly against his chest just like his brother and then whispered in my ear, "that Micah jumped me *before* I squeezed the trigger that day because I didn't realize what a treasure he'd found."

"Oh, yes, that reminds me." I pushed back to regain the proper distance; Micah was the only one who needed to hold me that close. "You will promise, swear on your brother's life actually, that no drugs will be involved; if she says no, you'll take no for an answer."

He got an odd look to his face, "Believe it or not, I couldn't do that to her—I can take a no."

The song ended and David leaned forward and slowly kissed my cheek. He squeezed my hands and thanked me and said he was going to get the next dance with Nadia before someone else got to her.

I watched him walk back into the room just as I felt someone touch my arm; Micah was there.

"I was wondering why he brought you out here?" he quietly questioned.

I smiled, "I was willing. I had to tell him something."

"What?"

"That I booked him a room with a guest door—to my mother's suite."

He grinned and gave a small chuckle, "You are never going to stop surprising me, are you?"

I pulled him into my arms and kissed him softly, "I certainly hope not."

At that moment we heard the sound of someone coming out to the garden, and, as we turned to see who it was, Ryan was standing there, but abruptly retreated to go back inside.

"Ryan," Micah called out to him.

He paused and looked at us.

Micah lifted my hand toward him, "Have you danced with the bride yet?"

He didn't say a word; he crossed the short distance between us and accepted my hand.

Micah kissed my cheek and went back inside, once again trying his wings out at not being jealous.

"I asked them to play a special song," he stated, a light blush came across his cheeks. "I don't know if they have—"

At that moment the music began to flow from the reception hall and I could hear the Michael W. Smith song, *Friends are Friends Forever*, begin to play.

"Would you like to dance?" he asked quite gallantly.

"You don't have to ask," I smiled and went into his arms. "I like the song choice; it's perfect."

He gave a heavy sigh and continued to dance.

"What's the matter?" I asked.

He looked down at me with those big blue eyes and said he had lousy timing.

"What do you mean?"

"I had the chance to start at PHS in the fall last year, but I drug my feet until March. If I'd have…" He shook his head and went silent.

It didn't matter, I knew what he was thinking and I was surprised at myself as the realization hit me that he was absolutely right. "If you'd have started sooner, I'd be with you instead of Micah?"

A half smile emerged, "Definitely. I liked you from the moment I met you in English class. I think I'd have had my work cut out for me, but I'd like to think you'd have eventually come around."

I blushed. "I would have," I confirmed for him. "But I'm sure God intended for us to just be friends, really good friends." But it was time to change the subject because the hold he had on me was getting firmer, "So you'll start back at school next week. What's after that?"

"I'll finish up at PHS since they have the Air Force ROTC program and then it's on to Colorado Springs."

I raised my eyebrows without thinking, "What's there?"

"The United States Air Force Academy; I have a full scholarship."

"Wow, that's pretty impressive, but…"

"But what?"

"What happened to Eglin? I thought you'd be staying in Florida."

"No, I just had family at Eglin."

An odd pang hit me hard in the chest as the thought of Ryan flying into a war zone crossed my mind, "H—how long does it take to become a pilot?"

"I'm already a pilot," he replied as smoothly as if he was telling me he was male, "but it takes a bachelor's degree from the Academy, officer's training and a lot of other things to fly in the Air Force."

I took in a comforting breath; a lot can happen in four years, and maybe the world will be a more peaceful place when the time comes for him to hit the sky.

"So how about you? Does your life end here tonight?" he asked.

I know the color drained from my face, "What?" The shock I felt was clearly communicated in my single word question.

"I mean are you forgetting about college and a career? I'm seeing him as a 'keep-her-barefoot-and-pregnant' kind of guy."

I rolled my eyes and felt the color returning to my cheeks, "He's already told me he doesn't want me to be a teenage mother and, to answer the first part of that question, I haven't decided yet exactly what I want to do, but whatever it is it won't be for the money—I have that covered."

He laughed, a big grin spread across his face, "Yeah, I know that's right." He spun me slowly in time to the music and then the smile faded, "So I guess this is gonna be it for us—I wish it wasn't."

"Why does this have to 'be it' for us? Can't we keep in touch?"

"No one ever does that, Leese. Everyone has good intentions and then they drift apart and the years slip by, and before you know it, we'll only be a memory for each other."

"Geez, Ryan, that's a depressing statement," I frowned. I truly didn't want this to be it. He and Micah were the most unique people in my life. Micah and I were pledged to having forever together, but how do you keep a friend from slipping away?

"It's true. You have a new life in front of you that doesn't include your friends. But," he added with a sweet look on his face, "I'll never, ever forget you." His lips came against my cheek and rested there for a long moment. "I don't suppose," he whispered, "You'd approve if I moved this to your lips, would you?"

I returned the kiss to his cheek, "No—these lips are for my husband. But I guarantee you that I won't forget you either." I wasn't expecting to cry, but I felt the sting coming on, "Are you staying at the Acqualina like most of the guests?" I was trying to find any reason for this not to be the last time I would see his face.

65

"I'll spend a couple nights, but then it's back to Pensacola." The song was ending and he gave me a firm squeeze and kissed my forehead, "Love you, Leese," he said, turning me loose and walking away.

One tear slipped down my cheek and I quickly wiped it away as Micah came around the corner to bring me back inside where our guests were waiting. I know he saw it, but he also knew I considered Ryan a good friend.

He pulled me on to the dance floor, "I think this will be our last dance tonight, here anyway," he added with a sultry look so hot I could feel it on my skin.

"Special request?" I asked.

"Definitely, baby. Your request."

"My request?"

"I think you'll remember," he smiled, centering us on the dance floor as the guests moved away and the lights dimmed.

As the music began, I realized it was the song I picked when he slow danced with me in my music studio at home. The blush felt as if it covered me from head to toe as *I'll Make Love to You*, began to fill the room.

"Are you ready?" he whispered in an echo to the singer's words, "I'll hold you tight, baby, all through the night...tonight is your night."

"Oh, Micah," I whispered back, "I didn't think tonight was ever going to arrive. I'm ready to spend the first night of the rest of my life in your arms. Let's go."

The next thing I knew we were running for the open limousine door as our guests blew a shower of bubbles over the walkway.

The hotel was only minutes away and before I could even collect my thoughts we were in the elevator and on the way up to our suite. Micah became very quiet, but his eyes were speaking volumes about what was going through his mind. I couldn't stop the constant blush that waved across my skin as he held me in his gaze.

When we reached the door, he opened it and then swept me off my feet and carried me inside, "We made it, baby—I can't believe we're finally here."

"Me either," I said, smiling up at him.

"I was thinking, since we've been so patient, there is no reason to rush tonight. I'd like to get comfortable and dance with you some more."

I was pleasantly surprised, especially since I was scared, but I didn't want to tell him I was feeling this way.

He came around behind me, his lips caressing my bare shoulders and neck as he slowly unzipped my gown. His mouth followed the zipper down to the base of my spine. He was kneeling on the floor when he finished, his steel hands holding my hips as he placed kisses on my lower back.

I turned and looked into those eyes so filled with love as I allowed the gown to slip to the floor. He offered me his hand and I stepped out of it. I could see the flush of heat on his skin as he looked at me in my lacy white bustier, panties, and garter.

"Go ahead and slip on something comfortable," he said through husky vocal cords.

I disappeared into the bedroom, putting away my gown and pulling out the silk, white baby doll outfit I had chosen for tonight. I hadn't realized how badly I was shaking until I tried to put it on.

When I returned to where he was waiting, I noticed he removed most of the trappings of his full tuxedo and was down to just the slacks and his dress shirt, untucked and the buttons undone. I hadn't shown him my outfit when I bought it; I wanted it to be a surprise and from the look on his face I knew he liked my choice.

He had the stereo softly playing love songs in the background as he opened his arms and pulled me in close, "Leese, I can't even begin to describe how much I love you—it may sound a little weird, but it almost hurts."

It didn't sound weird to me. I'd been feeling the ache and hurt inside me since the first time I realized I was falling in love with him, "I know what you mean; I feel the same way."

We danced around the living room for quite some time as the heat and the desire to take the final step into forever became overwhelmingly powerful.

His breathing became shallow and quick as he finally confessed he didn't want to wait any longer and asked, if I was ready, could he take me to the bedroom?

"Yes, Micah," I whispered, "I'm ready. Make love to me, baby." I looked into those eyes and knew there was no turning back now.

He was holding me to his chest as he carried me to the bed. The moonlit Atlantic sparkled beyond the large glass doors leading out to our balcony. I had two candles burning, but otherwise the room was dim.

He kissed me long and deep when he laid me back on the bed. His hands, hands that had always been careful not to be sexual, hands that had not caressed my breasts or inner thighs began to command my body. My back arched with need as he slipped the straps from my shoulders, kissing the places as he exposed them. His hot mouth suddenly suckling and caressing my breasts, and I felt all semblances of my control erode as I began to beg for him, to experience him, to give all I had to him.

His hands stopped as they gripped the sides of my panties, and he looked at me. I was lost somewhere in a place of tremendous need as I returned the gaze and begged him not to stop. I never expected him to kiss and caress what he was uncovering, but it was the most unique sensation I'd ever experienced as his mouth buried against the center of my desire.

I pulled away from him, sliding upward into the bed with what must have been a look of fright on my face.

"Are you okay, Leese? Did I do something wrong?" he whispered.

"I've never felt this way, Micah," I choked out. "I'm scared."

"I just thought you'd like to get off before—"

"Get off what?" I was down to bare skin; there wasn't anything else to remove.

His head cocked sideways as he pulled himself up to look into my eyes, "Leese, I know you've never had sex, but you've gotten off before—the shower in the bungalow, you…" An unusual look spread across his face. "All you did was take a shower?"

"What else would I do in the shower?"

"No wonder it didn't help you," he whispered, kissing the tip of my nose. "You've never had an orgasm? Baby, I didn't know you were *that* virgin."

All I knew was that an orgasm was a sexual experience and something I thought was to be saved for tonight, "Don't I need you for that?"

He smiled slowly, "No, but I'm certainly glad you've saved it for me."

"But, how could I—"

"That's why you stopped me. You were starting to feel it coming on weren't you?"

"I don't know what that was, but I was afraid I was getting ready to lose my grip on reality—because that wasn't real."

"Don't be afraid, baby, I promise you, it's real and you'll like it," he crooned.

"But I'll lose control," I started to tear up, that was the true reason why I had him stop; I realized something was getting ready to happen I couldn't control.

"Baby, we're both going to lose control tonight, but it's okay because that's all a part of making love. I'm going to take control of you and you are going to do the same to me."

"I don't know how," I cried softly, a tear running down my cheek.

He wiped the tear away and smiled, "You do, whether you know it or not. You've got control of me right now and I'd do *anything* to please you."

I nodded, "Then let me take your clothes off."

He rose from the bed and I followed, slowly removing his shirt and kissing and caressing his fabulous body. I knelt in front of him as I undid his waistband.

His hands reach down and stopped me, "I don't think I can handle you doing this part, Leese."

"No. Please, Micah. No boundaries tonight, let me take them off you."

I could tell he was fighting to retain his ability to be in charge of his desire so he wouldn't do what he threatened that morning in the Hyatt. I knew he was ready to grab me and collide with me in the bed, but with tremendous effort he permitted me to remove his slacks. He closed his eyes and I could see his hands clinch as I began to lower his boxers to the floor, but as I did, I permitted myself the first opportunity to touch his body intimately and he snapped.

I didn't even have time to react as my body was moved from kneeling on the floor to lying underneath him on the bed. My heart was pounding so hard it was painful, his teeth biting firmly but gently on my shoulder. He kept repeating "Baby, baby, oh baby," as he pulled me against himself, parts of our bodies touching that I had never experienced. He kissed me hard, and then broke the kiss.

He must have seen the fear on my face as he began to calm, "I can't hurt you, Leese. I've got to slow down."

"Micah, I'm ready for you to hurt me," I said with an unsteady voice, my hips rising to meet his and my calves keeping him from pulling away from me. "Don't stop. I need you."

He was still working on control as he lowered his body against mine.

The heat alone was enough for strange sensations to hit me. I felt his body push as my body resisted. I gasped for my breath.

He looked at me as a strange smile appeared on his face, "She's right. I feel like I don't know what I'm doing. I need you to guide me, Leese. You're going to have to show me where it feels right for you."

I was truly frightened to touch him intimately again, the last time was explosive enough, but I could tell he was ready for the sensation of my hand this time. He moaned deeply as I placed him where my sensations seemed to culminate, where need, desire, and heat centered themselves.

"Now, baby?" he asked.

I nodded as he pushed again. I didn't mean to sink my nails into his back, but I couldn't help myself as my body resisted him.

He knew what would help me forget the pain, as his mouth descended on to mine and he kissed me with all the emotion he had the very first time our lips ever met, stealing away my ability to breathe. His hips thrust and the barrier gave way.

I gasped and cried out, a mingling of pain and pleasure enveloped me.

"Are you okay?" he asked, his body stopped all forward movement.

I was still catching my breath, a feeling mounting that was completely foreign to me and it frightened me to the core. It felt as if someone inside me that I never knew had been awakened and was about to take over.

He pressed again and once more my body was resisting. I knew there was more of him waiting to enter as he pressed again. I was losing my fear of what was about to happen and instead I was building to some invisible anticipation of what was taking place inside me.

"I can't, Leese. I'm sorry, but it feels like I'm going to tear you in two."

"No, please…ah…Micah, don't stop," I panted. "I need you, baby…ah." The experience was beginning to overwhelm me.

He pressed harder and the barrier gave way.

I didn't mean to get loud, but I couldn't help myself as he moved rhythmically within me, shock waves of pleasure coursing through me. I couldn't breathe and I couldn't stop what he had put into motion inside me as I rode over the top of the new sensation.

He cried out, and I suddenly realized he was joining me in this feeling as our bodies no longer had a separation where one ended and the other began.

He held me for the longest time as he slowed his breathing, kissing my temple, my cheek, the tip of my nose, my lips, and chin. "Baby," he said, choked by emotion, "I've never… You are the most perfect thing I've ever known in my life and definitely worth the wait. I love you."

He began to pull away when I finally found my voice, "Please, can we stay this way for a little while? I don't want this to end just yet."

"Baby," he crooned in his velvety voice, "this is only the beginning; we've got a lifetime to enjoy each other."

My nightmare flashed in my mind and I tried to tell myself there was no reason to worry anymore, we made it, "Please," I begged.

He wrapped me in those steel bands and pulled me in tight, "Anything you want, *anything*."

Eventually, we became drowsy and relaxed.

"Would you take a shower with me?" he whispered.

I was so comfortable, but the idea was appealing and had been appealing since he asked me that same question back when we were staying in the bungalow. I looked up and smiled from some place cuddled deep against his chest, "I'd like that."

I sat up, feeling the soreness I hadn't experienced until I started moving. Micah came up behind me as I leaned forward to compensate for the ache, but he realized what I was doing. He pressed his bare body to my back and reached around and allowed his hands to rub my abdominals gently.

"Does it hurt, baby?" he asked, placing a kiss on my shoulder.

I nodded, pressing my hands to his and holding pressure against the cramping feeling.

"Do you want me to carry you?"

"No, I'll be fine," I whispered.

"You go ahead and get into the shower then and let the hot water start relaxing you. I'll join you in a minute."

I wondered why, and then I turned to see him folding up and removing the stained comforter from the bed. The cramping was getting stronger so I followed orders, sitting on the shower ledge and letting the hot rain pour down on me. Within moments the fogged up door to the shower opened and he stepped in. I started to rise, but he told me to stay where I was.

"I want you to relax and let me do the work," he said pouring shower gel into his hands.

What a unique feeling as his large hands slipped over my skin, soaping and massaging as they moved. I was actually feeling guilty to be relaxing and enjoying what he was doing without returning the pleasure, but he was insistent that I enjoy it and that was all. His hands worked lower, gently massaging and washing my lower abdominals and groin. I closed my eyes as he began to wash the more intimate areas. I was a little worried he might get soap in places that would be uncomfortable, but he was incredibly careful and slow as he worked. Eventually his hands slid down my thighs, calves and finished with my feet (which tickled, but there was no way I was going to laugh after such a sensual experience).

He lifted me from the ledge and placed me in his lap, leaning me forward as he began to lather my hair. He was literally removing every ounce of tension from my body as his finger tips massaged my scalp. He pulled the lever to divert the water out the waterfall ledge as he raised me to my feet and allowed the torrent of water to rinse me.

"You've got to let me do this to you," I whispered through heavy eyelids. I was so relaxed under the rising steam I could have laid on the shower floor and slept soundly.

"You can't even keep your eyes open," he chuckled as he turned off the water and began to dry me off. "How are the cramps?"

"I'm relaxed, but they're getting stronger." I wondered how he knew I was cramping, but then I became aware of my body language as I tipped forward slightly with one forearm pressed above my bikini line.

"Then it's off to bed and I'll get you some Motrin."

I nodded and attempted to step out of the shower, but as soon as the cooler air hit me, the cramps tightened. He picked me up and took me to the bed and placed me beneath the covers, tucking me in like a child. I drew my knees up against a pillow clutched to my stomach as the pain grew more intense. He was back with something to drink and three pills in his hand. As soon as I swallowed them, he blew out the candles leaving nothing but moonlight streaming into the room and crawled into the bed and placed his hot body against my back and wrapped me in his arms.

"Still bad?" he whispered thirty minutes later.

I nodded. The pain was like riding a wave, one minute it was rising and peaking and then I seemed to slide down to where I was almost comfortable and then it would build again.

"I should have been more careful," he began to chastise himself.

I laced my fingers through his and brought his hand to my mouth and kissed it, "You were perfect and it was better than I ever imagined it could be. The doctor said I'd be sore, Micah; this isn't your fault. Just keep me warm. I'll be better in the morning."

He kissed my bare shoulder and neck and then nuzzled into my hair, whispering how much he loved me and that was the last thing I remembered until sunrise opened my eyelids.

The cramps ended in the night and my sleep was dreamless and deep. Micah's arm was still wrapped around me as I smiled at the memories from last night. I don't know how, but he realized I was awake.

"Good morning, Mrs. Gavarreen," he said, his hand splayed across my abdominals. Just one of his hands felt as if it could cover me, "feeling better?"

I rolled over and kissed him briefly, "Good enough to make love again to my husband," I replied, then allowed the tip of my tongue to brush against his lips. I wasn't afraid of him anymore as my hand slid under the covers to forbidden places. I could tell it was still difficult for him, but he was managing the sensation, "I want to kiss you," I said barely loud enough for even myself to hear.

Immediately his mouth began seeking mine.

"Not your mouth," I said, keeping my voice soft. "I want to kiss you like you did to me when you pulled my underwear off last night."

His eyes filled with fright, "I'm not ready to handle you doing that, Leese. I'm still getting used to the touch of your hand. You do things to me, inside, that no one's ever done and it's incredibly intense."

"Umm…I like that," I answered, "but you will let me when you're ready?"

He smiled.

I knew that was a yes.

"I want to show you something," he said, smoothly rolling me back to my side and curling his bare form behind me. I was ready to be his eager student once more. He taught me how to shoot, how to kiss, and last night, how to make love, so I had no hesitation in allowing him control.

He propped himself against the headboard and pulled me onto him as if he had become a human lounger. His left arm and hand around mine and his right around my right, but as he brought my left hand up to my breast, I resisted slightly.

"Relax," he whispered, "I just want to show you how to get off."

"You showed me that last night," I said with mirth in my voice, my hand slipping out of his grasp and sliding around his bare thigh.

He gripped my hand and brought it back across my chest. "I mean on your own," he clarified.

"I don't need to learn how to do that. I'll just let you—"

"Baby, I know there'll be times when we're apart and I don't want you to think you need a man for this."

A stab of panic hit me as my heart began picking up the pace, "No, we aren't going to be apart, ever."

"I promised my Dad I would go with him next month to check out some businesses he is considering and—"

"I'll come with you," I interrupted.

He kissed the side of my neck, "That won't work, and I won't be gone long. It won't be often, but I know there are going to be times when we're away from each other. Now, would you please let me show you how to do this? *Please*," he added for emphasis. "Besides, I think it would be a turn on to watch you," he said as his hot breath filled my ear.

Turning him on I knew would become a passion of mine, but being apart, even for a day, I didn't like. I stopped resisting as he brought my hand back to caress my breast and my other was slid lower. Not resisting was going to prove difficult, but soon he was whispering in my ear and caressing my neck with kisses and things eventually became easier, and I found myself eager to do what he wanted me to do. Heat built from friction and need pushed me to the pinnacle as the shockwave gripped me so hard I literally doubled over and rolled to my side, pulling him with me.

"Stop! Stop!" I begged twisting my hand from his grip as the cramps returned with a vengeance. I was trying to catch my breath, trying to force my muscles to relax after the onslaught to my senses.

"Oh, baby," he said, pressing his aroused body hard to mine, "that was sexy." He must have realized I wasn't totally comfortable at the moment. "Are you cramping again?"

"Yeah, but it's already starting to ease."

"I'm sorry. I didn't think this would set them off again."

"It's okay, I'll be fine in a few minutes."

"So how was the orgasm?" he asked, curiosity clear in his voice.

"Hard," I whispered.

"Difficult kind of hard or—"

"Strong kind of hard," I whimpered, drawing up my knees.

"Harder than last night?" There was a funny, surprised sound to his voice.

"Yeah, this was a lot harder, but in a different way." I rolled over to look at him. "I liked last night better, it was more of a complete feeling, this was—I don't know how to describe it, but it was just straight on and intense. I like the feeling of this being part of love making, not just satisfying myself. Does that make sense?"

He gave a crooked smile as he looked up toward the ceiling, "Maybe it wasn't the best idea to show you how to do this. I may have just given myself competition."

The cramps were almost gone as I sat up and placed myself over him, letting my hair brush against his bare chest. "You have nothing to worry about because I prefer you to me anytime. But I want you to show me something else," I smiled.

I could see the amusement on his face, "What?"

I straddled his lap with my knees on either side of his bare groin, and I could see the deep sensation of pleasure wash over him as my body touched his. The steel grip grabbed my thighs and I sighed, arching my back and lifting his hands to my breasts. "Do you remember this, baby?" I said and then attempted to wiggle free. His hands moved swiftly from my breasts to my thighs, clamping down on me almost hard enough to bruise.

"Ooh, Leese, don't—" Then the big smile caused his lips to part, "Yeah, how could I forget."

"I wanted that moment so badly, but we couldn't. I want it now. Make love to me the way you would have that day."

His face pressed against my chest, moaning out my name; his hands lifted my breasts to his scorching mouth as he caressed them. "Leese, I don't know if we can do this without making you hurt again," he panted out the words as his body told me he was ready to enjoy me this way.

"I'm not afraid. Please, Micah."

He reached for the nightstand and grabbed the remote for the stereo; *I'll Make Love to You* came on.

He lifted me by the waist, as I helped by rising up on my knees and then slowly reseated myself, gasping at the feeling as he entered me, his hands showing me to lift myself ever so slightly as he began to move his hips under me. There was no painful barrier, only a firm fluid movement that took me by surprise. I struggled to remember to breathe as he became more intense. He wrapped his arms around me and then rolled me onto the bed, never breaking the rhythm that was perfectly timed to the music.

I danced with him to this song and now he was dancing within me. The sensation was overwhelming. I didn't expect this to be slow and gentle, and the feeling was extraordinary. The rise to pleasure was gradual and rich, as the music changed to *Back at One*, and he continued building a stairway toward heaven. His hips moving, at times, in an easy grind against me and I was slipping beyond the point of no return.

I'm not sure exactly what I was saying to him, except that I loved him so much I wanted him to join me as I crested. I curled my hips toward him so far that the small of my back was no longer on the bed. Then his rhythm changed to a rapid, hard pace and I couldn't wait any longer, my face buried against his neck to muffle my cry and within an instant I could tell he joined me and was experiencing the same pleasure.

His chest heaved as he gasped for air, a light sheen of sweat across his perfect body, "I'm never going to get enough of you, baby," he said, with a breathless kiss to my lips.

"I hope not," I breathed back to him, "but will it always be this good? You don't think I'll become boring, do you?"

He laughed out loud, his head falling back onto the pillow, "Of course you will," he said, flashing his beautiful smile, "in about a million years. No," he answered, all teasing erased. "I didn't truly believe that forever could exist until I met you and now all I can think about is that we're going to spend it together. You'll never be boring to me, Annalisa, so don't change anything. I love you just the way you are—except pregnant, *someday* I want to change you that way, just not now. I want you to get the chance to be young and happy for quite a few more years before we take that step."

"But if I end up pregnant from this Micah, it'll be okay."

"No," he was shaking his head, "she told us we had a small window, that's why this is it for unprotected sex. The next time I make love to you, I'm wearing a condom."

"But Micah, she said four or five days."

"I don't want to get you pregnant at eighteen, Leese. That's too young."

"And if I am right now?" I questioned, turning his face to me and making sure I had his full attention.

"I still say you're too young to go through that."

"Well, I don't believe in abortion, so I guess you'll just have to deal with an eighteen-year-old pregnant wife. God does everything—"

"For a reason, I know. I don't believe in abortion either and I'd never expect you to do something like that, so I guess, to answer your original question, we'd become parents nine months from now. But I'm not taking any more chances with you."

"Will it change things for us? The condoms, I mean."

"It'll change things a little for me, but you should stay happy."

"But I'm not happy if you aren't."

"Trust me, they aren't going to stop me from being happy with you; it'll just take me a little longer to reach my orgasm. By the way, any cramps?"

"If there were, they're gone and all I remember is how fabulous you felt. You were dancing inside me and—"

"Dancing?" he seemed surprised.

"You didn't realize you were timed to the music?"

He started to laugh, "I'm glad I didn't accidently have some hard rock mixed in with the CD's."

I grinned, "Well, I think you had a little hard rock going through your head at the end, but other than that you were my private dancer and I'll never hear those songs quite the same way again."

"How about breakfast and lunch in our room; then we can join some of our guests for dinner tonight?"

I looked at the clock, "That's about eight or nine hours from now. We'll have to think of something to keep us entertained," I said with a sly grin, "I get to wash you in the shower this time."

We both laughed, knowing the next hours would be just as pleasurable as the last.

Chapter Six

Giorgio, Celeste and Gwen were going down to Emeril's Miami Beach restaurant, but David and Mom had plans for a quiet evening at the Acqualina's Beachfront Grill Night, and they were more than willing to have us as company. I was surprised Kimmy wasn't with them when we arrived downstairs. The tables were arranged on the lawn with torches, lanterns and candles for lighting as the Atlantic lapped steadily at the shoreline.

We ordered our drinks and I tried not to frown when they ordered a bottle of wine. Both of them looked different tonight. Mom looked so young, in her gauzy beach dress, her hair pulled back at the temples in a ponytail and the rest was loose on her shoulders. She had gotten some sunshine today and her skin was slightly red, but I knew she tanned easily and by tomorrow she'd be brown. Her smooth, tanned legs were crossed at the knee and casually swinging her sandaled foot in the night air.

David was impressive. I guess he always was, but I had no reason to notice him before. Now I studied him carefully as he smiled and laughed and occasionally reached over and stroked my mother's arm. He was slightly taller than Micah, but the closer I inspected, I realized Micah had a bit of a muscular advantage over his brother. What impressed me the most was the fact that David was completely devoid of vulgarity and crudeness. He was proving he could be a gentleman when necessary, and I liked that side of him. My only problem was forgetting his other side.

"Where's Kimmy," I finally asked as the appetizers were brought to the table.

"They have a pool-side movie night," Mom answered, with the slightest hint of a grin, "she'll be there until about nine or nine thirty."

"By herself?" I was hoping I was wrong.

"Leese, she's six-years-old, of course she has someone with her."

"The hotel offers babysitting?" Micah asked.

"Yeah, but not this late," David responded before Mom could answer, "A friend of Leese's offered, so we decided to take him up on it."

"Him?" I said, clearly confused as to who was watching my little sister.

"Ryan," Mom clarified, "We asked him if he'd like to join us for dinner, but he offered to entertain Kimmy instead."

The conversation around the table continued, but all the while I thought about Ryan's tall, tattooed, macho persona sitting through a Disney film surrounded by small children, all to provide a quiet evening for my mother and a guy who looked a lot like my husband.

"Did you tell him Micah and I were joining you for dinner?" I asked, completely out of sync with what was being discussed.

Mom took a sip of her wine and put the glass back on the table, "Actually, yes, I think I did mention that to him."

I could see from the corner of my eye Micah was studying my face, so I looked at him and tried a smile. It still bothered me to think that Ryan, who should be scoping out the cute girls at the resort or on the beach, was instead 'babysitting.'

Mom and David ordered light from the menu and were soon excusing themselves from our company. I watched David place his arm around her shoulders as she leaned her head against him and they walked away. I felt a light touch on my arm.

"Are you okay?"

"They're both happy. I don't know how I couldn't be okay with that," I sighed.

He leaned over and kissed my cheek, "Why does Ryan watching Kimmy bother you so much?"

I rolled my eyes, "It doesn't bother—"

"Leese," he said, eyebrows rising as if to say to think twice before uttering a lie.

"He should be finding a date, not covering so someone else can have one," I confessed.

80

"He's a big boy. Maybe he wanted to meet a single mom at the pool and Kimmy was his ticket to do that," he gave a light laugh.

I frowned without thinking, "He's not that kind of guy."

"I'm trying hard not to be a jealous person, but you might give me a complex if you spend much more brain power on Ryan instead of me." There was no teasing to his statement.

I knew he was right. It had only been twenty-four hours since we said I do and the only person on my mind should be him. I gave him a sultry smile, "If I start thinking about you, we might be clearing the table for a little public exhibition."

"You know a hit man has to be discreet, but you could probably talk me into that one."

I could tell he was happy the subject was back on the two of us. After our meal, we walked along the shoreline and talked about the future, our future. We discussed houses and neighborhoods, states and relatives. We had been brought and kept together under such unusual circumstances that it was an odd feeling to enter a realm of normalcy.

We stopped and sat on the hard packed sand as the conversation ended and the tender kissing and cuddling began. I think if it hadn't been for the occasional beach walkers, he would have taken me right there, but instead he had to use some of the restraint that we had once been so good at.

"Are you ready to go back upstairs?" he whispered, his deep green eyes sparkling as the moonlight refracted off the white sand.

I nodded, staring into that perfect face and then suddenly found myself becoming overwhelmed with emotion, and the tears began to course down my cheeks.

"Annalisa, what's wrong?"

"I—I don't know," I answered as he tried to wipe away my tears, "all of a sudden, I'm afraid."

"Of me?" he said, clearly shocked.

"No—of course not," I sobbed. "It's just my nightmare—"

"You're still having that? I thought it was over when I moved into your mom's house."

"It's come back lately and I'm just afraid that something is going to ruin what we have."

He pulled me against his chest, "God, Leese, you're about to shake apart. You really are scared, aren't you? Baby, I won't let *anything* come between us."

He was trying to assure me he could keep us together by his own strength, but what he must have forgotten was that it was me in the dream that ran away. I pressed my face against his crisp cotton dress shirt, inhaling his Polo Double-Black cologne and relaxing in his grip.

"I know how you feel, though," he admitted, as he held me. "It so perfect between us, and I've done so much wrong in my life that I can't believe I deserve to have you. But the hard part is over with; you are my wife and I'm not letting go of you." He reached under my chin and placed a slow, sweet kiss on my mouth, "Are you ready to go back inside?"

"Yes."

It was a long night spent in his arms. The love was so gentle and I was so emotional that I must have pulled him into the emotions as well; several times he was overcome. It was the most sensual night we shared yet, touching, stroking, kissing, and needing each other on a level so deep it went beyond the physical and moved into a realm of spiritual. The sky was just beginning to show signs of dawn when we finally fell asleep in each other's arms.

It was two in the afternoon, before I felt him stir beside me. He rolled out and went to the bathroom as I pulled the sheets tightly around myself and wiggled into the warm place he'd left in the bed. He returned and placed a kiss on my bare shoulder, sending goose bumps down my arm.

I tried to get up, but he grabbed me before I could escape, "Micah, I've got to go pee—let me go, baby."

He laughed, but obeyed my request.

"How about break—I mean, how about lunch?" he called out to me. "I'll have it sent up to our room."

I was absolutely starving, but (apparently just like him) I didn't want to dress and leave the room.

Lunch was ordered and we enjoyed our meal in privacy until our room phone rang; it was his family. They were leaving to fly back to Louisiana within the hour and wanted a chance to say goodbye. We dressed and tidied up the room for their visit. We only spoke briefly, and Giorgio confirmed Micah would be joining him the week after we returned from Hawaii to go inspect some prospective businesses. Celeste and Gwen each gave me a teary hug goodbye, but I assured them we would be coming to New Orleans in the next few months to look for a house. Celeste said she would start the search and let us know if she found something suitable.

David pulled me in for a firm embrace and whispered in my ear that he would be returning in a week, and then he kissed my cheek. With the exception of Micah, the whole family looked at him rather oddly. Evidently David wasn't the sweet, touchy-feely kind of person and they were all surprised. I knew, in that moment, he had been very discreet with keeping his relationship with my mother from his family.

Micah went downstairs to see them to their taxi as I stayed behind and called Mom. I wanted to see if she and Kimmy might like to have dinner with us tonight, but I also wanted to see how she was doing now that David was stepping out of the picture for a short span of time. She said they'd love to have dinner with us, especially Kimmy who hadn't seen either one of us since the wedding. I asked about David, and she sighed, admitting she couldn't wait for the week to pass. I was just hanging up when Micah returned. I hate to admit it, but I think the fact that I stopped talking and put down the receiver just as he came into the room, caused him a moment of jealous suspicion.

"Mom," I said, pointing at the phone, "I just called to see if she and Kimmy would have dinner with us tonight."

"Oh," he said, clearly relieved, "so are we having dinner with them?"

"Yes, down in Il Mileno at 7:00 p.m." There was no reason to ask if he liked Italian food; I already knew the answer.

Dinner was enjoyable as we discussed our pending flight to Maui the following evening. Then Kimmy began to tell us about how much fun she'd had last night during the movie. I could see Micah tensing as she went on and on about how nice Ryan was to her and how much he talked about me.

"You were right," she said, smiling up at him as she placed a forkful of pasta in her mouth, "he really does like Leese as much as you do."

I know a little blush of embarrassment hit my cheeks, but then I remembered Micah's explanation of who Ryan was to Kimmy the morning I made the pancake breakfast.

"Can't you have two husbands?" she questioned me innocently.

"Kimberly Margaret!" Mom snapped. "No. Women don't have two husbands and men don't have two wives. Ryan is only Leese's friend."

I could see a moment of curiosity hit Micah as he leaned toward Kimmy, "Do you think your sister made the right choice?"

Mom froze, never expecting him to ask her such a question.

My mouth had gone dry and all I could think was Micah would be crushed if my sweet little sister preferred Ryan to him.

Kimmy smiled and then hugged his neck, "You're my favorite, and Leese loves you best, anyway."

He was smiling, completely happy with her response, but I couldn't help but think he opened himself up for a crushing blow had her answer been different.

"We're checking out in the morning and heading home. Do you need any help packing things up for the trip?" Mom offered.

I nibbled off the end of a bread stick knowing there was something I had wanted to ask her, but it had been forgotten, "No, I'm okay with that, but I keep feeling like I'm forgetting something."

"Well, don't stress over whatever it is because you aren't on a budget." Then she shook her head and laughed, "Matter of fact, if I were you, I wouldn't pack a thing. I'd just buy whatever I needed when I got to Maui."

"Mom, I can think of a lot better things we can be doing when we get their other than shopping." My original thought was hiking, snorkeling, and luaus.

She looked at us and flushed with color. "I can understand that," she laughed with a faraway look in her eyes.

I had a feeling it was a 'David' memory causing the look.

We finished dinner, then said our goodbyes and headed up to our room. We were both yawning by the time we closed the door to the rest of the world. Even though we'd slept six or seven hours after the sun came up this morning, it didn't take place of missing the entire night before. We crawled into the bed exhausted and knowing tomorrow wouldn't offer too many opportunities for rest either. Tonight was our chance to behave ourselves and get some actual sleep. We snuggled into our favorite position, which was me facing away and Micah pressed behind me with his arm around my waist, when I sat up quickly.

"That's it."

"What's it?"

"What I couldn't think of at dinner," I stated. "I never got the house key from Mom."

"You won't need it until we get back, baby," he said trying to pull me down into the covers.

"No—to the house in Maui—I forgot to get the key and I don't want to travel 5000 miles only to have to wait hours for a locksmith to open up the house."

"It's too late tonight. You can call your mom in the morning, baby. Come back to bed; we need some sleep."

I landed back amongst the pillows and sheets, but I didn't roll my back to him, I rolled toward him as I twined my leg over his and let my hand trail down his hot body, "You know we'll sleep better if we..."

He ran his fingers through my hair, sweeping it back away from my face, and then dove growling and snapping for my neck. I squealed far too loudly, and the new experience was on as we began to literally play with each other, until need overwhelmed us. We did get some sleep, and I was right about it being a better kind of sleep as we curled around each other and drifted off.

When morning came through the windows, I knew I'd have to get up and dress to catch Mom before they left, but I couldn't resist just a little teasing before climbing out of the bed. I rolled over and met his gaze, kissing him and then letting my hand travel down his perfect abdomen to rest just below his belly button and just above his inability to control himself.

"You can't be serious," he laughed, "Baby, you're gonna kill me."

I kissed him once more, but quickly this time and rose from the bed before he could get me in his grasp. He was up and after me as I laughed and ran for the bathroom. "I don't want to kill you," I said teasingly through the closed door.

"I can't think of a better way to go. Come back out here or I'm coming in there."

"Sorry, baby, but the door is locked. I've got to go see Mom today and then when I get back I'll see if I can put you out of your misery and—" To my utter surprise the door opened and he was right beside me. "Ah, I locked that! How did you get in?"

"I know how to do a lot more than aim straight under pressure," he chuckled as he came around behind me and moved my hair to gain access to my neck.

I could feel my resolve melting into a warm puddle. "I really do need to see Mom, and I've got to catch her before she checks out with Kimmy and heads home. Oh, Micah, don't stop," I said as he began to pull away.

"You're confused, baby," he whispered, "first it's stop and then don't stop. What's it gonna be?"

"Ah—stop, Micah," I chose reluctantly. "I really want to catch them, but as soon as I come back through that door, don't stop, and I really don't care what my argument is."

He gave a slow smile, "I'll be waiting and I don't care how long it takes."

I dressed, picked up my purse and left, wishing the whole time that I'd stayed. I was starting to wonder how we were ever going to go back to functioning normally in life when we simply couldn't keep our hands off each other. I pushed the elevator button and began my descent to the lobby. Would this whole fascination with each other eventually burn out or at least mellow? I couldn't see it happening; he was simply too mesmerizing. I could only hope he felt the same about me.

The elevator jerked hard causing my pulse to quicken. The lights dimmed and I could hear breaks being applied. It stopped between the third and second floor and panic gripped me. I wasn't claustrophobic, but my air felt as if it had been cut off. I'd never been trapped in one of these things. What do I do? I grabbed for the panel marked with a telephone symbol and opened it, but just as I put my hand on the receiver the elevator took off. This time I was going up instead of down.

Now, I don't know about anyone else, but the idea of falling from the second story wasn't as terrifying as the idea of dropping from somewhere higher. I was steadily climbing, passing our floor and still rising. I grabbed the phone and pressed the single button, but it was dead. My hand went for my cell phone, though I didn't know exactly who I was going to call, when the elevator stopped on the seventeenth floor. The bell dinged and the doors opened. A group of men stood waiting to get on, but I didn't care; I was getting off this mechanical menace!

As I started to push my way through them, I recognized, to my alarm, they were converging around me. I opened my mouth to scream as several pairs of hands took hold of me, one of them reaching around, covering my face with a rag. A sweet odor assaulted my senses and blackness hit me.

When I came to my head was still groggy. I wondered if this was just another strange bad dream, but, as soon as my focus returned, I knew this was reality. I was leaned back in a chair with a man on each side holding me upright and another man seated in front of me, studying me intently.

Clarity was returning as I tried to pull myself free. My battle was short lived, and they pushed me roughly back down into the chair.

"Don't be so upset Annalisa, not yet anyway, I just need to talk with you," the man across from me murmured in a condescending tone.

"Let go of me!" I growled, still trying to jerk myself free from the men around me. "This isn't how you tell someone you need to speak with them!"

"If you promise to sit still, I'll have them turn you loose. I honestly don't think you'll want to leave before you hear what I have to say, if you love your husband, that is."

That hit me harder than the rag that knocked me out. I stopped struggling immediately and the hands released. I think I'd have rather been plummeting to my death in the elevator than for this to have anything to do with Micah.

"What's this about?" I asked, calmness trying to replace my angered fear.

"My name is D'Angelo," he began.

I knew the name; this was deadly serious. In Micah's former mafia life, he obeyed this man's every command and the command was always to kill someone. As far as I knew, I was the only person to ever survive those orders.

"Do you know who I am?" he asked, low and even.

I could only nod.

"Good. I trust I can ask my assistants to leave and you won't cause me any problems, correct? We do need to speak in private."

"Yes," I tried to say confidently, but it came out as a whisper.

He looked up at the men and they left immediately. He was as unanimated as stone until the door clicked shut, and then he began, "It wasn't supposed to go quite this far." An odd smile spread on his leathered face. He was very much Italian. His hair was deep brown and graying along the sides, his eyes were a penetrating black/brown and they had that vacant quality that Micah's used to get when he had to kill someone. "You weren't supposed to get married until next month and when I found out it had been moved up, I couldn't get to you quick enough."

I was mute, not by choice, but by fright.

"You didn't move things up due to a pregnancy, did you? That would only complicate matters for Micah."

"N—no, we just…" I couldn't explain and he evidently didn't want to hear an explanation anyway, he just wanted to be certain I wasn't pregnant. My heart thudded against my chest. It was possible I could be, but I would only be days along and there was no way I was telling him that bit of information.

"Good, then maybe we can salvage this whole thing after all. Micah would never stop looking for you if there was a baby involved."

The heat in my body felt as if it had been drained and I was now aware of how very cold my hands had become as I unconsciously wrung them together, "What do you mean? Do you have plans to kill me?"

D'Angelo laughed softly, "Of course not, my dear, that simply wouldn't work to help my cause. I did consider that, but I want him angry, not heartbroken. You're going to leave your husband, and he's coming back to the family by his own free will."

"There is nothing you can do to make me leave him," I said through a quivering voice. In a matter of moments, I was going to discover how wrong I was about my statement.

"Of course there's nothing I can do, but I won't need to when you know what's at stake." He reached behind him and picked up a folder and pulled a handful of papers from it and laid one on the table in front of me, "Do you know what this is?"

I could see at a glance that it was a contract on David Gavarreen. I looked up at D'Angelo; there was no need to say the vile words when it was obvious the piece of paper represented the end of David's life.

"Yes, you know what it is," he replied when he saw the look in my eyes and took note of the fact that I was refusing to state it. "He should have died months ago, but the family recognized the serious flaw in removing him for his disregard of policy. Giorgio Gavarreen lost one son to you and he couldn't take losing the other for insubordination. He knows the rules, but he openly threatened the family should any harm come to his remaining son. Giorgio used his family's position to get them to release Micah, but he won't let go of David."

"What does this have to do with my leaving Micah?" I asked, wondering if I was about to become some kind of trade for David's life.

His hand went back to the folder and removed more papers and spread them on the table. "This is where you come in," he stated.

To my horror it was plain to see he was showing me contracts on Giorgio, Celeste and Gwen. I felt faint, every ounce of bravery and stubbornness washed out of me. It was a sick relief to me that Micah's name wasn't among the contracts. I reached out and separated them to make certain I was seeing it correctly.

"No, his name isn't there," D'Angelo answered what hadn't been asked.

"Would you have shown me if it were?"

"Our family gave the blessing for him to leave, and they don't go back on their word." He sounded angry for me asking that question. Evidently, he wasn't used to someone questioning his integrity.

"Why all of them?" My eyes were beginning to sting with the need to release the pain slamming my senses.

"His entire family knows too much about everyone in our organization. Giorgio has financial dealings with every person, the money they have, what they did to earn it, how they have invested it, where they have invested it; if he goes ballistic he could take us all down.

"And then there is the issue of his lovely wife, Celeste. She's created new lives for so many of our people, documents and records, complete histories. She helps create identities for those that do complicated hits so things can't be traced back to the family. If she loses her husband and son, she could wreak havoc."

He pulled Gwen's contract away from the others and tapped his finger on it for emphasis. "Gwen is truly the worst of them all. She is our inside connection to law enforcement. We have nearly free reign in Louisiana because of her knowledge about what is happening and where. She keeps heads turned the proper direction when we have a mess to clean up or records and evidence that needs to be, well, let's just say adjusted. She almost blew that trying to cover for Micah's escapade with you.

"The FBI is still curious and she's had to become more legalistic since then so she doesn't end up in the federal pen. She has a whole rank of officers that are loyal to her. She's played them like fools, but should she decide to change her ways, we'd be all but shut down in that state."

"Why are you showing me this?" My voice beginning to crack under the emotional strain.

"I'm going to give you the chance to change it. You see these contracts haven't been assigned to anyone, *yet*," he stated, without leaving any doubt he could issue them within minutes if needed. "If I can get Micah to return, on his own to the family, I can present the argument that he can keep his family together. I don't think you've grasped even a fraction of the kind of man you've married. Losing him was quite a blow to the organization. And, I must say, shook the confidence people had in the Gavarreen name."

"Why do I have to leave him? Can't I just convince him to return to the—the mob?"

He laughed and leaned back easily in his chair, as he seemed to size me up, "Do you really think you can convince him that you, of all people, want him back in a life of crime? A life where he is expected to go out and kill and then come back to a happy little home while you wait to ask him how his day went? Please, don't even try to insult my intelligence with that ignorant question. And besides, there are plenty of people in our organization that would be too leery to have you that close to what we do."

"He'll never believe that I've changed my mind," I stated honestly.

"Oh, I don't know about that, I mean you must be a pretty good actress to have stopped him from killing you. And, I know Micah well enough to understand he doesn't feel like he deserves you in the first place."

He was right about that. Micah plainly stated he didn't feel he deserved this shot at happiness. The pain inside was crushing me. I didn't want to let go. I stubbornly wanted forever with the man I loved, but what was the cost going to be? "And if I refuse to leave him?"

"You can do that; selfishness means you can keep him to yourself and the mob won't touch him. But I wonder when his entire family is dead in a few days, and he discovers you had the chance to stop all this, how will he feel about you at that point? Has he told you about his life before you met him?"

"I—I didn't want to know too much about—"

"The first person he ever killed was a woman," he hissed, cutting me off. "A woman he'd slept with."

Fear cut into me like a knife and I didn't want to hear more, "I don't want to—"

"Whether or not you want to hear this, you are going to understand something about him; when he snaps, and he will snap when this happens, you won't be able to control him no more than the first woman who tried to control him. Have you felt him on the edge of losing control, Annalisa?" He leaned toward me and the eyes narrowed, "He has a particular problem with women."

I wanted to call him a liar. I wanted to tell him how incredibly good Micah truly was inside. Yes, I'd felt his control erode, but that was in moments of passion. He'd always been able to reign in his actions. I believed my husband when he told me he could never hurt me, no matter what D'Angelo said about him.

"I personally know women who've slept with him and they are all afraid of him."

"Shut up, you son-of-a-bitch! Micah isn't—" I tried to stand when I uttered my angry words, but the back of his hand slapped hard against my mouth, knocking me down into the chair.

He snatched the papers from the table and shoved them in my face, "Tell me right now! Do I make these effective or are you going to be reasonable?! *Your husband is an animal, a lethal animal, and I need him back.*"

It was suddenly very clear; *he needed Micah.* The lives of the Gavarreen family members were incidental.

My face was stinging, but I refused to cower in pain, "What if I tell Micah what you're planning?" I grabbed my cell phone and flipped it open.

He looked at me and laughed, "Go ahead. I've got enough snipers in this building that he won't get far. His name doesn't have to be on these papers for him to lose his life, Annalisa. How about if I call him? Huh? Would that make you happy? I'll bet he'd be here in minutes and I would kill you both. But this I promise you, you'll watch him die first."

My heart shuttered to a stop and then took off as if I'd just run a marathon. I couldn't allow his family to suffer this fate, even if it meant letting go of the one thing I wanted more than life itself. D'Angelo was right, unarmed, Micah would charge up here to try to save me and I would be responsible for his death. My own life after that would mean nothing to me.

"I'll let you live long enough," he continued, "to know the rest of his family is dead—then I'll kill you, personally." He reseated himself and straightened his jacket, "It's a shame really. I've known Giorgio and Celeste before they were even married. I was at the Christening of each of his children and I've helped train them to be what they are. I would hate to see so much waste. Tell me right now; can you leave him and make it convincing or am I wasting my breath on you?"

"I can do it," I said, my voice quivering, but completely confident, "but I want one thing in exchange for preventing what would have to be a huge loss for your sick, demented family." I rose from the chair and put my purse under my arm.

He leaned forward in is chair, his elbows on the arm rests, his lips were pressed against his index fingers as he clasped his hands, "Do you really think you are in any position to ask something of me?"

"Yes, actually I do—if you want this to work."

"Name it."

"David doesn't die," I uttered.

"That might be difficult, I—"

"Not for you. I know in this 'family' a lot of weight is put on a man's word, I want your word that David won't be harmed. I think you can find a way to convince the others that he should live."

He took in a deep breath, still studying me. He'd been intently studying me ever since my eyes opened, "Agreed." And then he smiled, "I hope you are a convincing actress, for Micah's sake. But, if you try to get back with him or if you ever tell him what's been discussed here today, his family won't last 24 hours, is that understood?"

"I'll do what I promised and you'll make sure no one in the Gavarreen family is harmed. Do I have your word?"

"Yes," he stated, seemingly relieved we reached an accord. He put out his hand to me. I knew he wanted to seal this deal, but the idea of touching him repulsed me. When my hand slipped into his, it was as if I had just shaken the hand of Satan. My world was over and now I had to destroy my perfect new life that was only days old.

Chapter Seven

I headed for the elevator, realizing now he had someone watching our room all morning and as soon as I stepped on the elevator alone, someone assumed the controls. If I was really lucky, they'd cut the cable and I'd fall seventeen floors.

I called for a taxi and then exited on the second floor, using the stairs to descend out the back of the hotel. Thankfully, not too many people parked in the back. A hand gripped my arm—don't let it be Micah was my millisecond prayer.

"What are you doing out here?" came Ryan's voice. He was carrying a duffle, and that was when I noticed the back of a classic black car sticking out several vehicles to my left.

My mouth had gone dry; I couldn't speak. I hadn't planned on forming lies so quickly.

"Leese, are you okay? What's wrong?" The look of concern was etched hard across his face.

A cab turned the corner and started down the long alley toward us.

"I've—I've got to go," I wanted to say more, but I was ready to break down and I couldn't; I had to get away.

"Go where? What are you doing?" His eyes were telling me he knew something was terribly wrong.

"I've got to go to the bank," I finally managed to say. "I'm really glad you could make it for the wedding." I was trying to put some normalcy back in my voice. "I thought you went home yesterday."

"No, I didn't plan to leave until today."

94

I could see he wasn't buying my acting as the cab came to a stop and I tried to open the backdoor.

He held the door shut, "I'll take you where you need to go." It didn't sound like an offer, but more like a statement.

"NO—I—I'd rather take a cab. Micah is still pretty jealous when it comes to me being around you and I wouldn't want to—"

"He'll live," he said, blocking my way.

"Lady," the cabbie interrupted, "do you need a ride or what?"

"Yes, I need to go to the First National Bank downtown."

"No, she doesn't. I'll take her," Ryan asserted.

"Make up your minds. I'm on the clock here!"

Ryan grabbed his wallet and flipped the cabbie a hundred dollar bill, "You can leave, now."

"No," I was trying to rebut, but the cabbie hit the gas and was gone. "That jerk! I can't believe he left me." I turned my anger toward Ryan. "You have no right to—"

"I'm giving you a ride so get over it. Where's First National?"

I couldn't afford to argue any longer as I hoped and prayed a hotel camera wasn't recording in this area. I was trying my best to force back the tears as I told him where we were heading.

The bank wasn't far and even though he was pummeling me with questions, I simply told him I couldn't discuss it right now because I was too upset. I wanted him to wait in the bank lobby when I went back to speak with the president, but he refused and stayed at my side as I unemotionally requested a quarter million dollars in hundred dollar bills.

"I don't think we can handle that transaction this morning."

The banker was stalling and I knew it. I could see suspicion written clearly across his face as he looked from me to Ryan. There was no way he would suspect Ryan because the look on his face was clearly just as shocked as the banker's.

"Don't lie to me, Mr...." I glanced to his desk plate, "Mr. Archer. I have multi-millions with your bank, and if you can't handle a simple request when I need it, I'll move my money to another—"

"No, no, that's okay, Miss Winslett. We don't usually do this size of a transaction with such immediacy—we have the funds available, it's just a matter of putting it together."

I hated the sound of my former name—I wanted to tell him it was Gavarreen, but that dream was over. He was still lying to me, "Mr. Archer, I don't think it will be difficult to have a teller count out twenty five packs of hundred-dollar bills. I'll expect you to put them in a bank bag for me as well. You have fifteen minutes or I'll close my account."

He handed me the withdrawal form and quickly left the room.

"What the hell are you taking a quarter-million-dollars *cash* out of the bank for?" Ryan demanded as soon as we were alone. "What does he have you doing?"

He was accusing Micah of being behind this and it felt like the invisible knife was starting to work its way through my heart as he blamed the man I loved.

"This has nothing to do with Micah," I croaked, fighting to keep my fragile composure. "Please, Ryan—not now. Wait until we're out of here. I can't handle anything else."

He swallowed as he looked at me. He knew this was big trouble and I was ready to crack, "When we get in the car, you're telling me everything."

We left the bank and he drove to a waterfront park and pulled under a shady tree, turned off the engine, and looked at me.

"Ryan, I don't want you involved in this." I was actually afraid at this point he may have already been deeply entangled. Cameras would be checked at the hotel and the bank. Micah would know who had been with me and he would find Ryan to get the answers he had to have.

"I'm involved already," he admitted, evidently suspecting what I already knew about cameras. "You've got to tell me what's happening."

"If I drag you into this, I'm gonna get you killed—I can't handle being responsible for that. Please, Ryan, just leave it at this. Take me to a rental lot and drop me off. You can't get hurt if this is all you know." It was too late to stop the tears.

"You're running away from him, aren't you?" His head cocked sideways slightly as he realized this had nothing to do with Micah, but everything to do *without* Micah.

"Please, I've got to get out of here and he's got to believe I wanted to go."

He pulled me against his chest as I began to sob. He had become my best friend and he was willing to do anything to help me, even if it cost him everything. An hour of arguments, tears and reasons, and he finally understood, but I had sworn him to absolute secrecy.

"You say he's jealous about my being with you—it's the only thing that will convince him you wanted to leave."

I was blank for a moment, then it hit me; he was suggesting we run together. It would look like I had been torn between the two of them and chose Ryan. I didn't think Micah could believe it because I was sure he knew my love was true, but jealousy has a way of blinding a person.

"Ryan, he'll kill you if he gets the chance. He's the top hit man in the south and he will track us down and kill you—I don't know if I can stop him."

"You can't go alone, I won't let you."

"You've got school, you've got the Air Force, you've got a whole life of dreams in front of you; don't throw it all away on me," I pleaded.

"I don't think I could count being with you as throwing my life away."

I realized he assumed he and I would become more than friends at this point; I couldn't lead him to ever believe that. I wouldn't let him risk his life thinking he and I would become lovers.

"It can't be that way between us. You're my best friend, but I'm never going to stop loving Micah. If I never see his face again, it won't matter because I can't betray what I committed to him when I said I'd be his wife. We'll never sleep together."

"Then just let me help you get away. I can deal with him when the time comes."

"That's a fool talking," I whispered. "You don't know him like I do." I remembered when he killed Jack and Ricky; there was no pause in his fury. He simply drew and fired with deadly accuracy and without questions and without regret.

"He has to believe you wanted to leave him, Leese. If your plan is going to work, I've got to be in it."

I didn't want to agree, but he was right. I could only pray I didn't just assign him a death sentence—he didn't deserve that for helping.

"Take me back to the hotel. I've got to write a couple notes and leave them at the front desk. Wait for me out front by the security camera. Wait outside your car, and forgive me when I have to make this look convincing. Don't read more into what I do when I come out than to know this has to look believable."

He didn't ask questions; he just followed my directions and headed back to the hotel as I grabbed paper and pen from my purse and wrote the most difficult words of my life. As long as Micah wasn't downstairs, as long as neither he nor Mom caught me, I'd get away and the rest would be left up to jealousy to decide about my sincerity.

Ryan parked where I instructed and got out of the car and came around and sat on the front bumper on my side as I ran indoors and gave my notes to the clerk. He was waiting patiently, but nervously as I came back to the car. I walked up to him and his arms automatically opened to hold me.

"Forgive me," I whispered, but what I was about to do was unforgivable. I brought my lips to his and began to kiss him. I know he didn't expect the kiss. He was assuming he would just embrace me for the camera, but Micah had to believe. Jealousy would be the only thing that would keep him from killing himself over what I was doing to the two of us. If he was angry enough, he would vault himself back into his old life with a vengeance.

Ryan's kiss was different from Micah's. His mouth was tender and soft and filled with hesitation about what to do. Surely I wasn't his first kiss, but I didn't know if he had ever gone for the kind of deep passion I wanted to display. His arms, tense at first, relaxed and then he pulled me tighter against himself; one hand slid into my hair as the other slipped low on my hips.

The kiss broke for a moment as he moaned. This time I allowed him to be the aggressor and come back for a second round of treason. My hands gripped his shoulders as the kiss became deeper and hotter—it had taken him a stunned second to find the passion I needed for this to be convincing, but when it hit him, he took my breath away with his sensitivity and ability.

For a second time the kiss broke, but he kept his forehead pressed to mind, "If this is all I ever get from you, it's worth it Leese. Just once more and we can go."

My face tilted upward to his, tears streaming down my cheeks as he gave me the final kiss. Softer this time, pleading with his lips for me to respond once more. My lips parted and I answered his plea.

When we stopped, I made sure my face was far enough away from Ryan's for the camera to record what had to come out of my lips, "I love you, Ryan." I was hoping he understood why I said it, but with no possibility of the camera recording the movement of his lips, he told me he loved me, too.

It was time to go. Just like the nightmare that had haunted me, I was leaving, but it felt as if I shoved the blade into my own heart when we drove away.

Chapter Eight

Micah watched her go out the door and sighed to himself as he returned to the bed. The place where she had been was still warm. He smiled as he buried his face into her pillow, inhaling her lingering scent. He wasn't exactly sleepy, but he was very, very comfortable as he drifted toward unconsciousness.

An hour later he rolled over and glanced at the clock. Surely she would be back soon and when she came through the door, she wouldn't get far. He'd never in his existence believed he could feel all the emotions she brought to life inside him. She was the most incredible creature he'd ever found and he simply couldn't believe she was his wife. He changed everything to be with her and he knew, without doubt, it was all worth it. She opened him up to the possibilities that God truly cared about redeeming his once worthless, hell-bound soul and put him on the path he felt he never deserved to be treading.

Another hour passed and, as reluctant as he was, he dressed and decided to go down to the restaurant and grab a bite to eat. With any luck, he'd catch her down there still talking with her family. He had developed a regular need to see her face, to touch her skin, and to hear her laughter, and he had gone too long this morning without it.

The elevator opened in the restaurant, and he was making his way to the hostess, when he saw Nadia and Kimmy heading toward the exit on the other side.

"Table for one?" the hostess asked.

"Hold on a second, I'll be right back I've got to catch someone." He sprinted across the room. "Nadia!"

She paused and turned, both of them smiling, "Hey, I was wondering if I was going to see you before we left. We thought about coming up to your room, but didn't want to disturb anything." She blushed.

He looked confused. If Leese was with Nadia, how would they interrupt anything? "Where's Leese?" he asked.

"She's not with me. I thought she was upstairs with you."

His face went pale, "You did see her this morning, right?"

"No, I haven't seen her since we saw you two last night."

His hand went immediately to his cell phone and he began dialing.

"Why?"

He listened as the recording came on immediately saying she wasn't available and went to voicemail. This could only mean she was either on the phone or her phone was turned off. Leese never turned off her phone.

"Hey, baby," he said, trying to stay calm, "call me as soon as you get this message—I just *need* to know where you are right now. Call me back." He looked into Nadia's distressed gaze, "She left me about two hours ago and said she wanted to see you and Kimmy before you left for home. She forgot to get the keys to the house in Maui."

Now it was Nadia's turn to look upset, "Does she have the car keys? Could she have changed her mind and driven somewhere?"

He patted his pocket; the keys to the Corvette were there.

"She's got to be here somewhere. Ask the hotel if they can page her and tell her to call the front desk."

"What's wrong, Mommy?" Kimmy asked. The worried expression from the adults was causing her to tear up.

"It's okay, Kimmy." Micah reached out and pulled her to his side. "We just have to find your sister."

"Check the pool," Kimmy said confidently. "That's where I'd be."

Micah smiled outwardly, but inside he was in a state of panic like he'd never known; his wife was missing.

"Excuse me," he approached an older man at the front desk, "I need to page my wife, Annalisa Gavarreen. Can you do that for me?"

"Yes, sir, if you'll give me a moment."

"She left you a message," a young woman behind the counter interrupted, "about 15 or 20 minutes ago."

"Thank God," Micah relaxed, breathing a sigh of relief as he watched the woman retrieve it.

"She left two actually. Are you Nadia Winslett?" she asked with an extra piece of paper in hand.

"Yes, thank you," Nadia said taking the other paper.

Micah opened the message at the same moment as Nadia, and both of them immediately caught their breath. It was Leese's handwriting, but the notes were scrawled as if she had been in a hurry. Tears stained the paper and the first words on both notes were, "I know you'll never understand, but…"

Micah nearly collapsed as Nadia gripped his arm.

"Sit down, Micah." She led him to a nearby chair. "This is wrong—something is really wrong. She wouldn't do this to you—she loves you too much, I know she does.

He broke down in tears and covered his face. Her words that God has a purpose for everything came back hauntingly clear—he made her keep her date with Ryan, he purposely left her alone with him more than once and now it seemed the whole reason was to open her eyes. But she couldn't love Ryan more than she loved him, it just wasn't possible. Nadia was right. She wouldn't do this to him, not after everything, this just wasn't her. He dried his tears and the old Micah came back with a rush of commanding authority as his emotions dried up and withered away.

He walked back to the desk, "I need to see your head of security, now."

He didn't want Nadia to view the tapes so he asked if she and Kimmy would consider heading home, just in case Leese should go there. Nadia wanted to call the police right away, but Micah assured her he was more capable than even the police in finding her. He promised he would call her as soon as he figured out what was really going on.

He sat in the dim control room watching the tapes from the time she left him. There was footage of her in the hallway getting on the elevator, but the camera in the elevator wasn't working. He watched the lobby camera but the next time anyone stepped off, it wasn't Leese. He was getting that gut feeling that something was very wrong.

He continued to watch tapes and finally saw a glimpse of her heading down the hallway on the second floor to the stairwell. It had been a forty-five minute lapse since the first shot of her on the elevator. The stairwell tapes showed her going out the back of the hotel and waiting in the alley, but then a man entered the picture and grabbed her arm. He knew who it was immediately, and his blood boiled.

A cabbie pulled up, there seemed to be an argument, and then he watched Ryan pay off the cabbie who left without her. They went out of camera range for a moment and then they appeared again as a black Trans Am backed into the alley and sped away.

But she had returned to the hotel. The young woman said the notes had only been left 15-20 minutes earlier. He continued to watch.

"There she is," the hotel security officer said, pointing to the screen for the hotel's entrance camera. He watched Ryan seat himself on the fender as she ran for the lobby clutching paper in her hands. Then she returned and he opened his arms. Micah unconsciously braced his hand against the desk as he watched.

"No, Leese, no," he whispered as he witnessed the long kiss. The way Ryan's hands moved through her hair and down her back made him want to knock the monitor completely off the desk. Again, they were kissing. The third time he was ready to snap in two. He noticed something and used the video controls to zoom in on her as she upturned her face to his for the last kiss. He could see the glistening tears on her cheeks and he felt in his heart she didn't want to do what she was doing. But then all doubts seemed to erase as the final thing he saw was her lips moving with the words, "I love you, Ryan."

There was more to this story. She couldn't have simply changed her mind and her heart. She wanted them to have a commitment in front of God. That was why they waited for marriage before taking the next step. And, he knew he was the first person to experience that with her.

He called the cab company. His photographic memory was very clearly recalling the number on the cab from the video. He had to meet the driver to see if he remembered anything that might undo this knife in his heart. He thought about her nightmare and how afraid she was, saying nothing could drive her away from him, nothing could make her destroy her relationship with him, but now something had and he had to know if it was love for another man.

The cabbie didn't seem interested in cooperating as Micah stood outside the hotel and questioned him about the fare he didn't have to earn. He was wishing he had his pistols because one would be pressed to this little maggot's head right now and he would gladly tell Micah what he needed so desperately. He'd had enough. There was another way to get what he wanted as he jerked the cabbie halfway out the window to face him.

"Listen to me you insignificant piece of dirt; that was my wife that you left in the alley! She's missing and if you don't tell me everything you remember I'll kill you even if I have to snap your neck with my bare hands!"

"Whoa! Whoa! Whoa! Buddy, I'm sorry—I didn't know. Yeah, I do remember—she wanted to go to the First National Bank, but the guy said he'd take her. She acted like she knew him. I'd didn't think she was in no danger."

He let go, almost causing the man to fall out the cab window. He had another lead and he was on his way to the bank.

The bank president was about as helpful as the cabbie although he openly said he knew why she'd come in, but he wasn't privileged to disclose it. Micah had a way of convincing people to change their minds.

As he let the banker's feet touch the ground, still gripping the man's lapel, his final words were very clear, "You better hope to God you have all those serial numbers!"

"Ye—yes, Mr. Gavarreen. They were new bills, all consecutive. I'll get you the list."

Whatever she was doing, there would be a trail and the trail would lead him right to her door. He needed the best person in the world at chasing a paper trail; he just didn't want to call home and tell his mother what had happened.

He would be on a plane tonight for Louisiana. He was going home and stepping back into the world he shunned for her, but now it was the only world he could turn to. He called Nadia and told her that evidently it was true. He told her about watching the tape, about the kiss, but he was going to track her down and as soon as he found her he would have her call home.

"Micah," Nadia said before hanging up, "I don't think we have all the pieces and I know how much this is hurting you, but..."

He took in a calm breath. He had put his emotions away and felt nothing now—at least not love, and certainly not pain; anger was still there and growing stronger, but everything else had faded.

"Don't hurt her, Micah," Nadia finished, evidently realizing by his unemotional voice that he was changing.

"I could never hurt her," he said evenly, but deep down he was starting to wonder how much longer he could believe that lie.

Chapter Nine

"Do you have an idea where you want to go?" Ryan asked as we pulled out of the hotel parking lot.

I wasn't in any condition to talk, but I knew I had to come to my senses and start planning or this could go horribly wrong. I wiped my eyes on my sleeve and took a ragged breath. "I haven't thought that out yet; I just planned to grab a car and head out of state. I got the cash because I know Micah will find me if I use a credit card. He's—he's got plenty of ties to people who know how to track someone down, and I can't leave a trail."

"Were going to my house."

"No, Ryan, that's the first place he'll look!"

"Calm down, Leese, I'm just going to pick up a few things and then head for the airstrip." He could tell I still looked worried as he pushed down the accelerator. "Don't worry, we'll be there and gone before he gets there. I—I've got to say goodbye to my mom and then I'm flying you out of here."

I remembered the pain of not being able to say goodbye to Kimmy when Micah had taken me to Louisiana. I wouldn't argue the goodbye he wanted. "You mean hire a private plane?"

"No, I mean I'm flying you out of here. I fly all the time. I told you I've got my pilot's license and I own my own Cessna, but I don't think it's smart to take my plane. I've got a good friend who won't have a problem letting me use his."

"I just never thought about you actually flying."

"You knew I was planning on joining the Air Force." He stole a glance at me as he dodged traffic. "My dad was a colonel and took me flying all the time when I was little. I could pilot a plane by the time I was ten, but I couldn't get a student license until I turned 16 and then I started flying solo. I got my regular pilot's license when I turned 17."

I was glad for the conversation, anything to take my mind off the crushing pain working its way through my heart. Just as I dreamed, I was taking off, not knowing where I was going, but simply that I had to get away. I could only hope the rest of the dream had been a metaphor, because I already felt the knife in my heart and with every mental image of Micah's face, it shoved deeper.

"You never mentioned your dad," I said, trying to keep talking so my mind wouldn't wander back into the painful thoughts, "he's in the Air force?"

"Was," Ryan said quietly.

He stopped talking for a moment and I wondered if I should press him for anything more.

"He was killed in Iraq when I was 15."

I could tell he struggled to get those words out. It was obviously still very painful for him. I reached over and put my hand on the back of his as it rested on the shifter, "It sounds like you two were close."

"Yeah, we were—he was a great dad," his voice starting to crack. "He had so many people that really respected him, his career and everything he stood for. They told me I have an opening in the Air Force Academy whenever I'm ready, full military scholarship. Mom is against the whole idea, but that's because she knows why I want to join."

I remembered his words when we were at Pensacola High School about the Air Force being the only legal way to kill someone. Now I understood. Without thinking my hand trailed softly up the intricate colored tattoo covering his right forearm.

"Yeah, I got it after dad died. Mom still hates it and I really can't say I blame her. I—I wish I hadn't done it, but it's too late to change it now."

I thought about Micah's tattoo. I broke down sobbing so hard, I couldn't get a breath. I kept hearing Ryan saying it was going to be okay as his hand warmly rubbed my back.

"You didn't have a choice, Leese. You made the right decision, hard as it was, it's the only way."

"But why?" I sobbed into my palms. "All we wanted was to be together. Why did it have to end this way?" I pulled away from my hands and stared at the beautiful diamond wedding set on my finger. I had pledged my life to Micah Gavarreen for better or worse; I just had no concept at the time how bad the worst could become.

We hit I-95 and he kept our speed around ninety miles an hour until we pulled off into West Palm and made it to his house. I hadn't met Ryan's mother, and I certainly wasn't in any condition to see her at the moment, but I could tell he didn't expect me to come inside.

He was gone about ten minutes when he emerged carrying another duffle, with his mother following close behind. She was a petite blonde with eyes the same shocking shade of blue as her son's. She looked toward me and I could see the worry hit her. She knew who I was. Actually, there weren't many people who didn't look at me and remember my face from the news, but this was a different kind of look. She knew I married a few days ago and now her son was getting ready to fly away with the bride. He paused to embrace her, as she looked at me once again and nodded. It was as if she was letting me know, for whatever the reason, she was okay with him leaving with me.

We pulled into the Palm Beach International Airport, through the guarded areas as Ryan displayed his identification, and up to an area where numerous small aircraft waited.

"Which one is yours?" I asked, glad to finally have something to say since we had been silent from his house to here.

He pointed toward a sleek looking small plane with a silver bottom and a black stripe. "That's mine. It's a Cessna Corvalis 400, but what we're flying out in is that one." He pulled near a small jet that appeared to be big enough for at least six. "It's a Cessna Citation Mustang and belongs to a good friend of my family. That's him there," he said, as an older gentleman with a military crew-cut came around the plane. He was smiling as we approached.

"Does he know you want to use his plane?"

"Yeah, I called him when I was at the house. He's a great guy and he flew with my dad back when my dad was learning how to be a pilot."

Ryan grabbed both of his duffle bags from the trunk as he waved to the man. "Harvey, I really appreciate the loaner," he shouted over the drone of a small plane taxiing away from the hanger.

"No problem, Ryan. I've told you before all you have to do is ask. I know I can trust you to take care of her."

The man winked at me and I was wondering if he was discussing the airplane or me.

"Harvey Pinchon, this is Annalisa..." He evidently didn't know what last name he should give me, but Harvey didn't appear fazed that I had no last name at the moment.

"Annalisa, nice to meet you."

I reached out to shake his hand and watched his eyes snap immediately to the wedding ring on my finger.

"So," he said, quickly looking away from my hand, "I need a flight plan for you, Ryan. The FAA frowns on people without them. Where were you planning on stopping?"

"Well, I was kind of hoping you might let me take her to Heaven's Landing. I can leave her there in your hanger and then we'll just get a taxi over to Greenville and rent something else from there."

"Bullshit!" Harvey snapped.

That shook me from the comatose feeling that had been creeping into my system.

Ryan's eyebrows rose, but he apparently couldn't come up with a response.

"I told you all you had to do is ask. If you're flying out from there it'll be in my plane. Rent something? Ryan, I can't even believe you'd insult me that way."

"But I didn't want you to have to fly across country to get her back."

Harvey was fishing in the pocket of his slacks and pulling out a wad of keys. "Here," he offered, pulling two keys off the ring. "Here are the keys to my house and my truck in case you need to go anywhere when you get to the Landing. But, when you take off from there it better be in my plane or I'll be pissed. It doesn't matter how long you need it, either. Heck, if I want to go anywhere, I'll use yours."

Ryan handed him the keys to the Trans Am, "One more thing, Harvey. I have a feeling you're going to have a really big, angry guy coming around here asking questions and wanting to know if my plane is here. I know I've got to file a flight plan, but he can't know I flew out of here with Annalisa—it's really important. Can I use your name on it? And, I need you to take my car back to your house as soon as possible."

Harvey's eyes cut back to the wedding ring on my finger and then back to Ryan, "Your mom's okay with you doing this, right? I don't want her mad at me."

"She knows what I'm doing and she's cool with it."

"Load your gear in the plane," he stated. "Annalisa, I think it's best if you go ahead and get in the plane and sit down, honey. You look like you've had a rough morning."

I nodded numbly as he took my arm and led me to the open cabin door. It was very plush inside and I gratefully sank into one of the deep comfortable chairs as Ryan loaded his duffle bags and went through a preflight check. He paused to talk with Harvey and, although I couldn't hear what they were saying, I could see the serious expression on both of their faces. Harvey finally clapped the back of Ryan's shoulder and then shook his hand.

Ryan came aboard and closed the door. He was smiling at me and asked if I was tired.

"No, I don't know exactly what I am right now. I just can't believe I'm really leaving."

"How about a flying lesson then?" he asked, the smile getting broader. "Would you like to sit in the co-pilot's seat?"

I finally found my ability to react positively as I grinned. I knew what he was doing; he was going to try to take my mind off my problems for a little while. "Why not," I stated and then moved up to the nose of the plane.

He put on his headset and instructed me to do the same as he began talking with the tower. "Okay, Leese, I'm going to let you start her. See the start button? Okay push and release it. Now take the throttle and pinch the trigger. That's good. Push it forward over the gate, now release the trigger and pull it back down to idle."

The engine began to whine to life as he explained what was occurring by showing me on the big display in the center of the console. He began to explain about the pedals and the yoke, but then he got the approval from the tower and the airplane began to move forward. Next thing I knew, we were moving smoothly down the runway as Ryan pulled back slightly on the yoke and I could tell that we were no longer on the ground, but had become airborne. He made a large arc and turned the plane north as I watched Florida shrink smaller below us.

"Okay, Leese, take your yoke very gently. I want you to slowly pull back until the altitude indicates 35,000 feet." He pointed out where the altimeter was among the controls and as I gripped the black instrument, he released his side and showed me that I had control of the plane. "Hey baby, you're flying!"

I smiled outwardly, but having him call me baby caused a pang of regret that I was here with him. I knew I had made the right choice, but my heart was still screaming full volume to turn around and go back, to find another way, any other way, other than to leave Micah behind. I brought the plane to 35,000 feet and stopped.

"Now you want to know something really cool? You like to drive fast, but right now you are flying at 390 miles per hour—pretty awesome, huh?" he was beaming behind those blue eyes.

"Yeah, pretty cool," I said, trying to have enthusiasm in my voice. "How long will it take to reach this place—Heaven's Landing?"

"It's in the mountains in the very northern part of Georgia. My mom and I vacationed there with Harvey and his family last Christmas. It should only take us about two hours in this plane."

"So, what's after Georgia?"

"Well, this is your escape, but I was thinking we could fly out to Colorado after a couple days at Harvey's place. I know some people out there and I think we'll be pretty safe." He reached over and gently touched my arm as I held the controls, "You can relax, Leese. We're going to be fine."

"What did you tell your mom?" my voice sounded strange as it came across the mic.

"I told her that you were in a tight spot and needed my help," he said, settling back in his seat and watching the horizon.

"And that was enough for her?" I couldn't mask my disbelief.

"I told her this was going to give me some time to decide about the military. She's nagged me to change my mind ever since I decided to follow in Dad's footsteps. So, to tell the truth, I think she's hoping you'll put me on a different path."

I swallowed hard. I had put him on a different path, one that was just as dangerous as flying into a combat zone.

The next two hours passed quickly as Ryan explained every instrument on the displays, talked about a few of the crazy things he had done when flying, and spoke more freely about his dad. It was obvious how much he loved his father and, at one point, he simply went silent to keep from getting emotional.

I marveled at the beautiful mountains below us when I saw the landing strip appear in the distance. I wasn't expecting anything impressive, after all this was supposed to be a housing community, but it was a straight, smooth 5,000 foot concrete strip on top of a mountain done as well as any commercial airport.

"Okay, Leese, I think I'd better handle this part," he said as we lined up with the runway.

He set us down as gently as a feather gliding to earth and then turned and taxied to a group of hangers in the center of the strip.

Once the airplane was secured, one of the men that assisted us getting it into the hanger offered us a ride up to Harvey's house. He had a small pickup truck, so Ryan said we'd ride in the bed. I've never ridden in the back of a truck and it was actually fun, but what made it even better was the fact that we weren't sitting in the cab making up stories as to why we were here.

The house was a single story ranch with a lot of natural stone and wood on the exterior, set on a landscaped acre of ground with a long range view down the mountainside. We waved goodbye to our 'country taxi,' as Ryan called it, and went inside. The interior of the house was like stepping into a log cabin. There was a huge stone fireplace, rough sawn beams across the cathedral ceilings, heavy wooden furniture with oversized cushions, and a large kitchen with pine board cabinets and granite countertops.

Ryan set down his bags and said we'd better head into town if I wanted to have something different to wear by tomorrow.

"I know you may think I'm being a little dramatic, but it might be a good idea to see if Harvey's got a couple ball caps or something so we don't look so much like—like us." More importantly was that I didn't look so much like me. Over the last several months it wasn't odd to see my face on the front of a tabloid or newspaper. I had been offered to be featured in People magazine when I came out of the hospital, but I wasn't ready for the world to completely jump into my life.

It didn't take him long to find a pair of caps. I ran my fingers through my long hair, pulling it away from my face and into a makeshift bun at the back of my head and secured it with the cap. Ryan slipped on a Cessna cap over his silky black hair and asked if I was ready. I nodded and we went out to the garage.

Harvey's truck was much bigger than what we'd ridden in to his house. It was a Dodge Ram 2500, with over-padded cloth seats and a plush interior. It felt as if it took up half the road as Ryan carefully backed it out of the garage and turned it toward town. It left me wondering what it would be like to drive something so big. Every vehicle I'd had was small compared to this, and Ryan made it look easy as we drove down the mountain.

By one-thirty we were pulling into a Super Wal-Mart. We locked the truck and headed inside as I gave a sigh.

"What's wrong?" Ryan asked as he snagged a buggy from the parking space beside us.

"I'm going to have a complex about Wal-Mart," I said, shaking my head.

He gave a half laugh and asked why.

"It seems that every time I'm on the run, I end up at a Wal-Mart, once with Mom, Micah and now you."

"They say the third time is the charm," he said, flashing his dazzling smile, "So I must be the charm."

"Well, come on Charming, we've got a lot of stuff to buy."

We picked up enough groceries to last us three or four days and then I grabbed two new duffels, jeans, skirts, shirts, shoes, and a *big* purse. I did find it interesting that Ryan would *not* go into the ladies unmentionable aisle with me as Micah had once done (without so much as a blush). Ryan stood far away by a display of apples and acted as if he were thoroughly inspecting each piece of fruit.

When we rolled up to the pharmacy area where the cosmetics, bathroom items, and feminine products were kept, he made a beeline for the blood pressure machine and must have taken his pressure three times as I walked around picking up things I needed.

I finally grabbed his hand and pulled him away from the machine as I explained that I needed his help with something. He looked petrified until I took him down the hair color aisle and asked for his opinion on what to dye my hair.

"Black, definitely black," he stated grabbing a bottle of color.

113

I pulled it from his hand and placed it back on the shelf, "No. I want your opinion on what shade of blonde to buy. I'm cutting it, too," I added as I grabbed a pair of shears and threw them in the buggy.

He picked up an electric trimmer and said he guessed he needed to change his appearance as well. He grabbed a bottle of light auburn hair color and put it in the cart.

"Red?" I was trying hard to keep the funny lilt out of my voice, "I can't picture you with red hair."

"Well, I can't picture you as a blonde, but you will need streaks he said grabbing more hair products.

"I don't want streaks," I protested, afraid I'd come out looking like an odd type of skunk if I let him get carried away.

"Too bad, you're getting them. I mean, if you aren't going to let me dye it black then you're going to, at the least, have great blond highlights."

I frowned and started for checkout before he decided I needed a little bit of blue or pink streaks, too.

We loaded the counter as the cashier began scanning our items. She kept looking at us and smiling.

"Ya'll must be newlyweds," she finally bubbled out, as her eyes went from my spectacular rings back to our faces.

"Yup," Ryan lied, putting his arm around me and giving me a squeeze, "her luggage got lost on our flight from California to here, which sucks for a girl." He was covering quite smoothly for the fact that we were buying a tub-load of clothes for me and nothing for him.

"Aah! I know what you mean, honey," she said as she gave that little southern flick of her wrist. "My sister lost her luggage when she flew in from Vermont last year. Lordy, it was terrible how long it took before they finally found it. It had gone all the way to Washington State. How long ya'll been married?"

I couldn't speak, but that was okay because Ryan was on a roll.

"Since yesterday; this is our honeymoon," he winked at the cashier.

She blushed and kept ringing up items, "Where ya'll stayin'? Up at the Dillard House? I hear it's real nice there."

"No. My uncle loaned us his cabin up in the mountains to the east so we can have a little piece and quiet."

"That's real sweet," she was saying, enjoying the fact that the handsome guy with me was chatty while I was about as talkative as a patio chair. "You got yourself a quiet one," she said glancing from Ryan to me, "You don't say much, do you, sweety?"

I shook my head as Ryan leaned toward the clerk, "She lost her voice last night—a little too much screaming."

The cashier was blank for a second and then turned scarlet, "Oh, sakes alive! She got herself a wild one when she got you." She gave a giddy laugh.

"Ah!" was all I managed to squeak out as I slugged his shoulder.

He laughed, rubbing his arm, "See I told you, no voice."

"That'll be $434.27," she stated as she dropped the last item into a bag.

Ryan was going for his wallet when I smacked him again, "I've got it," I growled as I peeled five one hundred dollar bills from a $10,000 stack tucked in the bottom of my purse. I had left the rest of the money at Harvey's house since my purse wasn't big enough to carry it all, but my new purse would be more than adequate.

"I guess I didn't get all her voice last night," he continued teasing the cashier, "but that's what the honeymoon is for, right?"

She just laughed as she handed me back the change, "Ya'll have a nice time in Georgia, ya hear."

"Oh, we will," he called back as I was shoving him toward the exit.

"Geez, Ryan, you're an idiot!" I snapped, but I was starting to laugh under my pretense of anger.

"Hey, you've just got to have a little fun with people sometimes," he said as he grabbed the bags and put them on the back seat, "See, I even got you to smile."

He was right. I couldn't wipe the stupid grin off my face if I tried.

All the way back to Heaven's Landing, Ryan was cracking stupid jokes and I was laughing in spite of the dismal mood I wanted to wallow in.

"Okay, home sweet home." He pulled the truck into the garage and pressed the button for it to close. "It's just you and me now, baby girl."

I tried not to let my heart go wild on me. He and I spending time alone would be different from when Micah and I pulled off this feat.

Micah was under the promise of being a perfect gentleman; Ryan and I had no such agreement. I wasn't afraid of him; the problem was I was afraid of myself. Inside I was hurting so badly from what I'd done today, that I craved understanding and gentleness. Ryan embodied both those qualities.

It had only been a few hours ago that I had kissed him, and the feel of his tender mouth against my own hadn't diminished. I needed tenderness so badly and I wondered how my heart could be so completely crushed, and my body could have these irrational needs. Learning about satisfying needs with Micah, set my body on a path I'd never traveled, and right now I hated my body and all the thoughts that came with it as I followed my handsome friend into the house.

I put my bags on the kitchen table and rummaged through them looking for the scissors as he put away the groceries. I hated the idea of cutting my hair, but it had to go, and I needed something to do to get my mind off the Ryan dilemma.

"You're ready for a transformation right now? Don't you want to relax a little bit?"

"The longer I look like me, the more likely someone will notice, and I don't plan on leaving a bread trail to wherever we happen to be."

"At least let me do that," he said following me into the bathroom.

"You? Have you ever cut hair before?"

"Actually, yes. I cut my sister's hair. Of course, I was eight and she was sleeping, but it looked pretty good considering I only got half of it."

He took the scissors from my grip. At this point I didn't care and I wasn't expecting salon results. I only hoped he could at least make it even.

"Close your eyes," he whispered in my ear.

"Gladly," I said with a cringe.

I was facing toward the mirror as he began, but I never once peaked. One thing I knew was that he was cutting it really short. I could feel the cold blade of the scissors near the bottom of my ears and around the top of my neck as he worked. His fingers were running through my hair now, short as it was, and I could feel him pulling it upward, making cuts as he went. This was going to be a disaster. He turned me to face him, but I still didn't open my eyes.

He was pulling hair in front of my face and cutting somewhere around eyebrow height.

"You're not giving me…" I had to spit hair off my tongue. "…bangs are you?"

"Bangs are cute and don't talk unless you want another mouthful of hair," he warned.

Several snips later and a few more times running his fingers through my hair, he turned me to face the mirror, "Okay, see what you think."

I still didn't open my eyes.

"Leese, you can look now."

"I don't know if I want to," I whined.

"Come on you big baby."

I didn't budge.

"If you don't look then I'm going to kiss you while—"

My eyes flew open. I wasn't in a proper frame of mind to fend off a kiss from him. The sight in the mirror was a total surprise. "Oh, wow! Ryan you're—you're actually good at this. It's adorable." It was a slightly longer version of a pixie cut and he had pulled it with his fingers and made it somewhat spiky.

"I just wish you'd let me dye it black instead of blond. I think you'd look good with black hair."

"It wouldn't be that you are a little partial to black, would it?"

He smiled. "Time to shave mine off," he sighed, handing me the scissors and leaving for the kitchen to get the electric trimmer.

"Do you really have to like shave your head? Couldn't you just cut it a little bit shorter? It's going to look different when we dye it."

"I was going to have to shave it off for the military anyway," he said, returning to the bathroom with the cutter in hand and found me crying.

"God, I can't believe I managed to screw up your life, too."

"You didn't screw anything up," he said, cupping my face in his hands. "I was going into the military for the wrong reasons and you are just slowing me down a little and making me reevaluate if it's what I want to do or not." He kissed the tip of my nose, scaring me in the process because I thought he was going for the lips.

He released me and plugged in the hair trimmer, selected a short attachment for the blade and sighed, "Would you care to do the honors?" he asked, offering me the trimmer.

117

"I've never cut hair and you will look bad if I do it," I admitted.

"You can't screw this up, Leese. You just put it against my head and slide it through the hair."

Gingerly I accepted, but he was almost too tall for this to go smoothly. I could see him studying my hesitation from the mirror; he dropped to his knees.

"Better?" he asked.

"I can't believe I'm doing this," I said turning on the trimmer and placing it against his forehead. "Do you want to close your eyes?"

We looked at each other for a moment in the mirror.

"No."

I took a deep breath and slid the trimmer forward, watching as all that black silky hair hit the floor. He was right about one thing; it wasn't difficult although it hardly looked like he'd been in a barber's chair. He was actually smiling, which I found completely odd. I thought he'd dislike losing one of his most popular features, but he seemed unaffected as the new Ryan emerged.

I hadn't realized until I was finished how terribly my hands were trembling. It only became noticeable to me when his very steady hands removed the trimmer from mine.

"I'll finish it up around the sides. You might want to find a broom; it looks like we scalped a yeti in here."

I left and went to the kitchen to see if there was a broom. I found it and the dust pan and returned to the bathroom and began sweeping up the piles of brown and black hair.

"There," he said, turning off the noisy trimmer, "how does that look?" He had removed the guide and trimmed closer in some places, but that gave it a finished look.

"Can I feel it?" I asked. I'd felt a buzz cut years ago and remembered how interesting it was.

He leaned his head toward me.

"Oh, that feels so cool," I said, laughing as my hands slid over the soft, yet stiff ends of hair.

His hand went up immediately to feel the stubs, touching mine as he did. He looked at me and smiled. I removed my hand and went back to sweeping.

"Are you ready to dye?" he asked.

I didn't intend to show my reaction when he uttered those words, but he caught my momentary expression of panic. "Yea—yeah, sure," I said, trying to leave the room.

He gripped my arm, "I think you and I need to talk." All his teasing vanished.

"About what?" I replied, trying to let the color return to my cheeks.

"You just freaked when I asked that question. I saw the same reaction when I asked you at the wedding if your life was ending. Has Micah ever threatened to—to kill you?" His eyes narrowed at me and I knew he was going to want an answer.

"There is a lot about Micah and I that no one knows," I said, holding back the tears forcing their way to the surface.

Ryan gripped my shoulders, "You know there are no reasons for you and I to have secrets from each other—not now anyway."

It was a long, long evening, as I told him everything about Micah and me. How he had been hired to kill me and then almost did. How he agreed to let me buy a few weeks of life to stop whoever was hurting my family, and his agreement to be a gentleman. I told him what exactly was going through my head when I collapsed just before Micah took me away the day at the diner. I replayed my frightening first encounter with David, shooting lessons, his family, being drugged, and our time spent at the small motel becoming too close. I told him about the final call that shortened my life to mere hours, Jack and Ricky's executions, and ending with being in the hospital.

"So this is the same D'Angelo guy from the hotel today? He was the one pulling Micah's strings about killing you?"

"Yeah, he is like the banker, I guess. Someone comes to him with a hit, and he holds the money and assigns the hit man. When the job is done, he makes the pay-off."

"If you hadn't gone to the hospital that day to try to help your mom, you would have waited for him to come back, wouldn't you, even though he said he was going to kill you?"

"I didn't have a choice, Ryan. If I'd run, then Micah would have been killed. I don't know if he could have actually done it, but I'll never forget the way he looked at me when he told me my time was up."

"Why," he asked with his eyes large and round, "did you get back together with him?"

"I told you, I am so honestly in love with him. He's not really that way. It's just how he was raised. He's changed everything to—to…" I had done well up until this point in only allowing a few tears to fall, but as soon as I considered everything Micah had done to change his life, to make a new life with me, I collapsed inside. It was like an implosion of the worst kind. Suddenly I couldn't breathe and what was worse was I didn't want to breathe.

He had changed his world for me and now I had pushed him away—I had no choice, but at the moment all I wanted was to be selfish and run back to him. To keep him for myself and the consequences be damned, but I knew if I did then one day very soon he would hate me for what I'd done to his family. "Oh, God, Ryan, what is he going through right now? He knows by now that I'm gone. He thinks I'm some trashy whore who couldn't make up her mind about which guy to sleep with. He must hate me so badly. Oh, Ryan… Oh, God," I sobbed, my shoulders convulsing from the depth of emotion coming to the surface.

He pulled me into his arms as I disappeared into my pain. In all the points in my recent life when I had felt broken, nothing ever, ever hurt so badly as what I was feeling now. All I could see was Micah's face and the hurt, pain, anger and betrayal. All I wanted at that moment was to disappear from the planet earth, but I didn't know if even Heaven could heal the gaping wound inside my heart. The full effect of what was irreversibly put into motion this morning was like the impact of hitting cement after jumping from a high rise, obliterating everything inside me.

I must have literally cried into unconsciousness because when I woke up it was dark and I was tucked into a bed—alone. I got up and found Ryan asleep in the adjacent bedroom. It was two in the morning and I couldn't sleep. I imagined Micah was awake wherever he was at the moment.

I pulled the cell phone from my purse and sat there for another hour trying to decide if I should turn it on. I wanted nothing more than to call him, to hear him answer his phone as he breathed out my name. I would at least tell him how very sorry I was for what happened. I wanted to tell him I loved him with all my heart, but that wouldn't make much sense when I needed him to believe I left him for Ryan.

I finally turned it on and noticed I had twenty-seven new messages. I didn't want to play them, but I knew his voice was waiting for me at just the push of a button. The first message began the slow tearing of my heart from my chest.

"Hey baby, call me as soon as you get this message—I just *need* to know where you are right now. Call me back."

"I don't know what's going on, but I *know* you love me, Annalisa. Don't do this to us, please baby. I can forgive you for anything, just don't leave me."

"Why won't you at least answer the damn phone? Tell me what I did wrong—and then tell me what I can do right to fix this. You've got to at least talk to me, Leese, please. I know you're listening to this message—if you ever loved me, call me, baby."

There was a message from my mother begging me to think about what I was doing to everyone, Micah's family, her and Kimmy, and even to Ryan, "I never thought of you as selfish, honey, but this was the most... God, Leese, what's gotten in to you?"

There were twenty three more messages, two more of them from Mom as she balled her eyes out and asked me to come home, and twenty-one more messages were from Micah's cell number, but they were all silent. The silence hurt worse than the pleas.

I was still awake when dawn broke. There was no need to go back to bed as I groggily walked to the kitchen. Even though I wanted food, coffee would do for now. I think the sound of me in the kitchen must have disturbed Ryan's sleep because I could hear him moaning and tossing around, but he didn't wake.

The coffee finished perking and I poured myself a cup and unlocked the sliding doors that led to the back porch. A mist was lying down the intensely green mountain side as I sat in a rocker and watched a hummingbird by a large flowered bush at the end of the porch. It was so peaceful to look out upon when my inner self was in total shambles. I heard the sliding door as Ryan appeared carrying a cup of coffee; he didn't appear to be fully awake.

"Not a morning person?" I asked. Micah and I had both been early risers.

"Absolutely not," he said, rubbing his sleepy face, "but you? I figured you were a morning person; morning people always seem to be so bubbly."

"Jewels is bubbly, I just like to get up early no matter what mood I'm in."

He laughed, "Yeah, you're right. She was off the charts bubbly most of the time—it drove me crazy."

"So was there ever any chance for the two of you to get together?"

"No. She wanted to try her wings out at—at sex, but I wasn't—"

"Jewels?" I said, clearly surprised. "She wanted—"

"Yeah, like majorly bad. I think I was the complete opposite of what her parents would approve of and that was a big turn on for her." He shook his head at the memory and breathed in the vapors rising from his coffee cup.

"Well, I'm impressed with you. Most guys would have been happy to oblige her, especially if it was her first time."

"I suppose you're right, but I honestly didn't want my first experience to be in the back of my Trans Am with her cheering me on to make the goal."

I wondered for a moment if I'd heard him correctly. Did he say his first experience or hers? I stopped the rocker and stared at him, mentally reviewing what he'd said.

"Big shocker, huh?" he laughed lightly.

I still hadn't found the speech button for my mouth. This 6'3" tattooed, Air Force bound, electric-blue-eyed, raven haired angel was exactly what I had been four days ago—virgin. Now I really heaped a huge pile of guilt upon the ashes of my life. He risked everything and ran away with someone who could never be with him the way he was hoping to experience. And, for that matter, how was he ever going to find the right girl as long as he was in my company?

"That wasn't your—your first kiss back at the hotel, was it?" I was cringing hard.

"I've kissed girls before…" he said.

I took a breath.

"…but never the way you kissed me, Leese. I usually back away if a girl wants to try getting that hot and heavy."

I rolled my eyes heavenward as they filled with tears.

"Don't be upset about it," he continued, "they were the best kisses of my entire life."

"God, just send down a lightning bolt right now and fry me," I whimpered, still looking up.

He looked up at the sky and then back down at me, "Don't talk like that." He grabbed my arm and made me go back inside. Yeah, he and I both knew I deserved that lightning bolt.

"We're doing your hair," he stated, setting down his cup of coffee and grabbing the boxes of color and frost on the table, "come on."

I think I was still numb up until he rinsed out the first batch of dye. He was towel drying my head and had gotten a little too rough when I snapped out of it.

"Yikes, give me that towel. You're about to remove my scalp!"

"Oh, sorry," he said and then went for the blow dryer.

"I can do that part myself." I handed him back the towel. It usually took me twenty minutes or more to dry my hair when it was long, now it seemed to be dry in five.

"Okay, now we'll streak it," he stated matter-of-factly, getting the product out on the bathroom counter with all the little foil papers. "Crap, this looks complicated."

"I don't have to have streaks," I argued.

"We bought it, you'll look good with them so you're getting them, got it?"

"All right hair-god, but if my head goes up in flames, it's your fault." Why did I worry? He could work in a salon, even if that isn't what he considered macho enough for his persona. I looked fabulous when he was done with me.

The red dye didn't go quite as smoothly as the blonde. He just didn't have enough hair to keep from getting it on his skin. Once the time was up and I rinsed it off his head, it wasn't so bad, but it was certainly different. I didn't, and I don't think he did either, consider the shocking contrast with the red hair and the blue eyes.

"I look freaky," he remarked as he studied his reflection in the mirror.

"We're dying you back to black before we leave here."

"Nah, it's cool."

"Ryan, it looks like your heads on fire—you're going back to black."

He grinned as he put himself cheek to cheek with me as we looked at the blonde and the redhead in the mirror, "Whatever you say." He kissed my temple and walked away.

The rest of the day was spent lounging on the comfortable couches in the living room and flipping between the news and the weather channel. Ryan snoozed most of the time. He wasn't kidding about not being a morning person. At the rate he was sleeping, I'd be lucky if he was a late afternoon person.

It didn't surprise me there was nothing on the news about me, especially since we'd kept every detail about the wedding hush-hush from the press. I chuckled to myself as I considered we had the tightest security possible during the wedding because it was provided for us by the mob; even the most die-hard paparazzi would have been dissuaded.

D'Angelo had not been on the guest list because Micah felt having the person who hired him to kill me there, would have been like bringing Robert to the wedding. The reason for the change in our wedding date was now abundantly clear to me. Had we tried to keep it September 15th, D'Angelo would have gotten to me before Micah and I had the opportunity to experience each other. I wondered if it was possible that I might be pregnant. What a sad, but beautiful way to keep a part of him with me.

When nighttime came Ryan was fully awake and I was exhausted from not sleeping the night before. I felt bad leaving him sitting there with nothing to do, but I had to go to bed. I honestly don't know why I even tried. Within an hour, I was awake again. I tossed and turned and finally got up and watched a late movie with him until one a.m. and then tried once again to go to sleep.

I needed my sleeping pill; he was just over six feet tall with muscles and a way of crooning my name, and wrapping his arm around my waist as I drifted off to sleep. But there was no Micah to lull me into the rest I needed, only his memory; and a memory of him could never replace what I needed.

The next morning, the effects of two sleepless nights were starting to show. Ryan was up by ten and rather chipper for having risen before noon, but he could tell immediately I hadn't done well through the night.

"I think you need to get out and get some fresh air and exercise that way you'll be so tired you'll sleep tonight. I found a trail last Christmas that leads to a waterfall, wanna go?"

"Give me a few minutes to pull myself together," I said as I stumbled to the bathroom and got ready.

He was right about the walk, I felt so much better as we took off down the mountainside. We discussed leaving perhaps by Friday and going to our final destination, final as long as there were no signs that Micah had figured out where we went. We were both pretty sure our location here had been a good choice and that was why we wouldn't leave for another three or four days.

The waterfall was tucked off to the side of the path, but the sound of the falling water could be heard for a good distance away. It was small, but still impressive as it poured over the rocks and continued as a small stream running down the mountain. We splashed around and acted like a pair of kids for a while and then finally started the journey back up the mountain.

Okay, now I understood what he was saying about being tired enough for sleep tonight. The trip up the trail was arduous where as the trip down had been pleasant. We were both sweaty and drained of all the positive energy when we reached Harvey's place. Ryan took a shower and flopped on the couch, passing out almost immediately. I took a shower and tried passing out, but as tired as I was, I simply couldn't sleep. When he rolled over two hours later, he found me sitting there watching him.

"I made you some lunch," I said as he looked at me expressionlessly.

He blinked a couple times, yawned and rubbed his sleepy face, "Did you take a nap?"

"I tried; no luck."

"Crap, Leese, you've got to get some sleep before you turn into a zombie." He sat up, putting his feet on the floor and running his hand over his shock-red stubble, "If you don't sleep tonight, we're going back to town and getting you some sleeping pills."

"I don't take pills," I retorted.

"Well you got to do something. Did you have problems sleeping before all of this?"

"I did until Micah started staying at the house. He was my 'sleeping pill,'" I said, smiling for once at a memory instead of crying. "Some nights he'd slip in my room and—"

Ryan's hand went up to shush me, "I don't know if I want to hear about what he did to get you to sleep."

"Ryan," I stated with surprise, "we didn't have sex until *after* we got married. He would just crawl in bed and hold me and then we could both sleep. It's like we became so bonded when we had to stay together because of the contract that now it's as if something inside me is actually..." The tears were coming to the surface as I looked away so he wouldn't notice, but it was too late.

He reached over and turned my chin toward him, "It's okay to cry, Leese. Go ahead and finish what you were saying."

I sighed as I let the tears fall, "Something inside me is missing and I have to wonder if he's been able to sleep at all either."

"So how does he hold you when you sleep together?"

His hand gently caressed the side of my face and then swept slowly through my hair. I closed my eyes in response to the touch, "We'd... Why?" I asked suddenly more alert than before the soft lull snagged me when he touched my face.

"How about a replacement?" he whispered.

That caused a heated flush through my system as the thought of Ryan holding me in bed hit me, "No—I don't' want to give you, or me, the wrong idea."

"Just tell me how he holds you? Please, Leese. I'm not going to try to jump your bones. I've got a little more restraint than that."

"But what if I don't," I said softly.

I could see that took him completely off guard as a light smile came to his face, "I could only hope, but I think we both know you're more level headed than that."

"Usually, yeah, but I swear it hurts so bad that I just feel..." It was time to shut up and not tell him what had been going through my head when I focused on the physical instead of the mental. Mentally I was strong enough for a lifetime of denial, but physically? That had become another issue entirely.

"Tell me how he holds you," he repeated, "or I'm buying you some sleeping pills, and I am big enough to make you take one."

I was thinking there was no way he was big enough to do that, but right now I wasn't up for the challenge, "I'm usually on my side and he just fits behind me and wraps his arm around my waist."

"Tonight you and I are going to see if we can get you to stay asleep."

He wasn't leaving room for rebuttal, but I had to have a little more from him than the simple statement that he was going to be my 'Micah' stand-in, "If I'm not comfortable with this Ryan, you—"

"I'll get out of the bed and leave you by yourself," he finished for me.

"And," I said, coming to the real crux of the matter, "If I'm *too* comfortable, you won't let me cross any lines."

He rolled his eyes, "I'm just curious, but if this is a permanent situation between you and him, and you honestly change your mind about—about us at some point, how will I know you aren't just getting 'too comfortable' as you put it?"

I had to think about that. He had a valid question, but I wanted to believe, in my heart of hearts, God would work something out for Micah and me. I'd seen His plan unfolding all along, and I was amazed how He had gotten me through what should have been the end of my life to the point I was at right now, but what if His plan changed? What if I felt honestly led to embrace more from Ryan than friendship? This was a deeper thought than I planned to tackle anytime soon. What if Ryan was the new plan for my life? I looked at him and knew he sensed how difficult this question was for me to answer. But, I could answer it.

"First, you've got to promise me you won't stop looking for the right girl to come along. I don't want you holding your breath, waiting for me to change my mind. God will put the right person in your path someday and, if it's not me, I don't want to be what holds you back if you find her."

"I can promise that, but tell me how to know it's for real between you and me, and not just because we get a little too comfortable with each other."

"If I ever, wide awake, ask you to make love to me, I'll mean it. But if I ask you, it'll mean I want the rest of our lives to be together; I don't go for the one-night-stand concept."

"I don't know how any man could ever want only one night with you," he finally gave me that big smile and said he was ready for lunch.

I could tell he was anxious to put our plan into action tonight; I couldn't help but think this wasn't the best idea. The closer it came to bedtime, the less sure I was of trying this.

"If you don't mind," I said as it became late, "I'd like to go to bed by myself. I can fall asleep; I just can't seem to stay that way. Once I'm out, slip in beside me and we'll find out if this is going to work or not."

He nodded as I left the couch and went to bed. I was afraid I might not be able to drift off, but exhaustion took over and unconsciousness crept in. I wasn't sure if I was dreaming or if I actually felt the moment he slipped in beside me. I had that wonderful sensation of Micah's strong arm gathering me against his body, a soft kiss against my neck and then a feeling of peace filled me.

It was after ten in the morning when my eyes fluttered open. It had worked and I actually had gotten a full night's sleep. A warm arm was wrapped around my waist and I could feel his breath against my hair. It only took an instant to remember I wasn't in Micah's embrace. Being awake, together, in this position wouldn't be good so I attempted to slip out from under his arm and get out of the bed before he stirred. He was a late sleeper so I didn't think this would be a difficult feat, until I tried to move his arm. His grip tightened, hard. I heard him moaning and making some unintelligible sounds, but he never lightened his hold. I grabbed his wrist and put a little more force into trying to lift his arm.

"No." His hips pushed firmly against my butt as his arm moved slightly lower to keep me from pulling away.

I couldn't see his face so I didn't know if he told me no in his sleep or if he was awake and refusing to let go of me. "Ryan," I whispered.

He inhaled deeply and moaned again.

I was certain at this point he was still asleep, but that didn't change the problem of me getting away. Just as I made another attempt, the arm moved but not the way I expected as his hand came up and clutched my breast. "Ryan!"

He jerked awake, "Huh? Wha—shit!" He quickly withdrew his hand when he understood why I was making a loud complaint. He rolled onto his back, putting both hands in front of him as if to show he wasn't touching anything he shouldn't, "Sorry, sorry, I'm clear."

Being 'clear' was a pilot's term as if it was propellers on my chest instead of boobs. "I didn't realize I was an airplane," I laughed.

He rolled away and buried his face down into the pillow, "Damn, I hate waking up fast. I always say something stupid," then his head lifted as a tiny smile pulled at the corners of his mouth, "but you slept all night, didn't you?"

"I did—*thank you*." I hoped he could tell how very sincere I was, I didn't think I could go three days without rest.

"Sorry about the…" he made a motion with his hand like he was squeezing an invisible ball. "I didn't mean to…" His face was red.

"We've got to get that hair dyed back so it doesn't match your face when you blush."

He laughed as he rolled out of the bed and onto his feet. Just as he was rising, Harvey's house phone began ringing. We shot each other a worried glance as he moved toward the nightstand to answer it.

"No! It might be Micah. I—I can't talk to him."

"Leese, he doesn't know we're here. It's got to either be Harvey or my mom." He picked up the receiver slowly and said hello. "Harvey," he sighed with relief. But I could hear the sound of the caller's panicked voice as the look on Ryan's face changed, "Shit! When? Are you sure he's headed here? When did he leave?"

I didn't know what the outcome was going to be, but I was already up grabbing my clothes and items and throwing them into my duffle bags.

"Do you know what he's flying in? Damn, Harvey, that doesn't give me more than thirty minutes! All right, yeah I know. I hate to say it but we're leaving right now, we won't have time to straighten up the house and I'll probably leave your truck down at the hanger. Yeah, that sounds like a good idea. Okay, we're out of here. I'll let you know where you can find the plane when—all right, bye." He slammed the phone down and started grabbing his things.

He didn't have to say a word; there wasn't time as we threw our bags together.

129

"Let's go," he said, pushing the last of his clothes down and pulling the zipper.

I was going through my mind making sure I had everything. I had my money and my clothes and other items, so there was nothing I was forgetting as we jumped into the big Dodge and fired it up. We backed out and took off at breakneck speed. There were a few other pilots down at the hanger when we pulled up.

"We've got an emergency," he said as he approached them, "can you guys help me get it out of the hanger?" The men hooked the small tractor they kept at the hanger to the plane and pulled it out into the sunshine. They evidently didn't like the idea that Ryan was ready to jump into the plane without a preflight check, but then he told them it was a matter of life or death. They helped load our bags and then convinced him that no preflight might also be a life or death matter, but they would help him complete it quickly.

"You can't just leave the truck parked here," one of the men said to him as we prepared to board.

"Harvey will be here in about three hours and he'll move the truck. If that's not fast enough for you, I left the keys in the ignition, but we have to go," he said, practically pushing me up the steps into the plane. I went to the front and sat in the co-pilot's seat. Ryan joined me, starting the engines and then waiting impatiently as they came to life. The men gave him the thumbs-up and he began driving the plane to the air strip. We taxied from the center down to the end and then he turned the plane around and it was only a matter of moments and we were airborne.

As soon as we had climbed thousands of feet and were pointed to the northwest, I was ready to ask.

"Micah is on his way here, isn't he?"

Ryan glanced at his instrument display, "I should have fueled before we left. We've only got enough for another four hundred miles or so." He was touching the display changing items on screen, but he wasn't answering my question. "Murfreesboro has a small municipal airport, we'll stop there. We'll be there in about forty minutes."

"Ryan, please."

He looked at me for the first time since we had boarded the plane, "Yeah, he found us."

"How?"

"I don't know. Harvey got a call from a friend of his at the airport and said a guy had flown in this morning from Louisiana and had a cop with him. They wanted to know about my plane and then about any small planes that took off in about a two hour time span on Monday. There were only five and they were asking if I was piloting any of them."

"But you used Harvey's name on your flight plan, how—"

"I know, but one of the guys in the control room mentioned that Harvey and I were good friends and then someone else mentioned the flight plan couldn't have been right because they saw Harvey that afternoon. I guess it was all he needed. He's in a Gulfstream 350, and Harvey said they flew out of there around 8:30 or 8:45. If someone hadn't called Harvey, you would have seen Micah this morning, and I don't think he would have been happy to see me."

My head went back against the seat as my heart continued to pound in my chest, "I never, ever should have agreed to let you help me," I choked. I could feel the emotions wadded up in my throat, but nothing was rising to my eyes. If Micah didn't show up with his pistols strapped to his sides, it wouldn't matter because he would beat Ryan to death, and I know I couldn't stop him.

"Don't worry about me," he said, his hand reaching over and squeezing mine.

"He's just going to follow us to wherever we go and—"

"Only if he's a freaking psychic! He can't follow us this time; we don't have a flight plan."

"Will you be in trouble for that?"

"The FAA wants every trip to have a flight plan, but for small aircraft it's only strongly recommended. They can't pull my license or anything for not doing it."

My heart was beginning to slow from its fast pace and air was returning to my lungs. Running away from Micah I had known all along wasn't going to be easy, but I never expected him to find me so quickly.

Chapter Ten

Micah studied the property records on his laptop. He found Harvey Pinchon's information at Heaven's Landing. He knew exactly which house he would be going to when they landed in a few moments. He turned off the computer and closed the lid.

Gwen gave him a sympathetic look as they descended onto the mountaintop airstrip.

He hated that look. He didn't want sympathy. In fact, he didn't want her along at all, but he'd made himself bring her so it would be easier to get information at the airport, and so when he found them, she could talk him out of killing Ryan.

They landed and taxied toward the hangers where a group of men were standing.

Micah wasted no time in concocting a believable story. "Hello," he said as he and Gwen disembarked. "Harvey sent us up here to check on some friends staying at his place."

"You just missed them," one man quickly offered. "They flew out of here about fifteen minutes ago."

"Do you know where they were headed?" Gwen asked.

"No," another man answered, "but they were in a hell-fire hurry, said it was a matter of life or death. The guy wasn't even going to do his preflight check, but we talked him into it."

"He didn't even fuel up," the first man added. "He only had about a third of a tank so he won't go more than a couple hundred miles before he has to refuel. And," he added, pointing to the big black truck, "He left Harvey's truck sitting here with the keys in the ignition."

"I'll take the truck back up to Harvey's," Micah said smoothly.

No one was going to argue with someone his size, nor with a cop, as they watched the two of them get in Harvey's truck.

Micah had the information from the computer memorized, so it was no problem for him to pull into the right driveway.

"I'm going inside," he simply told Gwen.

"That's breaking and entering, Micah, I don't think—"

"Then stay outside," he growled back. "See if there is a garage door opener in the—"

Gwen already had it in hand. She had found it in the seat when she climbed in, but hadn't shown it until now. She hit the button and the door went up.

Micah smiled at the open door inside the garage leading into the house, "You don't have to come inside."

Gwen didn't say anything as she followed.

The house wasn't messy, but it was obvious they left in a rush. Micah inspected each room; pausing the longest as he looked at the unmade bed. He went into the master bath and then left the room and headed to the kitchen. He pulled out the kitchen garbage can and took off the lid and began pulling out empty Wal-Mart bags. Eventually he found the bag he was looking for as he removed a receipt and put it in his pocket. A little further down, below a couple more bags he stopped and stared for a long moment.

Gwen started to walk toward him when he spewed out an obscenity and slammed his fist through the kitchen wall.

"Micah!"

Three more powerful punches to the wall and she was struggling to get a grip on his arms. "Stop. Quit being an idiot! You're going to hit a stud in a minute and break your hand!"

"Damn it, Gwen—Damn it all to hell," he didn't sound furious at the moment, only defeated. "Do you have," he tried to say, but his voice caught on the words. He took a choppy breath and tried again, "Do you have an extra hair tie or a rubber band?"

Gwen reached up and pulled the hair band from her short pony tail and handed it to Micah.

He reached into the trash and removed a big lock of shimmering brown hair about eighteen inches long. He wrapped the end of the hair carefully and tightly with the band and then shook it as the intermixed black hairs fell away. He smoothed the hair between his fingers until it was straight and then slowly lifted it to his face and inhaled deeply, "It smells just the way it did the morning she left me."

Gwen had no words to comfort him, as she rubbed her hand softly on the back of his broad shoulder.

He coiled the hair and placed it carefully into his shirt pocket and then reached back into the trash and pulled out several bottles of hair color and their boxes, "I believe my wife is a blonde now, with highlights." He grabbed a half-filled bottle of red. "And the asshole is now a redhead."

He looked around the house for a few more minutes and then walked outside. He had the sales receipt in hand and was dialing the store's phone number, "Yes, can you tell me where you're located if I'm coming from Heaven's Landing? And is April working this morning? Thank you." He closed the phone and opened the door to the truck as he started to get in.

"Micah, you can't just take this truck. We've got to call a cab."

"Can't a police officer commandeer a vehicle?"

"Yes, I can, but—"

"Good, then you drive," he said, handing her the keys.

Within fifteen minutes they were approaching the customer service desk as Gwen showed them the receipt pointing to the name of the cashier on the paper, "Hello, I'm police chief Gavarreen and this is detective—"

"Michaelson," Micah said, reaching out and shaking the manager's hand. "We need to speak to April regarding a missing person that came through her line a few days ago."

"Oh—oh sure, I'll go get her." The slight-built man hurried off to relieve her from her register. It didn't take long for the twenty-something, gum chewing, curly haired cashier to greet her visitors.

"Hi, ya'll. My manager said you needed to see me about someone that I rang up a couple days ago, but there are a lot of folks that come through—"

"You might remember this couple," Micah interrupted, showing her a picture of Leese and watching her reaction as she earnestly studied her face. Then he handed her one of Ryan.

"Those two! Oh, Lord, yes. Who could forget those blue-eyes? He was a real card, half crazy, I think. I thought there was something wrong about them."

"Why?" Gwen asked.

"The girl, she was real quiet, but he was talkative enough for the both of them. He said they got married the day before—I mean the diamond on her hand didn't look like nothing he could afford, but she never denied it, never said a word. And then he got kinda nasty-talkin', sayin' she lost her voice from screamin' on their weddin' night. I couldn't believe he said that."

Micah inhaled and his muscle mass seemed to double in size.

"Anyway," she continued, apparently enjoying the fact that she had something to tell, "she hauled off and slugged him in the arm, hard, too. It was no love tap, honey."

Micah smiled slightly, losing a little of the anger.

"But when he started to pay, she spoke up and said she had it, and then pulled out brand-new hundred dollar bills."

"Was that all?" Gwen pressed.

"Did they mention anything about where they were headed after here?" Micah added.

"No, I don't recall, but he did say they flew in from California, if that helps."

"Thank you for—" Gwen started to say.

"So did he like kidnap her? I knew that boy wasn't right in the head."

"We'll be in touch if we need anything else," Gwen dodged.

The flight back to Louisiana was quiet for the first hour.

"Micah, I'm sorry, but I think you need to seriously consider what Mom told you last night."

"I'm not divorcing her, Gwen."

"It's not a divorce, it's an annulment."

"I don't care what it's called, I—"

"You worked too hard to risk your fortune on—"

"She has more money than me," he said raising an eyebrow at his sister.

"Maybe she does and maybe she could care less about your millions, but you also thought she was going to be a faithful—"

"Shut up, Gwen. It isn't right. I still don't believe she left me for Ryan. He may have been helping her, but he *isn't* the reason. You heard the cashier about how Leese was acting in the store."

"Micah, wake up! Didn't you notice something a little odd in that house? If she wasn't after Ryan then—"

"Don't say it. Of course I noticed the—the bed."

"They left in a hurry and they didn't take time to make the bed—there was only one bed that was—"

"Stop it! I'm not an idiot, Gwen."

"You've been denying what happened since she left. It's time to see the truth. She left with Ryan *on her own*. I'm sorry, I thought she was the real deal too, but in the end she's just a rich, spoiled, eighteen year old girl who didn't realize she already had the greatest guy on the planet."

Micah cut his eyes at her. They didn't speak to each other again.

As the plane approached the runway in New Orleans, Micah pulled out his cell phone and hit the speed dial, "Hey Bill, I need some legal work. It's not too late for an annulment, is it? No, I'm afraid it didn't work out, she—she ran away with another guy a couple days later. Yeah, but not as shocked as me. I'll stop by your office tomorrow."

They walked off the plane as Micah thanked his sister for helping him. His cell phone went off again and a strange look came across his face as he looked at the caller's identity.

"Who is it?" Gwen asked, worried it might be the person she just convinced him to get an annulment from.

But it only took one name to realize she would have preferred that it was Leese.

"D'Angelo," he said, answering the phone and walking away.

Chapter Eleven

After we fueled in Murfreesboro, it was a three hour run for Colorado Springs.

"That's about our maximum range," Ryan commented as we left the Tennessee runway. "We'll be pretty close to empty by the time we get there."

"So you say you know some people out there, but you never said how."

"I lived there when I was younger. My dad was an instructor at the Academy for about three years before he went back to flying combat missions."

"Wow, that's pretty impressive. You're mom doesn't look that old, was your dad—"

"A little—ten years; he would have turned fifty one next month, he was forty seven when he was killed."

I watched his brow furrow and I knew it was time to change the subject, "So you were living with your sister in Pensacola? I never met her, how old is she?"

"Dianna is twenty-two. Her husband, Clyde—"

"Clyde?" I was trying not to giggle, but it sounded funny.

"Yeah, I know and what's even funnier is that's his nickname. Did you ever see the movie 'Every Which Way But Loose' with Clint Eastwood?"

My smile got a little broader, "No, I'm afraid I never watched any of his movies."

"You're kidding, right? You've never seen a Clint Eastwood film?" He was genuinely surprised.

"I'm not a big movie buff, but go on and tell me what the connection is between them." I was getting the feeling from the expression on Ryan's face that it was going to be funny, however it ended.

"Eastwood's character in the movie is a boxer named Philo Beddow who travels with an orangutan named Clyde."

"He's named after a monkey?" The laughter was beginning to roll up from somewhere in the middle of my stomach.

Ryan was trying to keep a straight face, but he was already chuckling, "Orangutans are apes, not monkeys. And no, his mom named him Philo after the boxer, but he had such shock red hair that everyone said he looked more like Clyde the ape and that's how he got the nickname."

"That's awful! You're kidding about this, right?"

"Swear to God, it's the honest truth—his hair is redder than mine."

"He's at least a handsome redhead right; he doesn't look like an ape in the face?"

"Hey, that's a girl's department to judge. I don't rate guys, but it's just the color of his hair that earned him the nickname. My sister likes his looks. Man, when we land I've got to get some Clint Eastwood movies for you to watch."

"Finish telling me about Dianna and Clyde; you got side-tracked."

"Oh, yeah. Anyway, Clyde is thirty and he's a master sergeant with the 46th Test Wing at Eglin. They live off the base and Mom thought I needed another male influence in my life so she decided I should stay with them for a little while. Well, that and the fact I could be in the Air Force ROTC at Pensacola High."

"I thought you said your mom is against the idea of you enlisting?"

"She is, but she said she can't live my life for me, I've got to make my own choices, so she let me go."

"She sounds like a good mom. Where does Palm Beach fit into all of this?"

"She is. Mom is originally from there. Her family is old money and no matter where we moved with Dad when he shipped around the states, Palm Beach was always home base. We moved back there when they sent him overseas."

"So you still have friends out here?" I asked as we neared our destination.

"Yeah, I have a couple buddies that are already enlisted and a few that are finishing up high school—like *us*," he emphasized, letting me know he still wanted both of us to get our diplomas.

"I don't know how we're going to do that, at least not for a little while until we make sure we don't have to move again."

"We're going to be okay here, Leese. He only found us because of what happened at the airport."

"You don't know his family," I said, trying not to let the pain hit me. "His mother is an expert when it comes to tracing people and finding out every detail about their lives. I wouldn't be surprised if Micah knows every place you've ever lived."

"Maybe, but until then we're going to settle in and get comfortable here. If we have to go, we'll pick someplace that neither of us has ever been."

I was thinking if it came to that, I was leaving here without him. He looked at this as a game until this morning when we actually had a near encounter. He didn't know Micah like I did. He'd never watched him empty himself of emotion and become the person he was trained to be. Ryan would hate me for running without him, but it would be one time I would leave a big enough trail that Micah would come straight after me and leave him alone.

We landed at COS and I gave Ryan a roll of cash to cover the costs for storing the airplane. He left me for a little while when he went to talk to the guys at the office. I dug into my duffle while he was gone, realizing I never even brushed my hair this morning, but it was so short I could straighten it out with my fingers if I had to. I looked in the mirror and still couldn't get over how good of a job he had done. I put on my makeup. Then, making sure no one was around, I changed my clothes. I folded and repacked my bags and then sat there wondering what was taking Ryan so long. I considered opening his bags and folding his clothes, but I didn't want it to appear that I was simply snooping through his things.

Finally, my wild redhead appeared at the door of the plane.

"Wow, leave you alone for a little while and you get all dolled-up."

I smiled, "I'm not 'dolled-up' I just put on a little makeup and some decent clothes." I passed him the bags as he reached for them.

"Did you call for a taxi? I'm sure there are some hotels here at the airport that—"

"We're covered. I've got a couple friends coming to get us, we're going to stay with them tonight, and tomorrow we can start looking for our own place. And by the way," he said as everything was unloaded and he put out his hand to help me down the stairs, "You are a doll with or without the makeup."

He let go of my hand and placed both hands around my waist and lifted me off the stairs and set me gently on the tarmac, surprising me as I looked up into his happy expression. He was evidently enjoying our time together no matter the circumstances.

I heard a car approaching as Ryan reluctantly let go and grabbed up the bags, "Okay, here we go baby, get ready for some wild people."

"What?"

"Just smile," he said out of the corner of his mouth.

A white Chevy Caprice barreled toward us with two massive young guys in the front seat. They were built like Micah, wide chests, thick necks and burly biceps, but they both had crew-cuts and were whooping and hollering out the windows before the car even stopped.

"Who did you call?" I questioned through gritted teeth.

"Friends," he gritted back. "Take off your rings," he whispered and then stepped in front of me to provide a little cover.

I quickly pulled the wedding set off my hand and slipped them into the pocket of my jeans.

"Andy! Ty! How's it going!" he shouted at them as they rolled out of the car and headed our direction.

They practically dog-piled Ryan, which isn't easy to do to someone his height, but it was no problem for these two monsters. He got slugged a couple times, in teasing of course, but I could still tell it hurt. They were laughing and asking what happened to his hair as they roughed his head.

"My hair?" Ryan scoffed, "You guys are ones to talk. What happened to your hair?"

"We got ours cut, but someone didn't turn our asses over and dip us in friggin' pumpkin colored paint!"

"It's red, not pumpkin," Ryan rebutted, defending his color choice.

"It's my fault," I spoke up, causing all three heads to snap my direction. "I'm responsible for the color job, but we're dying it back to black tonight."

Both guys straightened up and big smiles came across their faces. "Damn, Ryan—you've done all right for yourself, son," the largest one stated.

I felt the blush hit my cheeks.

"Andy, Ty, this is Leese, she's—"

"A good friend," I finished for him, reaching out to shake hands. I didn't expect to get grabbed but the one Ryan referred to as Andy, pulled me next to him and wrapped his arms around me.

The smile fell off Ryan's face.

"Well, girlfriend, if he's just a buddy, I'm your new man," he laughed and gave me a brief hug and turned me loose.

Ty reached out and took my hand and brought it to his mouth and kissed the back of it, "Not if I have anything to say about it," he quipped. "Nice to meet you, Leese. And don't mind my brother, he's a dipshit, but I know how to treat a lady."

Ryan pushed them both away from me and stepped between, "Back off you idiots, she's here with me and she's not looking for a Romeo—or a pair of clowns."

"Ah, man, you're just jealous because we look better than you, Pumpkin Head," Andy laughed.

"Maybe we'll look for that apartment *today*," Ryan growled, turning to me.

"The hell you say!" Andy responded. "Momma's got a room ready for you and supper planned. She'll kick your ass if you bail on us now."

The trunk was opened and our bags were tossed inside. The guys tried talking me into sitting between them in the front seat, leaving Ryan alone in the back, but I politely refused. I think they were kidding, but it was a little hard to tell.

I wasn't usually afraid in a vehicle, but Ty drove like a lunatic. I found myself clutching Ryan's arm to stay upright as Ty took curves and corners too fast. Ryan wrapped his arm around me and braced his legs against the back of the front seats to keep us from sliding around.

"Do you guys know of any good cars for sale," Ryan asked as we exited the airport. He could tell I wouldn't want to ride any more than necessary with these two.

Andy turned around to answer and got a funny look on his face as he watched Ryan's grip on me tighten, "I know a guy that has an awesome 1969 AMC Javelin. It's all original with the 390 engine and a four speed, but he wants like ten grand for it."

"Is it on the way?" I asked, my arms twining around Ryan's waist.

Andy leaned forward and smacked Ty on the shoulder, "Hey, stop at Pearly's house, they wanna check out the Javelin."

The car took a sharp left and Ryan landed on me as we flopped over in the seat. He was grinning as we righted ourselves. "Ty, do you think you could drive a little less like Bo Duke? Leese's gonna have bruises by the time we get to your house."

"I don't know," Ty laughed as he slowed his pace, "I had a big crush on Daisy Duke. If you can talk Leese into a pair of short-shorts and high-heels I might actually drive civil."

The guys laughed. I didn't think it was that funny.

We pulled down a shaded street filled with older homes and drove down to the end and turned into a driveway. Andy went up and knocked as we waited in the yard. An older black man answered the door and then came outside.

"You interested in my car?" he asked Ryan.

"Yes, sir. Is it in good condition?"

"I'd say. I bought her back in '69 right off the showroom floor. I've put 78,000 miles on her and that's all. Come on around to the garage."

We followed him to a dilapidated detached building around the side of the house, but when the door was lifted, there sat a shining red Javelin with a black stripe.

"She ain't got no rust. The seats are perfect except for one little burn hole in the backseat from my stupid cousin Clair. The floor is solid and the mats are original. She runs like a scalded-ass ape."

"When's the last time you cranked her up?" I asked.

"I crank her at least once a week and I take her out on the road about once a month. I've won a couple awards at the local car shows for her," he added proudly.

"So why are you selling it?" Ryan asked.

"Why does anybody sell anything?" he quipped. "I could use the money and my pickup truck gets me back and forth to work just fine. She's just for show."

"Well, stop jacking your jaw, Pearly, and crank her up," Ty said impatiently.

"You damn boys might be MP's but you ain't the boss of me, so you can just hold your high horse," he said fishing around in his pocket for the key. "Besides, I see this lady here seems to have an eye for fine cars." He watched me looking it over. "She might like to crank it. It's stick though, honey, so you're gonna have to push in the clutch and put her in neutral.

"I can drive stick," I smiled, taking the offered key.

Andy and Ty made a collective noise like they were impressed that I could drive a manual. Ryan just laughed. He'd ridden with me and he knew what I could do behind the wheel.

"Give the gas one tap, before you turn the key," Pearly stated.

I did as instructed and the engine came immediately to life. I liked the sound right away. "Can we test drive it?"

"I don't know," Pearly stated, giving me and Ryan a hard look, "can you afford it? I want eighty-five hundred for her."

"Do you have a current tag on it?" I asked.

"Yup, just renewed it about five months ago."

"Yeah, we can manage the price—if it runs good."

"Well, come on, darlin' let's take her for a ride." He motioned Ryan around to the passenger's side. He looked at Ty and Andy. "You boys can wait here, cuz the trunk ain't big enough to hold both of you!" he laughed. He had me lean forward as he tipped the seat up and crawled into the back.

I could see the disappointment written on their faces as they watched me drive away.

"Which way?" I asked reaching the end of the drive.

"Turn right and then I'll show you where you can stretch her out a little."

Within a few blocks we were in an area that had a few closed up warehouses and basically no vehicles in the street.

"Okay, you've got about eight blocks of nothing, so check her out and punch her d—"

He didn't get to utter the last word before I dropped the pedal to the floor and burned down the street. The transmission was in excellent shape and the engine responded like a dream. There was plenty of room in an empty parking lot as I neared the end of the vacant road and I slid her into it, spinning one-eighty and heading back down the way we'd come.

Pearly made no comment about my driving, but he was grinning from ear to ear when I looked into the rearview. Now I could see why they called him Pearly—he had the whitest teeth I'd ever seen. I slowed before turning onto the street that would take us to Ty and Andy. "Ryan, you want to give it a go?" I asked, unable to get the smile off my face.

"It's your money, Leese. You're the boss."

"I'm paying, but I'm not getting the car for me, it's for you."

"How about I get to drive it to Andy and Ty's house?"

"Deal," I said, reaching over and squeezing his hand.

We pulled the car up behind the Caprice and followed Pearly inside to pay him and get the title. He pointedly told Andy and Ty they could wait outside.

His house wasn't well lit and the curtains were drawn, but we made our way to the couch as Pearly left the room for the paperwork. I pulled out a pack of hundreds and tucked them behind my purse.

"Leese, how are we going to transfer the title and get insurance on the car?" Ryan quietly questioned.

"Let me handle that for now," I whispered my response as Pearly returned to the room.

"Okay, I don't take checks," Pearly began.

"I'll pay cash, but I need a couple favors from you."

At this his eyebrows went up, "I knew you was gonna be too good to be true," he said, shaking his head.

"No, it's nothing bad. It's just that we're trying to stay out of my crazy ex-husband's reach. Can I pay you ten grand and I get to keep the license plate? I'd appreciate it if you didn't drop it from your insurance for several months, so we'll have time to figure out how to insure it without sending up a red flag that says 'here we are,'" I finished.

"Crazy ex-husband, huh?"

I could tell he wasn't totally buying my story, so I reached into my pocket and pulled out my rings.

"Damn, he's probably crazy 'cause he wants those back! Not that you ain't a package worth reclaiming yourself, but them rings cost a pretty penny, I can tell."

I returned the rings to my pocket and took the bundle of hundreds that had been hidden by my purse, "So, do we have an agreement?"

"Is that his, too!" he exclaimed. "I don't want him looking for me if he's got that kind of dough."

I laughed, "No, the money is mine."

He reached into a drawer in a small table beside him and pulled out what appeared to be a magic marker. "Not that I don't believe you, but I've been burned before," he said, reaching toward me.

That was when I realized it was a counterfeit marking tool. I handed him the money as he put it under the light from the table lamp and marked a random sampling of bills.

"You got a deal, lady," he chuckled, flashing his bright smile.

We shook hands and left with the title.

"Did you buy it?" Andy asked with a hint of excitement in his voice.

"Sure did. We'll follow you guys," Ryan confirmed, taking the key from my hand.

I tried to talk him in to stopping somewhere so I could pick up some black hair dye, but he said we would do that later because he didn't quite remember where he was headed and he didn't want to lose the crazy driver in front of us.

Twenty five minutes later we pulled up to an older tri-level home with a stone façade and an ancient tire swing in the front yard.

"I used to live in that house there," Ryan pointed to the large brick house next door. "These idiots were my neighbors."

"I'm surprised you survived it."

Our bags were in the trunk of the Caprice and Ty had already unlocked it and was pulling them out. "Which ones are yours, Leese?" he asked.

I tried to grab mine, but he slung them over his shoulder.

"I don't want you to have to carry them, I just wanted to be sure I wasn't carrying Pumpkin Heads," he said, throwing the other two bags at Ryan.

I could hear the air leave Ryan's chest as the bags smacked into him. "Thanks a lot," he gasped. "You're a real great host."

We walked into the house and a familiar odor hit me. Garlic bread? Lasagna? It was some kind of Italian food being prepared.

"Ma, were home!" Andy yelled out.

A heavy set woman with a kind face and an oven mitt on each hand came around the corner. "Ryan? Is that you? Good Lord, baby, what did you do to your hair?"

"Hey, Miss Naomi." He dropped his bags and gave her a warm embrace.

"I know it's you, 'cause it's the same handsome face and those perfect blue eyes," she said, with an oven mitt cupping each of his cheeks.

"Ouch! Hot, Miss Naomi," he whined.

"Oh, Lord, I'm sorry. I forgot I just took a big pan of lasagna out of the oven with these dumb things." She pulled off the mitts and tucked them under her arm. "You've grown a foot since I seen you last. How's your momma?"

"She's fine," he replied. Both of his cheeks were as red as if he'd been out in the sun too long.

She looked at me waiting patiently behind him and she smiled, "Well, who is this pretty young woman you've got with you?"

"This is my good friend Leese. Leese, this is Naomi Saint-George, mother of thing one and thing two," he said pointing to Andy and Ty.

"It's just George," Naomi corrected him. "I'm no saint."

"Sure you are," Ryan continued, kissing her cheek, "You've had to put up with those dummies for twenty-some-odd years."

She suddenly seemed a little worried, "I—I only have one extra bedroom, unless we put you on the couch, Ryan," she mentioned with a little flush to her cheeks.

"Leese and I can share a room," he said throwing a cocky glance at Andy and Ty.

"Sure we can," I said, a little miffed that he blurted that out, *"Pumpkin Head can sleep on the floor."*

Andy and Ty burst out laughing.

Pumpkin Head withered under my stare. Maybe I didn't have to get that black dye tonight after all.

"Well come on," Naomi said, "Let me show you to the room so you can put down your bags—oh, I know what we can do. Ty, go down to the garage and grab your old twin bed. We can fit it in there

146

so Pum—Ryan doesn't have to sleep on the floor," she said, giving me a wink.

It was only four in the afternoon, but Naomi said the food was done and we might as well have dinner. The only thing Ryan and I consumed today was donuts and coffee at the Murfreesboro airport when we fueled up, so I was starving. She made a big pan of lasagna, which I thought was enough to feed ten people instead of five, until I watched Andy and Ty take their servings out of the pan. Wow, those guys could eat! When we finished they went back for seconds and wiped out the remainder.

I learned a little more about them around the dinner table. Ty had just turned twenty and Andy was twenty-one. They had lived in Colorado Springs all their lives and their parents were divorced. Naomi had been raising them, single-handedly, for the last ten years. Both joined the military right out of high school and they worked as MP's at Peterson's Air Force Base.

With the meal finished, I asked if there was a shopping plaza or a drug store nearby so I could get some dye to correct Ryan's poor, color-flawed hair. We drove to a nearby Walgreens and grabbed a box of Just for Men black hair color and returned to Naomi's.

I offered to help Ryan do it, but I think he didn't want the guys to tease him so he opted to do it himself. It was five minute hair color and he was going to shower when he washed it out, but he must have spent an hour in the bathroom, and I was starting to worry what went wrong.

We were all seated in the living room watching the six o'clock news when he emerged. His hair was glistening black and damp. He had a towel over his shoulders, and just a pair of jeans, no shirt. It was the first time I had seen his bare chest and I now regretted I said one bedroom would work. He wasn't thickly muscled like Micah, but he looked more like one of those guys you'd find carrying a surfboard down to the beach. He had softly defined six-pack abs and a light tan and I was considering he would be a great model, when he waved his hand in front of my face.

"Hello? I asked how you like the hair," he had this big smile on his face because he knew I was checking out almost everything except his hair.

"N—nice job," I managed to say.

"Yes," Naomi spoke up, "you look better sticking with your natural black, honey."

"I think he looked better as a pumpkin," Andy smirked and then jumped up and said he called the shower next.

By the time eight o'clock rolled around, I was surrounded by shirtless bodies. Andy emerged from the shower shirtless, toweless, and practically pantless. All he had on was a pair of swim trunks. Next Ty took a shower and followed the example, coming out equally undressed. They were all really hot and I had a feeling that the parade was solely for my benefit. Andy kept catching me glancing over at him, but it was hard to help since he was the one that had the closest 'Micah' body.

"Is my air conditioner not working?" Naomi asked as she finally stirred from the movie on the television.

Ty rose up and looked at the thermostat, "It's seventy-two, isn't that what you normally keep it on?"

"Yes it is, but why the Sam-hell are all you boys practically naked?" she scoffed.

"Would it be okay if I used your shower, Miss Naomi?" I asked. I was ready to hit the bed, but I really wanted a chance to clean up first.

"Of course you can, honey, but I have to warn you we only have the one bathroom in the house so I can't promise that these knuckle heads left it in decent shape."

"That's okay," I replied, but inwardly I knew we'd have to find a place to stay real soon, because I loathed the idea of showering behind that many people.

"You can come out shirtless, too!" Andy yelled as I headed down the hallway. I heard the loud smack as he yowled, "Ouch, Momma! What did you hit me for?"

I smiled.

The bathroom was fairly small, but the troops had been decent about not leaving it nasty. I grabbed my shampoo and soap and stepped under the running water. It had been a long day and I was hoping I could fall asleep tonight without Ryan's assistance. I was grateful he helped me last night, but surely I could manage tonight by myself.

I toweled off and put on a pair of shorts and a tank top and went back to the cramped bedroom. There was one queen-sized bed and the small twin they brought up from the garage. I decided Ryan wouldn't fit so well on the twin, so I took it and left the larger bed for him. I could still hear the guys in the living room, laughing, talking and reminiscing.

I drifted off, but within an hour, my eyes were open. I grabbed an extra pillow off the large bed and tried wedging it behind me for a stand-in, but it wasn't warm and there was no strong arm to slip around my waist. I heard Ryan coming down the hallway as he told everyone good night. He came into the dark room quietly, the only light being the red display on the clock and a seashell night light on the other side of the queen bed.

"Leese," he whispered.

I tried faking sleep so he wouldn't know I was struggling with it again, and then I tried not to crack a smile as he began to talk to himself. He was speaking lower than a whisper, but I could still hear him.

"This isn't going to do," he said. "She should be in the big bed, not me. If she wakes up, how am I going to fit on that little bed with her? All right, baby girl, let's see if I can move you without waking you."

I was ready to roll over and tell him I was awake, but his arms were already under me as I began to turn toward him. I guess he assumed he woke me.

"Shhh," he breathed softly, "Go back to sleep, I'm just moving you to the other bed."

There was no opportunity to argue with him as he had already lifted me. He turned to the other bed and realized there was a problem as my head was now pointed at the foot of the bed.

"Put me down," I whispered. He was still shirtless and I was finding it unsettling to have my hands against his bare skin.

"Can you go back to sleep?" he asked as he put my feet on the floor.

"Sure," I lied. I wasn't prepared to argue the issues of who should be in which bed. I immediately felt a big difference between the thick pillow top queen mattress and the thin, uncomfortable twin that Ryan was now settling onto. "That bed isn't very comfortable; sleep up here, but you don't need to hold me."

I didn't have to ask twice as he rose and pulled back the covers, stretched out and sighed, "Much better. Good-night, Leese."

"Good-night."

I lay on my side watching the bedside clock tick by.

"You aren't asleep, are you?" came a whisper in the dark.

I thought about ignoring him, but I finally whispered back, "No."

His body came up behind me, warmth flooded my skin and his tattooed arm wrapped around my waist. I didn't expect the kiss on my neck that sent shivers through me.

"Get some sleep."

I really needed to be asleep *before* he attempted to replace Micah. It seemed though he found sleeping with me to be relaxing enough that he drifted off and within fifteen minutes, I could hear his deep, steady breathing, just short of trying to snore.

I laid there and wondered if Micah was sleeping right now? I cried silently. My heart ached to hear his voice, to feel his touch, and to taste his lips against my own. I was ashamed to be lying here in Ryan's arms, knowing I wanted to roll over and let him have his first experience with a woman, but I couldn't make that fatal mistake. It wouldn't prove fatal to my physical body, but my heart and soul wouldn't recover from the betrayal. Somewhere around four in the morning, I managed to fall asleep and, once asleep, I was comfortable and safe in Micah's arms.

Chapter Twelve

There was a knock at the bedroom door around eight in the morning as Naomi's voice came through saying that breakfast was ready. It scared me bad enough that I jerked upright in the bed, almost pulling Ryan with me.

"Yes, I will," he blurted out as he coiled back into the covers.

"You do say funny stuff when you wake up," I chuckled.

"It can't be morning yet," he whined.

"Sorry Sunshine, but it's breakfast time."

He moaned and sat up, "It's gonna take a quart of coffee to get me awake."

I sat back on the bed beside him and leaned over and kissed his cheek.

His eyes fully opened as he looked at me, "What was that for?"

"Are you awake now?"

He blinked a couple times, "Yeah."

"Good, let's go have breakfast before Andy and Ty eat it all."

He grinned and we left the room.

We were enjoying bacon and eggs when someone knocked at their door. I jumped hard.

Ryan's hand immediately touched my arm, "It's okay."

Ty was already in motion toward the door when Ryan asked him to make sure he knew who it was before he opened it. That earned him a strange look.

"Who is it?" Ty asked.

"Candace, you idiot. Open the door."

Now it was Ryan's turn to jump. The front door opened and in walked a young woman about my age. She was shorter than me, maybe 5'6" with straight, sandy blonde hair and brown eyes, slim built, but she definitely had me beat when it came to bra size. I was a healthy c-cup, but she had to be a double-D.

"Oh, I'm sorry, I didn't realize you had company," she paused and then recognition hit her. "Ryan? Oh, my God. I don't believe it!"

Ryan rose and met her half way of the living room as they gave each other a hug.

"What the heck are you doing back in Colorado Springs? It's been, what: five or six years? You look great."

"Thanks. You, too. I can't believe you're still here? I thought your dad shipped to California?"

"He did and then he fell off a flight deck and broke his back. He's okay, but the military gave him a medical discharge and we moved back here. Miss Naomi, why didn't…"

That was when she looked around Ryan to the table and saw me. I was smiling, but I could see she immediately assumed I was someone significant to Ryan.

"Oh… Hi, I'm sorry; I didn't know anyone else was—"

"Candace, this is Leese. She and I are—"

"Good friends who flew in yesterday," I finished for him. I got up and she met me part way to shake hands.

"Nice to meet you…" she let the words trail as she looked at me as if she knew me, "Did you grow up around here? You look so familiar to me."

"No, I'm from Florida."

"I swear I've seen you before," she continued.

She was figuring out who I was even with the new hairdo.

"So, you grew up with these guys?" I said, hoping to get her to stop staring at me.

"Yeah, but Ryan of course was only here from like fifth grade to seventh, but he left quite an impression on all the girls with those pretty eyes of his. He was considered the hot ticket in middle school," she laughed.

"Now I'm the hot ticket," Ty spoke up flexing his bare chest.

"No, you're pretty much still an idiot," she stated, deflating him, "but you're an idiot that I need at the moment. I came over because I need a ride to work; my car won't start. I think the alternator is out on it again."

"We can give you a ride," I offered, remembering how terrible Ty drove yesterday.

"Sure," Ryan added.

"I don't want to impose," she started to say when Ty frowned.

"You don't mind 'imposing' on me!"

"That's because riding with you isn't imposing, it gives you another chance to figure out how to drive."

I liked this girl; she could put those boys in their place and, more importantly was the reaction on Ryan's face when he saw her.

"Come on," I said touching Ryan's arm and waking him from his daydream. I grabbed my purse and the three of us went out to the car.

"Pearly's car? Did you buy this?" she was clearly impressed.

"Yeah, yesterday. But Leese actually—"

"Worked out the deal," I finished for him. "But it's Ryan's car."

Candace started to go into the back seat, but I told her to sit up front so she could show Ryan the way to where she worked.

Ryan's brow furrowed as he watched me slip in the back seat.

I noticed that Ryan remembered Pearly's instructions as he hit the gas once and then turned the key. I stayed quiet and let them talk as she pointed the way to the JC Penney's in the Citadel Mall.

"So did you graduate high school?" Ryan asked.

"No, this is my senior year, but we go back after Labor Day. We were in the same grade. Did you graduate?"

"Not yet, I mean we will, but that depends on where we decide to stay."

I was wishing he hadn't said it that way because she became noticeably quiet.

"We are just friends, though. Nothing more," I added from the backseat. "He's been really great to help me get settled somewhere before he moves on with his life." I got another nasty glance in the rearview mirror from him. "Hey, Candace," I continued, "Do you know of any places around here for rent?"

She twisted in the seat to look at me, "Are you looking for a house or an apartment?"

"I prefer a house, but anything at this point would be good."

"There are some houses near the historic district that they recently renovated. I'd love to live over there; all the shops and restaurants are within walking distance."

"That sounds perfect. Do you have some paper so you could write us some directions?"

"Yeah sure." She pulled out a small note pad from her purse and drew a map to show how to get there from the Citadel. "I could show you guys around there after I get off work at three today, if you'd like?"

"You're going to need a ride home anyway, right?" Ryan finally spoke up.

"That would sure save me from having to bum a ride from someone at the mall."

"Great. Then we'll pick you up at three," I said, leaving no room for an argument as we pulled into the large parking lot and drove around to Penney's.

Candace thanked us for the ride. I climbed out of the back seat and into the front.

"What are you doing?" Ryan snapped.

"What?"

"Don't 'What?' me—you—you're trying to put me and Candace together, aren't you?"

"She's adorable and I saw your face when you heard who was at the door. I'm betting you had a thing for her at some point."

"Yeah, Leese, I did—when I was twelve! You haven't given yourself enough time yet for me to know if we have a chance."

"Hey, you promised I was not going to be what holds you back from finding the right girl."

"But, that doesn't mean you get to play match-maker. Okay?"

"Okay, but—"

"No buts!"

"I was just going to ask if you find her attractive," I said, putting out the bait.

"I don't like discussing that with you."

"Do you find me attractive?" I'll start with small bait.

"You know I do. If you asked me right now to—"

"Then what's wrong with telling me if you find her attractive?"

"You can be relentless, you know that? Yes, Leese—I had a huge crush on her in middle school. When we moved, I…"

"What?"

"Never mind," he snapped.

"You know I'm going to bother you until… Ryan, pull over!" I said as I motioned to a gas station coming up.

"Why?"

"I've—I've got to get to a bathroom—now!"

He whipped the car swiftly off the roadway and into the station, as I grabbed my purse and ran around to the ladies room.

I had been expecting this, but I was trying to mentally will that it wouldn't happen, now that it had, I was caught off guard.

I came back to the car ten minutes later; I didn't have myself together. I didn't realize how hard it was going to hit me and I couldn't stop crying.

Ryan's face was pale as he watched me clutching my abdomen. "Leese," he said softly, "are you okay?"

I handed him Candace's paper and just asked that he drive there, I wasn't ready to talk. He made it to the historic district and located where the developer had a section of homes remodeled. We found the office as I dried my tears and tried to open the door to the car.

"Tell me what's wrong, please," Ryan pleaded, gripping my arm and preventing me from leaving.

"I'll tell you, but I can't do it now or I'll never make it through talking with these people and, as much as I like Naomi, Andy, and Ty, I don't want to stay at their house any longer than necessary."

"All right, but you promise to tell me before the day is over, okay?"

"I will," I stated as I took a ragged breath and opened the car door.

There were about fifteen houses left to choose from and it only took a glance for me to decide which one I wanted to see. It was a two bedroom, two and a half bath stone house with a 1,700 square foot open floor plan. It came with all new appliances, including a washer and dryer and was available for immediate occupancy. The sales woman drove with us the block and a half to unlock it so we could go inside and look around. It was clean and crisp with new hardwood floors and fresh dry wall. The kitchen was a rich cranberry with deep mossy green granite counter tops. The bedrooms were each designed to be suites with their own bathroom. The bathrooms were a little smaller than I liked, but they were new and private. The half bath was situated just off the living room so company didn't have to traipse through the house to get to it.

"It's only two blocks to one of the area's best little sidewalk bistros and there is a farmer's market just a little further down from there every Saturday morning," the woman explained.

"It's perfect. We'll take it." But then I rethought my statement, "Wait—I'm so sorry," I said, touching Ryan's arm and getting his attention as he was looking around the room smiling, "I didn't even ask if you like it."

"Leese, do you see the smile on my face? Yes, of course I like it. We'll take it," he said, slipping his arm around my shoulder and facing the sales woman.

"I—I haven't given you the price yet," she stated. It must have surprised her that I never asked that question. "It's fifteen-hundred per month; that includes everything except gas and electric. We require a minimum of a six-month lease and I'll need a first, last and a security of a thousand dollars."

"Okay," I said quickly doing the math in my head. "That's four thousand, correct?"

"Yes."

"Can we start moving in today?" I continued.

"Well, yes, but—"

"Leese, can I talk with you, privately for a minute?" Ryan asked, looking at the sales woman who quickly took the hint.

"I'll wait outside so you two can discuss it; it is a big decision."

As soon as the door closed behind her, he gripped my shoulders and pointed out the obvious, "What if you put all this money into this and—and Micah finds us? Shouldn't we give it a few days, before we slam several more thousand out of your purse? I mean at the rate you're burning through that cash, you might be broke pretty soon."

"First of all, I agree, I'd prefer to give it several more days, or even a week or two before we know for sure if we can stay here, but I can't spend another couple nights like last night. Secondly, I have access to my account, I'd just have to have you fly me to another state to make a withdrawal, and you know as well as I do that I can't burn through *that much money*. So let's do this. I hate to say it, but I'm ready to 'play house' with you and—"

"Whoa, baby girl, does that mean what it sounds like?" he asked with a smile tugging at the edge of his lips.

His grip on my shoulders was changing and I could tell he was getting ready to pull me against him. I put my hand on his chest to stop him. "I didn't ask you to make love to me. I'm just saying I want this whole 'Ryan and Leese's place' kind of thing."

"How about we celebrate finding this place with a kiss?" his voice dropping into a husky range.

I could tell the idea of 'our place' was a definite turn on for him and he was getting ready to step over a line as the distance between us began to erase. I turned my face without a moment to spare, but he eagerly went for my cheek and then his mouth was moving toward my ear and neck. His hot breath became as soothing as a caress on my skin. He was kissing my neck as he tucked me against his chest. I was caving in without thought, my arms starting to slide around to his back, when reality slapped me hard.

"Stop it!" I snapped, pushing him away. "This isn't what I was… Don't do that again!" I couldn't help the fresh tears that rose to the surface.

"I'm sorry, Leese, you just feel so damn good to me. I didn't mean to—"

"You are sleeping in the other bedroom when we move in." My trembling hands moved to wipe away the tears.

He sighed, "I'm sorry, really I am."

I turned and walked out to where she was waiting for us, "Let's get this done because I want to be in here by tonight."

"I've never seen anyone move in that quickly," she laughed. "It might take you—"

"I'll be in by tonight," I stated firmly.

When we sat down to complete the lease she tried unsuccessfully to get our driver's licenses, "I can't accept checks or charge cards without—"

I pulled out twenty thousand dollars and laid it on the table, "Would twelve months rent in advance make this a little easier?"

She sat there with her mouth open.

"The name is Smith," I said pointing to the line for our names. "Ryan and Michelle Smith. I'd really like to hurry this up because I've got a lot of shopping to get done if we're moving in by tonight."

She filled in the names as I instructed and we signed the lease and left with the keys to our new home. I asked to use her telephone book before we left, copying down the addresses to three different furniture stores. We stopped at the first store and went inside. As mad as I was over what he'd done, I was excited to let the shopping trip begin.

"First question, how do you expect to get furniture delivered today and secondly, who is Michelle?"

"Later, Ryan, just follow me," I headed straight back to customer service. "Hello, I want to purchase a complete houseful of furniture this morning, but I want it delivered by five or six o'clock tonight, can your store handle that or do I need to shop somewhere else?"

The young boy just stood there and looked at us for a moment and then said, "You're serious?"

"Yes."

"Let me get my manager."

Within moments a medium aged-dark haired man came to the counter and shook my hand and asked what he could do to help me.

"I'm furnishing a house today," I stated, laying the paper with the three furniture stores names and addresses on the counter. "If you can't deliver today, I'll have to choose one of your competitors. Can you help me with this?"

"How are you paying for your furniture?"

"Cash," I said, folding the paper and returning it to my purse.

"If you'll take floor models, since they're unboxed, assembled, and ready to go, I think we can rework the schedule for this afternoon to get what you need delivered. There is a standard delivery charge that applies."

"I understand, and floor models are fine with me."

"I'll have Charlie walk around the store with you and he can mark down everything you want, but please look it over before you decide to purchase it. Floor models are sold as is and might have damage."

I don't think young Charlie ever had customers quite like the Smiths. It took a total sum of forty minutes to pick out two full bedroom suites with mattresses, a dining room set, living room furniture, an entertainment center, lamps, tables and accessories and a couple area rugs.

158

Thirteen thousand dollars later, we had a furniture delivery scheduled for four-thirty that afternoon. It was five minutes to eleven in the morning and we were headed back to the Citadel.

"So who is Michelle?" Ryan asked as we climbed back into the car and pulled out onto the road.

"Me. Annalisa Michelle Peterson Winslett… Gavarreen," I added, knocking myself right off my shopping high.

"You want to tell me what happened back at the service station," he asked softly.

I mumbled what I didn't want to say, but it was enough to send the Javelin off the road and onto the shoulder.

I braced as we came to a sudden stop.

"Pregnant? Did you just say—"

"I said I'm not pregnant," I sobbed.

"You wanted to be?" he asked incredulously.

"Micah didn't want me pregnant and to tell the truth, no—I don't think I'm ready, but we knew there was a chance."

Ryan's face was turning red as he was struggling to say something to me, "So you're not on anything—no bir—birth control."

"No, I didn't want to take anything."

"If we cross any lines then… I mean if you asked me to… We'd be taking the same chance?"

I nodded, still crying over the fact I had been secretly hoping my period wouldn't start. I'd ignored my calendar and today was the day. I knew the moment I asked him to pull into the service station that any hope of carrying Micah's baby was gone.

He leaned across the seat and held me for a few minutes, "You could have told me about this sooner, Leese. I wouldn't have changed my mind about helping you if you thought you were pregnant. Matter of fact, if you were and you decided we had a chance, I'd love you either way. I don't have to be the first guy, I'd just be happy to be the last." He kissed my temple as he straightened in the seat and put the car back in first gear. "Maybe we should do this shopping thing another day. The furniture is all we need for tonight."

I dried my eyes, "You know who ever turns out to be right for you, she's going to be a very, very lucky person." Then I gave a smile and told him I was fine and we should continue shopping.

We met Candace in JC Penney's just before three o'clock and took her back to her house in the cram-packed car. Poor Ryan was exhausted, but shopping only seemed to give me more energy. We had bought dishes, cookware, utensils, bedding sets, bath and kitchen towels and such to the point that we literally had no more room in the car. The trunk was packed and there was only a small space for me in the backseat as I was surrounded by bags. Even Candace had to give up a little space because there were a few bags on the floor board by her feet.

"I'd love to see your new place, and I don't mind helping you unbag everything and set things up," she offered. We had pulled into Naomi's driveway as we crawled out from the bags and boxes.

"That would be awesome to have some help," I admitted, accepting her offer. Besides it was another chance to see how she and Ryan were around each other.

"Great, then I'm going to go change my clothes and I'll be back over at Naomi's in a few minutes." With a wave of her hand, she crossed the street.

Another wonderful aroma hit us when we stepped inside.

"Where the crap have you two been all day?" Ty exclaimed when he saw us.

"Blowing wads of money," Ryan replied as he literally flopped into a nearby recliner. "Don't ever go shopping with Leese. She can kill a mortal man."

"Ah," Ty said with a sly smile, "I think I could handle a day with her."

"But could you handle a night with me?" I asked. I had spoken it before I realized how very badly it came out. Both he and Ryan looked like their eyes were going to pop out after I uttered it. "What I mean is that I was hoping you and Andy could help me and Ryan tonight get moved into our new place."

"You guys got a place *today*?"

"Who's got a place?" Andy asked as he came into the room.

"Leese wants me to spend the night with her," Ty laughed lightly with a wink to me.

"Whoa," was all Andy managed to get out of his mouth.

"That's not exactly what I said."

At this point Ryan and Ty were starting to double over with laughter as they confirmed I actually did kind of say it that way. I snatched up two throw pillows and hit them both.

"Would you be willing to help me and Ryan get some furniture moved around our new place this evening?" I asked, turning to Andy.

"I don't know. Do I get the same deal as Ty?"

Men! Lord, now they were all laughing. I was glad to hear Candace's knock at the door; at least I had some female assistance to help control the male population in the house.

Naomi insisted we all eat before heading over to the new place. No one would argue with that. She had made oven roasted chicken, real mashed potatoes, gravy, and sweet peas. She had even baked a big pan of double-chocolate brownies for dessert. A person could get used to eating with this family. Well, if you didn't lose a limb at the dinner table as Andy and Ty dove for the food.

We had no space in the Javelin for our duffel bags, but Andy offered to take them in the Caprice. And, even though Ty and Andy had plenty of room for Candace in their car, I told her, for safety sake, she'd better ride with us; she agreed.

We pulled up to the house at four fifteen and everyone grabbed an armload of boxes and bags as I unlocked the door. They all thought the place was really cool, but then the delivery truck pulled in right behind us and the real work began. Between our guys and the delivery driver and his assistant the truck was unloaded quickly.

Candace and I unrolled rugs and placed the smaller furniture while the guys brought in and set up the larger pieces. It was a lot of work, but by nine p.m. we actually had a house that looked livable. The beds were made, everything was arranged, and it was totally perfect, until I looked at the windows.

"Ah, nuts!"

"What's wrong?" Ryan asked.

"Nothing is wrong—if you're an exhibitionist. I forgot to get stuff for the windows!"

"Just put a sheet over them for tonight with a couple thumbtacks," Candace explained. "Then tomorrow you can buy curtains."

"We really appreciate all the help," I said, speaking for both Ryan and myself. "We haven't gone grocery shopping yet so I can't offer you guys a drink, but it is Friday night and I hear there is a great bistro a short walk from here. It's my treat if everyone wants to go."

The rest of the night was a blast. We walked in the cool night air to the café and then sat around and laughed and joked until about eleven. Andy and Ty said they would drive Candace home.

"I had a really good time," she said just before she got into their car.

"Oh, I almost forgot. Do you need a ride to work tomorrow?" I asked. "I don't imagine your alternators been fixed since we've tied you up all evening."

"Thanks, but no. I've got the day off. I'll get someone to help me with it."

"Momma kept me and Ty busy all afternoon or we would have fixed it for you. Tomorrow we go back on twelve hour shifts at the base so it'll be Wednesday before either one of us gets a spare minute."

"What are we doing tomorrow?" Ryan asked.

"Shopping, of course. We've got window treatments to buy, groceries, and—"

"I have a great idea," Ryan interrupted. "I'm basically shopped-out, but I am mechanically inclined. Why doesn't Candace help you shop and you two can leave me up to my elbows in grease and parts."

Candace looked at me and smiled, "I'm game."

"Sounds good to me, too."

We waved goodbye and wearily walked inside and locked the door. I had no thumbtacks, but the second bedroom was windowless and we decided we were both too pooped to be of any trouble for each other tonight so sharing the bed was viable.

I changed into my shorts and tank, and Ryan slipped into a pair of shorts and we crawled into bed.

"Leese."

"Yeah," I yawned.

"I like the house."

"Me, too," I whispered back.

"Can I hold you? I'm starting to get a thing for sleeping this way."

"Would you give me a few minutes to fall asleep? Last night I couldn't—I mean being awake is harder for me because I know it's you."

"You don't like knowing it's me?"

"The problem is that I do like it, but I just can't let myself cross that line."

He leaned against me and kissed my ear, "Goodnight."

It wasn't long into my dream state when I felt the comfort my tired body craved. It was a very good night.

Chapter Thirteen

Micah pulled up to the small office he once regularly visited, but it had been six months since the last time he was here. That was when he accepted a file on a beautiful young woman who was to be his next target. In a matter of weeks, she changed everything he ever knew about himself. He threw everything away for her, only to have her throw away all he offered. It was as if he became the target because she absolutely blew him away.

The annulment had been finalized. His attorney informed him the judge would not accept the abandonment issue, but he was able to get the annulment by claiming she abandoned Micah because he had forced her into the marriage and put her under duress. Micah didn't like the sound of any of that. He didn't force it on her, but his parents insisted he take the steps to annul the marriage so his assets would be safe.

The problem was he didn't care about his assets anymore. He already planned what he was going to do with his millions and it would leave him nearly broke, but, in his mind, it was a gamble worth taking.

He walked inside, nodded at the young woman who sat at the desk and walk to the door behind her. There was no need to be announced. He had been called so he was expected.

D'Angelo was ready as soon as Micah came through the door.

Two files were on the table in front of him so Micah expected this would be a double homicide. He took his seat and waited for D'Angelo to speak to him.

"I'm sorry to hear what happened to you, Micah. Women are far more treacherous than men give them credit. I'd use them for making hits, but I haven't found one I can trust," he finished with a little mirth to his voice.

Micah didn't respond.

"I am hoping you plan on returning to what you do best. You aren't going to bother with this girl anymore—am I right?"

"I haven't decided exactly what I'm going to do at this point. I'm still planning on facing her over her..." he paused and took a breath, "decision."

"I wouldn't do that if I were you, because—"

"You aren't me." Micah knew it was borderline insubordination to speak that way to D'Angelo. He watched the anger flush the man's skin, but then he seemed to cool.

"As I was saying, the only thing facing her will do is to put you in jeopardy of killing her and the man she ran away with. That would be a waste of *your* life, because I doubt you'd do that job neatly."

"I won't kill *her*. I just need to know why she changed."

"Women change their minds like their clothes, Micah. But I didn't call you here to discuss your foolish waste of time pursuing a tramp."

Micah's eyes flashed with a fire that momentarily worried his commander. That was who D'Angelo was in all reality to Micah. He commanded; Micah obeyed.

"I want you to rejoin the family..."

Micah started to speak, but D'Angelo silenced him with a simple movement of his hand as he slid a folder down to him.

"Take a look."

Taking a look was very dangerous in this business. A look at something could create obligations you couldn't simply turn away from. He steeled himself as he opened the folder. It only took a second for his blood to boil under his skin, "You'd be crazy to think I'd take this assignment."

"No, Micah, I wouldn't ask you to kill David. But someone is going to—if you don't intervene. I've been holding that file for months and the family is starting to get annoyed with my hesitation. I've told them he can be trusted. I told them he only did what he did to help *you*, but we both know actions speak louder than words, especially in this business. I never particularly like David..."

Micah gave what sounded like a low laugh. It was true. D'Angelo didn't like someone who didn't follow orders exactly as given. He also didn't like having orders questioned. David tended to get under D'Angelo's skin, and if it hadn't been for the rest of the family being so valuable, he would have disposed of David a long time ago. Not that David wasn't an excellent hit man, his methods and accuracy rivaled Micah's, but he had a stubborn, insubordinate streak that pissed off people in high places.

"...but, that doesn't mean he doesn't have value. I want you and David to help me with a new member we're bringing into the family. I think this will go a long way in reinstating his loyalty."

"Who's the target?" Micah knew it would be someone big, if it was going to 'impress' the family.

The second folder slid down the table into Micah's waiting grip. He opened the folder and the picture that met his gaze was of a middle-aged Hispanic man. He was ready to scan quickly over the document, but the first thing he noted about the man stopped him. He was a diplomat to the U.S. from Bogota.

"Government leaders aren't usually our concern."

"No, but this one has crushed the supply of a certain product provided by a group willing to be an exclusive supplier to us at a very tempting price."

"Drugs, D'Angelo? My personal family has stayed out of the drug market. You know how my parents have felt about it since the influx from the seventies."

"True, but this new supplier will add billions to our revenue and open a whole new venue in our family. We're getting stale, Micah. Other families are edging into our territory and they are out pacing us. We either make a move and re-dominate, or we fade." D'Angelo leaned forward as his eyes narrowed, "I'm not going to let that happen."

"So this job is as much for you as it is for David. You have a personal interest in seeing this group come in through Louisiana and no one has catered to your personal interests quite as well as me." Micah had done things to help D'Angelo stay in a position of power that even his own family didn't know about. One of them had left a scar on his shoulder.

"I like having a man I can count on. I can count on you, Micah. That's why I was against you leaving the family to chase after that spoiled little girl."

You could almost hear the growl rising from Micah's chest. He knew one person had been in stubborn opposition to him leaving the family and it almost cost him his chance to be with her. Now he knew who that one person had been. As rough as it had been to watch her run from him, there was something about the experience he would never be able to regret for having gone through it.

"Of course you can forget about today, you're not under any obligation by mob rules to do anything I ask of you. But I am obligated to do something about your brother."

"I'll do what you need done, but only if I have your word the contract on David is never executed. And he can't know that's why I'm doing this hit."

"You're both going to have to do this hit. It's probably the most complicated you've ever tackled and he is the only one who has enough brains to help you do it. The two of you went out of this family at the same time and it's going to take both of you coming back in to make this work. The price is right for the job. The supplier is willing to pay ten million U.S. to reopen their business routes."

D'Angelo rose and stretched out his hand toward Micah, "Do we have an agreement? You save your brother's ass, we get a new influx of revenue, and *I own you again*. There will be more personal business to attend to when this is done and you're the only person who can handle my most delicate situations."

Micah looked at D'Angelo as he stood up, dwarfing the man who had a propensity for impious scheming and self-promotion within the ranks of their orderly society. This would slow down his own plans he already put into motion, but if his plans failed, well the money from this job would keep him in the lifestyle he had grown so very accustom to over the years. He shook his hand, picked up the folder, and walked away.

Chapter Fourteen

It had been three weeks since we had moved to Colorado Springs and things were going remarkably well. There was no evidence that Micah had discovered our location, and our home had become a safe haven to enjoy with our friends and each other. Candace became a regular visitor and Ryan started teasing me, privately, that he should take us both to Utah and become a polygamist.

I politely declined, but I was glad he was starting to think of Candace in that way. I had a feeling there would come a place in our near future where Ryan and I would part ways and she would become the significant person in his life. All the signs were there; they teased each other relentlessly, and the last few days they had begun to touch each other, not in a sexual way, but little things like watching her reach over and touch his arm when she would say something to him, or slug his shoulder if she didn't like something he said. Sometimes he would reach over and squeeze her shoulder or grab the back of her neck like he was going to rough her up, but of course it was all in teasing.

It was weird for me because I was fighting jealousy every time they got a little bit closer. I wanted him to find someone, but I still felt some kind of ownership to my security blanket. We didn't sleep apart and over the last week, I didn't need to be asleep for it to work. Some nights we would just lie awake and talk until the wee hours. He liked kissing my neck and I finally admitted I enjoyed it, but it pushed the line between us every time.

"So why do you like it so much?" he asked me as we cuddled preparing to go to sleep.

"Because it tingles all the way to my belly button," I laughed as he placed another slow kiss on my neck. "The sensation is almost electrical."

"It shocks?"

"Not exactly, look let's try something, but don't get the wrong idea."

"I love it when you tell me not to get the wrong idea about something because I know I'm getting ready to get the wrong idea about something," he snickered in my hair.

I rolled over and faced him, which was something I didn't do when in bed with him, "Roll over."

"You mean you want me to—"

"Yeah, you roll on your side and let me hold you for a little while. You're going to tell me if this feels anything to you like it does to me. Let's see if I can generate a little of this electrical feeling for you."

"Maybe this isn't a good idea," he said, suddenly sounding very unsure about being the recipient of affection.

"Yes or no?" I asked simply. I didn't want to do anything to make him uncomfortable, he was much too important to me to ruin a beautiful friendship.

"Okay, but if you lose your level head we're both in big trouble."

I didn't know why he was concerned about it. It was true I'd only been on the receiving end of affection from him, but how hard could it be to draw a line and stop? "I'm not going to flip out and jump your bones, Ryan."

"Okay," he said softly, still sounding unsure, but rolling to his side.

"Well, it certainly isn't going to be easy," I laughed, trying to fit against him. "You're like a giant from this perspective." I slipped my arm around his waist, but had to move it up to his chest so I could get a good angle on his neck. And then I started laughing.

"What's so funny?" he asked seriously.

"I feel like a freaking vampire getting ready to bite your jugular!" I teased as I made a lunge for his throat.

"Damn that tickles," he said, scrunching his neck.

"Okay, okay, I've got it under control. I swear all I'm going to do is kiss your neck and you tell me how it feels."

He was still laughing, "You know this is kind of fun, Leese."

169

"Be quiet and be still," I warned as I prepared to kiss his bared skin. I didn't think I was going to get into this, but as I breathed, nibbled, kissed, and suckled against his skin, I lost all sense of what I was doing. His reaction as he moaned and whispered my name only made me want to do more to him.

My hand, which was supposed to only be holding around his waist, was feeling every gloriously muscled and softly sculpted part of his chest. My body had become molded to his as my hips began to move in a once familiar pattern against his body and the heat flooded me. I was breathing hard as I rolled away and began pulling his shoulder to roll him toward me.

When he turned to me, I was over the invisible line and I didn't care. I knew the words I was afraid to utter were resting on the tip of my tongue.

"Leese, baby, are you okay?"

I took his hand and brought it to my breast and then closed my eyes as I permitted his touch. I could feel him gather above me, his muscled arms came around each side of me. My breathing was getting faster, as I felt his lips barely brush against mine.

"Shit, Leese, this is really going to happen, isn't it? You're going to let me do this when I don't have a frickin' clue what I'm doing. But you've got to ask me, baby girl, you have to do what you said or I can't go any further."

Micah, Micah, Micah, was all I kept screaming inside my head. "N—no," I said pushing him away, my other hand went to my own forbidden places as I remembered Micah's words that I didn't need to have a man for this moment. In seconds the shockwaves hit me so hard I doubled over, turning away from Ryan and crying out at the sheer magnitude of the first orgasm I'd had since the last time Micah brought me to this point.

"What the hell was that?" came his stunned words.

I was still in a ball and crying my eyes out. I tumbled out of the bed and ran for the bathroom, nausea flooding my senses over what I'd done right in front of him. I washed my face, splashing the cold water on my skin and simply wanting to drown myself.

I felt his hands on my waist. Crap! I hadn't locked the door. He never came in on me in the bathroom.

I grabbed a washcloth and buried my face into it, I couldn't look at him. I was so ashamed. "I'm so, so sorry, Ryan—I'll sleep in the other room and tomorrow I'm getting out of here."

"Whoa, don't you dare start talking like that."

I straightened slowly and finally looked at him, "I was just a freak show in the bedroom and I can't—"

"Freak show? Baby, you were so freaking damn sexy I thought I was gonna die watching you. I just never knew it was *that* intense for a girl."

"Well, trust me I have no clue if I'm normal or not. I blew it, Ryan—I totally blew my control and if you hadn't asked me to actually say it, I would have been your first and I can't do that with you—it's just wrong. I promised him forever. I can't promise it twice." I broke down sobbing, flinching as his arms encircled me.

"Shhh, it's okay. I know you're trying to do everything right, but baby you're forgetting something really important," he said, as he tipped my chin up, "you're still human."

"But I'm so ashamed."

"I thought you were beautiful, not to mention you had the strength to push me away."

"How can you stand me? I satisfied myself and left you laying there."

"Go back to bed, Leese. I'm going to take a shower."

I looked at him wondering if he was telling me something with his remark.

"Yeah, I know how to take care of me. I'll be in there in a little while. Goodnight."

I climbed in the bed still unable to believe what happened. I was awake when he returned to the bed and cuddled up behind me with his arm around my waist.

When morning came, I woke early and dressed and grabbed my purse. I was going down to the Saturday Farmers Market. Besides, I needed something to clear last night out of my head. Ryan would sleep until noon, so I locked the house and began a slow walk toward the market.

The café was on the way and I decided I'd stop and have a coffee and a muffin. I kept getting this odd feeling someone was following me. There were quite a few people out this morning doing the exact same thing I was doing, but I couldn't shake the feeling. I stopped at the café and sat at an outside table for two as I sipped the piping hot Hazelnut coffee and picked at a blueberry muffin. I was glancing through the local newspaper when a shadow crossed my morning sunshine. I turned and my heart lurched hard against my chest; David Gavarreen was standing beside me.

I panicked, and started to stumble away from the table when he reached out with a steel grip and put me back in the chair.

"I need to talk to you," he said in a low voice. "Your mom is worried sick."

"Micah—where is Micah?" All I could think was if David was with me, Micah might be at the house doing something unforgivable to my best friend.

"In Louisiana," he said simply, "I talked him in to letting me do this."

"Do what?" I asked, straightening in my chair and gathering back my courage.

He reached under his arm and pulled out a manila envelope, "He wanted you to have these so you'd know you can go on with your life. You don't have to run or try, pitiful as you are at it, to hide."

"I haven't used a credit card or a cell phone or—"

"You left a cash trail all over the place. I guess you didn't realize the bank had all the numbers on those bills you took. Micah threatened the banker and got the list and all we had to do was wait for them to start popping up. You've dumped a shit-load of them here and the fact that Ryan lived here for a few years made this too easy. I've been watching you for three days. But I have to admit the hair did throw me for a few seconds."

"How's Mom?" I changed the subject, but I had been aching to talk with her.

"She's wonderful. You of course are on the biggest shit list I've got—you ripped my brother's heart right out of his chest, and if I wasn't so crazy about your mother, I'd probably go ahead and waste you for hurting him that way. You know he's back in the mob and bad as ever. That's one reason I'm here now, he and I are leaving the country tomorrow on a big job and I hope like hell we both make it back alive, although I don't know if he really cares if he does or not."

"Don't—don't say that. I didn't want to hurt him—I—"

"You've sure got a funny way of not wanting to hurt someone." He picked up my coffee and took a long drink, "Open your envelope. He wanted to be sure you read it and didn't simply throw it away."

"I wouldn't throw it away," I growled, tearing open the seal and pulling out what appeared to be legal documents. "An Annulment?" My breath caught in my lungs as I said the word. Suddenly I felt dizzy and sick all at the same moment.

"Yeah, he had to say he forced you into marrying him, but it was the only way to get it."

I stared at him blankly. I couldn't believe Micah had annulled our marriage; it was as if it never happened.

"I have to ask you something and you'd better tell me the truth. Did you do anything with Micah's money?"

"His money? I've never touched his money—I don't even know what bank he keeps it in. Why?"

"When he got out of the mob, Dad sold every business Micah owned and liquidated all his assets. He had a hundred and twenty-three million in the bank. Now, he has less than three million. It's a little hard for a hundred and twenty million dollars to simply vanish and he won't say where it went. You honestly don't know what happened to his money?"

"No, I'd never do anything like that. Can I—"

"Yeah and none of us figured you'd run off days after that wedding you were so determined to have, either."

"I have my reasons and I can't change them."

"I know, blue-eyes and black hair, I've seen him."

"He's..." I stopped myself. We had been so careful to tell everyone here in Colorado Springs that we were just friends that I almost said the same thing to David. That would have caused more suspicion than I could handle when Micah showed up to get the rest of the riddle solved. "Please, David, if you're going with him on this—this job, please don't let him get hurt. I know you think I'm some kind of nut case, but I really still love him with all my heart, just don't tell him. I'd die if something happened to him. Please keep him safe and bring him back without another gunshot or knife wound."

"That's my intention. I've got to go," he stood up and pushed in his chair. "Call your mother. Oh, and Micah said to tell you to start 'living your life,' whatever the hell that means. Goodbye, Leese."

And he walked away as I sat there and watched him get into a dark sedan and drive off.

I never made it to the market. I walked in a daze back to the house and put the annulment papers on the coffee table and simply crumpled up on the floor. It was around eleven when I felt a touch on my arm.

"He found us, didn't he?"

"It's over, Ryan. He isn't coming to look for me. He's leaving the country tomorrow."

"He annulled the marriage—I saw the papers," he was trying to be as gentle as possible when he uttered it. "Did he give these to you?"

"No, he didn't want to come, so he sent his brother instead," I said, still lying on the living room rug as Ryan tried to coax me off the floor. I wasn't budging, so he joined me.

"Leese, I know this hurts, but it means you can get on with a normal life now. We can finish our last year of school. You can go out and buy a car for yourself. We're going to be fine and you don't have to jump every time someone comes to the door. We—"

"I can go home," I said quietly, but evidently loud enough to cause him to go silent.

"I don't think that's a good idea, baby girl, because if you go home and I stay here it'll only be a matter of time before he thinks you're available and shows up. You said this guy forbid you to get back together with him or else—"

"I know the or else, Ryan. Please, don't remind me."

"Leese, I have to know. Do you really want to go home? Because I'd like to think you'd rather—rather stay here with me. With the marriage annulled, your promise to him isn't—"

"Yes it is, Ryan. I made the promise, not the piece of paper. I love him more than ever, I just never expected him to give in and walk away. I guess he was telling me the truth the day in the hospital when he said he'd rather give me to you a thousand times over than for something to happen to me."

"Me? He said he'd rather give you to me?" Shock and surprise were clear.

"It's a long story and I can't discuss it now," I said, wiping my eyes. "But to answer your question, no I don't really want to leave here, but I've got to call my mom." My cell phone had a full battery the night when I listened to all the phone messages and then turned it off and put it away. I was pretty sure the battery would still be good as I sat up on the rug and drug my purse beside me.

"I'm—I'm going to go outside and let you talk."

My cell phone powered up and I hit the speed dial for Mom. Two rings and I sighed as I heard her voice. It was a long conversation. I couldn't tell her any of the real reasons for me leaving because she might say something to David, who would tell Micah, and who knew what Micah would do if he knew the real person who caused all of our problems. So, I had to stick with the lie that I simply loved Ryan a little more, but didn't realize it until I met up with him the day we left together.

She was angry with me, chewed me up and spit me out actually, but it was still good to hear her voice. Once she finished berating me, she began to forgive me and then to plead with me to come back home. She did pointedly mention Ryan was not welcome in her house, at least not for a while.

"No, I'm sorry, Mom. I love you, but I'm staying in Colorado with him. I won't be coming home, at least not to live anyway, maybe just for a visit. I'm honestly out of the nest this time and I guess it's time to start really living my life."

We said our goodbyes and I clicked the phone shut. Ryan returned after another twenty minutes, carrying coffees and a bag of pastries from the café.

"Would you like to call your mom," I said, offering my phone to him as he set everything down, "I'm sure she's just as worried as mine."

He smiled and accepted the phone.

By the end of the night, I purchased a pair of laptops for the house, a new cell phone for each of us, picked up a rental car, and placed an order for a new car.

It was late by the time we hit the bed, but we had church in the morning and Candace was supposed to be joining us so we needed some sleep. I got up once at six a.m. and unlocked the front door so she could get in while I was in the shower. She would be here around seven-thirty and she normally just came right in and relaxed while we finished getting ready. Ryan was zonked out in my bed which simply wouldn't do, even though our relationship was platonic, no one would ever believe that we shared a bed without sex.

"Hey sleepy-head, time for you to go get in your bed," I yawned, lying back down beside him for a moment. He hadn't moved a muscle. I let my hand gently stroke across his jaw line and then allowed my finger to brush his lips. The eyes fluttered weakly open as he stared at me through his blue orbs.

"Don't tell me it's morning," he said as if there wasn't enough strength in him to get the words out.

I yawned again, "Yup, time to move to your room."

His arm flopped across my side as he attempted to pull me toward him. A frontal embrace wasn't a good idea, especially after the other night. I rolled my back to him and allowed him to pull me in tighter. It was late September and the weather had cooled to the point where being cuddled against his warm body was perfect.

"What time is it?" he whispered.

"Six-fifteen."

"We have time for a little more sleep. Set the alarm for another thirty minutes, please, Leese."

I didn't argue. I was as tired as he was as I reached over and set it for six-forty-five. I was going to pull away from him in a few minutes and slip into a hot shower, but my eyelids drooped and the soft bed and the warm body lulled me to sleep.

The next thing I heard was, "You son-of-a-bitchin' liar!"

The alarm had not gone off and Candace was standing in the bedroom doorway with Andy and Ty standing behind her. She told us she was inviting them, but I didn't know for certain they were coming.

I jerked up right, pulling Ryan with me.

"She's married!" was the first thing out of sleepy-heads quick-draw mouth.

"This isn't what it looks like," I said, tumbling from the bed.

Ryan was still trying to clear his brain as he stared at all the people looking at us, "We didn't do anything," he finally managed to say.

Andy and Ty were all smiles, but Candace was on the verge of an explosion.

"You both said you were just friends! You led me to believe... Aaah!" she turned to storm out and I knew I had to catch her before she got out the door. "Get out of my way!" she bellowed as I ran around to block her path to the front door.

"Candace, do you know who I am?"

"Yeah, you're a freaking liar just like him!"

"No. I know you recognized me when you met me—I'm Annalisa Winslett," I said hoping it would give a moment's pause before she tore out of the house.

"The runaway princess?" she said, stopping and staring at my face.

The title was one I absolutely hated, but the national tabloid had dubbed me that after all I'd been through. They attributed Pensacola to me running away (although it wasn't), my disappearance after the school shooting as running away, and, more recently, they published that I had married and then run away from my new husband with a mystery man. I was making the press a lot of money.

"Ryan is the guy you... Why didn't I realize this when I knew he was from Palm Beach and you have all this money to spend? So it's true then, you dumped your husband for Ryan. You're a real cheap piece of work, bitch!"

"No she's not," I heard Ryan's now fully awake voice. "You can haul ass out that door and never know the truth or you can sit down and let me explain. But if you go out the door then that blows the chance for us to be more than friends, Candace."

Her eyes got big, as well as Andy and Ty's. It was the first time Ryan made any reference to the fact that he had a 'thing' for her.

We didn't make it to church as we sat around the living room and explained to them as much of what really happened as we could. I couldn't give details, but I did let them know that the mob was threatening his whole family if I stayed. Ryan had put his life on the line to get me out of there. I told them how much I loved Micah and that I couldn't sleep for days until Ryan offered to be his stand-in.

"And now it's just become natural for us to sleep in the same bed, but we've never made love to each other." I blushed a little which I'm sure to my audience was for uttering those words, but for me it was because we had come way, way too close to not being able to state this as the truth.

"Damn, Ryan, you've got more will-power than freaking Superman," Ty stated honestly. "I hate to admit it, Leese, but I couldn't handle *that*," he said gesturing toward my body.

"So you haven't had sex together?" Candace wanted to confirm. Ryan shook his head.

"And you are honestly available to have a girl friend?" she continued.

"Yeah, I am."

"Okay, I'm cool with all of this, but Ryan I don't know if I can get used to the idea of you sleeping in the same bed with her. Can you try sleeping on your own, Leese?"

I smiled, "I'll do you one better: how about if I get my own place?"

"No!" Ryan snapped, "We can sleep in separate beds, but I don't fully believe Micah isn't keeping tabs on you. As soon as I'm out of the picture, he'll be back and then what the hell are you going to tell him?"

"He annulled the marriage, Ryan. I—I don't think—I don't think he wants me ba—" I bolted for the bathroom. It hurt so bad to say it out loud, but I was pretty certain ever since David delivered the papers, Micah had completely let go. The hard cold reality was it was over between us emotionally. I knew I couldn't go back to him, but it hurt worse to know he probably didn't love me anymore anyway. Damn, D'Angelo—I hated that man.

Candace joined me in the bathroom and tried to comfort me. She told me I didn't need to move out. Ryan was right about that. "I guess this proves you can't believe everything you read," she said as she rubbed my back. "I had this impression you were just some selfish, spoiled brat, but I don't think I could have done what you did. This hit man of yours must really be something if you're willing to go through all of this for him."

I dried my tears and tried a smile, "He was the most perfect thing in my life, even if he didn't believe it himself."

"It's kind of funny, but I look at Ryan the same way—he's so perfect and I'm such a nothing in comparison."

"Don't go selling yourself short, I think he's had a crush on you since middle school. Just do me a favor and take it slow with him. I know this whole business of watching over me has rattled his brains. If he acts a little confused between the two of us, just give him a chance."

She hugged me really hard, "Leese, I hate to say this when you're so sad, but damn I'm happy."

I squeezed her back, "Let's go tell the guys we want to go out for breakfast."

It turned out to be a great day in Colorado Springs.

Chapter Fifteen

"So what car did you order?" Ryan asked again, for the hundredth time as we sat at a sidewalk table at the bistro. This had become our favorite place to hang out. Besides having good food, the atmosphere was carefree and fun.

"I'm not telling, you'll just have to wait and see. But I promise you this, I'll kick your ass in anything you want to match against it," I laughed. I knew he hated the idea of a girl whipping him in a race, but his pride was just going to have to take a beating when my new car arrived.

"Yeah, I hear you," he said, sounding doubtful that I was telling the truth, "I'm having my Trans-Am shipped out here you know, so you might be in trouble."

"Do you see me shaking? You better bring a soft pillow."

"For what?"

"Because I'm gonna bruise that male ego of yours."

He pushed my head as if he were going to knock me off my chair. It had only been three days since I ordered my car and it was being rolled off the showroom today and getting ready to take a cross-country ride in a semi-truck and be sitting at our door by Friday afternoon. I couldn't wait to see Ryan's face, or Andy and Ty's for that matter. But the car wasn't my only secret.

I didn't tell him, but I was looking for another house. I knew how he felt about me moving, and his reasons why it wasn't a good idea, but I was starting to feel like an intruder when he spent time with Candace. Since she knew the whole story between us, she had become more aggressive in staking her claim to him. She hugged him now when she greeted him, leaving her arm around his waist and staring into his eyes when they talked. And then last night, just before she left to go home, I watched her place a brief kiss on his lips. I was jealous and I couldn't help it. He was the perfect catch and I had thrown him back.

I had brought my laptop and was just signing off on an assignment as we finished the last of our lunch. Ryan thought about going back to high school with Candace, but he finally opted to complete the few credits he needed online, which was what I was doing as well. I was just a little further ahead than he was because I started my classes' right after I got out of the hospital back in March and then stopped when Micah came back into my life. I was only weeks away from my diploma and finally anxious to close that chapter of my life. I snapped the lid shut and asked him if he was ready.

We were just about to get up and leave when a gentleman approached our table and stated my name as if he knew me. I had no clue who he was. He was about my height, slender built and in his mid to late thirties with graying hair and a salt and pepper close trimmed beard and was wearing a pair of small, expensive sunglasses.

"What did you do to your hair? Annalisa, that will never do," he continued. "We're going to have to get some hair extensions and dye it back to brown." He stated as if I should know what he was talking about.

"Excuse me, but I don't know you." I was getting a strong suspicion he would end up being a reporter.

Ryan stood preparing to get this guy away from me.

"No, but I do know you," he said extending his hand.

I refrained and he withdrew as Ryan moved toward him.

"My name is Don Bollson, I'm working for a production company in L.A. and we've been trying to find you."

"For what?"

"We're putting together a new show for ABC and you're on our hit list, girlfriend. Do you mind if I sit? We've got a lot to discuss."

"A television show?" Ryan questioned.

"Yes, it's called Remake. We debut this November and it will be prime time."

"I'm not going on a television show. I've got enough problems with the press."

"Well, just answer me one question because you might not even fit our needs anyway," he stated and then leaned toward me from across the table and asked quietly, "Can you sing?"

"Like an angel," Ryan replied, before allowing me to speak.

"Perfect!" was the exuberant response.

"I'm not going on a television show!" I snapped. Heads began turning our way.

"Could we at least discuss this somewhere privately? I can give you all the details and you can give me an informed refusal."

"Sure, you can come back to our house."

"Ryan!" I said, slapping his arm. "No, I don't—"

"Leese, you could at least hear the man out. I mean this might benefit, I don't know like starving children in Africa or something, right?" he asked looking at the man.

"Sure, you could donate the million dollar prize to your favorite charity. That would be fine."

"See. It's charity work, Leese."

"I'll donate a million dollars and skip the show," I growled.

"Please, just a chance to tell you about it, that's all I want."

Ten minutes later we were seated in our living room as Mr. Bollson explained the concept. "We're getting people from all over the United States who have captured the interest of the American public. The only thing they can't currently be are singers, nor can they have or have had any singing contracts. We'll start with a total of twenty-four contestants. The first show, you'll choose a song to sing and our judging panel will decide if you make it to the next week."

"Wait," I stopped him, "what makes this different from American Idol? It sounds like the same thing."

"No, our contestants are famous or infamous in their own right. Then we pair you up with the original group, singer or band and let you remake their song. It's more like a cross between Idol and Dancing with the Stars.

"The next week, the same thing happens. On the fourth week there will only be twelve of you left. The weeks after that are themed and you'll choose songs from the era or genre selected. You'll get to work with some of the greatest artist of our time, if they're alive and agree, of course. That is one thing we can't control is the song choice for your first two performances. So, if you pick an Elvis song, and we pray that you don't, we have to get permission from his estate and then you can only get a feel for how he performed by watching old video. Does that make sense?"

I nodded. Even though it sounded like it could end up being fun, it would also increase my problem with going out in public.

"America votes each week when the live shows start, and we dwindle down until we have the final two contestants. The last song will actually be a surprise the night of the live show and you'll only have a short amount of time to prepare for it. We're a little concerned how this is going to work, but we're still discussing this point with ownership.

"If you win, you get a million dollars and recognition as the first star on Remake. We don't promise any recording contracts, but I can almost guarantee that if the public wants to hear more from you, record companies will be breaking down your door to get you to sign."

"And that," I stated with my first amount of enthusiasm since I met Mr. Bollson, "is exactly why I don't want to do it. I don't need the publicity, nor do I want people breaking down my door trying to find me."

"Ah, come on, Leese. It sounds like fun and I know you'll be fabulous at—"

"NO!" I shot back at Ryan. I looked at Mr. Bollson, "I'm sorry, but I'd prefer to stay as obscure as possible."

"Well, if you are positive you don't want to do it, I'll leave. But here is my card, just in case you change your mind," he said, rising and walking away.

Ryan showed him to the door when Mr. Bollson stopped and turned around, "You know a song is a great way to get a message across. Isn't there someone in your life, maybe someone you've lost touch with or haven't seen in a long time that you'd like to choose a song and send that message out?"

"N-no," I stumbled on the response. Of course there was someone I'd like to sing my heart out to, someone who I'd like to sing my apology to, someone I loved so much yet couldn't have anymore.

Ryan opened the door as I watched my opportunity preparing to exit. "Wait!"

I had a feeling I was going to seriously regret this decision.

Mr. Bollson turned to me and smiled, "I need you in L.A. on Monday morning. We can fly you in—"

"I can fly her in," Ryan stopped him.

"I need an idea of the first singer or band we're going to need to call."

"Rascal Flatts," I breathed out.

Two sets of eyebrows raised my direction.

"All right, then I'll see what I can do to either have them flown in or have you fly out to wherever they are."

He produced a single paper with the time, date and place in Los Angeles where I was to go on Monday. He said the other paperwork would be completed at the studio.

"And by the way, I'll have a stylist waiting for you because America doesn't know this short-haired, blonde version, so don't be offended."

Mr. Bollson left.

Ryan stared at me after closing the front door, "Rascal Flatts? He's country right? I just figured you'd pick something different."

"*They* are country; it's the name of their group not a singer. They have the perfect song and it's the only reason I agreed to do this. I'm actually hoping the other contestants are really good and they'll give me the boot after the first week. I just want a chance to sing one song for Micah."

"Which song?"

"*What Hurts the Most*," I said as my eyes began to tear.

"Will you sing it for me first?" he asked as he came and sat beside me on the couch, wrapping his arm around my shoulder.

I shook my head, "I don't think I can, not right now. But, I know there's a song that fits how I feel about you, too. If I make it more than a week or two, I'll sing it for you."

He leaned over and kissed my forehead, "So that only leaves me one question to ask," he breathed as he lifted my chin and pierced me with those blue eyes.

The look was so deep and hard that I was afraid of what the question might be. His hand slid slowly around the side of my cheek, cupping me warmly as his mouth reached the opposing ear. He was being so deliberate that my pulse was beginning to quicken as he very slowly whispered, "What kind of..." He took another breath, "...car did you order?"

"Ah!" I pulled away and smacked his shoulder. "You jerk!"

We laughed and tousled against each other until I pulled a few martial arts moves on him and made him beg for mercy. I don't honesty think he was trying very hard to defend himself, but it was fun anyway.

Friday, a few minutes after noon, my new baby arrived. It was just going to be the two of us to see it first. Andy and Ty were pulling guard duty and, although Candace got out of school at twelve-thirty, she had work right after that, so he and I would get to enjoy my car alone for a little while.

The sleek black semi-truck bore no marking to spoil my surprise. They opened the back doors and lowered the ramp as the sound of a high performance engine resounded from somewhere inside the box trailer.

"What color is it going to be?" Ryan asked, obviously not wanting to wait for the suspense of seeing it roll down the ramp.

"I liked the paint job on the Javelin."

"Red?" he sounded surprised.

The back of the car emerged and then she rolled down the ramp and into the street.

"It's a... What is it?"

"It's a Shelby Ultimate Aero," I stated proudly, "The world's fastest production car." I sounded like a commercial. He wasn't speaking as he walked slowly around it, so I continued, "It packs 1,287 horsepower—"

"Shit! Leese, you don't need that much engine! I don't want you killing yourself," he snapped as a worried expression washed away his smile.

I ignored the remark as I gave him a few more tidbits, "It goes zero to sixty in 2.78 seconds, redlines at 7800 rpms and tops out at 256 miles per hour."

He was still frowning.

"Wanna go for a drive?" I said twirling the key from my index finger, and giving him a wink.

The frown was losing ground, "You drive first, but I want a turn behind the wheel, too."

I squealed with delight as I charged for the driver's side.

I would have to be content with civil driving as we moved down the city streets, but Ryan was on his cell phone with Andy begging for a favor.

"Head for the Air Force Base. Andy's going to see if he can get us a runway for a little while."

I was surprised he actually did get permission, but it turned out that Andy's Colonel was a big fan of Shelby cars and we were told that the military would turn their heads for a couple trips down the runway.

It was like being strapped to a rocket as we blurred across the strip. We had gathered quite a crowd by the time we decided that we had taken up enough of their time. Their Colonel came out just as we were ready to leave, but I offered to let him take it for a test drive as a thank you for the use of their roadway.

He declined at first; I guess he thought I wasn't really serious. When he realized I meant it, he accepted my offer and took it for a gentle ride. We thanked Andy for his help and told him we'd see him and Ty later at our house.

Candace was the first to make it to our place when she got off work, but she was the last to see the new car. I told Ryan to take her for a ride, before Andy and Ty showed up. I needed him out of the house for a little while anyway because I had to make a call to my realtor.

I had chosen a place a couple miles to the south in a beautiful neighborhood with awesome views and quiet streets. I had been deciding between purchasing or leasing. The purchase price was two and a quarter million which was fine with me, but purchasing had a certain permanence to it and I was starting to understand why my mom usually opted to rent what she liked instead of committing.

The year-long lease was a hundred and twenty thousand with an option to buy at the end. I decided on the lease and I needed to let her know I would be ready to sign the paperwork when I got back from L.A. on Saturday. Ryan would be pissed at me, but I needed to get out of his life before I got weak and made a serious error in judgment.

By the end of the night they all knew about my pending television debut. I could see the concern on Candace's face when Ryan said he would fly me to L.A. on Monday and stay with me for the few days I was going through the first phase of the show. I know how she felt as it seemed Ryan was in this unintentional tug of war between us. He wanted to continue helping me and at the same time he wanted to begin this budding relationship with Candace. Before the end of the night, I had a feeling this would be the last time I used him as my private pilot.

Ty and Andy left, and Ryan was taking a long time to tell Candace goodnight as I turned off the lights and closed the drapery. They were talking outside by her car. I had no intention of seeing what they were doing, but just as I started closing the kitchen blinds, I saw them kiss. This was not the brief kind of kiss they shared before; this was the kind of kiss that he and I shared when I was running away from Micah. I went to the bedroom and, for the first time, I closed my door.

It must have been another fifteen or twenty minutes before I heard him come into the house. We hadn't slept together since Candace asked us not to six days ago. My first couple nights had been rocky, but he was in the house and that was comforting enough that I finally managed to start sleeping alone. The funny thing was he told me he was having withdrawals on trying to sleep alone.

My door cracked open slightly, "Leese, you asleep?"

"Not yet," I replied.

"Can I come in?"

"Do you really need me to answer that?"

The door opened and he came and stretched out beside me on the bed, "Candace asked me to go with her to her house tonight," came his soft words in the dark.

I rolled toward him. "I'll be fine by myself," I assured him, thinking he was getting ready to leave. I was going to be a nervous wreck instead of fine, but I would never tell him. I'd never been truly alone in my whole life. When I wasn't with Mom, I was with Bev and Matt, then Micah, and now Ryan; but just me by myself was a scary concept.

"No, I'm not going. I told her maybe another night."

"Why? And don't tell me you don't know if you really care that much about her because I've seen the look on your face and it looks a whole lot like someone falling in love."

"You and Micah waited for marriage, but I don't know if—"

"Micah didn't," I corrected him, "I did. There were other women, plenty of other women I'm assuming, before I came along. I guess I was the only one to say I had to have forever first."

"I keep asking myself if I can see her as my wife because I don't want to hurt her; I don't see it yet."

"I can't speak for other women, but I know if you made love to me I'd feel the need to commit my life to you. I think Candace might have the same expectation, so don't take making love to her lightly."

"I just want to get to know her better to make sure I want her, not just to be able to finally say I got laid."

I laughed softly, "Ryan, you just aren't that kind of guy. Does she know why you want to take this slow? Does she know you've never—"

"I've left a few hints, but I haven't come right out and told her."

"If you don't tell her she's going to take this hesitation to mean something else. She's already worried about you and I going to L.A. together."

"Yeah, she kind of told me that tonight."

"If I have to go out there anymore, I'm hiring a pilot. I don't need to make her jealous."

"I think that's ridiculous—I'm not doing anything, I'm just flying you out there and staying a few days."

"If she left for a few days with another guy would you be worried?"

"That's not the same."

"Oh yes it is. You need to realize she feels this way every time you and I are alone. I imagine she's wondering what we're doing right at this moment."

"So you're saying you would have wanted me to go with her tonight?"

"All I really want is for you to be happy and in love, because I can't be that person for you—you deserve to be more than a Micah replacement."

He leaned over and kissed my forehead. "I—I love you, Leese."

I reached out my hand and rested it softly against his cheek, "More than anything, I want you to be happy."

"I don't suppose you consider letting me sleep in here for old time's sake?"

I laughed and gave him a push, "Not that kind of happy—no, and I hope the next time you are in a bed with someone she rocks your world and doesn't tell you no."

He rolled off the bed, his feet hitting the floor with a light thump, "Goodnight."

"Goodnight, Ryan."

Monday morning, after Ryan consumed a half pot of coffee at five a.m., we flew out of Colorado Springs. We touched down at LAX, forty-five minutes before I needed to be in the studio. I considered a rental car, but opted for a taxi since I didn't know their roads or traffic. Someone at the studio made us reservations at the closest hotel, and we would only have enough time to grab our room key and toss our bags inside before continuing our journey.

Mr. Bollson was the man to greet us as he ushered me back to the waiting stylists. There were two of them because they were going to try to speed the process from four or five hours to less than two as he explained that the other contestants would be arriving at noon. Ryan was seated in a comfortable chair with a ringside view as the man and woman worked on me, but it wasn't long before I saw his eyelids droop and he fell asleep—so much for all that coffee.

Two hours later, I gently touched his arm. Surprise was written all over his face when he saw me.

"Leese?" His hand reached out and gently touched my long brown hair, "Wow, it feels so real?"

"It is real—real human hair anyway. Amazing isn't it?"

"I didn't realize how much I missed seeing you like this until now—yeah, pretty amazing."

It looked like my natural hair and even the color was perfect, but it was definitely fuller.

Mr. Bollson asked us to come out to the studio and have a seat in the audience chairs as more contestants were still arriving. They filed in, several brought companions or friends with them which I know helped Ryan feel a little more at ease.

I recognized some of them; Kitkat was from a reality television modeling show; she made a name for herself by being a total witch to everyone; Shana Weaver was a women's tennis pro; and then Carrie Wakefield showed. She'd had a short career as a television wrestler; she was loud and crass and known for starting trouble. She immediately began staring at Ryan, and I could tell it was making him uncomfortable.

Nicole Fletcher was a soap opera star and by all accounts a very nice person. The oldest contestant was Dobrey Stewart. I recognized her from all the charity work she received recognition for doing. There were a few other women; some looked familiar to me and some didn't look familiar at all.

It did surprise me though when a pair of bouncy, blonde twins entered the room and Ryan told me they were play bunnies, Melissa and Melanie Nielsson.

"How do you know who they are? And please don't tell me you read Playboy."

A grin lifted the corner of his mouth, "No, but Nate does. He brought one to school and had it in his gym locker. He's got their centerfold taped inside."

"Ah! Poor Natasha, I bet she—"

"She bought it for him," he said with a light laugh.

"You're lying, Ryan Faultz. There is no way—"

"Honest," he raised his right hand. "He told me she gave it to him and said that better be the only way he ever sees what a white girl has under her clothes. I don't think she had a clue he put it in his locker, but he did."

I just shook my head and leaned back against the chair as more people entered.

I only recognized a handful of the male contestants. Rashad Smith was a professional baseball player, and Sergio Mendez was a motivational speaker, Lexington Overhill was an actor, and one other guy was really familiar, but I couldn't quite figure out who he was until they called his first name, Sadarius.

"Do you know who he is?" I whispered to Ryan.

"Isn't he the one who beat up those guys that were robbing a family?"

"Yeah, Sadarius Collins. I think it's pretty cool that they've got him on the show. I hope he can sing."

"You're supposed to be here to win this thing, not rooting for the other contestants," he whispered with a light chuckle.

"I don't want to win. Matter of fact, I don't even want to be here, but between you and Don, here I sit."

"All right," Don began, quieting everyone, "it's time to lay out the ground rules and get started."

For the next hour he covered confidentiality, how the eliminations would work, introduced the judges, and discussed some dos and don'ts on the stage. "We won't be live for the first four shows, but we will have an audience. The live shows will air on Tuesdays and Thursdays starting the first week in November. The taped shows will be women on Wednesday and men on Friday, and you are expected to be present for the tapings even if your group isn't performing. We'll cut three contestants by the end of each taping. You'll get a two week break and then, after two more tapings, another six will leave until we have twelve contestants. There is another two week break before the live shows begin."

"You are on camera all the time you are with us, with the exception of the changing area, so be aware that anything you do may make it on television. Keep that in mind, and yes, you will sign a waiver that you can't sue us if you don't like how we portray you from your extra clips.

"Some of you will be here this week to work with your singer or group, some of you will be flying out of here to meet elsewhere to do your remake, but we'll all be back on Wednesday and then again on Friday for our first taping. Fill out your paperwork and turn it in for today and you are free to go until eight a.m. tomorrow morning."

Ryan read over my shoulder as I went through the contract. There were several people who brought lawyers, but I didn't think this was horribly complicated. I finished reading and reluctantly signed my name. If it wasn't an excellent opportunity to sing my apology to Micah, I wouldn't be here.

"Okay, let's turn this in and go do a little sightseeing," I said smiling up at Ryan as he offered me his hand.

Kitkat was standing impatiently as she waited to hand in her paperwork when she turned and looked at me and began to laugh. That was a little unsettling.

"You must be Annalisa Winslett," she said quite loudly, "the Runaway Princess."

"That would be me," I replied as I held my head erect and stared back at her, "but don't believe everything you hear."

"Shit girl, I don't but I'm guessing this is the piece of candy you ran off with the last time—I'd run off with a guy that looks that good, too."

Ryan was trying hard not to blush, I could tell, but he was losing the battle.

Carrie came up behind us and began openly handling him as she grabbed his jean belt loops and gave his pants a light hoist to improve her view of his backside, "Yeah, I agree, he's got a nice ass on him." And then she goosed him.

His face was getting dark as he tried to step away.

"Please, don't do that," I asked calmly.

She was not a small woman. She was at least two inches taller than me and very muscular, but she didn't frighten me. She may have liked wrestling, but I had sparred with some tough people in my martial arts training, and I was sure I could take her. And, with a title that included the word 'princess' in it, I knew she wouldn't expect me to pack a punch.

"I do whatever I please, little girl, and you better be happy I'm touching him and not you. Now baby," she said, addressing Ryan. "When you want a girlfriend that knows what a man like you is for then—"

"He has a girlfriend," I stated, stepping between her and Ryan as we made our way closer to the table. The camera crew was focusing on the two of us, and I was beginning to grit my teeth. She liked having her 'I'm so bad' reputation and I'm certain she wanted to keep it up for this show, but she was picking the wrong person to mess with.

Kitkat laughed lightly as she stepped away from the table. I know she thought I was getting ready to get my butt kicked, but I was going to show Carrie that no matter what title they stuck on me, I wasn't running away from her challenge.

Carrie appeared to be reassessing me. I stepped up and handed them my contract. Out of the corner of my eye I saw her getting ready to grab another pinch of Ryan when I startled her by turning swiftly and blocking her attempt with a sweep of my arm. As soon as we made contact, she was ready to start throwing punches. Ryan barely had time to turn around as I blocked two of her swings and the stage crew jumped in to pull us apart. She never even ruffled my hair, but I know she was dying to get at me.

"Try something like that again and I'm gonna rearrange that pretty face for you!" she spewed after me.

The stage crew still had a hold of her as I gave a light laugh and took Ryan's arm and walked away.

"Yeah, you'd better run away," she sneered.

I ignored the remark. I knew who I really was underneath the title, and I was sure she'd keep pushing my buttons and then she'd find out, too.

When we stepped outside, Ryan began the apology, big time. "I had no idea what this was going to be like, Leese. I'm so sorry I talked you into this."

I waved down a taxi as he continued to tell me that he would fly me out of here right now. We slid into the back seat of the cab as I turned to him, "Rodeo Drive or Venice Beach?"

"You don't want to stay and actually do this—you want to go home, right?"

"Venice Beach," I decided for him, tapping on the cabbie's glass panel. The car pulled out into traffic.

I laughed. "No, I'm fine. I overheard some of the guys saying that the bookies in Vegas have already started a pool over whether I'll run away before the show airs. Somebody's going to lose a lot of money, because I'm staying."

He smiled and looked out the window as the buildings blurred past. "Thanks for the help in there," he said sheepishly. "I have no clue what I'm supposed to do when a woman pulls something like that—I couldn't hit her and I didn't have any idea what to say."

"I could tell. Unfortunately, so could she. I'm thinking she's going to be a thorn in our side for the next several days."

He groaned, but she was forgotten quickly on the streets of Venice Beach.

We were at the studio right on time the next morning as Don approached and said we had a plane to catch. "You're going to Tennessee with a film crew to shoot your practice with Rascal Flatts at 2 p.m. today. You'll be back by about 9 p.m. and then it's back here tomorrow at noon for the dress rehearsal. Doors open for our first taping with an audience at 6 p.m."

"I can fly her to—"

"Sorry, Romeo, the flight is already scheduled," he said dismissively.

"His name is Ryan," I sternly reminded Don, letting him know I didn't like his remark.

He gave a half smile, "Sorry, Ryan—I'll remember that next time. We have a plane and a crew ready. By the way, Annalisa, I need your song choice for next week. Have you given any thought about what you'd like to sing?"

I had actually been thinking about it ever since I agreed to do the show. If these people were going to give me an opportunity to send a message to Micah, I would make sure the message was clear, "'Everything I Do' by Bryan Adams."

"Oooh," Don remarked in a very drawn out manner.

"Why? Is there something wrong with that song?"

"No, I think it's a little old for someone your age, but Bryan Adams lives in London."

Now I understood the 'Oooh' remark.

"Don't worry about it, Annalisa. If that is your song choice, we'll make it happen. He may not even be in London this time of the year. Go to Tennessee and have a good time and we'll figure this out when you get back."

It was a little different to not have Ryan at the helm, and it would have been nice to just sit together in the back of the plane and relax and talk except for the camera crew, Pete Claxton on camera and Jason Kelley on sound. I tried talking them into turning it off, but that was a lost cause.

The jet was roomy and comfortable and our seats were side by side so we just reclined, turning our backsides toward the camera. Ryan's arm draped over the seats to rest across my waist. It had been a while since I'd felt the comfort of sleeping under his touch and it didn't take long before I dozed. Just before I drifted off, I was thinking about Candace. If a clip of this made it on the show, even though we technically weren't sleeping together, it would probably still qualify in her book as the same thing. Hopefully, she wouldn't get mad.

We woke just as the wheels touched down on the Tennessee airstrip. Our meeting would be at a studio in Nashville.

"You nervous?" Ryan asked as we were about to enter the building.

I know he could tell, but I put on my braver-than-I-felt front and smiled, "Of course, not."

He laughed—he knew I was terrified.

I'm not really sure what I expected, but it ended up being a blast. The guys from the group, Gary, Jay and Joe were down-to-earth, very personable and fun to be around. They made me immediately comfortable as they ran through the song once before I sang it with them.

"I'd like to change the lyrics just a little bit to fit my situation, if that's okay?"

The guys looked at each other and shrugged, wanting to know what I wanted to change.

"When it comes to the chorus and says, 'watching you walk away,' I want to change it to say, 'having to run away.'"

The guys laughed. Running away was supposed to be my modus operandi anyway, and Micah wasn't the one who left me. I wanted the song tailored to reflect my feelings for him.

They agreed to try it with me singing my revised lyrics. Ryan sat smiling and watching as the music began.

The song went very well, even if I did shed a few tears before the end, but the adjusted lyrics worked perfectly. The guys were impressed with my singing, but I wasn't happy with the ending chorus.

"You hit that last part, '…was being so close' with so much feeling and I don't think my version has the same intensity as yours, but I want that intensity."

Gary and I practiced the final chorus a few times until I felt like I knew how to hit it correctly and then it was my turn to try singing the song alone.

I was even more emotional when I sang it by myself, but the emotions worked so well to evoke all the feelings the lyrics deserved. I was wiping away the tears, as I hugged and thanked them all for their help.

Two hours in Nashville vanished quickly, and, before it seemed we had a chance to breathe, it was back on the plane and back to Los Angeles. The camera guys warmed up to us in studio, so the cameras were turned off for the return trip. We actually had a good time talking and getting to know one another.

Wednesday's taping went well with the exception of Carrie still trying to cause problems and rattle me. Ryan was a little more vocal in his efforts to keep her at bay, but she wouldn't be dissuaded. She wanted to pick a fight with me so badly and Ryan was her ticket to the match. After the first three contestants were cut and the audience left the studio, everyone met back stage to say goodbye to the girls. Carrie was being loud and laughing about my tears while I performed on stage. It didn't bother me about crying while I sang, and even the judges said I had given the best performance of the night, but she wouldn't let it go.

"I'd be worried if I were you, sweet-cheeks," she crooned to Ryan as she continually tried to touch him, "I think your little runaway might be regretting her decision."

He had become more at ease with all the contestants, including her. She simply caught him off guard the first day. He smiled as he dodged her attempts to reach the more personal areas, "I love her no matter what happens, so I'm good with whatever she decides."

"Oh, I'm sure you are 'good,'" she remarked as she licked her lips and made a grab for his crotch.

He stepped back just in time as I moved between them for what seemed like the hundredth time, "Would you just back off?"

"And just what, little girl, are you gonna do if I don't?" she said, puffing up and putting herself in my face.

Ryan had my shoulder and was attempting to move me behind him, when she put her hand on my chest and pushed me into him.

"If you want to fight me, then come out and say it," I growled as I pulled out from under his grip. "You're bold enough about everything else—like trying to intimidate people who are too nice to tell you to keep your damn hands to yourself!" At this point I was advancing into her and actually caused her to take a step back, but I wasn't finished with what I had to say. "I'd really like to know what the problem is," I continued as my fury over her constant needling built, "don't you have a man that will put up with you?"

"That does it!" And she started swinging.

I blocked the punch, and swept her leg out from under her with mine, knocking her to the floor. She grabbed my ankle and I went down on top of her. Ryan and the crew were on us in a flash as she tried to head butt me, but I managed to slam her cheek with an elbow strike. The blow rendered her senseless long enough for them to separate us.

Now she was taking swings at the crew as she threatened me. She and a stage hand went tumbling over a chair as others jumped into give him a hand.

"You okay?" Ryan asked as I straighten my clothes.

"Yeah, I'm fine. Let's go before they turn her loose and I end up actually having to hurt her. Geez, I'm starting to think this show is going to be more like Jerry Springer meets American Idol."

He laughed lightly, "You've got her as long as she doesn't close the gap between you two. If she does, it'll come down to wrestling and I think she'll have the advantage."

Thursday and the majority of Friday we had free time to do what we wanted. I managed to talk him into Rodeo Drive, but he wore out on the shopping trip pretty quick.

"Let me at least buy you a nice silk suit. They have Gucci and Prada and—"

"First of all, why in the world would I need a suit? And secondly, Leese, why do you insist on blowing money on me? I have money—nothing like you, but I've got a couple million in a trust fund."

"I don't know, I guess I feel like I owe you so much for everything you've done for me and I just want—"

"I got paid," he stated matter-of-factly, "three of the best kisses of my life, remember?"

"That wasn't much of a payment for offering your life," I frowned.

"You're right. I think my life might be worth another three kisses."

I slugged his arm, making him yowl, "Candace would rip your head off if she heard you say that."

"True, but we are over a thousand miles away and—"

"Ryan Faultz, I am shocked! I thought once you kissed Candace those lips of yours would be sealed for her alone. Don't tell me you're going to be a run-around."

"I'm not a *run-around*; I just happen to be crazy about two women—and you had a piece of my heart first. And, I only mentioned a kiss, that's not like asking if we can sleep together? Although, by the way, I really miss sleeping together."

I shook my head and laughed, "You are being bad today. I think Carrie has rubbed off on you."

"Carrie would like to rub a lot of things off me. She is possessed. But, thank God for my bodyguard." He knocked his shoulder into mine, which wasn't easy since he's seven inches taller than me.

"You aren't going to be like this after you and Candace finally…"

His face blushed a little, "How am I supposed to know what I'm going to be like after that?"

"Will this be her first time, too?" I timidly asked as we continued window shopping.

His face became somber, "Can we discuss this some place a little quieter?"

I immediately knew the answer was a no, but there must be something more to the story so I agreed. We had lunch and headed back to the hotel. I wasn't sure if I should ask him anymore about Candace, but he was the one who decided he wanted to talk, I just didn't expect him to ask if we could lie in the bed together while we did.

"I slept so good on the plane just because I was able to keep my arm on you—I won't ask to sleep this way tonight, but does a nap really count?"

"We'll talk—I think a nap does count, but we were in separate chairs on the plane."

We curled up on my bed and I had to admit it was wonderful to be cuddled against him. He put a soft kiss on my neck and then relaxed against the pillow.

"Candace started dating a guy last February who worked with her at the store. He pressured her really hard about letting him be her first. He claimed that he loved her and said if she loved him, she'd let it happen between them."

I had a feeling I wasn't going to like the outcome of this story.

"He bought her a cheap promise ring and told her everything a girl wants to hear. She finally decided she'd take the step, but not before she got on birth control pills. I'm so glad she at least knew better than to believe him when he said he'd 'take care of everything.'"

"What happened?"

"A Friday night, a cheap motel, and a couple drinks and it was all over with. The next time she went to work, he'd told all the guys what he'd done and he didn't want anything to do with her."

"That's sick, Ryan. I mean I know those kinds of guys are out there, but it's so hard to understand how he could treat her that way. What did she do? Does she still have to work with him?"

"Candace is like a little sister to Andy and Ty, so when she came home crying and upset and they found out why, they showed up in the parking lot after he got off work and they roughed him up. He quit and she hasn't seen him since."

I could picture Ty and Andy doing that and, due to their size, I'm sure they scared the crap out of the guy. "I can see why that worked," I gave a light laugh.

"I don't think I could have been happy with just roughing the bastard up. He would have had some broken bones if I'd gotten my hands on him. But I don't understand why she's so willing to put her trust in me. She wanted me to go home with her and it's been years since she's seen me."

"You're one of the good guys, Ryan. I think any girl can tell that about you once she gets past the tattoos and the wise-cracks. Did you do what I told you? Did you tell her why you're hesitant?"

"Yeah, when she and I went for that drive Sunday before she went home, I told her. I thought it might freak her out a little bit, but she was—well, I think it was a turn on because she was all over me."

"It is a turn on, you nit-wit," I laughed, squeezing his arm tightly.

"Why? I'm not going to have a clue and I'm pretty sure I'm not going to start right out the gate being a rock star."

Now I was really laughing. I never would have thought he would have stated it quite that way.

"What's so funny," he demanded.

"She'll remember it for the rest of her life and I'm sure it won't take you long to be her personal 'rock star.'"

"So were you—were you Micah's rock star that first night?" he whispered quietly in my ear.

"That's a little personal, Ryan," all my teasing evaporated.

"I have a feeling you were," he continued, not realizing just how uncomfortable he was making me.

I pulled away from under his arm and got up and went into the bathroom. Washing my face and trying to keep from breaking down as I recalled my few days of heaven in Micah's arms. I missed him so badly that, just like the love in his heart he described for me, it hurt, physically inside.

"I'm sorry, Leese," he said, standing in the doorway. "I had no business asking you that."

I broke into sobs as he wrapped his arms around me. "I miss him so badly. I thought it would get easier the longer we're apart, but I swear I think I could actually let his family get slaughtered, just so I could have him again for a little while."

"No, you wouldn't. You're stronger than that, but I hope someday you'll realize you can't keep going on alone. Micah would understand if you—"

"Only if he knew why. But, if he knew, he'd kill D'Angelo and then the mob would kill him and his family anyway. I can never tell him why," I choked. "I hope I never have to face him because I don't think I have enough strength to turn him away. You have no idea how hard it is to want to see someone with every ounce of your body and, at the same time, want to avoid that person just as badly."

"I had a taste of it, but you're right, I guess I don't know what you're really going through."

I looked up into those penetrating blue eyes and searched, without words, for what he was referring to by saying he'd had a taste of it.

"When you got married, I knew my chance was gone. I had to force myself to go to the wedding and I nearly lost my courage to find you and dance with you, because I just knew it was pointless. Then when I saw your mom and his brother at the hotel and she invited me to have dinner, I opted to take your sister to a movie instead because, even though everything inside me wanted to see you again, I knew I couldn't take it—I knew you'd been with him and... I just couldn't take it."

"And who knew we'd end up here, huh?" A small grin finally tugged at the edges of my quivering lips.

"That's what we should do tonight!"

He was so enthusiastic about it, and I didn't even know what 'it' was. "What?"

"Go dancing," he beamed.

I winced and he noticed.

"You can't tell me you don't like to dance?"

"I love dancing, but... Well, it's just that I... You'll get the wrong idea and since we're sharing a room, this might not be the smartest thing to do. Kind of like letting me kiss your neck." I

200

reminded him, hoping he would understand. He got the reference to his neck, but other than that he seemed mystified. "Okay, fine. I'll just say it: I dance dirty."

He busted out laughing, "You? Sweet, little innocent you? You dance—"

"Like a pole dancer," I finished for him.

"This I gotta see. Now I wish I'd let you buy me that suit, or at least the slacks and a dress shirt."

Before the afternoon was over, he had a pair of black silk slacks, dress shoes and a crisp white dress shirt. I still wasn't convinced this was a good idea, but I bought a dress and heals to go clubbing in and away we went.

I called Don and asked, since I didn't want to end up in the wrong club, where was a good place for a night of dancing; he told me to hit Hollywood. He recommended two clubs in particular and said to have fun. I called for a limo and away we went.

I wasn't sure what to expect out of Ryan on the dance floor, but he stunned me with the fact that he could dance—I mean *really* dance. After the first song, I had to ask if he was a natural or if he'd had lessons.

"I don't think there is any kid from Palm Beach that hasn't been enrolled in a dance class—yeah, my mom insisted. I did it for a year just before my dad died. By the way, I don't think you dance dirty. I'm guessing you aced expression dancing."

I just laughed and pulled him back out onto the floor. By the end of the night he determined that we had a song that fit us, or at least from his perspective. It was new when we were both in elementary school, but it didn't matter. The DJ played Kryptonite by 3 Doors Down and we burned up the dance floor with a variation of a fast jitterbug.

"So," I asked as we rode in the limo back to the hotel, "How does the song fit us?"

"Okay when it says 'I watched the world float to the dark side of the moon, after all I knew it had to be something to do with you.' That's the moment when I knew I had to help you run. And, 'I really don't mind what happens now and then, as long as you'll be my friend at the end.' That statement is fact as far as I'm concerned. I'll keep your secrets, so we've got that one. I don't honestly think you've taken me for granted, but the 'if not for me then you'd be dead, I picked you up and put you back on solid ground,' was getting you to Colorado Springs and helping you start over."

"But I'm kryptonite to you then. Isn't that something his enemies used against him?" I felt like we were back in AP English dissecting poetry.

"Definitely," he grinned. He was exhausted as he leaned back into the plush seat and stretched out his long legs.

"I don't actually get that."

"You're my weakness. I'm not a run-around, as you mentioned earlier today, and I'm falling hard for Candace, but you are the one person who could make me change everything—you are my weakness. I think I can handle almost anything, unless it involves you. If something happened to you, I—I couldn't take it." He dropped from fun and teasing to serious on that last sentence.

I guessed it would be wise to put a little humor back into this conversation before he went too deep on me, "And you can fly, and you can cut hair, and you can dance like a maniac—yes, I think you're right; you are superman."

"And, if Micah catches us, we'll see if I'm faster than a speeding bullet!" he said, bursting into laughter.

The smile fell off my face, "That's not funny."

I was going to refuse to laugh, but he tickled me mercilessly until I was nearly in tears.

"So now that I've got you," he panted, pinning me to the seat, "how about those three extra kisses?"

"I never agreed to that, Superman," I stated as I tried to wiggle free from his hold.

His face descended, but I turned my cheek to him. He readjusted for my mouth, as I dodged for a second time.

"You aren't serious?" I asked as I struggled to avoid him, "Ryan, stop."

He pulled back slightly, but didn't let me go, "Yes, I am. I don't want you to keep blowing money on me and three kisses are what I want instead."

"I'll stop 'blowing' money on you then, but I don't think we should get this—" I was going to finish by saying 'close,' but he had taken my chin in hand and wasn't going to allow me to turn his last attempt away.

His mouth was on mine just as soft and gentle as the first time I kissed him. The tip of his tongue, like a piece of silk, stroked my lips, begging me to give in. I missed kissing almost as much as I missed sex and I felt defenseless to refuse. My lips parted as I accepted his invitation to share the intimacy of the moment. I'm not really sure how long the kiss lasted, but we were both breathless and wide-eyed when our lips parted. I don't think he considered the fact when he had kissed me that he still had me under him on the seat, but realizing it now we were both flushed with heat and need.

"I don't think this is a—" I started to say.

"Good idea," we finished together.

"Damn, Leese. I'd forgotten how awesome you are at this. If I go for two more, I'm afraid we won't stop."

"I agree—please, get up—I can't take—"

He rose and took my hand, righting me in the seat.

We finished the trip in silence, went to our separate beds in our room, and tried to sleep. I watched the clock from one a.m. to three a.m. when I heard him whisper in the dark asking if I was awake.

"Yes," came my quiet reply.

"If we don't sleep together, we aren't going to get any sleep."

"Then stay up and watch the sunrise with me, but we aren't getting into one bed."

"Are you mad at me for kissing you?"

"Yes."

"I wish I could tell you I was sorry, but I'm not."

"Ryan."

"Yeah?"

"You said earlier I'm your weakness, even though you're falling for Candace."

He rolled over in his bed and faced me, reaching across the short distance between them to touch my cheek, "You are, and I think I'm always going to love you no matter what happens between me and her."

"I want you to know you're my weakness. I'm not going to have you fly me back out here next week. I've found a place of my own—"

"Don't, Annalisa—please, don't put distance between us."

"I'll still be in Colorado Springs. It's a nice place about two miles south of our—of your place," I corrected. "I couldn't get too far away from you. I'm just too damn weak for that right now."

"When are you moving?" I could hear the deep sadness in his voice.

"If everything is worked out with the lease when I get back, I guess it will be sometime next week."

"Don't expect me to stay away from you," he warned. "I'm not going to let my best friend be lonely."

"I don't want you to stay away. It's just at night, when we're alone, I'm—I'm just not strong enough to keep being this close."

"Leese, I know the day you ran away you told me you loved me, but I also know it was for the camera, not for me. How do you really feel about me?"

I had to be honest with him, but I knew it wasn't going to be easy. I slid onto the floor, resting on my knees as I knelt beside his bed. I cupped his face in my hands and lowered my lips to his. I know he wasn't expecting me to do this and all the while I was hoping I'd be able to stop, but I had to show him the emotions that were bottled up inside me. His arms encircled me, trying to pull me up onto the bed with him, but I couldn't. I released him from the kiss. He tried to come back for another as I placed my fingers over his lips. "I love you so much, Ryan Faultz—but the last kiss can never happen. I guess you'll just have to be happy with a piece of my heart."

"I wish things weren't so complicated between us."

"Me too, but God has a purpose for everything."

"I believe that too, but sometimes it's really hard to accept." He leaned toward me and kissed my forehead. "Sunrise isn't far away; maybe we should try to get some sleep. I can be good, if you can," he said sliding away from the edge of the bed and making enough room for me.

I told Candace I wouldn't, but…

I lay down in the warm place he left when he moved over, turning my back to him and feeling the wonderful sensation of him holding me close, "Goodnight, Ryan."

He kissed my shoulder and whispered, "Sleep tight."

It was a good thing I wasn't required to be in studio for the taping of the men's show until four p.m. because it was after one in the afternoon before I finally stirred. It was the first time that Ryan actually woke before me. He was on his back staring at the ceiling when I rolled over.

"Good morning," I yawned.

"Nope, baby girl, it's afternoon."

"What are you looking at?" I was trying to see what he was seeing in the ceiling tiles, because he seemed to be fixated.

He just kept looking up, ignoring my question.

"Okay," I said, deciding to head for the shower, but just as my feet hit the floor he spoke.

"You scared me this morning," came his simple statement.

I wasn't sure exactly what he was talking about. I didn't think it frightened him when I kissed him in the wee hours, nor when I finally told him how I really felt about him, so I was mystified, "About what?"

"You were talking in your sleep a little bit ago, but I thought you were awake."

I knew I talked sometimes in my sleep, but I wondered what I could have said to scare him. "What did I say?"

"It was around eleven when I woke up because you were getting wiggly so I kissed your shoulder and you, very clearly said, 'Make love to me.'" He swallowed, but continued, "It felt like my heart was going to jump out of my chest, so I asked if you were sure."

Now my heart was pounding with what I was obviously wanting in my sleep, "Go on." Yet, I could tell he didn't want to finish.

He took an unsteady breath. "You said, 'Please, I need you so badly,'" he paused. "Then you were calling out his name, begging for him to take you and I realized you were still asleep."

It was a strange sensation to be happy that Micah was still the man on my mind, and yet so sad to realize how it must have hurt Ryan to listen to me calling out for someone else.

I wanted to say I was sorry, but he'd known all along that I was deeply in love with Micah Gavarreen; I simply couldn't apologize for that.

He stopped staring at the ceiling and got up and headed for the bathroom.

"Are you okay?" I asked softly as he walked away.

"You know I've only got one thing to say about this," he turned and stared into my eyes.

I was a little concerned about the sharpness in his voice, but then I watched him wipe the corners of his eyes and I knew it wasn't anger coming from him.

"He is one lucky son-of-a-bitch."

Chapter Sixteen

"But I was told that the CIA wasn't going to make an official presence in this latest skirmish," the man said, studying the Americans with clear suspicion.

"We're not," David stated sternly, "but you can understand our concern about your success. You've managed to cut the flow of cocaine to the US dramatically, but when our operatives got a good lead about the latest effort to remove you from office, we decided to share the information. We are just here to offer you some suggestions."

"Our informants tell us they are planning an attack on your personal residence in less than two hours," Micah added. "I suggest you move your family to a safe house. We have a helicopter standing ready to take you there and you can order your forces to lay in wait for the attack. The first group will be small, just to see if you are trapped in the building. They are planning to send a second wave of five hundred men to surround the hillside by your home and they will cut down everyone who gets in their path.

"They aren't planning on stopping this time until they have destroyed you or at least sent a clear message to the people that they are tired of you standing in the way of their business. If your men take out the first small contingent, and then move to an air attack, you'll have the upper hand. The only ones who will be surprised will be their men," Micah finished.

"My intelligence people say I should be more concerned about a pair of hit men from the states posing as CIA trying to lure me away from the safety of my guards."

Micah's fingers itched to go for his guns, but he knew he'd be sentencing both he and David to death if he did. "Your lead intelligence officer, Montoya, was caught trying to send correspondence to the other side; I know he wanted to make sure you didn't listen to us."

"You can call Langley and verify who we are and why we're here—" David began.

"Better yet," Micah interrupted, "if you're thinking this is some kind of trick, we'll take the waiting helicopter. You have plenty of resources at your fingertips, call for your own transportation. Do you have somewhere you can safely wait to find out if we're telling the truth or not?"

"Of course I do, but I wouldn't be foolish enough to tell you where it is," he stated, causing the group of Uzi toting guards to laugh uneasily. The place he bunkered in when trouble arose was not known, and the only reason why he had lasted so long for someone who opposed the drug lords so vehemently.

"Fine," David said, standing and stepping away from the table, "just don't ignore the danger posed to your family. We want to see you to continue to succeed. We'll be at the Habitel Hotel until tomorrow at noon and then we are on a flight to Venezuela."

Micah stood slowly, "One more thing, when this is over with today, you may want to dig a little deeper into your intelligence people. Montoya wasn't alone in his efforts to help the other side and—"

The gentleman stood up and offered his hand to Micah, "I appreciate what appears to be an honest effort here to convince me that there is trouble within my organization, but I'm not even convinced that Montoya is guilty."

Micah accepted the offered hand, gripping it firmly in his right as he clasped the man's jacketed forearm with his left, allowing his hand to slide and pause. "That's the problem with a good liar," Micah stated locking eyes with the man, "he'll make you want to believe he's telling the truth. In a few hours you'll know he's the leak, but when you find that out, I would be suspicious of anyone loyal to Montoya."

"That would prove difficult, because that would be about half my staff."

Micah hesitated, expecting David to shake the hand of the deputy chief, but he was making no effort to make contact. David turned and opened the door and they walked out to the lobby. An attractive Spanish woman who appeared to be in her early thirties rose from the sofa, "Joaquin, what is this about?"

"You must be Mrs. Martinez," David said, extending his hand to her.

She accepted it cautiously, still looking toward her husband.

David clasped his free hand on her shoulder and slid it back and paused. "Nothing to worry you about, I'm sure your husband has this all under control."

It was quite clear that Mr. Martinez did not like David to put his hands on her as he came up and took her arm and turned her away from him, speaking Spanish as he did.

Micah didn't speak more than a few words of Spanish, but David was fluent.

They walked out of the office building and headed for the waiting helicopter. Micah and David boarded as the group watched nervously. The blades came slowly to life, but soon enough they had lifted off and were swooping over the city.

"Did you have any problems getting it off your palm?" Micah asked as they sat in the privacy of the cabin.

"No. I overheard some of the murmurings by the guards that she had arrived and I figured she was a more reliable person to pin it on. How about you?"

"It locked tight on to the sleeve of his jacket." Micah pulled out a silver brief case and opened it up, removing a piece of electronic equipment. He turned it on and watched the small blips on the screen.

"I'd really like to know how the hell the information about us coming down here leaked to Martinez." David growled. "It was beginning to feel like we were setup."

"True, and believe me, I'll be grilling D'Angelo on how that happened, but, for now, it looks like everything is going according to plan."

"Jimenez has twenty of his least valuable men going on the attack. When Martinez realizes we were correct, and that Jimenez is gunning for him, I'm sure he'll take his group into hiding until the guards take care of the insurgence. As soon as we see them on the move, we'll have him and then we can finish this job and get the hell out of here."

Within an hour, David and Micah transferred from the helicopter to a Land Cruiser and were following the tracking signals from the devices they slipped onto Martinez and his wife. The attack happened right on schedule as the guards open fire on the inexperienced fighters.

David captured the radio signals as they informed Martinez the attack happened as the American's predicted. His guard was being mobilized for an air attack. What the fighting forces didn't know was that Jimenez, with the help of a pair of Americans, had already sabotaged their aircraft and a terrible accident was waiting to befall them.

Martinez, his wife and their two sons, the deputy chief and two other officials were on the move with ten of his closest, heavily armed guards. They were going to the bunker until the battle was over and Jimenez and his men had been taught a lesson, again. Unfortunately, Martinez had no idea that he and his wife were bringing the enemy to their door step.

They followed the signal to a village on the outskirts of Bogota and watched from a distance as the group entered a small and seemingly unfortified home nestled against the hillside. Micah was putting grenades in his flak jacket and grabbing the SAG-30 grenade launcher, ready to move from the vehicle when David stopped him.

"They're not in there bro," he said confidently.

"You just tracked them," Micah began, but looked over at the screen. The green blips were on the move; David was right they weren't inside the house. The house was against the hill, so there was no rear exit.

They watched with the slightest amount of amazement as the green flashes continued moving at a semi-fast pace to the left of the screen.

"It's a cave entrance," Micah stated as he pulled his topographical maps up on his computer, "wow, a big cave system, too. We'll have to keep tracking and see if they come out at another house or if they're bunking inside the cave. They must have some type of transport because they're moving too fast to be on foot."

"Nothing gas powered I'm sure. Most likely they have an electric golf cart they use to move everyone quickly." David paused and looked at Micah. "I don't like spelunking, bro. And, we didn't bring the right equipment for going into caves."

"We aren't giving up. We'll give them a little longer and then start driving through the village and see if they come out at another house."

Micah removed the trappings of his jacket and placed it on the floor as they began moving slowly through the town. Several houses were easy to eliminate due to the fact that they didn't rest against the mountain. The blips continued to move as David and Micah looked for what might be a likely exit from the cave. The road turned to the north as it began a gradual rise up the mountain.

"Wait," Micah said, "They're right underneath us. The cave travels under the road and crosses to that..." He was looking up the side of the mountain and could see what appeared to be a large deserted house wedged into the rocks. "I think we just found our bunker."

David drove cautiously down to a small gully to the east as they loaded their gear on their backs and began the careful trek up to the house, ever vigilant for guards that might be hidden along the way. It was becoming apparent that Martinez had felt this house was so obscure that extra guards were unnecessary—a deadly mistake.

When they reached the building, they split up, David traveling up and over to the opposite side as Micah began looking for weaknesses on his side. He found the perfect place to watch through a small window. Within minutes, a door inside the back of the living room opened and the guards emerged cautiously inspecting the house and then motioning Martinez and his officials and family that it was safe to enter.

Micah could tell they were confident in the security of their hideaway as they relaxed and began to move about the house. He felt the soft vibration in his pocket as David signaled he was in place and ready for the invasion whenever Micah signaled back he was ready to attack. He had two options; pull his scoped pistol and take off Martinez's head and be satisfied with making the original target, or use the impact grenade in the launcher and aim for the roof support to the cave opening, effectively collapsing the exit and then cutting down everyone inside. One signal to David would mean making one target. Two signals would mean David should be ready to move inside the house right after the explosion.

Micah didn't respond immediately as he watched Martinez's wife and two young sons move closer to where he was hidden and watching. He placed the impact grenade into the launcher and moved to a place where he could get the best possible shot. His hand went to the button on his phone, as he softly clicked the button once and then again. He steadied his aim and suddenly the quiet hillside reverberated with the explosion in the house.

Micah heard a woman's scream as he vaulted through the window, he drew his fully automatic Glock-18's. He had the special 33 round clips loaded into each gun, but he knew if he wasn't careful he could unload the rounds in a blink of an eye and then would have to pause long enough to draw his two additional Glocks. But that wasn't Micah's style, fully automatic or not, his reactions were so precise that he would control the release of bullets by fractions of seconds. Even under tremendous pressure, he was deadly.

His first priority was the guards. Two were already down from the flying debris from the explosion and collapse and eight more fell to his guns in under two seconds. David was coming in from the other side of the room, taking out the deputy chief and another official. Martinez's hands rose defensively as Micah approached, but they offered no protection as the last of the rounds emptied into him and the remaining man. It had been less than eight seconds and dead men littered the floor.

Micah moved to the bedroom, a fresh Glock in his hand as he looked at the woman trying to cover her children with her body in a corner of the room. He felt the touch of David's hand as he raised his gun.

"We don't have to get this bloody, bro—no women and children today."

He could feel the emptiness draining and a little humanness returning; he didn't want to kill them, but it was an automatic response inside him—responses were something he was going to have to learn to keep under better control. He nodded to David and the gun was re-holstered. He moved to where Martinez's body was laying, grabbing the dead diplomat by the collar and dragging the body out the front door and down the hillside. He was so overloaded on adrenaline and testosterone that it didn't take him long to get to the Land Cruiser. David was already in the driver's seat as Micah threw the body into the back of the vehicle.

An hour later the body of Joaquin Martinez, the most successful Columbian diplomat to ever stem the flow of drugs from the rich fields of this South American country, was found lying in an alleyway in Bogota. A fresh shipment of cocaine was already in route to an awaiting frigate headed for the port of New Orleans.

There was an uneasy feeling that had been filling Micah since this mission had begun and it was becoming increasingly stronger. D'Angelo was up to something bigger than opening the vein of a new source of income. Micah and David had become the instrument by which D'Angelo would start a move for the top, Micah was sure of it. But someone else, whoever it was helping him reach his leadership goals, gave the information about their mission to Martinez. Someone wanted the brothers to make their last stand in Bogota.

It almost worked. He could still feel the pricking of his skin when Martinez exposed his suspicions. His training taught him if all was lost, make your target and accept your fate. It had been fated for him to draw his guns in that room and kill Martinez, but he overcame the urge and outwitted the death sentence. He had other plans to attend to when he returned to the States, but he would find out the answers he needed to this riddle one way or another.

Chapter Seventeen

We made it through the taping of the men's show without Carrie giving me any trouble. I think she was still considering that I met her challenge in a most 'un-princess' like manner on our last go-round. I knew I'd face more problems with her, but the next time she'd calculate her attack a little more carefully.

Sadarius, as I hoped, turned out to be one of the best male singers in the group, and I knew he'd go far in this competition. A couple of the others were good, but he made them look amateurish.

As soon as the taping ended, I found Ryan and got out of there before Carrie could catch up to us. I really didn't feel like a fight tonight, and besides, I wanted to get back to Colorado, back home to our place, a place I'd come to crave as a shelter from the rest of the world. Ryan appeared equally anxious.

Saturday morning I called my realtor, Jan Blakemoore only to discover someone put in an offer to buy the house I planned on leasing.

"It's not a full priced offer," she stated matter-of-factly, "I know you'd been trying to decide between buying or leasing, so if you are really interested in the house we could put in an offer to purchase it."

I wasn't concerned about the price, but more so the commitment I wasn't quite ready to make. "Is there anything else in that general area for lease? I don't think I'm ready to own just yet."

"I'll do a little research and call you back later."

Within thirty minutes my phone was ringing with an excited realtor on the other end. "I found something even better, same neighborhood, but just came on the market this morning—and this one is fully furnished and has a pool."

Ah, magic words to my ears. This time Ryan knew what was going on, so I invited him to come along. He was still against the idea of my moving out, but I could tell he liked the house.

"I'll be over here all the time in your pool anyway," he playfully threatened. "I don't see why you're even moving."

I shot him an annoyed glance. We'd been through this already.

"I love it," I told Jan. "How soon can we take care of the paperwork?"

"The owners will be completely out by next Tuesday, so you're looking at Wednesday or Thursday at the earliest."

"That works for me. I don't have to be in L.A. for another ten days, so I'll have time to get settled in before I'm out of here."

Tuesday, I packed my stuff and was ready to make the move when I got a panicked call from Don.

"We caught up to Bryan Adams. He's in Vancouver and will be flying back to London Thursday night. We've got a plane coming to get you. I need you in Canada by tomorrow morning."

I sighed; moving would have to wait a little bit longer. I could tell Ryan's feelings were a little bruised that he wasn't coming with me to Canada, but I had to start applying the brakes between us. I told him I thought I'd be back sometime Friday evening.

It was a good thing I had gotten a chance to get to know Pete and Jason a little better on the return flight from Tennessee because now at least I didn't feel totally alone. Vancouver was absolutely breathtaking. Once again, I was terrified to meet a legend in the music industry, but, although much quieter and subdued than I thought he'd be, Bryan Adams turned out to be a very inspiring artist.

The song was more difficult than I imagined, but mostly because I wanted to throw all my emotion so hard into it that I was overstressing it. He explained I needed less raw emotion and more control. He said I needed to open my heart without spilling the contents on to the stage.

It took practice to find that balance of control and emotion, but eventually he began to smile as I sang, and I knew I had finally attained what he had been explaining. We sang it as a duet, to each other, just to see if I could hold that control with his accompaniment. That proved to be a real lesson in digging down into the soul. It was as much a lesson on focused emotion as it was in singing, and I was awestruck by the power of the knowledge.

I got to spend a little more time with him just discussing music, the little bit about the show that I was allowed to tell, and what kinds of song choices I was thinking about for future shows, if I made it that far.

He assured me, if I could stay open to suggestions and be willing to stretch myself, I would end up in the finals.

It was five p.m. and I had the choice of staying for the night in Canada or flying home early. I decided to get a night's rest and head back to Colorado in the morning. Pete and Jason followed me around Vancouver for a little while filming me as I did a little shopping (drawing a crowd as they did), when I finally convinced them to turn it off and have dinner with me.

When morning came, I was ready to head home, but the plane wasn't. They had run into a problem with the hydraulics and I was told it would either be charter another plane or give them a day to make the necessary repairs.

"I've got a great idea," Pete had a big smile spread across his bearded face, "Whistler's."

"Yeah, now that would be cool to film, just like we did for the Bachelorette," Jason agreed.

I had no clue what they were talking about, but by the smiles on their faces I wasn't sure if I wanted to know. "What's Whistler's?" I asked, taking another bite of my breakfast.

"It's a town about 75 miles north of here. The Canadian Outback Adventure company does tours out of there. Have you ever traveled on a zip-line or bungee jumped?" Jason asked.

I smiled. They weren't things I had done, but they certainly sounded like something I'd love to try, "No, but I'm game."

Pete laughed, "Somehow I had a feeling you would be."

"Is that good or bad?"

"It's good," Jason answered for Pete, reaching over and giving my shoulder a squeeze. "Pete and I were discussing you not long after we got back from Tennessee, and we decided you're someone who loves life and never backs down from a challenge."

"Well, I'm only going around this world once, so why not live a little while I'm here."

Of course, that statement was a little harder to follow through with when I was standing on a platform a hundred and sixty feet in the air and ready to plunge through a forest down a mountainside on a thin metal cable. They had rigged it so that Pete would be following a hundred feet or so behind me on the cable filming my experience through the trees as Jason stood at the landing area with another camera to capture my arrival. This would have been something Ryan would have dearly loved to do, and just before I stepped off into air, I wished I had brought him along.

It felt like I was literally flying through the trees, with the only sound (besides my initial scream) being the sound of the equipment sliding over the metal cable. Pete told me to feel free to ham-it-up on the zip-line, so seconds after launching I went arabesque and then (praying the whole time the guy who hooked me up was telling me the truth about what I could do) I flipped upside down, flying head first over the river. I righted myself as I neared the landing, I could hear the cable brakes being applied and my 50 mile-per-hour flight was coming to an end.

"That was freaking awesome!" I yelled to Jason as they were unhooking me. Just then Pete arrived, laughing about my reaction to the adventure.

"Okay, Leese, are you ready to go bungee jumping?"

I nodded enthusiastically, my throat at the moment too dry for words.

We made it to the bungee jumping site and I had to admit this was a hundred times more frightening than flying down a cable. This was like suicide with a safety net, "I honestly don't know if I can do this," I admitted, trying to worm my way out of diving off the bridge.

"Come on, Leese, you'll love it. Give it a try."

"Oh, really? Have you ever jumped, Jason?"

"As a matter of fact, yes, I have."

"Great. You do it first and then I'll do it."

"I'll go you one better, I'll do it with you."

Worry shot through my mind. If I wasn't sure that I trusted (basically) a giant rubber band to save me from a smashing death, did I really trust it to hold two of us from diving to our demise?

"You're always in the palm of God's hand, Leese, no matter where you are," Pete added.

He was right, and my confidence re-bloomed.

Jason and I were tethered to a giant bungee line as we moved cautiously out onto the tiny platform. I was shivering uncontrollably, not so much from the cool air, but from terror. Jason wrapped me in his arms and asked if I was ready. It was at that moment I realized he might have ulterior motives for volunteering. He wasn't much older than me and he certainly seemed to enjoy an opportunity to body-hug me.

"Okay?" Jason asked.

Before I could open my mouth, he had pushed off from the platform and we were swan-diving to the shallow river below. I know my scream was piercing, but I didn't close my eyes as the earth rushed up to greet us. Suddenly I felt the tension in the line and our decent slowed as we neared the water. I stretched my arms over my head to try to reach it, but we were a couple feet shy of being close enough to get wet. The line pulled us back skyward and then sent us, once more gently toward the river.

I was laughing and crying at the same time. What an adventure Canada was turning out to be.

Jason was only laughing, but still holding me tightly as we dangled upside down. "Want to do it alone now?"

"No. Once was enough of a thrill. You guys are just going to have to show this with you in it. I'm done."

I could tell at that moment he wasn't going to mind being in the clip.

The plane was repaired by night fall, but they wanted to run a couple more tests and said we would take off about four a.m. We landed in Colorado at around eight in the morning as I told the guys goodbye and jumped into my Aero and headed home. I couldn't wait to pounce on the bed and wake Ryan and tell him what I had done.

I pulled up to the house and didn't bother to grab my bag. I was going to be loading the car for the new house in a few hours anyway, but I had to tell my adventure to him before I exploded.

I unlocked the door and headed straight for his bedroom, surprised that his door was nearly closed. He never closed his door. I could see his arm hanging off the side of the bed in what appeared to be in an unnatural position. Panic gripped me. I had the sudden feeling something was horribly wrong. My heart was lunging against my breastbone as I softly called his name and gave the door a gentle push.

The sight that greeted me froze me to the earth. It was not at all what I had feared to find—and for a jealous split second it was almost worse. He was asleep in the tangled bedding—with Candace.

The air caught in my throat as his sleepy face raised my direction. He tried to right himself in the bed, but she had crowded him too close to the edge and he fell out onto the floor—stark naked.

"Ah, shit!" I exclaimed, turning swiftly and then clamping my hand on my mouth over the remark. I jerked his door closed and headed for the front door.

"Leese, don't go," I heard his voice as I gripped the door knob.

"I'll—I'll be—back—I just can't…" I went out the door and jumped into my car; I was so dumbfounded I just simply drove without thinking.

I wanted him to find someone, someone who could mean to him what Micah meant to me, but why did it hit me so hard? If I could have Micah back right at this very moment, would I turn and leave Ryan without a second thought? I knew I would.

How could I be so selfish? He needed someone who could give him everything I couldn't, and I should be happy for them both. Then there was the embarrassing moment of seeing him nude. I was trying to stop seeing it inside my head and suddenly the humor of the whole thing hit me and I began to laugh. I was flying in there to tell him about my 'great' adventure and instead stumbled on to what had been his great adventure.

I turned the car around and drove to the bistro and bought breakfast for three and then drove the two blocks back to the house. My hands were shaking so badly I hoped I wouldn't spill the coffee before I got it inside to the table.

Just as I reached the door, he opened it for me. His face was deep red and I had to do my best not to look at him at the moment. Candace was sitting on the sofa in his tee-shirt and a pair of underwear. I didn't particularly care to see her dressed that way. She was taking a little too much liberty in what was, at least until I took my bags out of the house today, still me and Ryan's place. I ignored her attire and asked if they were hungry.

"Starving, actually," she spoke up, following me to the table.

I wanted to say, 'yeah, sex will do that to an appetite,' but I kept my mouth shut.

"So, how was Canada?" he asked, pulling out a chair for me.

"I really wish I'd brought you along," I blurted, not thinking that it would sound like I wanted to prevent what occurred between the two of them. "I—I—mean the plane had hydraulic problems and…"

I could see a worried expression come over his face at the mention of airplane trouble.

"Anyway," I continued, "Pete and Jason talked me into a day of adventure; I went down a mountain on a zip-line at about fifty miles an hour, and then Jason and I went bungee jumping."

"Bungee jumping?" Ryan raised an eyebrow at the same moment a little crooked grin appeared on his face.

"It was terrifying," I confessed. "You'd have loved it. So—Candace—you must have stayed the night," I said trying to keep the little quiver out of my voice. "You must be playing hooky today."

"No," she laughed. "It's a record day, so I don't have anything to do until three when I go into work."

"Oh," was all I could come up with.

"I'm going to go take a shower," she said, drinking the last of her coffee and rising from the table. "Do you want to take one with me?" she reached over and was tugging Ryan's hand toward the bedroom.

I could see the look of indecision on his face. He was debating about being a gentleman while I was in the house, or giving in to what Candace wanted at the moment.

"Go ahead," I said, hoping to help with his decision. "I've got stuff to pack up anyway."

Reluctantly, he allowed himself to be led away. I wanted to scream at myself for being such a jealous idiot, but I would have to settle for grabbing my bags and throwing them into my car. I was slinging them around with enough force to make up for not being able to scream.

Candace, on the other hand, was having no problem getting vocal in the other room. The more she screamed and moaned, the less I could take. I finally had enough. I grabbed my keys and made the first run to my new house. I fit everything except two bags into my car, but I wasn't going to bother to go back for them until well after three p.m. Consciously or unconsciously, she was flaunting the fact that he belonged to her now.

I called Jan and she told me the combo to the lockbox on the house and then she told me my new alarm code. I pulled up to the large craftsman style, two-story home. The house was a gray-brown stone façade with beautiful white columns framing in the front porch. They had done extensive landscaping and flowers lined the flagstone path up to the front door.

It was certainly bigger than anything one person needed with just over three thousand square feet and three bedrooms and three and a half baths. The upper story was a huge bonus area the family had turned into a game room. There was a billiard table, dart board, bar, ping pong table and even two full-size antique video arcade machines. One game was Centipede and the other was Pac-man. The pool was not excessively large, but more than sufficient for laps and there was an eight person built in spa that flowed into the pool. It had an outdoor kitchen and barbeque on the pool patio. This was definitely a party house, but I was a party of one.

After turning off the alarm and finding the remote to the garage, I pulled my car inside and drug my bags into the house. It was funny for them to seem so heavy now that I wasn't running on all the embarrassed energy that filled me while Ryan and Candace showered.

I got as far as the living room with the bags and flopped onto the couch. "It's okay, Leese," I said out loud, "you can cry now." I rolled over onto the pillow and began to sob.

I woke to the sound of a doorbell. For a stunned moment, I didn't know where I was. I stumbled toward the door, glancing at the time on my cell phone as I did. It was three-thirty. I approached the door cautiously, expecting to see Jan's petite figure through the stippled glass, but it was a man. I was pretty certain from the height and the darkness of the hair that it was Ryan. I looked through the peek-hole and he was there holding my last two bags.

I opened the door, but he stood there sheepishly, waiting for me to invite him inside.

"Hey," was all I could manage.

"When I realized you weren't coming back for these, I figured you might be waiting for someone to leave."

"Yeah, I guess it kind of sucker-punched me in the gut. I mean, I'm happy for you—both of you, I just didn't think it would be that hard to take."

"Candace didn't help matters any," he admitted.

"Well, I can't say I blame her. You are pretty much the catch of the century, especially when all those clips of you come out on Remake."

He rolled his eyes and stepped inside, "Where would you like me to…" His eyes went to the other bags lying on the living room floor. "Which bedroom are you sleeping in? I'll carry all these for you."

I showed him the master bedroom, grateful for him to move the bags for me.

"So did you bring your shorts?" I asked, pointing toward the pool.

He grinned and grabbed for the buttons on his button-fly jeans; two buttons undone and I could see his trunks.

I had to ask, "Did Candace know you were coming over?"

"Yeah, she did, but I swear now that she and I have… Well, let's say she's more insecure over me being around you than before. I finally had to tell her to just get a grip because you and I are still best friends."

"Well, don't get into fights with her over me," I said, clearly shocked she was still concerned about he and I stepping over a line.

"We aren't going to fight about it. She's just going to have to accept it."

I smiled, "You want to go ahead and get in the pool while I get my bikini on?"

He gave me the most unusual look. I had never seen that expression on his face before and I couldn't quite understand it. He turned and headed for the patio as I went into the bedroom to find my bathing suit and robe. It wasn't until I joined him poolside that the realization hit me I'd never worn a bikini in front of him.

Suddenly, I knew what the look on his face was reflecting. There were no secrets anymore. Ryan was a man who knew the intimacies of being with a woman and I was getting ready to get close to him with very little clothing on. Micah had given me a similar look as he waited for me the first time we swam together.

"This isn't going to get weird between us, is it?" I asked as he waited.

"Leese, I honestly don't think there has been anything between us that hasn't been weird since we met. You were an heiress in hiding, a hit man was getting ready to steal you away, you end up marrying him, I end up running away with you, we love each other but we can't make love, you work on hooking me up with an old flame, and now here we are, alone again—we are about as weird as it gets, baby girl."

I had to laugh. He was absolutely right. I pulled off the robe and dove in.

He caught me pretty quickly and I surprised him by hugging his neck and kissing his cheek. "Well, at least we're happy weirdoes."

"All right, so tell me what bungee jumping was like," he said with curiosity.

"I should have had you with me instead of Jason. They tied our legs—"

"You jumped with him—I mean, literally tied to him?"

"Yeah, he hugged me so tightly that—"

"Like embracing each other?"

I wrinkled my brow, "Don't tell me you're jealous," I teased.

"Baby girl, you are too innocent when it comes to men. Don't be so trusting because some guys have all the wrong intentions."

"I don't typically get that close to a man, but I was terrified to jump alone."

"Did you go head first?"

"Yeah, and, at first, you can't feel the bungee and it's like 'I'm gonna die, I just know it.'"

"It sounds like you had a great time."

"I—I did. So how was your—adventure?"

"Terrifying," he laughed, "at first, but after I got over my heart feeling like it was going to jump out of my chest, and then remembering to breathe, it was pretty awesome."

I wanted so badly to ask him something he asked me once, but I was struggling to get it out and he noticed.

"What?"

"Nothing."

"I can see it in your face, baby girl. You want to know something; just say it."

I grinned slowly, "So are you a rock star?"

The eyebrows went up as he grabbed me by my head and dunked me.

I came up spluttering as he laughed and said according to Candace, he was.

"So that means you have to answer the same question, because you never told me last time."

I took a deep breath, "He was the rock star, but he did say he'd never experienced anything like me." I caught and wiped the tear as it blended into the pool water on my cheek.

"That doesn't surprise me," he sighed. "I think you would be so different from Candace—she's fun, but she acts her age. But you? I have a feeling you would give a whole different dimension to making love."

"Let's swim, before we get too deep."

The rest of the afternoon we lightened up and enjoyed ourselves. I invited him to bring Candace, Andy, and Ty back to the house tonight for steaks on the grill, fun in the game room, and pool. He kissed my cheek and said he'd be back in several hours. I went to the local grocery store and did some serious shopping and came back to the house and got everything ready.

Candace didn't get off work until nine, so I didn't expect company until nine-thirty or ten. They showed right at ten p.m.

"You really need to be my girlfriend," Ty said teasingly after getting a tour of the house.

The guys grilled while Candace and I tossed a salad and cut potatoes to brown in the convection oven. It gave us a chance to talk as I asked her if she was happy.

Her eyes went huge as she smiled, "Who wouldn't be? He's about as perfect as perfect gets. I just hope he likes me half as much."

"Candace, don't worry about him—he never would have—"

"Yeah, I know, but I may have pushed him a little hard on that issue."

"Still, if he didn't want to, he would have found an excuse. Don't doubt yourself; he's crazy about you."

She giggled and thanked me for the vote of confidence.

It was a little wild after we all got down to bathing suits and jumped into the pool, but Candace and I survived all the testosterone and flexing.

Once everyone left and I locked the house and set the alarm, I got to try my wings out at being alone—really alone. I hated it. Within an hour, I was ready to jump in my car and drive back to our little place in the historic district, but I knew what I'd walk in on and I simply couldn't handle that. I laid down in the silence, but it was driving me crazy. I finally got up and found the stereo and turned on the music and went back to bed. Drowning out the silence was preferred, but I still couldn't sleep. Somewhere around five in the morning, I slipped into unconsciousness. Two hours later, I was having coffee and watching the morning sky, ripple across the hills.

I didn't see Ryan and Candace until late Saturday evening when they came over to swim, but I could tell Ryan was studying my face. I knew he wanted to corner me and ask how I slept last night, but I made sure he didn't get the opportunity.

Saturday night was no better and I simply couldn't, no matter the exhaustion level, get to sleep. I went out and did laps in the pool until I was so weak I could hardly drag myself from the water, but within an hour of dozing off, I was awake again. This was driving me insane. Before I met Micah, I didn't have trouble sleeping. After Micah, it was as if my ability to close my eyes stayed with him when I ran away.

I met Ryan and Candace for church, but I had to use extra makeup to cover the dark circles that were starting to form under my eyes. I had to get some sleep tonight because I was flying out Tuesday for L.A. and at the rate I was going I would never be able to perform. I was going to have to break down and buy a bottle of sleeping pills.

I went to the pharmacy after church and found an over-the-counter sleep aid and went home. I took two pills and laid down for a nap, I knew I'd have no trouble drifting off, but it was staying that way I needed help with. I woke two and a half hours later. They helped but now I was lethargic and unwilling to get up even though I was awake. I stayed on the couch for another hour and then got up and trudged around the house with no ambition to do anything. Ty, Andy, Ryan, and Candace showed a little bit later as we played pool and darts and they tried to talk me in to going out with them to the bistro.

"Nah, not tonight. I've got to get a good night's sleep. I'm heading out for L.A. early Tuesday morning."

Since it was only Sunday night they couldn't understand my dilemma, but I knew Ryan did. He sent them out to the car to wait for him as he finally asked me the question I'd been dreading.

"Are you sleeping?"

"I will be after you get out of here," I dodged.

"Leese, there isn't enough makeup in Colorado to hide those dark circles under your eyes. How about if I talk Candace into letting me—"

"Absolutely not! She's insecure enough when it comes to you, I don't need to send her over the edge. Besides, I bought some sleeping pills today and I managed a decent nap, so they should work for tonight, too."

"Prescription?"

"No, just some over-the-counter stuff—they helped, honest."

"I'm coming over after she leaves for school in the morning, and—"

"Is she—is she living with you now?"

His head wobbled slightly as if he didn't have enough neck muscle to hold it up, "I—yeah, okay, she is. Her dad is really pissed at both of us, but she said she can't stand being away from me."

"So how are you sleeping?" I asked, remembering how I found him the first time they slept together.

"Can you keep a secret?"

I leveled my eyes at him.

"Sorry, I know you can keep a secret—she's a bed hog. You always lie so still and let me cuddle you. She is like all over the place. I think I've got like twenty bruises where she elbows me or kicks me. I've fallen out of the bed at least twice."

"Maybe I should give you some of my sleeping pills so you can knock her out and make her be still," I said with a sleep-deprived giggle.

He kissed my forehead and told me to try for sleep, but he would still see me in the morning—early.

Once the house was locked up tight and the alarm was set, I took three of the sleeping pills and went to bed. It was just after nine when sleep hit me. One a.m., I rolled over wide awake—crap! I tried to go back to sleep, considered more pills, but to tell the truth, I was afraid to keep taking them.

When sleepy-faced Ryan showed at eight thirty, I could tell he needed sleep as badly as I did. He had to be home before two-thirty, so I set the alarm and he and I crawled into my bed, comfortable and secure in each other's hold. It seemed I barely allowed my eyes to close as five hours passed dreamlessly.

"It can't be time to get up," he moaned behind me.

"Thank you," I whispered.

He leaned forward and kissed my neck, "I just wish there was some way I could get over here tonight so you won't be dead-dog-tired Tuesday."

"I've got an idea. Can I have your shirt?"

"You mean like literally right off my back?"

"Yeah, I'm going to wrap a pillow with your shirt so I can still smell you."

"Do you really think that'll work?"

"Hey, it's worth a try. Besides, I like the way you smell. But you'd better hurry home or Candace is going to wonder why you're pulling in shirtless."

"As long as I come home with my pants on, she should be happy," he teased as he pulled off his shirt and gave it to me.

"Bye, baby girl," he said, kissing my temple, "I love you."

And he was gone.

Chapter Eighteen

I flew to L.A. early the next morning and was in studio for my rehearsals by noon. I could see the surprise on a lot of the faces when I appeared without my ebony-haired shadow, but I simply told those bold enough to ask that he stayed in Colorado this time. Carrie was probably the most disappointed, but she didn't let it stop her from being a thorn in my side. I was too tired to fight with her, so she pretty much walked over me, which delighted her to no end.

One of the stage crew, Thomas, who usually had to play bouncer between us noticed and asked me if I was okay. I thought it was nice of him, but I didn't want to get too personal so I simply told him I hadn't gotten much sleep over the last several days.

"Do you have anything to help you go to sleep?" he questioned, looking around to make certain no one was listening to us.

"Yeah, I picked up some Unisom at—"

He gave a small laugh, "That isn't going to help much. I meant some real sleeping pills."

"No, I haven't gone to a doctor if that's what you—"

"Well, you're lucky because the doctor is in the house." He reached into his pocket and produced a small bag of blue capsules. He removed one and pressed it into my hand. "Take that when you get back to your hotel and I guarantee you'll sleep eight to ten hours no problem."

I tried to hand it back to him, but he insisted I keep it.

"If it works, then you can lay a little money in my hand and I'll get you a bottleful."

I could see there was no use in arguing with him as I slipped the pill into my pocket, intent on throwing it away when I got out of the building.

Rehearsal went well and it seemed every time I sang the song, I improved my performance. Melissa, Melanie, and Dobrey invited me to join them for dinner in the hotel restaurant after we finished practice; I was grateful to accept. Anything was better than simply sitting around in my hotel room and waiting for bedtime, so I could sit around wide awake until sunrise.

We were a definite odd blend, the play bunnies, the philanthropist, and the heiress, but we had no trouble relating to one another. The twins wanted to know immediately where my handsome boyfriend was hiding.

"He's actually just a really good friend—my best friend," I said, sipping my ice water.

"You're kidding," Melanie exclaimed wide-eyed, "You mean he's not your boyfriend—*he's available*?"

I laughed, "No, he has a girlfriend, it's just not me." I watched her deflate.

"That sucks," Melissa added. "I mean, it's cool that you two are friends, but he is so hot I don't know how you could take just being friends."

"He is nice looking," Dobrey spoke up with a light smile, "but, personally, I like his attitude better than any of the guys here, other than perhaps Sadarius."

The twins looked at each other and giggled, "Sadarius is a gentleman." Melissa winked at her sister, "He's kind of shy, too—until you get him alone."

"Maybe they should make Ryan a contestant for next season," Dobrey suggested, trying to avoid the lip-licking look the twins were giving each other over Sadarius.

Now it was my turn to laugh, "They could put him on one of the dance shows, but that boy *cannot* sing."

We were just about to place our order when Sadarius and Rashad entered the room, waiting to be seated. The twins wasted no time in excusing themselves from our company and scampering over to invite themselves to dine with the men.

"Those girls certainly take the title of play bunny seriously," I joked with Dobrey.

"Those two? You and Ryan haven't stayed around here to watch them go after the guys. Sadarius seems to be their particular target, but Rashad, I guess, makes it a little easier for them to share."

We spent the rest of the evening getting to know one another and I found Dobrey to be fascinating. She had been born in Scotland, the daughter of very wealthy land owners. She came to America when she was still a baby. She said her family owns an actual castle in Scotland and she said she often goes back when she wants to recharge her life.

"That sounds wonderful. The Good Lord knows my life could use some serious recharging about now."

"I'm going there for at least a week while we're on break. I'd love some company, if you'd like to join me," she offered.

I gave a quick thought about my wonderful sleeping buddy who now had regular plans to visit me while Candace was at school. "No, I'm afraid I have trouble sleeping when I'm away from home."

"That's what it is," Dobrey exclaimed as she gave me a harder look. "I wondered what was different about you today, and it's got to be that you're tired."

"Is it really that obvious?"

"I'm afraid so. I think everyone is assuming something happened between you and Ryan, but I had a feeling it was something else."

"I'm exhausted and going somewhere to recharge sounds wonderful, but I bet when this show airs in a couple weeks, none of us are going to get any rest. We'll have more attention than anyone would want—except for perhaps Melissa and Melanie. I can't imagine taking off my clothes and letting someone take pictures of me for a million guys to view."

Dobrey giggled, "Me neither. But, I have several very private places to retreat if the press gets too bad. If you ever need a place to go, I have a fabulous cottage in northern California set on a massive hill overlooking the Pacific. No neighbors, no television, no telephone, just miles and miles of view, and peace and quiet."

I gave a huge sigh, "That sounds like heaven."

"And," she added, "you're guaranteed to get a good night's sleep. I don't know what it is about the air coming off the cold ocean water, but you go to bed under a thick down comforter and it's like tucking a baby in a cradle."

"I might take you up on that sometime."

"Anytime," she said, reaching into her purse. She handed me a business card. "That's my cell number. You call me whenever you need it and it will be available."

We finished our meal and talked a little bit about me. She asked if what the press reported about me actually being married and then running away with Ryan was true. I told her things weren't as they seemed. He was, I assured her, just a friend.

"Is your husband actually mafia?" she asked quietly.

The tabloids left many people thinking the stories had been greatly stretched, but for once much of the outrageous things they printed about me were close to correct.

"He was—I mean he is again, but…" I thought about mentioning the annulment, but I couldn't. It felt like such a long time since I had been overcome with these deep emotions. I set down my fork and picked up my dinner napkin and dabbed my eyes.

"I'm sorry. That's really none of my business."

"No, it's okay, I just can't talk about it right now."

We finished our meal and ended our evening as good friends. She gave me a firm hug and reminded me whenever I wanted a little time away from the world, to give her a call.

I found the little blue capsule in my pocket when I undressed for bed. I set it on the night stand, and stared at it for a few moments. It was stamped by Lilly so I knew it wasn't some kind of illegal drug cooked up in someone's back room, but I was still afraid to even consider trying it.

I tossed and turned, and by sunrise I had garnered perhaps an hour's worth of sleep. I had to get some rest. I had to be in studio by four p.m. and ready to perform in front of an audience by six. I dug through my bag and pulled out the box of over-the-counter sleeping pills, popped two out of the foil and swallowed them down and returned to bed. I managed two more hours of sleep and at least another hour of drowsy stupor. I pulled Ryan's tee-shirt out of a zipper bag and placed it on a pillow and hugged it tightly. Relaxation hit me as I inhaled his sweet fragrance. I wasn't sure what exactly he used, I knew it was one of those body sprays, but whatever it was it began to lull me until I drifted off for another hour and then someone coming loudly down the hotel hallway woke me. That was it. I was going to have to be happy with what I'd gotten and hope my performance didn't suffer too badly.

Everything went well during the taping. I had, gratefully, drawn the first slot of the night to perform. That was fine with me because the sooner I got off stage the better. The judges were very impressed with my remake of the song, '*Everything I do*,' and said they were seeing tremendous growth in me already.

"Our next show will be themed for pop music and I hope you continue to pick songs that are challenging because I believe we've only scratched the surface of your potential. Good job, tonight. Great way to start the evening," the most critical judge told me before I exited the stage.

I sat with the other contestants and watched the remaining performances. There were nine of us left and by the end of the night the judges would cut another three women. The three choices didn't surprise me, but they certainly surprised one of those cut from the show. They cut Carrie, and she was livid. She told the judges they didn't know what they were talking about. She said she had more potential than any of the other contestants. They disagreed. And, after giving everyone a vocabulary lesson in vulgarity, she stormed off the stage.

This was one time I was glad Ryan wasn't here. She was out for blood as she came backstage, pitching what amounted to a tantrum as she tipped over equipment and threw whatever she could get her hands on.

"And you," she said, pointing an angry finger in my direction, "you suck as a singer! You're just a spoiled little rich girl—a whore that ran off on her husband, and that's the only reason you're on the show!"

I was in no condition to challenge her over the remarks so I decided to let them roll over me. But, several of the guys decided she needed to stop as she got closer to me during the tirade. Sadarius, Rashad, and Lexington all got up from their seats and blocked her attempt to get near me.

They were telling her she needed to calm down, but that only agitated her further. The cameras were rolling and I hated the fact that all of this was going to make it on television. She finally seemed to relent, almost to the point of tears as she turned away from the group.

The line between us parted as Sadarius attempted to comfort her over being cut from the show. He was being impossibly kind as he spoke to her, but in a flash she turned and flew right at me. It had been a ploy to open a path. My reaction time was off as I missed blocking her swing and her fist smacked hard against my left cheekbone. I had never been punched in the face before, and I reeled backward, caught by Melanie and Melissa before I hit the chair behind me.

I was stunned for a moment, but the anger and adrenaline drown out my lethargy as I swung with a round-house kick straight to the side of her head and she hit the floor motionless.

I wiped the blood from the corner of my lip as I watched the crew roll her over and set her upright. I knocked her out cold, but she was coming around. Sadarius and Rashad got on either side of me and escorted me away before she made it to her feet.

"Sorry," Sadarius was saying softly, "I didn't have a clue she was playing me."

"That's okay," I tried to say, but my jaw felt funny. "Man that hurt." I reached up and placed my cool palm against my throbbing cheek.

Rashad laughed, "Yeah, well I think you definitely got in the better hit. She's gonna feel that one for days."

They took me back to the stage crew's kitchen area and found a plastic baggie and some ice for my cheek.

"Here," Sadarius said, as he wrapped the bag in a piece of cloth and placed it against the tender place on my face, "This'll make it feel better in a little while."

Don was there in a flash asking if I was okay. "She didn't break anything, did she? Does the jaw feel okay?"

"Shit, man," Rashad snapped, "the girl gets punched in the face and you sound like all you're worried about is if her mouth is okay so she can still sing. Why don't you just ask her if she's okay and leave it at that?"

Don ignored him as he gently pulled my hand holding the ice pack on my cheek away. "That's going to leave a bruise. There is a medic on the way in here to look at you and—"

"I'm okay," I said, knowing that nothing had broken (except a little bit of my pride).

By the time the evening ended, and Carrie had been removed from the building, Sadarius walked me to the hotel. I could tell he still felt really bad about the fact he'd let his guard down long enough for her to get to me, but it wasn't his fault.

The distance to the hotel was less than a block, but it gave us a chance to talk. I was mostly interested in his rise to fame when he came upon a home invasion and ended up taking on three armed intruders to save a family he didn't even know. He was extremely modest about what he did, but he said the press made such a big deal about it he ended up on several talk shows telling about his adventure, and then he was approached to tryout for Remake.

"What do you mean tryout? Didn't they just come and invite you?"

"Nah, I had to prove I could sing first. You know that, everyone had to audition at some point."

I remembered the day Don appeared in Colorado Springs and all he wanted to know was *if* I could sing. I never sang a note for him until my first time in front of an audience. That was a little strange, and I knew I'd have to ask some of the other contestants to find out if what Sadarius was telling me was true. If so, then why did I seemingly get special privilege?

Even though Thursday was a free day, I spent it trying to recoup from a lack of sleep Wednesday night. The sore jaw didn't help my efforts and I ended up with zero sleep time. It must have been near twelve noon when I finally relented, reached over and grabbed the blue capsule and reluctantly swallowed it.

When I opened my eyes it was one p.m. and I didn't figure that stupid pill did much good other than make me have to pee like I'd drunk a quart of water. I was woozy as I made my way to the bathroom to relieve my bladder. At least the one hour's sleep left me feeling rested. I flipped on the television and watched some news when I noticed something in the corner of the screen that caught my attention; the date. What? I grabbed up my cell phone and stared at the display. It was Friday, and I had slept twenty-five hours!

"Ah crap!" I said jumping out of the bed. I was scheduled in the studio in three hours! I rushed through my shower, and dressed. I was absolutely starving, but that was understandable since I'd missed a day's worth of food. I went down to the restaurant and had a late lunch and then started out the lobby for the studio. Sadarius was heading out at the same time and offered to walk with me. I honestly think he was worried Carrie may have lingered in town and would be lying in wait to jump me or run me over.

"I tried calling you yesterday. I was going to see if you wanted to hang out for a little while, but you never answered."

"No, believe it or not, I slept through yesterday."

"Wow, that punch in the jaw must have been a little harder than I thought."

"Yeah," I agreed, the light purple bruise was still on my face under my makeup, but I wasn't about to tell him the punch wasn't what put me down for the day.

Thomas found me not long after I got to the studio and privately asked me if I tried his sleep-aid.

I scowled, "I slept an entire day!"

"But how do you feel today?" he continued, unaffected by the fact that I had an extended rest.

"Well, I feel great, but—"

"You don't have to take them all the time, just when you really got to get some sleep. I brought you a bottle of them, but they aren't cheap. Do you have five on you?"

"Five dollars?"

"No," he laughed lightly, "Five hundred dollars—and that's cheap."

"I really don't think I'd want to take another—"

"Ah, come on, girl. You don't know all the trouble I went through to score this bottle for you. I'm already out the money and I've got rent to pay and—"

"All right, all right," I said to get him to shut up. "But I never told you to put yourself out to do this for me."

"I know, but I figured you looked like you could use some rest, you know."

I opened my purse as Thomas unabashedly peered inside while I pulled out five, one-hundred dollar bills. I still had a considerable amount of cash I had not re-deposited, and I realized it was foolish to carry it around, but I would eventually get it to the bank.

He produced an unlabeled prescription bottle and dropped it into my purse, "Nice doin' business with you, Leese. You let me know when you need some more, but five hundred was the cheap price. If we do this again it'll be eight-hundred."

"Trust me; I won't be doing this again."

He gave me a strange smile as he stuffed the cash into his pocket and simply said, "We'll see."

I felt absolutely dirty after the transaction, like I needed to go back to the hotel and shower. And, having a bottle of pills inside my purse was unnerving me. It was almost like having to carry a gun to dinner so very long ago. We each had a locker area and I secured my bag and went to make-up for my touch up and to see if they could do a better job of hiding the bruise on my cheek.

The doors opened as the music played, each of us taking our turn to wave to the camera as they panned over us. The men gave their performances and three more were cut. We were all brought out on stage during the last five minutes of the show so they could recap who made it to the final twelve.

For the women, it was Kitkat, Dobrey, Melanie and Melissa (who did everything as a duet so they counted as one person), Nicole, Shana and me. For the guys, it was Sadarius, Lexington, Rashad, Todd, Allen and Pierce.

The commercials letting the American public know about the new series had been running, but in a few days they would give the public glimpses of who made it as contestants. I would have to call Mom tomorrow and let her know what was getting ready to happen because she had no idea I had been doing this.

The shows would begin airing in two weeks, but the first four were taped so we'd have almost a month off. We were all backstage getting ready to go our separate ways when I started asking about how the other women auditioned for the show. I was shocked to learn everyone had to prove they could sing before they earned their spot in the original twenty-four contestants. I never told them I didn't have to audition, but the fact that I appeared to be separated from the other contestants was starting to worry me.

I had the option to stay the night or fly home; I opted for home. It was after one in the morning before I pulled into the driveway. Once again, I was exhausted, but couldn't sleep. I pulled out the bottle of capsules and opened it up, pouring the contents into my hand; there were twenty pills. I wasn't about to take another one and end up missing another day of my life, but I would keep them just in case. I placed them in my nightstand by the bed, lay down and watched the clock tick by.

I dozed before dawn and then got up and headed into town to the farmer's market. I drove past my once happy home, knowing that Ryan and Candace were probably still sound asleep, unless she had to work today, but that was unlikely since her car and the Javelin were both parked in the drive. I picked up my fresh fruits and veggies and headed back home, noticing their cars were missing when I went past the house the second time.

I turned onto my street fifteen minutes later and could see his car was in my driveway. My cell phone was going off. "Hello, Ryan," I answered, slowing my approach.

"When are you getting back in town? I was kind of thinking it would be today."

"They extended our taping for another few days so I won't be back until next week," I teased and then pulled in behind him.

"Very funny, Leese," he said and the line went dead as he stepped out of the car.

He came over to help carry in my produce when he got a look at my face. "Ah, Crap—what happened? Did that witch club you?" he said as he inspected the tender place gently with his fingertips.

"Yeah, she got cut from the show and went ballistic."

"I knew I should have gone with you!"

"It's okay. She managed one good punch before I knocked her out."

He started laughing, "You mean like honest-to-God knocked her out?"

"I caught her with a round house to the side of the head and she dropped like a rock."

"How did you manage to miss blocking the punch? You're usually pretty good at that."

"My reactions were a little slow," I admitted.

"No sleep, huh? Come on, baby girl, that's what I'm here for. Candace has a full shift today, nine to five and I need the rest as much as you do."

It was so great to be home.

I called Mom the next day and told her about the television show. She was excited, but (knowing how much I disliked public attention) surprised I did it. I told her I'd really like to see them, but I wasn't ready for all the emotions of coming home, even if it was only for a few days. She offered for her and Kimmy to come visit me and I quickly accepted, telling her I had plenty of room. She didn't ask about Ryan, but I knew her well enough to know that she had begun to accept the idea that I knew what I was doing, no matter how much she or anyone else for that matter, didn't.

The weather the next day was overcast, and, before I left to go pick them up from the airport, snow began floating to earth. When we got back to the house the snowfall had become steady. Kimmy was happy to see me, but I think she was truly happiest to see the snow. She had seen snow twice before but she was too little to remember it very well, so this was like a whole new experience. She went out in the yard and began collecting handfuls of it and started making a very small snow man as Mom and I watched from the window.

It didn't take long, just the two of us inside the house, before she began cautiously asking me questions about what happened that caused me to run from Micah.

"I don't believe it was Ryan—he was just an excuse, not the reason. I'd really like to know, and I won't say anything to David," she added.

"I can't tell you."

"Was Micah—was he abusive or did he do—"

"No—he was perfect—it was me."

"So where is Ryan?" she asked. "Or did he leave because I'm here."

"If I tell you something you can't tell David, Micah, or anyone in his family."

She nodded.

"Ryan doesn't live here," I sighed. I didn't dare tell her we weren't lovers; I simply left that subject alone. Ryan was planning on making an appearance each day, but I already told him he didn't have to go so far as to come over and sleep with me.

I could see the surprise written all over her face, "You mean he's not living here while we're here. David said you two were—"

"No, I mean he really doesn't live here."

"But, Leese, this is a big house and you expect me to believe that you are living here all alone?"

"That's the truth."

"I don't like you being alone," she said honestly.

I wanted to tell her I didn't like it much myself, but it would only serve to worry her. "Just do me a favor when he comes over, don't treat him like an outsider. None of this is his fault."

"Do you love him, Leese?"

I sighed, "Yeah, actually I do."

"More than Micah?"

"I hate to tell you how screwed up your daughter is, but I'm in love with both of them—what I feel for Micah is just a little bit stronger."

She came up behind me and wrapped me in her arms, kissing the side of my head, "Your cheek looks bruised," she whispered. "There isn't something going on here that you don't want to tell me, is there?"

"My cheek is bruised because I got punched in the face, but it was on the set of the show."

She turned me to face her, a frown etched hard into her expression, "I thought you said this was a singing competition?"

"It is, but I got into it with one of the other contestants."

"As long as this isn't Ryan's handiwork."

"He is one of the kindest people on the planet, Mom. He'd never lay a hand on me. Let's go out in the yard and give Kimmy some help."

We were chilled to the bone by the time we had scraped up enough snow to make a small, but decent snowman. He was perfect in all other ways. We used twigs for his arms, a carrot nose, and plum halves and slices for his eyes and smile and some fat, red grapes for his buttons.

Ryan pulled in just as we were finishing him up. "He looks pretty good," he said as he climbed out of the car.

"Ryan!" Kimmy squealed with glee. She was oblivious as to what had happened over the last two months, but she remembered all the fun she had with him at the hotel. She ran and threw her soggy arms around him.

"Wow, kiddo, you're pretty wet. We'd better get you inside before you catch pneumonia out here."

I could see his concern for Kimmy's welfare put a smile to Mom's face, "He's right. We'd better all go inside before we turn into snowmen."

Kimmy laughed, "Ryan would be the snowman, Mom—we'd be snow-girls."

Ryan wrapped his arm around my shoulders and softly kissed my bruise. Mom observed, but never showed any signs that it bothered her.

We made hot chocolate and then I took them upstairs to the game room. Kimmy was in heaven as Ryan showed her the proper way to kill centipedes and gobble ghosts. Mom challenged me to a game of pool, telling me she had once been pretty good at it. I'd never really studied or practiced it, but I was up for the match. Ryan stated he'd play the winner.

The next game was Ryan and Mom, because she kicked my butt on the pool table. Ryan had his work cut out for him, and I could tell he wasn't going to fake inability so she could beat him. It seemed to impress her that he wasn't going to try to bolster her confidence with a false show. They were evenly matched and it finally came down to who was going to make the eight ball. Mom had a difficult bank shot if she was going to get it in the pocket, but, after a tip from Ryan about the angle at which she was holding her cue, she made the shot.

Originally, we were going to grill, but it was too chilly tonight to leave Ryan out on the pool deck cooking, so he and I cooked in the kitchen instead.

When it became late, I took Kimmy down to the room I prepared for her and tucked her into bed while Mom and Ryan had a little alone time in the living room.

"I've missed you," Kimmy yawned as her head hit the pillow. "When are you coming home?"

"Well, I'm a grown up now so I get to have my own house."

"Oh," she looked glum at my response. "Where's Micah?" she perked up slightly.

That hit me hard, my throat knotting immediately, "He and I—we're going to be apart for a while—I've been busy with the television show and he's—he's busy, too."

"I'm glad Ryan isn't too busy. I can't wait to see you on TV; I'm telling all my friends to watch you."

I kissed her forehead, said prayers with her, and told her to get some sleep.

I was coming out of the hallway and into the living room as I heard Mom ask Ryan if he loved me. He raised his head as he watched me approach. I sat down beside him as he refocused on Mom, "More than she even knows," he said, his eyes getting misty, "but, it's late and I've got to get going or…" he let his sentence drop.

I knew what the rest of it was going to be '…or Candace will be pissed,' but he caught himself in time.

"I'll walk you out," I said, following him to the Javelin.

I could see my breath in the cold air. The snow had stopped falling, and a blanket of moon-kissed white covered the lawn. "Thanks for everything tonight. I hope Candace understands."

"Yeah, she does—she doesn't particularly like it, but she understands. Try to get some sleep tonight." And then he kissed my cheek and was gone.

I stood outside and watched as the red taillights disappeared down the street and turned out of sight. Mom was waiting as I walked in.

"You really should tell me what's going on, Leese."

"I can't, Mom, maybe someday, but not now."

She still had a funny look on her face.

"What?"

"It's just strange to me that the two of you never kissed on the lips. You couldn't stop kissing Micah when you two were together. Things aren't what they seem, are they?"

"Just remember, not a word to David. By the way, how is he?" What I really wanted to know was if they were back in the country, but I was too scared to ask.

"He is absolutely wonderful and I never thought I'd fall so deeply in love again—this is just like it was between your dad and me. He—he just mentioned before I flew out here that he'd like to marry me someday, but he is still upset over this whole thing between you and Micah."

"Wow—Mom, that's a bomb-shell. Would you be willing, I mean have you considered it?"

"I had no intentions until he mentioned that your marriage was annulled."

The tears hit me fast and hard with just the sound of the word. The word screamed, 'It's over!' every time I allowed myself to think about it.

She moved over to the sofa and wrapped her arm around my shoulder.

"Have you seen Micah? I mean, they are evidently back from their—trip," I said, still sobbing.

"No, I haven't seen him. David says he's still just too hurt to come by. David is so angry at you. I wish you'd let me tell him how torn up you are about this whole thing."

"NO—please, Mom. Just leave it the way it is. I can handle him being angry with me. It's not important the kind of person he thinks I am."

"Yes it is, honey. If he only knew—"

"If he knew, then Micah would know, and I can't face Micah. I don't want to talk about this anymore. I'll see you in the morning." I rose quickly and headed for the safety of my bedroom. I had already shown Mom where she would be sleeping so I wasn't being completely rude. I just couldn't keep up the conversation any longer.

They could only stay two more days, because Kimmy was missing school for this adventure, but they were two terrific days. We spent one of the days at the Garden of the Gods, and then the last day was spent at the Cheyenne Mountain Zoo and the Seven Falls Park. Ryan joined us for each adventure, and by the time they were ready to head back, Mom seemed to understand how I could be enamored with two men. I was relieved she no longer had a bad impression of him—he didn't deserve to be the scapegoat for what happened; it just simply had to look that way to make it work.

Chapter Nineteen

The days passed too quickly and it was finally time for the first show to air. Ryan said we needed to have a party and he volunteered my place to have it. Naomi, Andy, Ty, Candace, Candace's dad, and Ryan all came to my house. I ordered catered food simply because I was too nervous to get any cooking done.

It was so completely different to watch the show than what it had been to do the show. They made everything so seamless. It was a two hour special and they included lots of clips. Candace's reaction to Carrie putting her hands on Ryan caused her to flush with anger immediately. Ryan told her what happened, but it still seemed to take her by surprise. I watched, even more carefully, as the airplane trip to Tennessee came on screen. They included the shot of the two of us asleep, Ryan's arm draped across me, but she didn't seem upset. Her dad, on the other hand, sent an annoyed glance Ryan's direction (which Ryan pretended not to notice). They had clips from my practice with Rascal Flatts, and finally, all the stage performances. Everyone agreed I had done an outstanding job. All I could do as I watched was to hope and pray that Micah was also watching, and he would know how incredibly hard it had been for me to leave him.

Our party ended and we made plans to get everyone together on the following Tuesday for the last women's taped show. I would be leaving the following Friday to stay in L.A. for the five solid weeks as we geared up for live shows and the count-down started toward the final two.

But, the next day, I wasn't prepared for so many people to suddenly recognize who I was. I had the feeling that every person in Colorado Springs had watched the show. When I got to the grocery store, everyone wanted to say hello, get an autograph, or take a picture with me. All of them wished me well and said they hoped I'd be the winner.

Ryan showed later that afternoon and he was completely flustered. It wasn't the whole fame thing that bothered him. It was the fact that when he took Candace to work and gave her a kiss goodbye, an elderly lady approached and smacked him with her handbag and told him that he shouldn't be two-timing on me!

"This might get really sticky, baby girl, because people think I'm your main squeeze."

"You'll just have to be careful out in public when you're with Candace. I'm sure you two will end up on the front of the tabloids if you don't. Wear a hat and sunglasses; that should help."

He sighed, "How are you going to sleep when you're in L.A.?"

"I don't really know. Your tee-shirt helps, but I might need you to visit me once in a while—if Candace doesn't get too mad at us."

"I've told her that I love her, but I've also told her she's got to give me a little leash when it comes to you."

"Come on leash-puppy, let's get in a nap before she gets out of school."

He laughed and followed me to the bedroom.

The time to make my temporary move to L.A. arrived way too soon. I wasn't going to be staying in a hotel. They rented a mansion and put all of us in it—men and women. The house had eighteen bedroom suites and a huge, Olympic size pool, but it was a little unnerving for me to know we were all going to be together. They hired a pair of full time chefs to keep us fed and, of course, they kept a full time camera crew in the mansion. We had a weight room, sauna, and four limousines with drivers in case we felt like getting out of the house for a while.

Our first two weeks of live shows were still going to be divided as women on Tuesdays and the men on Thursdays, but, when we got down to four men and four women, the final eight would be singing together and it would no longer be an elimination of one from each side. Instead America would simply vote and every show the person with the least votes from the previous show would be let go.

We could still choose what we wanted to sing, but the live shows were themed and we had to pick from within the genre chosen by producers. The first week was pop. I made my choice and, for once, I didn't have to go anywhere; the artist was coming to a private studio in L.A. for the practice. I had chosen the slow version of 'Bleeding Love,' by Leona Lewis. Kitkat and several others told me I was making a grave error by choosing one of her songs.

"She is like the next Mariah—you never touch the biggies like Streisand, Dion, Houston, Carey, those are the divas of death for someone to imitate—no one can compare to them."

"Well then, I'll be out of your way and you can win the competition," I said. I honestly was ready to get out of all of this, but I certainly wasn't going to back down from a challenging song. I was going to put my all in what I was doing and if I failed, then I got to go home, but if I succeeded then I'd prove my worth as a singer.

I never practiced quite as hard as I did with Leona to get that breathless kind of sultry, smoky quality to my voice. By the time I felt like I had the song down really well, I understood this was a song that had to be sung with as much sex appeal as I possessed. That wouldn't be hard; all I had to do was think of Micah and the sex appeal came gushing out. I had a fashion designer help me with my outfit, and I spent extra time in the makeup chair. My hair didn't need much more than a simple wave look because it was going to get a lot of hand-tousling on stage as I sang. I also needed a stage prop; I decided on a long, black leather couch.

My rehearsal turned a lot of heads, all of them male (and a few of them female). Don was telling me I was going to put our already soaring ratings completely through the roof if my performance went off as flawless as my rehearsal.

The night of the live show I was nervous, but I had hugged Ryan's tee-shirt all night and managed five hours sleep, so I was rested and ready.

The lights were low as I started with the first whispered breaths, and then the lights came up as I slowly rose from the couch, running my fingers through my hair. My full-length, red dress had a slit all the way to my upper thigh, a rhinestone band ran around my hips and one strip of stones went up the center of the dress, but other than that the entire midriff was totally sheer and then the rhinestones branched out and made a bikini type top and went over my shoulders as thin straps. My scar showed on my chest, but that was okay because the song contained the lyrics, 'I'll be wearing these scars for everyone to see.'

I looked at the camera as if it were Micah's face as I continued to pour out the emotions the words begged for, "...something happened...the very first time with you. My heart melted to the ground, found something true. And everyone's looking round thinking I'm going crazy. But I don't care what they say. I'm in love with you. They try to pull me away, but they don't know the truth. My heart's crippled by the vein that I keep on closing—you cut me open and I keep bleeding, keep, keep bleeding love."

I danced slowly to the routine I had rehearsed so well that it was now completely natural. I finished the song as I laid back on the couch, my back arched and my hands clasped over my heart. The lights dimmed and then came back up to the roar of the crowd. I immediately rose and took my place in front of the panel of four judges. The comments ranged from, "This is what I was talking about stretching yourself," to "You've set the bar tonight for the remainder of this competition. We might be looking at our winner."

I hated the feeling of over-confidence, but I was on a natural high when I walked off the stage. The guys in the contestant waiting area were more than enthusiastic. Kitkat told me I did a good job, but she still seemed really annoyed that I had pulled off what she told me would be impossible.

Kitkat and the twins did a great job when it came time for their turns on stage, but Dobrey and Nicole both had an off night, and I knew one of them would be going home by the next show.

When I got back to the mansion it was eleven p.m., but I told Ryan I was going to call him and see what he thought about the show. It was one ring and he answered his cell.

"Hey," I said, still feeling the euphoria pumping through my veins, "so what did you think?"

"Well, I got in a fight with Candace over it."

"What?" I couldn't imagine why they had a fight over my performance. It was then that I could hear the occasional swish of passing cars and I realized he was driving, "Did she toss you out of the house?"

"No, of course not, it's our—I mean it's my place, but I volunteered to go for a drive, so she could cool off."

"Did you say something to piss her off?"

"No, baby girl, I didn't have to say a word; the problem was body language."

I was still stumped, "What do you mean?"

"You remember the night you were kissing my neck and we got a little too—"

"Yeah, I remember," I stopped him before he could say more.

"I said what you did was so freaking sexy that I thought I was gonna die—well, that performance was right up there with the one in the bedroom and I must have, unconsciously, got a little too excited watching you. When she noticed, she slugged the crap out of me."

I kept reviewing what he said as I tried to get the meaning. It finally hit me as he began to explain.

"I ended up with a—"

"Don't say it!" I stopped him, "I got it. I wasn't going for trashy," I started to say, thinking my performance may have not been exactly what I had hoped.

"No, no, no, baby girl. You were not trashy. You were sexy—sexy like some hot Hollywood starlet. You were fabulous. It's just that I kept thinking I've been in the same bed with you and never realized exactly what I was holding on to."

"Ah nuts, Ryan. Does this mean we aren't going to be able to manage sleeping together anymore?"

He laughed hard, "Man, I hope not. It might take me a little longer to fall asleep, but…"

I told him to go home and apologize profusely to her and get out of the cold weather. He agreed, told me he loved me, and hung up.

Everyone wanted to stay up and talk, but I excused myself to my room and curled up with Ryan's tee-shirt, inhaling deeply and smiling as I thought about him. I managed to fall asleep and stayed that way until four a.m. Then I got up and hit the weight room down stairs, with plans to hit the pool afterwards. I was pumping some light iron when I realized I wasn't alone; Sadarius had joined me.

"What are you doing up so early?" he asked.

"I don't sleep very well when I'm away from—home." I almost said Ryan.

"How about you? Are you normally an early riser?"

"Sometimes, it just depends on what I did the night before. I've been wanting to ask you something and I don't want to like scare

247

you off or anything, but are you and Ryan real serious? I mean, you haven't been bringing him along so I wondered."

"He's my very best friend, but he actually has a girlfriend—just please don't mention that to anyone else—like the press."

"No way, girl. I don't talk to those people willingly. But, if you and him aren't dating, I was wondering if you'd like to go out some time?"

"Ah—no, I—I don't date," I answered uneasily. I wasn't willing to explain my reasoning to him because this conversation would lead to exposing some private matters.

"You don't have an issue with color, do you?" he didn't say it rudely. He seemed genuinely interested in knowing if I had racial preferences.

"No, I have husband issues," I said softly as I put the barbell carefully back into the cradle and sat up on the bench.

His eyebrows went up, "I thought you ran off from him?"

"I did, but it is more complicated than what I want to get into."

"I read that he was like some big shot in the mob. Is that true?"

"He was out at the time, but he's back in the mob and... I really don't want to discuss it. I'm sorry, I just can't." My eyes were giving away the pain that was piercing me.

"Hey, it's cool. You seem to treat your friends pretty good, so how about just being friends?"

I smiled, "I kind of thought of you as a friend already."

He straddled the neighboring bench and began doing curls with the dumbbells, "Are you coming to watch the guys practice today?"

"Should I?"

"Akon is gonna be in the studio helping me with my song for tomorrow."

"Which one are you doing?"

"*Beautiful*," he simply stated.

"Ah, I love that song. Yeah, I'd like to come to the practice."

"And then we could have lunch together—just as friends, of course."

Boy, I got suckered into that one. I grinned and sighed, "Yeah, I think we could manage lunch."

Chapter Twenty

"Are these all the cameras we have in the studio?"

"Yes sir, boss man, but I can install more if you want. I can put them anywhere and no one will know." Cedric watched the owner as he focused on one particular female contestant, "I could even put one in her dressing room, if you like," he grinned. "She needs someone to keep an eye on her because I think she's going to get into trouble in the big city."

"Why is that?"

Cedric backed the video to the last taped episode. He pulled up the feed where he caught Leese buying drugs from Thomas, and then watched the owner's face grow furiously dark.

"What the hell did he sell her?"

"I'm not sure, but she paid five hundred dollars for it, so it must have been something good."

"I want him fired—today—within the hour, and I want to know what he sold her."

"Yes, sir. Anything else?"

The owner gave him a mildly annoyed glance, but continued to study her, "If you put a camera in her dressing room, that feed better run only to my office, nowhere else, is that understood?"

Cedric had actually been kidding, but it wouldn't be the first time in this business someone wanted to be a voyeur. He almost wished he hadn't mentioned it; he liked Leese. She was a sweet girl and not fake like so many of the women he had met in this business. But, she wasn't the one making sure the bills got paid around here, so what would it hurt to let the boss get a little peek? "I'll install it tonight."

He and the owner watched the cameras as Sadarius began rehearsing the song '*Beautiful*' by Akon.

"Capture that," the owner said quickly, pointing to camera twenty-seven.

Cedric brought the camera view to full screen as he watched what had intrigued the owner, actually it would intrigue anyone with an ounce of sex drive. Leese had begun to dance backstage as the music pumped through the studio. She was wearing a pair of straight-leg jeans with high heels and a button up the front white cotton shirt with the first three buttons undone and a nice view of her cleavage. She was laughing and smiling, running her fingers through her hair as her body swung and swayed to the beat of the music. She was dancing like some kind of lithe nymph high on life. Sadarius was, of course, oblivious as to what was happening backstage, but every time he would sing the repetitive verse, "You're so beautiful, so damn beautiful," the two men watching would reflexively moan their approval.

"I want that playing on the screen behind Sadarius when he sings tomorrow night. Work your magic on it so the backstage is blended out and it's mostly just her."

"Boss, I don't know if that's gonna be cool with Sadarius. I mean it's his song and she's going to be stealing the spotlight."

He could tell from the look on the owner's face that he didn't care what Sadarius would think about it.

"Don't you have something else to do, right now?"

The hint was quickly taken that the boss wanted to watch her privately so Cedric left the room.

"You are beautiful," the man replied as he watched his personal dancer, "So damn beautiful."

It was a sold out live show as the men took to the stage to sing. There were full bands tonight to enhance the performances, and Sadarius had drawn the final slot for the night. Leese sat with the other women, although she was about to come out of her seat as the music began; she loved the song.

The audience was having quite a reaction as they cheered and screamed while he perfectly executed the lyrics.

"Well, I'll be damned," Kitkat exclaimed.

Leese looked up and suddenly realized what was taking everyone by surprise. There she was, full screen behind Sadarius dancing to the song.

"Ah, crap!" she exclaimed, but there was nothing she could do about it.

They called the women on stage for the voting results from Tuesday's show, and Nicole had the least amount of votes and was eliminated. The women's final four had been determined.

The show ended as everyone met back stage, and it didn't take long for Sadarius to find Don. "Hey man, that was not too cool to put my competition looking sharp behind me when I'm singing."

Don would have told Sadarius that he absolutely agreed, but he had nothing to do with it. Producers may run the show, but the money that pays the producers calls the shots. "You did a great job and I don't think her performance is going to lower your votes, if anything I think she'll give you a boost.

About that moment, Leese approached the two of them. "Sadarius, I had no idea they filmed me yesterday, I'm so sorry—"

"It's okay, baby-doll," he said as he wrapped an arm around her and pulled her in for a light hug, "I didn't figure you had anything to do with it. And damn, girl, the only problem it caused for me was the fact that I kept wanting to turn around and watch you dance," he smirked.

"Don, did you plan this?"

"No, Leese. But, you signed the contract allowing us to film you and who knows, this may work out well for both of you," he stated trying to keep a positive spin on things.

Later that night Cedric finished the install of the hidden camera in Leese's dressing room, making sure it was angled properly for the widest possible shot. He thought about running the feed to his panel as well and simply keeping it turned off except for times when he knew the boss wasn't around, but getting caught was a very unpleasant thought. The feed went to the boss's office as instructed.

Chapter Twenty-One

The next week was country week, and I prepared to sing my song for Ryan. I told him from the start there was a song that expressed how I felt about him. He already knew my feelings, as I thought about the intimate kiss I gave him when I told him that I loved him, but he didn't know the song. I was back on a plane to Tennessee, but this time I was headed to Pigeon Forge.

I had one more surprise for him. I mailed him an envelope with explicit instructions he wasn't to open it until after my stage performance, and it would be best to open it in private.

When Tuesday night came, I knew the judges expected to see me sing some top forty country hit, but what I had chosen was a very old song. This time I wasn't thinking about Micah's face. The song could have just as easily have been for him, but this was for Ryan.

I looked deeply into the camera with all the honesty I possessed as I sang the Dolly Parton version of 'I Will Always Love You.' I couldn't stop the soft tears as I sang the final words.

The judges liked my performance although they were commenting on the fact they would have chosen something more current, but my reviews were still positive.

I went back to the contestant area and waited as Kitkat finished the last song of the night. I wished the whole while I could have my cell phone to find out what Ryan thought about my gift, but it would have to wait. I made the decision, since I told him I'd never give him the final kiss, I would pay him (so to speak) for it. He had told me to stop blowing money on him, but I owed him that kiss and found it hard to put a price tag on it.

I was in the limo riding back to the mansion, and my cell was softly vibrating in my purse. When I pulled it out, I had six new messages all from Ryan's cell. I didn't really want to call him with all the ladies in the car, but I was anxious to talk to him, so I hit the speed dial and took a breath.

"You shouldn't have done that," was all he said when he answered the phone.

"Well, considering what the price was, I thought it was a fairly even trade."

"Leese, I…" His voice cracked as he paused. "I loved the song, but you didn't need to buy the house for me."

"The lease is going to end in less than a year and then you'd either have to re-up or find some place new and I hate to think of someone else owning our first place." The line was silent so I continued, "Of course, that doesn't mean I'm against you selling, if you and Candace decide you want to live somewhere else."

"You aren't moving again, are you? The whole business in the song about, 'so I'll go' you aren't trying to tell me anything, are you?"

I took a small breath, "Someday, but for right now, no."

"That someday better be far, far away, because I'm not ready to have you go—not right now, anyway."

"I've got one free day on Friday, since they're making us miss Thanksgiving—is Candace working?

"It's Black Friday, so she is working an extended shift eight to four—unless you want me to come out there?"

"No, I think she'd kill you. I'll see you sometime Friday morning."

"By eight," he added. She'd be at work by seven-forty-five and he wasn't going to waste any time.

They wouldn't give the results of the women's or men's eliminations during the Thanksgiving show, but would make everyone wait until Tuesday when we did our first combined show. I would have to spend the weekend wondering if I made it or not, but that was okay.

Saturday afternoon I had a big practice in L.A. for my next song, but I would relish the opportunity to sleep in his arms for the few hours we were able.

He was at the airport waiting for me when I landed because my little Aero was parked in the garage at home. I climbed into the Javelin and hugged his neck long and hard. I had gone two weeks without my Ryan-fix and I needed him like I needed a breath of fresh air.

The only problem was the excitement of seeing him was canceling out the sleep I actually needed to get.

"I could use another one of your tee-shirts," I whispered as he cuddled against my back in the bed. "I've just about drained every ounce of you out of the other one." I gave a light laugh as I pulled his tattooed arm tighter around my waist. He put a slow kiss on my neck, sending tingles to my belly button.

"Close your eyes and go to sleep, we only have about five more hours." His voice was deep and throaty, it almost didn't sound like him.

"I'm trying," I said earnestly, "I'm just glad to be home."

"Stop talking," he breathed into my hair.

I closed my eyes and slowed my breathing. I became so still I could feel the beat of his heart. The next thing I remember was him gently waking me. Our time had ended and he was going to meet Candace at home and bring her back to my place for a little while. He pulled off his tee-shirt and tucked it into my hands, then slipped on his jacket and was gone. I actually fell back asleep with his shirt pressed to my cheek. I woke to the doorbell, they were back.

"Hey," Candace was saying as she came through the door with a box in her hand. "Miss Naomi said she couldn't stand the idea of you not getting a Thanksgiving dinner so she made you up a big take-out box." It was more than enough food for all three of us.

Saturday morning I was the only person who got to rehearse in the studio and on stage with my group. Tuesday's show was music from the 70's and I chose to do a remake of Bob Seger and the Silver Bullet Band's '*Old Time Rock and Roll.*' The fun part was that I decided to do it in Tom Cruise fashion. It was a little scary at first as I took off running and then slid, in my socked feet, onto the stage gripping an electric guitar. Slipping and falling would be a disaster, but after a couple tries I knew my balance was good enough to keep me upright. It would look like I was only in a man's dress shirt and socks, but I had a white bikini on underneath.

The song had a gritty kind of quality that was difficult to master and by the time I was finished my vocal cords were a little strained, but I got the essence (even if I did think it sounded much better when Bob Seger sang it).

The pace of the show was now feverish as everyone had two songs a week to perform. On Thursday, the theme was the 80's and I worked with Foreigner to do the song, '*I Wanna Know What Love Is*,' and then the next it was working with Aerosmith for Tuesday's show and I sang '*I Don't Wanna Miss A Thing*.'

When the Christian/Gospel night theme arrived, I felt like I was finally in my true element. I decided to sing '*Praise You In This Storm*,' by Casting Crowns and everything was set for my practice when Sadarius approached me and asked for a favor. He decided to sing '*Born Again*,' by Third Day, but he wanted to keep the female part in the song and he asked if I would be willing to accompany him. Don wasn't real keen on the idea, saying that one of us might suffer votes because of it, but, if we really wanted to, we could do it as a duet. I would be the person with the majority of the stress because it meant I had to perform twice that night. If it had been anything other than Christian music, I would have really struggled, but this was easy for me.

The only tricky part was using a falsetto for the needed high pitched female part in the duet. We practiced with Third Day and Lacey Moseley from Flyleaf until we felt we had it right.

We were down to the final four: Sadarius, Kitkat, Lexington, and me. The last week would be rock for two days, and then the last show would be a two hour results show. The final three contestants would sing for the first hour, phone lines would open for one hour of voting, and the two finalists would be announced to return two days before Christmas for the final contest.

The duet went perfectly. Sadarius and I sang the uplifting lyrics as images of baptisms, crosses, infants, and breath-taking scenery played in the background. But, what had been a spiritual and uplifting evening ended up appearing on the cover of the tabloids saying I had dumped Ryan and was now dating Sadarius.

The last week I sang '*Kryptonite*' by Three Doors Down, and the last song for the two hour results show was '*When You're Gone*,' by Avril Lavigne. The final three were Lexington, Sadarius and me. They played a montage of all the songs we had sung up to this night as the three of us waited nervously to see who would be the final two. When the results were tabulated, the finalists were Sadarius and me.

The show was pulling in the biggest ratings of the whole year, and a celebration party was planned for the Saturday before the last episode. I dreaded going alone and also dreaded what the next round of tabloid news would be spreading about me. I was coming home the Friday before the party, and I finally accepted Ryan's offer to come out to L.A. I had turned him down every time to prevent problems between him and Candace, but I wanted him to attend the party with me. I needed the tabloids to get off the kick about Sadarius. I had to get Ryan back in the picture before it looked like he was out of my life.

I didn't know if Micah even cared what I had been doing since we had parted four months ago. He never made any effort to contact me other than when he had David deliver the annulment papers. I was beginning to wonder if my original reason for doing the show in the first place even mattered; he might not have even watched any of the episodes.

Ryan agreed immediately, but I wanted to hear it from Candace, myself, that she was okay with me 'borrowing' him for the night.

When I flew into Colorado Springs, I was surprised that she was the person who picked me up, but I tried not to let it show, "Hey, I appreciate the ride. What's Ryan up to?"

"He's out looking for a suit," she answered, but wasn't smiling.

"I—I hope you don't mind that I asked him to go with me. It's just that—"

"Leese, I'm not going to lie to you—I hate the idea of him even being around you," she confessed as she turned onto the main road and began the trek south toward my house.

Boy, this was not going to go as I had hoped, and I began to feel I should withdraw my request before I caused a breakup. "We're only good friends, Candace. I—"

"No, you're not," she stopped me. "You two are in love and I've been ignoring that fact ever since he came back here."

"He loves *you*," I began.

"I know he loves me," she sighed, showing that she was quickly getting exasperated, "I just wish I wasn't competing with someone like *you*. You're beautiful, talented, sexy, kinder than anyone I've ever met, and the fact that you're richer than two-foot up a bull's ass doesn't hurt things either—hell, if I was a guy, I'd be in love with you!"

"I'm sorry I asked him—I'll tell him—"

"No, you aren't going to back out of the invitation. He's really looking forward to going to a big L.A. party and who could blame him? He loves the spotlight—and I hate it. I don't honestly know how he can stand being with me."

"He's not the kind of person to string someone along. You've got to stop putting him up on a pedestal and thinking the whole time you don't deserve him," I responded with a little sharpness to my voice.

She cut her eyes toward me and I could tell I ticked her off, but I continued, "When he and I went to Pensacola high school, he had the captain of the cheerleading team drooling over him like he was edible. She was gorgeous, fun-loving, and—and a virgin. She wanted him, but he turned her down. Do you think, for one minute, if he wasn't crazy about you that he would have, under any circumstances, slept with you? Every hot chick on Remake melts when Ryan gets near them—and he's yours. You are that special person in his life and you need to start feeling that pedestal under your feet a little bit. Start letting him adore you, because sex isn't the only reason he's staying."

She wasn't answering; she was just watching the road and gripping the wheel. I knew I'd hit what was at the heart of this matter. She was feeling used, but he just wasn't that type of person.

"You've been sleeping together, haven't you?" she stated as if she hadn't heard a word I said. "I know you have because whenever you show up in town and I'm either at work or school, he ends up with your scent all over him."

"You know I don't fake sleep issues to crawl into a bed with him. If I didn't have him to…" My voice caught and the burn was beginning in my eyes. "I'd be in the nut house by now," I said turning my face toward the window. "He's the last piece of sanity in my life and I'm trying—trying hard, to turn loose of him."

"Don't turn him loose, Leese," she softly replied as her hand reached over and gripped mine. "You're right. I need to start valuing myself a little bit more. I'm naturally insecure and watching him turn heads doesn't help. I'm holding on to him so tightly I know I'm about to chase him away."

I looked over and could see she was on the verge of tears as I squeezed the offered hand.

"That's why I told him to go with you. I'm the one who needs to turn loose because I'll never find out if he really loves me if I don't." She swallowed hard, "I'm going to try to take a lesson from you and be a friend to him, a real friend and then wait and see what happens."

"You aren't planning to move out of the house, are you?"

"No," she said, eyes getting wide, "I'm hooked like a junkie on him. I'm just going to back off on issues where you're concerned and let him be himself for a while. I'm tired of making him have to slip around behind my back to be with you. I've got to stop trying to control everything about him, and show him a little more trust, a little more honest-to-God love."

I finally smiled, "You know I think the new and improved you is going to impress the crap out of him."

"I hope so, but you know what, if it doesn't and he realizes he's not happy with me... Well, let's just say I'm starting to understand I love him enough to want him to be happy, even if it isn't with me."

"Wow."

She finally turned and glanced at me, "What?"

"Now that's starting to sound like real love."

She laughed, "You know I have you to thank for that. I mean I've been thinking about you a lot lately and I realize there is a certain amount of vulnerability and sacrifice that has to be part of being really in love. If it's not there, then all I'm doing is trying to be in control of someone else."

She turned on to my street; I was suddenly so glad she came and picked me up. She was gaining the maturity that I knew Ryan wanted so desperately to see in her, and I wasn't going to worry about tip-toeing around her emotions any longer—she was growing and he was going to end up so desperately in love with her.

We had a little free time together before he showed up, and I asked if she'd like to play a little dress up while we waited. Candace hardly ever wore make up and she always wore her hair loose and a little unkempt, but I wanted to give her a make-over that would knock his socks off when he arrived. She agreed and the fun began.

I did her make-up and then brushed out her blond hair and made a single French braid down the back, leaving a little loose near each ear. I gave her a pair of my diamond stud earrings and loaned her a soft cotton tank and crisp white over-shirt. She couldn't button the shirt because she was chestier than me, but that was okay, it looked great unbuttoned. She kept her jeans, because I was a zero and she was a four. It didn't matter though; she looked like a model with her pouty pink, lip-glossed mouth and lightly blushed cheeks. It was an hour later when he finally showed. His reaction was perfect. He was all smiles and couldn't seem to take his eyes off of her.

We made our plans to leave out Saturday afternoon. Then Candace surprised us both when she told Ryan she'd head back to the house if he wanted to help me get some rest.

"I know you probably won't sleep tonight," she said turning to me, "but I bet he could help you get at least six or seven hours in before he comes home tonight."

Ryan's mouth was open, but nothing was coming out.

"Would you mind?" I asked, turning to him.

"N—no, but..."

Candace went up on her tip toes and kissed him lightly and said she'd see him at home by nine. She was walking away when he turned and looked at me like he didn't know what to do. I mouthed for him to walk her outside and motioned him to follow.

"Let—let me walk you out to the car," he stated and then sprinted to catch up to her.

I could see the smile spread across her face.

When he came back inside, he wanted to know one thing, "What did you do to my girlfriend?"

"Other than a little makeup, I didn't do anything. She is just growing up—and somehow I think you're going to like the grown-up version."

"Damn right. I can't wait to get home now—at least I know it won't be a fight waiting to happen. But you told her about us sleeping together?" he seemed genuinely surprised.

"No, actually she has apparently known all along and was tired of making us think we were sneaking around. She's very special when you peel off the hard outer layer."

He got a certain kind of dreamy quality to his eyes, "Yeah, she is."

"Are you sure you even want to stay?" I needed my relaxer, but I wasn't going to hold him back if he wanted to go.

"No, I think the anticipation will do me good. Come on, baby girl, let's get cozy."

Candace was one lucky woman.

I don't think he slept too much; he had his mind on other things, but I got a relaxed several hours tucked safely in his warm arms.

Saturday afternoon he arrived and he was quiet, but all smiles as we drove to the airport.

"So you seem really happy today. I take it you and Candace did not have a fight when you got home."

"You know this is so weird that I want to tell you about my night, but talking to you about sex with her seems a little—well, inappropriate."

I figured that was why he was smiling, but I had no intentions of being nosey, "You don't have to tell me anymore; I get the picture."

"No, I don't think you do. Would you be like offended or jealous if we did talk about it?"

I reached over and touched his cheek. He looked so handsome in his basic black tux. "I can handle it, if you can. That's what having a best friend is for, right? When you're dying to tell about something that rocked your world."

"She definitely did that because last night was the first time I've made love," he breathed out the words with a sound of pure amazement in his voice.

Whoa—that hit me square in the chest. "But—but—it couldn't have been." I must have really missed something in what he'd just said because I knew last night wasn't his first time.

His smile grew broader, "We've been having sex, Leese, but last night she was on a whole different playing field. She wasn't like 'do me now, I want it.' She was vulnerable and timid. She let me hold her instead of crawling all over me. I don't even know if I can describe it." He sounded like he was struggling. "I finally got to *really* make love to her and it was beautiful and peaceful and sexy and... You're going to have to forgive me for saying it this way, but it was how I've assumed all along it would be like to have you."

I couldn't stop the tears, although I was grabbing a tissue and trying to catch them before they ruined my makeup.

He looked over at me with an alarmed expression, "I'm sorry. I shouldn't have."

"No, no, it's not that. You don't have any idea how happy I am for you—both of you. This is all I've wanted for so long was for you to be really, really happy. This *is* what you've deserved all along."

"So you're not like freaked out about me telling you this?"

"You have no idea how long I've been waiting for us to have this conversation," I said as I kept catching the downpour.

We pulled up to the hanger and he leaned over and wrapped me in his strong arms and kissed me gently on the temple, "I love you, Leese—someday you're going to be happy again because God knows you deserve to feel this way, too."

The rest of the trip to L.A. was pure fun. The best part was that I told him, since we were both familiar with L.A. now, I had rented a car. His eyes lit up as he asked what I had rented. I wasn't going to tell him that I'd called the exotic car rental and had a Lamborghini sitting on the tarmac, so I said there wasn't much available and we would have to be happy with a Ford Taurus. He deflated. I knew what he was thinking. 'We're going to pull up to the red carpet in a Taurus?'

We spent the rest of the time laughing and discussing the tabloid tales, and then he got serious and asked if there was anything I needed to tell him about Sadarius.

I got a little Candace in me when I slugged him, although not too hard because I wanted the airplane to remain on a level course, "No, you idiot. He and I have gone out twice, once for lunch and once for dinner, but I've already told him the only thing I'm in the market for is a friend."

"I'm a friend and I get to crawl in bed with you," he said giving me a sharp look.

"Ryan Faultz, I do believe I hear a little jealousy in your voice," I smirked.

"But—I—"

"You are a very special friend and there isn't anyone else like you in my world. Superman can crawl under my covers," I teased, "but other than that, everyone else can forget it."

"I'm just making sure. Just want to know if I've got to be prepared for a fight when we get there."

I laughed, "No, no fights unless Micah should decide to track me down."

We were walking off the plane when I saw the beautiful, blue-as-his-eyes, Lamborghini. What was hilarious was that two cars away sat a plain white Taurus. Ryan sighed as he headed for the economy car. I pressed the key into his hand as we approached. They had over-nighted it to me, so that I could leave as soon as I was ready.

He didn't look down until he got to the door, "Hey, this isn't a key for a..." His eyes grew brighter when he saw the symbol.

"Yeah, I know it sucks, but they were out of Taurus' so I had to get a Lamborghini."

Chapter Twenty-Two

The party was in full swing when we pulled up to the red carpet. Ryan was reluctant to relinquish the keys to the valet, but he finally turned them loose and took my arm as the cameras flashed and reporters shouted out questions to us wanting to know if he and I were 'back together,' and how was Sadarius handling it. He was good at this whole fame business, comfortable even. But I hated it. He flashed his dazzling smile as he walked with me, looking more like the star than the starlet's date, and showing no discomfort with the attention.

He couldn't get the grin off his face as we walked into the roomful of people dancing, laughing, and enjoying the party. Remake had become the smash hit of the year and sponsors were lining up to spend millions of dollars promoting it. Whoever had been the brains behind this show would reap in substantial financial benefits.

Sadarius was one of the first to greet us and ready to steal me away from Ryan, but Ryan politely refused, "Hey man, we just got here. Let me wear her out a little bit, before I have to turn her loose."

They played many of the hits that made the show popular, some were our versions and some were the originals. Akon was making a guest appearance as well as several other artists that had coached our crew of fledgling singers. Ryan only left my side long enough to make a special request which was for the DJ to play Kryptonite. When we began our dance, the floor opened up as the majority of the people made space for the two of us to take over. I was having the time of my life.

We stopped long enough to grab a drink, Ryan was grabbing for champagne, but I reminded him he was flying us home tonight and I might be able to keep us in the air, but I needed a sober pilot for take-offs and landings. Besides, I didn't want to see what the effects of a drink or two could do to one's reflexes behind a Lamborghini.

The lights lowered as the DJ's voice came over the microphone, "And now we have a special request for Miss Annalisa."

I arched an eyebrow at Ryan, "What did you request?"

"I didn't request anything, I swear. I've been with you the whole time except for asking them to play Kryptonite."

Akon came on stage and the music began. He was singing '*Right Now.*'

"We can't waste a special request," he said taking my hand and leading me back onto the dance floor. He was smiling as he lip-sank to the song. That was one thing superman couldn't do—he couldn't hold a tune.

"You had to have requested this song," I stated. "I wish you could fly with me? I miss how you lie with me? I wish you could dine with me? Ah, the grind part though…"

"I didn't request the song, but I do recall the grind," he smiled, pulling me close.

"I never—"

"No, no, no, Annalisa, think before you say never. Remember the night you were kissing my neck? You had those hips working against me pretty hard and I'll never forget that."

I know my face turned deep red as I recalled I had done exactly that the night I went a little too far over the line, "So you're saying you did request this song."

He laughed, again, "I'm sorry. I don't know who is sending out this dedication, but baby girl, it wasn't me."

I was puzzled, but the mystery faded from my mind as the next song began. The twins, Melissa and Melanie, approached and said they wanted a turn with the hottest guy on the floor. He was blushing as I watched them dance him away from me.

"My turn," came a male voice. Cedric was standing there pulling my hand toward the opposite side of the floor.

I hadn't spoken to him very much, it seemed he spent most of his time running interference between ownership and the producers, but I knew him well enough to dance with him. The only problem was he kept pulling me farther and farther away from the crowd and I was starting to get nervous. I finally had to refuse. "Cedric if we go much farther we'll be down the hallway—I'm not going down the hall to dance."

"Well, Leese, I have to admit I'm setting you up."

The next song changed as they said it was an anonymous request to a special lady. 'Far Away' by Nickelback began to play.

My heart began to increase in speed, "What do you mean?"

"I had strict orders to separate you and Ryan on the dance floor so the owner could finally get to meet you. He's kind of private, but he's had his eye on you for a while. He requested this song for you."

I didn't like the sound of this. I didn't know who the owner was, but a creepy guy who stays in the shadows and watches from afar didn't sound like someone I wanted to meet. But, then again, it was the owner and I supposed it would be extremely rude to refuse.

Cedric had me spinning as he continued toward the office door. One more spin. I heard the door open and then I was caught in a steel embrace.

I never heard Cedric walk away, though I knew he was gone. I couldn't hear the music or the party going on because my world simply stopped as I stared into the most beautiful green eyes on the planet. "Micah," I whispered the name that my heart had been begging to hear for so long.

"Baby," came the velvet reply. He was singing to me, "...I love you. I have loved you all along. And I miss you, been far away for far too long... On my knees, I'll ask, last chance for one last dance, 'cause with you, I'd withstand all of hell to hold your hand."

My legs came out from under me, but he knew me well enough to expect the reaction as he held me up, suspended by a fraction of an inch from the floor. His mouth closed the gap between us and I floated into heaven; my arms encircling his neck, my fingers running through his hair. It was real. He was in my arms and his kiss was stripping me of all the reasons why I had left him. I didn't want it to end, but he eventually pulled breathlessly away from me.

"Oh, Micah," I whispered as our lips parted, "I've missed you so badly." My tears were flowing freely down my cheeks.

There was a look of confusion on his face, pain intermingled with the expression, but it didn't stop him from pressing me against the wall with his body as he came back for another kiss.

"Take me—" I started to say when something broke the spell I was under. Micah's expression went deadly blank immediately as his head turned to what had ended my words.

"Stay the hell away from her or I'll kill you," he hissed with so much intent that it sent a chill like ice being injected into my veins.

I turned my face to see Ryan's stunned expression as I was locked in Micah's hold.

"Leese, baby girl, you can't."

Micah pulled away from me as he growled out for Ryan not to call me baby. The explosion was about to take place, and I knew what would happen to my best friend if it did.

"No, Micah," I cried, holding on for dear life to his shirt, "don't touch him."

"You've got to let her choose, Micah. This isn't about me or you, it's up to her."

It wasn't wise to talk to Micah when he was in such a volatile mind set, but I could see Ryan's words were breaking through the void.

He was right. It was up to me and only he and I knew the repercussions of what that decision would mean for Micah. I had never expected to be face to face with him and make the choice between right and wrong.

Micah could read the indecision on my face, the hurt and the pain I was suddenly in as I looked from one to the other.

He was afraid, but willing as he backed away to give me a moment to decide, "Don't do it. Je t'aime, Annalisa. Please, baby, don't leave me twice—I couldn't take it. Tell me now that you want to be with me. I'll take you away from here and make love to you until the world fades—don't leave me, again."

The tears welled over my eyes and poured down my cheeks because I knew there was only one right decision to make. I could feel my heart being ripped out of my chest as I gripped his wrists to keep him from encircling me. I raised up to put a tender kiss on his mouth; then I backed slightly away. I couldn't take my eyes away from his even though I didn't want to be looking into them when I knew what I had to say, "Get me out of here...Ryan," I breathed.

Ryan was reaching for my arm as Micah suddenly exploded to get to him.

"NO MICAH!" I yelled, putting myself in harm's way to keep the animal inside him from attacking. My hand was firmly on his chest as I pushed him back. He was struggling hard to regain control over his emotions as he looked at my face.

"I made my decision; honor it, *please*... I have to leave."

I watched defeat crush him as he slumped away from my hand. Ryan grabbed my free hand, and we ran for the door.

I didn't remember getting into the Lamborghini, or even getting into the airplane. I do remember lying on the floor in the back of the plane feeling like I was going to die. I must have laid there for the entire flight back to Colorado because the next thing I was conscious of was Ryan trying to get me to sit up.

He was holding me and shushing me, whispering that it was going to be okay.

How could it possibly ever be okay? How could anything stop all the pain I was in?

"You!" I snapped, suddenly feeling an angry, boiling tide rising up inside me. "Why did you come looking for me?! A few more minutes and I—I would have been gone!" I yelled at him. I balled my fists and thrust them hard against both sides of his chest, pushing him back against one of the seats. "Why didn't you turn away when you saw that he had me?! Damn you, Ryan!" I hit him again and again, but he didn't try to stop me. I looked into his beautiful eyes and finally saw the tears running down his face. "I'm sorry," I sobbed as he pulled me into his arms and held me. "I'm so, so sorry—it's not your fault—I'm so sorry."

We sat there together for several long moments as he rocked me gently back and forth, "I'm going to take you home," he finally whispered. "I'll stay with you tonight and—"

"No," I refused, a little bit of sanity returning to my muddled brain. "I'll be fine."

"I'm staying with you until—"

I pulled back and, even though having him help me through the night was what I wanted more than anything in the world, I lied with all the sincerity I could dig out of my soul, "I—I *really* want to be alone."

He smoothed my hair away from my face and looked at me with his still teary eyes, "Are you sure?" His voice was quivering, so I knew my refusal was causing him pain.

"Yeah, I need some time by myself."

He didn't say another word; he just took me home and walked me inside.

The house felt horribly empty and hollow—so very, very lonely. I shuddered as I looked at my surroundings almost as if it was the first time I'd ever seen it.

"Please, let me stay with you, baby girl," he pled.

"Go home, Ryan." I was trying to sound convincing, "I'll be okay."

"Candace and I will pick you up for church."

"No—I—I'd rather stay home. I don't think I'll be ready to see anyone tomorrow."

"Well, you're going to see me because I'll be here after church. You can talk and I'll listen, or we can both be quiet and I'll just hold on to you, but I'm coming over."

I nodded numbly as he embraced me, but kept my arms folded in front of me. If I hugged him back, I'd break down again. He kissed my temple, my ear, and then my cheek, whispered he loved me, and then he was gone.

Chapter Twenty-Three

Micah had never known the kind of pain he was experiencing. He thought the first time was the worst, until he actually held her in his arms and felt her push away. He heard it from her own lips that she chose Ryan. But, that wasn't what he experienced before Ryan showed up. She yielded to him immediately, actually wanting him to kiss her. She didn't want him to stop, and she asked him to take her, but she never got to finish the sentence.

There was a plethora of venomous obscenities caught in his throat as he remembered Ryan's words. 'Baby girl'—he actually was calling her baby and that was so ludicrous and unacceptable to Micah. She was his and no one should be allowed to call her that. He tried to let the fury inside him subside. He had been completely irrational since he met with D'Angelo earlier in the day. His emotions were so raw and impulsive he had barely been able to stop himself when she stepped between them; and they were becoming harder to control by the minute.

He wondered if D'Angelo had done something to him when they had lunch because he hadn't felt right since. His heart had begun to beat faster and a light coat of sweat seemed to perpetually wash over him. D'Angelo tracked him down the day before and was furious about the entire affair. In particular, he wanted to know how long Leese had been aware that Micah owned the show. Why he needed to know that Micah couldn't understand, but D'Angelo never asked anything without reason.

"She doesn't know anything," Micah stated as they had a private late lunch meeting. "I haven't shown myself, but I will during the party in a few hours. *I'm going to get her back.*"

"You're a fool if you think she's going to come back and live the life of a mob wife."

"I'm not staying in the mob. I've gotten out once and I can do it again."

"You aren't going anywhere—we have unfinished business and I am not releasing you from your obligations to me. You agreed to do what I needed in exchange for David."

"South America was for David."

"No," D'Angelo growled, "I said he would help you with that job to reestablish his trustworthiness, but I told you that you would belong to me again. I have been looking for you for weeks and I don't like being ignored."

"Then I'll do what you need done, but I've got to finish *this job* first."

"Are you going to kill her boyfriends—all of them?" he sneered.

Evidently D'Angelo had been following the tabloids and was referring to Ryan and Sadarius. Micah knew that the stories weren't true. Not that Sadarius wouldn't like to be with her, that was obvious, but Micah had kept a careful eye on the two of them. He could tell Leese wasn't looking for a boyfriend. "I don't think she could forgive me for that, but all I want is to confront her about why she left me and beg her to come back."

D'Angelo had an expression that was difficult to read, it seemed to be a cross between fear and disgust, "Begging hardly seems your caliber, Micah."

"It depends on what's at stake—she is worth begging for."

"So you're telling me after you confront her, no matter how this turns out, you will come see me and finish what I need done?"

"I'm finishing this season's shows. Just what do you need?" Micah said with his suspicions exposed about what D'Angelo was really after this time.

"You're taking out a boss."

"No," came immediately out of his mouth. The boss was the very head of the family; a man to be respected at all times and to be obeyed at all costs. D'Angelo wasn't second in line so what could he possibly benefit by taking out the head of the family?

"Not the head of our family," he clarified. "There is another family that is receptive to uniting with us, but their Boss is against it. It won't be easy, but you've handled things more complicated."

"Which family?" There was something very wrong in all of this and Micah wanted to know who was behind it.

"No need to give out too many details right now. No one else could be trusted to do this for me and I won't give up if the family has to convene *again* about letting you out. I don't need to remind you about your secrets."

"They're your secrets, too."

"Don't threaten me, Micah. You aren't *that* valuable."

"Evidently I am," Micah stated finishing his meal. He stood from the table and downed the last of his glass of wine, "I will finish what I'm doing with this show which, by the way, has proven to pay out more than anything I've ever made with the mob."

"Sit down, Micah."

Micah seemed to be locked at the knees.

"Sit," D'Angelo reiterated.

Micah slowly lowered himself back in the chair as D'Angelo poured him another glass of wine, "So, you've aroused my interest. You've done well with the show. How good has the investment been?"

"I've tripled my money—so far."

D'Angelo finally smiled, "I will admit your little whor—girlfriend," he corrected, "is an excellent singer. She may have a future doing this. Did you know all along she could sing?"

"I heard her sing just days after I got the job to kill her. She thrives on music and I even used an iPod when I proposed to her."

D'Angelo's eyebrows went up, "Really? You recorded your proposal?"

"No," Micah said shaking his head, "I downloaded one song that told her how I felt about her and then had it delivered. I waited to see what her reaction would be before I approached her and proposed."

D'Angelo was giving his evil half smile, "I never knew you had a romantic side."

Micah's pulse was picking up and he could feel the cool sweat coming over him, "Murder doesn't lend to that emotion."

"On the contrary, Micah. You should remember that murder is the highest crime of passion. *Remember that when you catch up to her.*"

He didn't like the remark, or the insinuation, "There is no passion in making a mark, not anymore anyway."

Their meeting ended abruptly as Micah's pulse continued to rise.

When she ran out of the party, Micah called for his private plane to be fueled and ready. He was possessed with the need to get to her and find out why she was willing and then suddenly chose Ryan. It was late, but he would make sure a car would be waiting for him at the Colorado Springs airport in the morning. But before leaving, he needed to rest. He was still feeling the ill effects from lunch. It was worth investigating, and he wouldn't put it past D'Angelo to poison him. He was valuable alive, but there were reasons for D'Angelo to eliminate him as well.

Micah pulled out a familiar black case and opened the bag pulling out a hypodermic and a rubber strap. He tied off the band, using his teeth to pull it tight and then plunged the needle into his vein, filling the syringe quickly. He wouldn't waste time getting it to a lab now, but he knew the blood would say usable for at least five days. He wrote a short note and wrapped it around the syringe, then opened his office refrigerator and carefully placed it out of view. If anything should happen to him, David would find the note and the vial; D'Angelo would pay.

By 7 a.m., Micah was ready to leave. He had all the information he needed. She had one home in Colorado Springs in Ryan's name and one in her own. He would try her address first. He wasn't sure if he should trust himself to bring his guns, especially not with the odd effects he was still feeling, but he didn't debate it long as he strapped on the harness.

He developed a new symptom as he sat in the quiet cabin area of the jet. He looked down and noticed his hands were shaking. He was starting to wonder if what he was feeling was actually a case of nerves. He'd been rock-steady his whole life and now, when he needed composure, he had the shakes. He opened the bar and stared at the bottles of alcohol. Surely she would smell it on his breath, but he needed something to stop the tremors as he poured himself a Jack and Coke that was mostly Jack. The cold sweats had returned as his trembling hand lifted the glass to his lips and he chugged down what he really didn't want to drink. His emotions were slipping beyond his control as he fought the urge to grab the bottle and lose every ounce of reason he possessed.

Chapter Twenty-Four

Sunrise on Sunday morning found me on the pool deck watching the sky change colors over the white landscape. I had determined that I wasn't going to back out of Remake. There were only three days until the final show, and I would finish what I'd started. But I would question Don first and make sure all the voting results hadn't been tainted by the 'owner' trying to keep me on the show.

I hadn't slept at all last night, but I needed some rest before Ryan showed after church. I knew it would be just the two of us; he wouldn't bring Candace. I grabbed the most recent tee-shirt that he'd given me and crawled into the bed, willing my aching heart to sleep.

I woke to a strange noise just before twelve. It sounded as if someone was in the house, but it was too early for Ryan to show up unless he skipped out on the worship service. I got up and glanced in the mirror. I still had dark circles under my eyes from crying so much last night.

"Ryan?" I called out as I emerged into the living room.

"He's not here," came a male voice from my kitchen area.

I screamed before I could stifle it as I turned and saw Micah standing inside my house. "Wha—what are you doing in here?"

"I came to see you," he stated as if I should have expected him.

This wasn't good. Ryan would be showing up in the next fifteen to twenty minutes and I could clearly see by his unzipped jacket that he was armed. I would have to be strong and I would have to get rid of him in a hurry. I couldn't show any weakness and I couldn't fall as easily as I did when I ended up in his arms last night.

"You need to leave," I was trying to be firm, but not panicked.

"Why? Last night you were ready for me to take you and now you want me to go away?"

I studied his eyes. I could tell the level of danger by watching those green barometers. He was on an edge; anger was in place of the deadly emptiness that I feared more than anything.

"Please, leave Micah. We settled this last night."

He began moving toward me as I backed slowly.

"Nothing was settled last night, Leese. You wanted me, you needed me, and then you ran away. All I want is to know why? Why Ryan? I don't believe you love him."

"Don't doubt that, Micah. I do love him."

"More than me?"

I could feel the stab to my heart, "I'm here."

I couldn't back anymore as I had reached the couch and was ready to turn and move around it when he swiftly reached out and grabbed my arm.

"*Don't* keep walking away from me."

I could smell his breath and I knew he'd been drinking. He wasn't drunk, but he was definitely not in his right mind. I had never seen Micah in this state, and fear was spiking inside me as I desperately tried to remain calm. "Please," I re-asked. "Please don't do this—I need you to leave."

"Will he be home soon, Leese? What did he do? Did he go out to get you something to eat? Did you get your thrills with him last night?" He was so close to going over the edge, it was almost visible.

"Out! I want you out now," I demanded with a shaky voice.

He grabbed my upper arms so hard that I could feel the bruising as he jerked me to his chest, covering my mouth with his. I could taste the alcohol; I could taste the hate and the need he had to kill someone. I pushed hard against his chest, breaking the kiss and slapping his cheek. It was as if I had placed the blade to my chest just as in my nightmare. To hurt him, was to kill myself.

I could see my reaction stunned him and then he seemed to unravel with fury as the back of his hand hit me hard in the face and I flew backward onto the coffee table sending the items on the table scattering. I rolled off the table to the floor and covered my cheek with my hand. It had been a powerful hit and it stung horribly. I could taste the blood in my mouth.

I was rising from the floor when I looked back into his eyes. I couldn't tell who he was. He had given into the animal part of himself and he didn't care that I had just been knocked across the room.

"Tell me why you left me," he growled, snatching me by the wrist with a steel grip.

I tried to twist out of the weakest part of his hold, but at the moment there were no weaknesses. Again he was trying to kiss me, but his mouth was so hard and unyielding that I could feel my lips being cut by my teeth as he slammed into me.

"Stop it, Micah, please," I begged as I pushed away from him.

"Why? Don't you like this, baby," he said mocking me. "Is that it, Leese? Is he better in bed than I am?" He was grabbing at my body roughly as I struggled with him. "Maybe you just need a refresher?" He grabbed the front of my blouse and quickly ripped it open. I could hear my buttons skittering across the floor.

I was crying out for him to stop, but I could tell he wasn't hearing my pleas as he pushed me violently back onto the couch. I was no longer dealing with Micah; I was dealing with pure rage. I was shocked that he was actually undoing his jeans as I rolled from the couch and scrambled on all fours to try to get away. He grabbed me brutally by my calves and jerked me back.

"No!" I screamed at him as he flipped me onto my back. I was kicking and sliding backwards as he continued to grab at me as if I was nothing more than a piece of meat. He was bruising my thighs as he pulled me to him. He lowered himself toward me and I took the only opening I had to punch toward his face. I was aiming for his nose, hoping to stun him enough that I could get out before his weight came down on me, but he was too skilled of a fighter as he turned his face and I hit his rock-hard jaw. His hand came around my throat and tightened so hard I thought he would crush my windpipe. He slapped my face twice, open handed, but shockingly hard.

I was passing out. I couldn't breathe. His hand moved just before I lost consciousness. I gasped and sputtered for air. Then he was on me, his weight crushing my already air deprived lungs. He was tearing the last of my clothes and under garments, my body screaming in pain as the elastic on my bra cut into my skin. Then he was biting me, not the way he used to when he would make love to me, but literally sinking his teeth into skin. I was crying and pleading for him to stop. I was saying his name over and over, hoping it would shake him out of his inhuman state before he did the unthinkable.

It was too late. I screamed out in pain as his body tore into mine. I wasn't prepared for his entrance and even if I had been, his aim was skewed and my body seemed to split under the punching drive of his hips. His massive hands were gripping my shoulders too hard and it felt as if he had bruised every inch of my body has he raped me on the floor.

I was convulsing with sobs, as the violence slowed. The rage was releasing its hold over him and he began to call out my name. He was becoming controlled as he found his rhythm inside me. "Leese, Leese, I'm sorry," he cried, tears now coursing down his face as he continued to bring himself back to the human side. "I love you, baby—I'm so sorry—I need you so badly—please, please don't cry." He lifted slightly as he looked into my bloody, shocked face. His mouth came down again, but this time softly, kissing my eyes and my cheeks, my chin and my mouth.

My body was starting to respond to what was now turning gentle. I didn't want to let my physical side win this battle, because that was what it had been, but the needs I'd had stored away for so long were now being brought to life.

His mouth was begging me to part my lips and respond. With tears rolling down my cheeks, I accepted the kiss; the taste of my blood mixing with the flavor of the alcohol. His hips were grinding so deliberately and I couldn't fight the feeling any longer as I cried out and thrust my hips upward to meet his strokes. He cried out at the same moment and we crested together.

I didn't want to open my eyes and look at him as he observed the damage he'd done to me. "God, Leese, why did it have to be this way?" he said with a stunned, choked sob, "I never meant... I didn't want to hurt—"

At that moment, I heard the sound of the Javelin and terror flooded me. Micah raised himself, pulling up and refastening his jeans. His human side simply vanished as his eyes went blank; he reached in his jacket and pulled out his pistol.

"No," I begged, gripping his arm, the gun pointing dangerously toward me, "Don't hurt him, Micah. I swear if you hurt him then you might as well kill me right now."

His eyes were still blank as I heard the engine turn off. He looked up and then looked back at me.

I grabbed the barrel and pressed it to my chest. "Go ahead," I choked, "pull the trigger, Micah, because I won't live if you hurt him."

"I—I can't."

My finger went into the trigger guard and I was poised to finish this.

"Don't Leese," he said pushing the safety back on with his other hand, "He's not worth it, is he?"

"He's worth every breath left in my body. Take his life and you've ended mine, too."

I could hear as the key was turning in the lock. Micah was up and away from me in an instant, the gun still gripped in his hand. The scream strangled in my throat as Ryan opened the door and Micah jerked him inside and slammed him against the wall so hard I thought he would knock him out.

Ryan's eyes blinked a couple times, not really understanding what had just happened. The gun went against his head as Micah spewed out the two bitterest words I'd ever heard in my life.

"Your turn," he growled, then slammed his shoulder into Ryan's chest, knocking the air out of him and then letting him fall to the floor. Micah was out the door. A car cranked and I heard it screech away from the house.

"Leese?" he coughed and gasped out my name.

I was so relieved that Micah hadn't killed him that I couldn't speak. I couldn't move from where I'd been drilled to the floor; my body beginning to cramp and burn and ache.

Ryan rose, shaking his head as if he was trying to bring his brain back to life. He looked toward the couch and he saw me. I think he thought at the moment I was dead, because the look on his face was horror struck. He rushed to my side as the ability to sob returned to me. I didn't want him to see me stripped down naked, but there was nothing left of my clothes to cover me.

"Oh, God, baby girl, oh, God—what the hell did he do to you?" he said reaching under me as gently as possible and picking me up from the floor. He carried me to the bedroom, tears pouring down his face as he laid me down and used the corner of the sheet to cover my body.

"That son-of-a-bitch is going to jail," he snarled, grabbing his cell and flipping it open.

"No," I choked, reaching out and stopping him, "No cops—*please*, I don't want anyone to know,"

"You've… God, Leese, you've got to go to the hospital. You're bleeding, baby girl, pretty bad. I—I don't know what to do."

"I'll be okay—I just need—"

"Leese, I'm freaking out here—*I don't know what to do to help you.*"

"I—I—need to wash off and get some clothes. Can you help me to the bathroom?" I pleaded, the pain growing stronger and I was starting to double over.

He removed the sheet and reached underneath me as I wrapped my arms feebly around his neck. He lowered me into the tub and turned on the warm water, allowing the tub to fill as he used a washcloth to clean my face and neck. He was crying his eyes out as he washed each cut, bruise, and bite mark. He worked lower, but I took the washcloth away from his trembling hand and I washed my most private area. It stung so badly to clean the tear. He drained the pink water and helped me stand as he wrapped me in a towel and carried me back to the bed, placing me on the opposite side to avoid the stained sheets and then went to the dresser.

He returned with a button up the front top and a pair of underwear.

"I need a—a pad. Would you get me one from under the bathroom sink?"

He returned and helped me swing my legs over the side of the bed as I slipped on the underwear and placed the pad inside and pulled them up. He took the bloody sheet away and came back with a fresh blanket and covered me up, crawling in behind me and trying to find a way to hold me that wouldn't cause me any further pain.

"You can't let him just get away with this," he whispered, smoothing my hair away from my temple. "You've got to turn him in."

"No—I know you won't understand this, but something was wrong. He wasn't himself."

"Leese, I think you're wrong—I think you just met the real Micah."

"No," I sobbed, refusing to believe him. "I know him well enough, he didn't intend for this to happen."

"Don't say another word. Don't cover for what he did. I want to kill him bad enough at the moment; we've got to stop talking about him."

He held me for a while and I began to drift. When I woke up, I was alone and I heard voices. All I could hope and pray was that he hadn't called the police.

"Ryan?" I called out.

He entered the room with Candace, "I had to have someone, Leese. I can't handle this."

Candace sat gently on the edge of the bed and by the expression on her face I must have looked pretty bad.

She pulled back the covers to see the rest of me and I could see her flinch. "He's got to go to jail," she stated matter-of-factly.

I touched her hand as I shook my head, no.

"Leese, this was worse than a beating, he—he raped you."

"No," I whispered. "No one except the three of us is going to know anything about this—I couldn't take it if this got to the press. My mom..." I choked up, but stopped before the tears spilt over my lashes.

"We can't leave you here like this."

"I'm staying," Ryan stated with a hard edge. "I won't be coming home until she's—"

"Bring her to our house," Candace said gently. "You said the crazy son-of-a-bitch pulled a gun on you, and I don't want the two of you here and have him show back up."

"No!" Ryan snapped back at her. "I don't want to take a chance of him showing up with you around. I want you to go stay at your dad's for a few—"

"No, Ryan, I—"

"Please, Candace. This is bad enough. I couldn't take it if something happened to you, too."

I could see his concern for her safety washed over her like a wave of love, and then the tough exterior peeled away and she began to cry, "I don't want anything to happen to you either."

He dried her tears and held her close, "Don't worry, please. I'll turn on the alarm and I'll call the police if I even suspect that he's around. Stay at your dad's—for me—Candace, please."

She finally left and he went around and locked every door and window, set the alarm and crawled in beside me. I had drawn my knees up which made it difficult for him to hold me the way he normally did, so he let his hand rest on my shoulder as I fell back asleep.

The next day the cramping was worse and I was still incredibly sore. My body looked hideous like I'd been tossed over a mountainside and had rolled all the way to the bottom. Ryan tried to get me to eat, but I honestly didn't want anything. By noon he said he was going to go get me something for the pain, but he would be back as quickly as possible. Within thirty minutes, he sat beside the bed with a glass of dark amber liquid.

"Sit up, baby girl," he was trying to help me up from under the covers.

"No, wait. I don't have my shirt on," I said looking for wherever it went. It felt like it was cutting into my bruises last night and I had pulled it off, now all I had was a bra that Candace helped me get on before she left the day before.

"Leese, you were absolutely naked yesterday. I can handle your bra and underwear. Drink some of this."

I was in so much pain that I was cringing as he propped the pillows behind me. He brought the glass to my face; the strong aroma of alcohol hit me. I pushed his hand away, "No—what is that?"

"Brandy. Drink it."

"No," I refused.

"Leese, when I was little I'd get terrible stomach aches and my dad would give me sips of brandy to ease the pain. It always worked. Please, drink it—I wouldn't do anything to hurt you."

I knew that as I allowed him to bring it back to my mouth. It was strong, yet had a strange, smooth quality that warmed my throat and stomach immediately. "I can't drink all of this," I protested.

"It's like seven or eight ounces; it's not that much and it will help."

He encouraged me to continue as I sipped until nothing remained in the glass. I was warm all over, but not the same as when David doped me with ecstasy. This was a different kind of warm. The cramps seemed to blend away in the heat and my eyelids drooped heavily as I realized I had consumed enough to pass out. The last thing I remembered was moaning softly that I wanted to sleep as he slid me down in the bed.

"I'm sorry," I heard him whisper as he kissed my forehead, but I was too sleepy to care what he was apologizing for as I drifted away.

I woke eight hours later to the sound of my cell phone going off. "Who is it?" I asked weakly.

"Don't worry about it."

"Ryan, who is it?"

"It's Don—at least I think it's Don unless Micah is using his phone."

I put out my hand.

"No."

"Give it to me. He's calling about Wednesday."

Reluctantly he handed it to me as I caught it before it had gone to voicemail.

"Leese," came Don's panicked voice, "you were supposed to be back in L.A. last night. We've got—"

"I can't—I can't get back for the special Wednesday. I've—"

"Can't! We're talking the finale, here! What do you mean can't?!"

"I was in a—a—car accident," I began. The line was silent so I continued, "I'm really banged up and I can't go on stage looking like this. I can barely stand up for that matter."

"I'm sorry, Leese, I didn't know. What happened? Was anyone else hurt?"

"No—no—it was a deer in the road," I lied. "It went right through the windshield. I've got cuts and bruises everywhere."

"Don't worry about a thing. I'll either get the network to run a Christmas special or Remake reruns. I'll let you know as soon as I work it out."

The next day, he was standing at my bedside, "Geez, a deer did this? It looks more like a grizzly. Are those bite marks?" he said looking at my shoulder.

I pulled the blanket up to cover the mark, "No, just lots of glass."

"Well, you're lucky it didn't take your head off. That little Aero must be tougher than it looks."

"It was a rental car," I stated quickly. My Aero was in the garage without a scratch on it.

"I just wanted you to know you've got two weeks to recoup. The network is doing a Christmas special and then the next week they're doing a top 100 music count down. I tell you if our show hadn't been so popular they would have cut our throats for—"

"Don, I've got to know something about Remake. Is there anyway someone could have tampered with the voting results?"

He looked confused and a little upset at the question, "No—we have an independent accounting firm that takes care of the tallies. We aren't allowed to have anything to do with that part."

"Good," I sighed.

"Why? Did you think we were cheating?"

"I just wanted to be sure that I earned my spot and it wasn't the result of—of ownership."

"Absolutely not. The owner doesn't—"

"Micah Gavarreen," I stated. I could see it shocked him that I knew who owned the show. "He's my ex-husband and I had no idea—"

"Ah, shit! You're kidding, right? But, you're a Winslett."

"You honestly didn't know who he was to her?" Ryan asked, butting into the conversation.

"Is that why I didn't have to audition like the other contestants?"

"He insisted you were going to have a slot, without an audition, but I didn't know he was... If the press gets wind of this we're sunk. We can kiss next year goodbye."

"Well, there are only five people that know and three of us are in this room. The other two are Micah and Ryan's girlfriend."

"I thought you were Ryan's girlfriend."

"No, that was a ruse. We're only friends."

"Good grief, are there any other secrets I should know about, like you're secretly a man or something?"

I laughed in spite of the pain. It was the only humor I'd felt in days.

"Where is he, by the way?" Ryan asked.

"He's at the studio. I mean he has spent most of his days and evening in his office, but just in the last two days he's actually started walking around the studio and meeting the crew."

"So he is in L.A.?" Ryan continued to press.

"Yeah, he practically lives in studio. Why?"

"Just curious."

When Don left, I told Ryan to call Candace and go home. Micah wasn't going to show back up at my house. I was able to move around and I didn't need him to be my mother-hen. We argued for another hour and he finally relented and called Candace and told her he was coming home.

Christmas Eve and Christmas passed quietly. Ryan and Candace visited for a while both nights, but we had sworn off of gift giving. I tended to go overboard and they said they couldn't compete, so we skipped it. Mom called and said she and Kimmy would like to come out for Christmas, but I turned her down with the excuse that the show was keeping me busy—even if they did move the finale.

I was healing on the outside slowly, but mentally I was crumbling. The more I considered what he had done, the more I thought about endings, the deeper and darker my mood became. I was refusing Ryan's assistance at every available opportunity, telling him I was sleeping fine and I needed private time to get my life back together. He couldn't make out the dark circles under my eyes for the bruises that were already in place.

I was like a hermit now. All I wanted was nothingness. I sat in my bed most of the time just weeping and wishing something I'd never wished in my life; I wished I'd never met Micah. I was still in love with him, but what he had called my 'innocence' that had drawn him hopelessly to me had been completely destroyed. It was like everyday my soul was being stripped down to reveal a vacant person inside me, and I didn't like that person.

I kept thinking about the fact that I had been so determined to finish the last show on Remake, but now I was dreading every minute it came closer. Micah would surely show himself this time and I couldn't face him. I was starting to seriously doubt my sanity as I sat in the bed and discussed my life with myself. I wanted to fall in to a deep chasm where none of this existed and I could find some peace. I had made it to the one week mark; one week since I had been brutalized by someone I had sacrificed my hopes, my dreams, and my life for.

I cried out to God and asked Him why? I had tried my whole life to honor Him and to do what was right in His eyes. How could He have allowed it to come to this point? I'd always believed in Divine purpose, but now it felt as if that hope had also been stripped away from me. I sat there weeping and yearning for the rest that wouldn't come.

I'd been awake for almost forty-eight hours since my last brief attempt at sleep and I knew if I didn't sleep soon, my sanity wouldn't matter because it would be gone. I dug in the medicine cabinet for my Unisom; the box was empty. Ryan's tee-shirt didn't comfort me anymore, and I was starting to think about jumping into my ice cold pool and just letting myself sink to the bottom, but it wasn't the way I wanted to leave the world.

I was leaning back on my pillows when I remembered what I had tucked away inside my nightstand. There was something that could transport me to the void I was yearning to find. I pulled out the unlabeled bottle and opened it, pouring the blue capsules into my hand. One capsule and I would sleep for a day. Two capsules and I'd sleep for perhaps two days. Three capsules and I'd most likely sleep forever.

"Hey," came a voice from my doorway. It frightened me so badly that I spilt the pills onto my bed.

I looked up to see Ryan standing there with a puzzled expression, "I didn't mean to scare you—I thought you heard me come in. I called out your name, but…" He looked at my face and then he looked at the capsules on the bed. "What are you doing?" he asked with clear suspicion.

I began gathering them up as he approached me. "Nothing, I was just going to take something to help me sleep," I breathed out unsteadily.

"What are these?" he asked as he picked one up and studied it. He took the bottle from my hand, "Where did you get these? There's no label on the bottle."

"I—a guy from—I… I don't have to explain everything to you," I snapped.

"Who gave these to you—and don't duck the question."

"A stage hand from Remake; he said they'd help me sleep."

"Have you been taking these?" A look of deep concern crossed his face, "Answer me, Annalisa."

He rarely used my full name.

"I—I—took one a couple months ago and then he sold me this bottle."

"Were you able to sleep?" his questions were becoming gentle, but he was still very suspicious as to why I had them out now.

"Yeah," I choked, "twenty-five hours worth."

The eyes went huge and round. "What did you pay for these?" he asked as he removed them from my hand. "Answer me, damn it! What did this cost you?"

"Fiv—five hundred dollars," I whispered.

"Shit! Leese, you bought dope! What is wrong with you?!"

"They're not dope. They're stamped," I argued, trying to take one from him to point out the lettering. "They're prescription. I just didn't—didn't go to a doctor."

"You bought drugs. Don't try to cover that up. I can't believe you even took one of these. What if he knew you'd be knocked out and planned to break into your room? Did you ever think about that? And what were you planning to do with a handful?" Suddenly his face went two shades lighter, "No, don't you even think about doing something stupid like that, baby girl—just how many were you going to take—enough to let me find you dead in here today?!"

"No," I sobbed.

He sat down on the bed placing the capsules back in the bottle and took firm hold of my shoulders. I wouldn't look at him as the tears fell down my cheeks. I felt his hand reach under my chin and tip my head back, "Tell me the God's honest truth, were you thinking about taking more than one of these?"

I couldn't answer. Yes, the thought was going through my mind, but he stopped me before I had a chance to make the decision.

His eyes welled with tears, "So that's it then. You were planning a Marilyn Monroe on me! Damn it, Leese," he yelled as he picked up the bottle and slammed it against the wall. The cap stayed in place as the bottle bounced to the middle of the floor. He ran his fingers into his hair as he grabbed a double-fistful, pacing a small circle on the floor. "Why?! Over him?" he shouted at me. "What about me? What about your mom and your sister and everyone that loves you? All right fine," he said, picking up the bottle and opening it. "You want to do this then let's do it together! Okay, how's that?" He put a small pile of capsules in my hand as he held the others. "I changed my whole life for you. Why not change the ending, too." And then he tossed the capsules into his mouth.

"NO! RYAN, NO! Please, please. God, please, spit them out!"
My pills scattered to the floor as I lunged for him. He refused to
open his mouth. "Please, baby," I cried out. "I'll do anything you
want—anything. *Just don't do this, please."*

He opened his mouth letting the capsules spill out into his palm,
"You're going to take every one of these to the toilet and flush them
down. You will *never* buy drugs again."

I was nodding my head furiously, "Yes, okay," I agreed as I
pulled the wet mass from his palm. My hands were shaking
uncontrollably as I dropped to the floor sobbing, trying to find all the
ones that had scattered.

Then he was on the floor with me, holding me in his arms as I
cried, "I love you, Leese—don't ever do anything like this again."
He kissed me, it seemed every available place; temple, forehead,
eyes, nose, ear, throat and then softly on the lips. "I don't know what
I'd do if I lost you. You've got a piece of me and I'm never going to
get it back. You've got to take care of it. Do you understand?" He
kissed my lips again, slower this time, but he wasn't seeking
something sexual. This was sweet emotion from an exposed heart,
"I'll be your sleeping pill for as long as you need me. I knew I
shouldn't have believed you when you said you were okay. That
crap about wanting to be alone isn't going to fly with me anymore."

He finished gathering the pills, "How many were there?" He was
going to make sure nothing was left.

"Twenty, I think—yeah, I'm pretty sure it was twenty."

He counted them and then placed them in my hand, "You're
flushing them, I'm watching."

I was trembling so hard, I could barely hit the opening in the
toilet.

"Have you been eating?" he asked as he tried to keep me from
shaking.

I shook my head no.

"I'm making you something to eat. Then I'm calling Candace
and you and I are going to bed." He left no room for rebuttal.

A little while later, safe in his arms, I went gratefully into
oblivion.

Chapter Twenty-Five

The only problem now was that Ryan was stuck to me like glue. He wouldn't let me do anything without him being present. Candace was spending a lot of time at my house, and I knew it was because she was missing him terribly and the only way she could get to see him was to be around me. It was wearing on her and I could tell he needed to give her some attention or his whole plan of helping me was going to hurt them both in the long run. I just couldn't figure out how to shake him loose again. I finally told Candace to stay the night at my house, so she could wile him away from me. That seemed to help because for the first time in a week, he wasn't focused on me as she teased him into one of the other bedrooms.

I sat on my bed, grateful it worked and I had some breathing room. I was restless tonight anyway because the show was only three days away. We were performing the day after New Year's, and the two week delay only served to build the public's anticipation for the finale.

My bruises and marks were nearly healed as I stood in the bathroom and studied myself in the nude. They were light yellowish green now and the bite marks healed to fine pink lines that, hopefully, would fade in time. I filled the tub with hot sudsy water and slid in, letting the jets relax me. I was totally relaxed, forgetting about the show, forgetting about what was going on in the other bedroom, forgetting about Micah, forgetting...

"Ah!" A thought struck me as I inhaled and sat up in the tub. Over the past fifteen days, I had forgotten some things too well. The longer I sat and concentrated on it, the more I began to see things clearly—especially things of God and things of purpose. Wow, what a difference a revelation could make.

I was up before both of them the next morning. My hair brushed, makeup on, and I was in the kitchen putting together a big breakfast. The scent of fresh perked hot coffee drifted through the house and mingled with the tantalizing aroma of bacon, eggs, and biscuits. It didn't take long for my aromatic wakeup call to work.

They came out together, sleepy faced and puzzled, but smiling as they entered the kitchen and sat at the island.

"Just in time. I've got breakfast ready," I said as I began filling their plates, "I put cheese over the scrambled eggs. I hope you guys don't mind." I placed the plates in front of the silent pair, "You two look like you could use some coffee." I poured two big cups and set them down in front of them with the sugar and cream containers, as I sat down and joined them.

"What got into you this morning?" Ryan asked. "By the way, you look great."

"You must be feeling—better," Candace seemed to be having a problem finding the right word.

"I am."

Ryan looked suspicious now.

"Honestly," I defended. "I'm okay. By the way, Don called me early this morning and he wants me in studio, at the latest, by Wednesday morning."

"I can't believe you're going to actually finish the show," Ryan stated. "I'm going with you. You know that right? I'm not taking a chance that he'll get his hands back on you."

"He's not going to bother me in a crowded studio and I don't plan on being alone. It's fly out, do the show, fly back the same night and..." I'd almost said a little too much.

"And, what?"

"And then I'm done. It'll be all over with and I won't be going back to L.A. ever again."

"I'm still going."

I could see the worry spread over Candace's face. "I have an idea," I said with a smile. "Why don't we all go? Candace couldn't go before because well, you would look like you were into polygamy, but she can now."

I watched her face brighten.

"No," Ryan snapped.

"Come on," I urged, pushing his shoulder. "We won't be in any danger during the show and we aren't going to hang around afterward."

"What if you win? They'll expect you to hang around for a while."

"Nope, win or lose, I'm out of there right after I say goodbye to my friends."

"Please," Candace asked, finally finding her voice.

He was out numbered and hopeless to turn down the women in his life. "All right, fine. But if I see him coming around, both of you are out of there."

All the Remake contestants were back for the finale to a packed house. Tonight's venue was completely different from how the show normally worked. The artists were to be a surprise. We would have less than a half an hour to meet and learn the song. Then we would perform with the artist and band, but we would be the lead vocal.

I wasn't surprised when I found out what we were singing. They had been hand-picked by ownership. I would sing '*The Reason*' with Hoobastank, and Sadarius would sing '*I'll Make Love To You*,' with Boyz II Men. Micah was either trying to make me remember what we meant to each other or he simply wanted me to breakdown and cry on stage. I wasn't crying tonight. The song he chose for me had too much meaning now to do anything else but give it my best.

I had drawn the first slot and I went on stage and gave a stellar performance. I looked for him as I sang. I had a feeling, if he wasn't sitting in his office watching on the monitor, he would be somewhere tucked away from the crowd and the cameras. Just as I was a verse away from the end, I saw him appear in the edge of one of the exit corridors. I knew he realized I'd seen him as he hesitated and seemed to be ready to back away from my gaze, and then he decided to stay as I finished the song.

I took my seat as Sadarius prepared to sing. I watched the whole time to see if he would leave or stay. Sadarius did an incredible job with his song as well; Micah standing off in the distance watching. When we finished our performances, they opened the voting lines and the public had one hour to vote while all the contestants came on stage for a music medley. They played numerous clips from the first show all the way through. I was being careful to avoid Carrie at all costs, but she didn't seem like her old self, she was actually smiling and happy.

The big announcement had finally arrived as Sadarius and I were called to center stage. I had planned all along if I won I was giving the money to him. He was a decent, moral and kind person who deserved everything this opportunity could afford him. And, if he won, I'd simply be happy for him because he was truly an awesome singer, and I hoped he would get to fulfill his dreams of cutting a record deal after the show.

Our emcee opened the envelope as the lights all around us dimmed and we were the only two remaining in the spotlight.

"By a separation of less than three percent, the winner of season one, Remake is… Sadarius Collins!"

The confetti and balloons were dropping from the ceiling as the crowd rose to their feet. Sadarius was hugging me so tightly, tears running down his face. He kept saying, "I don't believe it! I don't believe it!"

"You did it," I smiled over the roar of the crowd. But, what I didn't expect was him to plant a big kiss on my lips right there, live on stage with millions of viewer watching as he dipped me slightly backward. I know my expression reflected my surprise as he righted me. He smiled and said we needed to give the tabloids more to write about. I laughed in spite of my dislike for the tabloids.

All the contestants went back stage and Dobrey approached me and gave me a hug, slipping something in my hand as I thanked her and tucked it away. Ryan and Candace fought through the crowd to get to me. The three of us were taking off despite the huge party they were throwing at the Hilton's grand ballroom.

We were back in Colorado Springs by two in the morning, and they drove me home. Ryan was prepared to stay the night again, when I simply told him no.

"You two are going home—your home. I'll—"

"No way," he began.

"I'm going to make sure everything is locked up tight. I'm setting the alarm and I'm going to enjoy some peace and quiet—go home."

We argued for a little longer until he finally realized that I would not relent. My mood had been so upbeat that I gave him no reason to worry and fret over me, and I could tell he was starting to give in. Reluctantly, he and Candace left for home.

There was a lot to be done in a short span of time. I spent a couple hours packing and loading my car. Everything wouldn't fit, and what was left would be bagged and set on the curb for one of the charity organizations to pick up. The rest of the time was spent cleaning the house and boxing food that I was leaving behind for Ryan to take home. I was finally getting away and he was not going with me. He had someone that changed his world and he needed to focus on her, not me.

I'd called a local salon the day before the show and made a private appointment for early this morning. The long brown hair extensions were going. I was getting a trim and going back to blonde, maybe even ultra blond this time. By seven a.m. I was in the hairdresser's chair and losing my famous appearance; then it was back to the house by nine.

I had just sat down to compose my letter to Ryan when a UPS truck pulled into the yard. The driver came to the door with a small package in hand. I signed and went back inside, wondering what it could possibly contain. I opened it carefully and pulled away the lid to the brown box to reveal a new Apple iPod with a note. The writing was Micah's and had evidently been scrawled quickly. All it read was "No one has to pay me for this job. Micah"

My heart was picking up the pace as I began looking around. He wasn't far away the last time he had one of these delivered to me. I hated being afraid of him, but after our last meeting, and this odd note that seemed to lean toward murder, I was terrified. I got up and locked the door and turned on my alarm system and put my cell phone beside me.

The iPod contained a single song. I knew the group, and the song sounded familiar, but I didn't remember it. It was 'Breath,' by Breaking Benjamin. I slipped the earphones on as the song began to play. My heart froze against my breast, a lump rising in my throat and my hands began to tremble as I listened to the words, '...So sacrifice yourself...I'm going all the way...You take the breath right out of me. You left a hole where my heart should be. You got to fight just to make it through, 'cause I will be the death of you."

He had gone from being remorseful after he attacked me, to now letting me know he was going to end my life and no one had to pay

292

him to get the job done this time. "Oh, Micah," I whispered, "Why baby, why?" I had my escape planned before I received his threat, but I would be extra careful now because I couldn't allow him to get anywhere near me.

I was prepared to write a farewell to Ryan, but now my heart was heavy and what should have been a happy moment to let go of him had been darkly overshadowed. I wrote it and left it lying on the coffee table. I made no mention of the fact that I was, once again, on the run from Micah. I simply told him I loved him too much to keep being the thing pulling him away from the life he should have had before he met me. Just as I was finishing the note, my cell rang. It was Ryan. I didn't know if I could get through a conversation with him without breaking down.

"Hey handsome," I said softly.

"Hey, yourself, baby girl. Candace is at work today and I've got permission to spend my free time with you. I'm on my way over and I don't plan on you turning me away."

I took a slow breath. I was really going to miss him. "Sounds good to me, just let yourself in when you get here." I paused for a moment, "Ryan…"

"Yeah?"

"I love you."

I could hear the smile through the receiver, "Love you too, Leese. I'll be there in ten."

I closed the phone and grabbed my keys. I would be long gone in ten minutes.

Chapter Twenty-Six

It had only been two days since the show ended. Micah was finishing up the details as he prepared to head back to Louisiana. What he really wanted was to see Leese and tell her how much he honestly regretted what he'd done that day. But, like the lady she was, she came back and finished the show with her head held high and wouldn't look away when she saw him.

His health was back to normal. Once again he was rock-steady and under complete control, but the toxicology reports on his vial of blood came back as a near overdose of anabolic steroids mix with amphetamines. He knew D'Angelo spiked the food and probably the wine to make certain he was filled with rage and aggression when he confronted her. But, he couldn't prove it, and D'Angelo had already denied any wrong doing when he questioned him. He couldn't do anything about it at this point, and he still was furious over his own ignorance for going to where she was when he knew something wasn't right, but what was done, was done. As far as he was concerned, no matter the reason or cause behind it, he made the worst mistake of his life.

If Leese harbored any doubts between loving him or Ryan, he was certain he destroyed any chance he had of winning her back. He didn't have a reason to live any more, but he knew the stigma and suffering it would bring to his family if he blew his brains out. He would keep doing the ever increasingly dangerous jobs D'Angelo had for him until someone took care of the problem.

He neared the stage when one of Don's assistants approached him. "This was just delivered for you, Mr. Gavarreen," the young woman stated, handing the envelope to him and then walking away.

He stared at the plain white envelope. There was no need to open what looked suspicious in the presence of others, so he headed down the corridor toward his office passing people in the hallway as he did. Curiosity wasn't going to be delayed for complete privacy as his finger slipped under the edge of the flap and tore it loose. They were photographs, and from the small piece of hip that was exposed they were of a woman with very little clothing on. He reached his office door, oblivious to those around him as he carefully revealed what remained of the first picture. Everything within him froze; unbearable wasn't the proper word for what he saw.

Suddenly he felt two men on either side grasping his arms. He knew he didn't have a chance. Their hold was like iron straps as they snatched the packet of pictures from his hand and pulled him into the office. He had no fight in him even if his reaction time had been faster. The pictures of Leese's battered and bruised body had taken every ounce of resistance completely out of him.

"Yeah, I thought a little reminder about your handiwork might make this easier," Ryan stated calmly. "This isn't going to be a fair fight," he admitted as Andy and Ty gripped Micah's arms. "But, then again, it wasn't a fair fight for her either."

Ryan started swinging.

By the time he finished, Micah wasn't much more than just a body on the floor. He lifted the bloody face up for the final time. "You are such an idiot! I can't believe she's thrown her whole life away because of you," he practically spit the words at Micah. "Are you really stupid enough to believe that she left you for me? You don't know her at all! If she hadn't been trying to save your... If she hadn't been forced, she never would have done it."

"W—what?" Micah slurred, "Tell me—please."

"You aren't worth it! At least I've kept my promises, but I never told her that I wouldn't kick your ass for what you did. She wouldn't call the cops and she wouldn't let me take her to the hospital after you finished with her. I had to wait until the next day to knock her out with brandy to get these shots."

"She doesn't drink," Micah spoke, clearer than before.

"There are a lot of things she doesn't do, but you... You son-of-a-bitch, if I have to bury her because you sucked out the last of her will to live, I will be back and I will kill you!"

Ryan threw the photos on the floor and the three of them left.

Micah rolled onto his back, everything was throbbing. He was sure several ribs were cracked, his gut was on fire and everything had a red haze from the blood that was stinging his eyes. He laid there for a few minutes and then made it up on his knees. His head swooned as he staggered up on his feet and stumbled for his bathroom.

He looked in the mirror with a strange sense of appreciation at the work-over Ryan had given him. He washed his face. The sting of chlorinated water in the cuts helped him become more alert. When he finally dried off, he assessed the wounds. He had cuts under both eyes, his lips were split and swollen, his nose was still bleeding, the side of his right cheek was thick and red and his eyebrow on the right was also split and still bleeding. He was right about the ribs, taking a breath was excruciating.

Grabbing a few more paper towels he went back into his office and picked up the photos off the floor. He sat at his desk and stared. He didn't know exactly how hard he had handled her in his fury. He had been filled with so much rage that he'd blocked most of that afternoon out of his memory, but looking at her, the images came vividly back. Her cheeks and eyes were black and blue from where he had slapped her so hard that he knocked her onto the coffee table. There was a shot of her back showing all the bruises she sustained where she hit it. Her lips were swollen and cracked just as his were now. Bruised skin covered her from where he'd gripped her throat and shoulders, to the places where he grabbed for her when he snatched her back from trying to escape. Ryan had even taken pictures of her ripped clothes and her bloodied undergarments. A wave of nausea hit him—what kind of animal had he been that day?

But then Ryan's words pricked his consciousness. What did he mean that she didn't really leave to be with Ryan? Who forced her to run that day, and what did he mean when he said she was trying to save someone?

There was only one person to get those answers from, but if she was willing to suffer through what he'd done to her and still not tell why she left, how would he ever get her to talk? And then another pain hit his chest; Ryan's last statement made it clear that Leese was a suicide risk. She seemed fine the night of the finale, but then again she left with Ryan immediately after the show.

He had to get to her. He had to find her and tell her he was sorry for doing what was unforgivable. But he had to have answers and he knew she'd still refuse him.

He waited for the bleeding to stop before he headed to the airport. He knew her well enough to know if he got close to her, she would be more concerned about his injuries than her own safety. He shook his head; how could things have gone from the happiest moments of his life to the darkest?

Hours later, when he arrived at her house, no one was there. He picked the lock and went inside to discover her belongings were gone. He called Nadia, cowering inside at the berating he was sure to receive, but evidently Nadia was in the dark about everything concerning Leese. She wanted to talk, but Micah had to cut the conversation short as he simply told her it was of extreme importance that if she called to please have her get in touch with him right away.

He staked out Ryan's house for several days, she wasn't there, but another woman was. This woman was as young as Leese and evidently Ryan's actual girlfriend. But, from the constant expression on Ryan's face, he was extremely worried about Leese. She had to be on the run again, but why? He'd made no effort to bother her since the attack. Why would she take off? Unless she was planning something she didn't want Ryan to witness.

He called his family, once again enlisting there help to find her.

"Forget about her," his mother snapped. "She's not worth any more pain."

"Please, Mom. I need your help. I found out something I didn't know before and—and I have reason to believe she was forced to leave."

"Son, stop torturing yourself—she went after another man and that's all there is to it."

"No, there is much, much more to all of this. I've got to know the answers. I've got to find her before—before it's too late."

"I think you should come home and stop—"

"I am coming home—D'Angelo has a job for me."

His mother paused, "I'll help you look for her, but I think it would be wise to stop taking so many jobs. We can look for her together."

Four months of dirty deeds for D'Angelo passed quickly. But, every free moment he had was spent following up leads that his mother turned up. Leese had done an excellent job of hiding this time. She had taken cash, but made sure no numbers were left behind. There had been no traceable phone calls home, and no credit card receipts. The only thing she had that might give her away was her car. There were very few Shelby Ultimate Aeros on the road, and you couldn't simply pull it into Wal-Mart to have it serviced.

His mother had begun conducting interviews with former Remake contestants saying she was helping the producers get next season's group ready, and she needed their opinions. Every time she turned interviews into conversations about Leese. When she got in touch with Dobrey Stewart, she got her first solid lead.

Dobrey mentioned loaning Leese a cottage in California so that she could get away from all the publicity. When Celeste pressed her for more information about the cottage, Dobrey became suspicious and ended their conversation. She couldn't find any records in California that showed Dobrey owned a piece of property, but Celeste was certain she was keeping it under an assumed name. When the court house is of no help, the newspaper archives are. She found a seven-year-old article about how Dobrey Stewart had given the money for a public library in the small northern town of Gualala. They mentioned that Ms. Stewart had been so enamored with their town that she had purchased a cottage in the vicinity.

Micah was on a plane and in Gualala by the next day.

"Yeah, I've seen her before," the man at the local grocery store admitted pointing to the blond version of Leese as Micah showed him two photographs. "She's a real sweet gal, kind a shy and quiet. I think she's living somewhere just north of here. She drives a red four-wheel drive, a Jeep Wrangler I think. Should I tell her you're looking for her next time she's in town?"

Micah smiled, "No, I was going to surprise her. We were friends in high school back in Florida and I wanted to see her before I head back to the east coast, but I'll find her." His lies were smooth as silk and had enough sincerity to make a believer out of anyone.

There was a small motel on the ocean side, right across the street from the grocery store. He could wait a day or two and see if a red Jeep came through town. He really wondered if the man could be mistaken because a Jeep just didn't sound like Leese's kind of vehicle.

By the second day he was ready to move a little further up the coast to show her picture and see if anyone else might know where she was at, but, as he was fueling up, he watched a red Jeep pull into the store. When the young woman with blond pixie hair and a flowery, flowing baby-doll top and blue jeans climbed out, he knew without a doubt he found her.

He parked his car at the far end of the grocery store lot and waited. Thirty minutes passed and she finally came out pushing a cart with a few bags. She loaded everything into the Jeep and headed back out on the highway going north. He would have to be extra careful tailing her; he knew what kind of skills she possessed behind the wheel, and if she suspected he was following her, she'd out drive him, even if she was in a Jeep.

The road was dangerously curvy, up and down and sometimes would break free on the edge of a cliff that dropped off to the mesmerizing Pacific. There were two cars between them and as he rounded a sharp s-curve in the road he realized she must have turned off, she was no longer in the lead. He traveled to the next turn-off and headed back south, looking for the sign of a driveway. He passed one so obscure and small it didn't look like a driveway, but more like an overgrown path. He saw it too late to make the turn so once again he had to continue traveling until he could reverse course. He made the sharp right and headed up the weed-ridden path. Surely there was another driveway that he missed. This didn't appear to be traveled very often. Just as he was considering turning around, the woods gave way to a cottage set on a hill in an open field; a red Jeep was parked out front beside her unmistakable Shelby Aero under a car cover.

He was sure she hated him for what he had done to her and, if his plan worked, and she allowed him to get close enough, she was going to hate him worse by this time tomorrow morning.

He parked the car and walked up to the front door. He looked back and couldn't see the road below, but it was a beautiful view of the ocean over the tree tops. He looked at the front porch, noticing all the flowers and the pair of rockers. Could it be that she had moved on to man number three? Perhaps Ryan didn't know what he was talking about. The front door opened before he could step up on the porch, and she was standing there behind the screen door.

"Don't take another step," were her words of warning.

He could see a pistol in her hand.

This might be harder than he imagined.

Chapter Twenty-Seven

I pulled up to the cottage and grabbed my bags of groceries. Today was absolutely glorious. The smell of the ocean mixed with the fragrance of pine trees and wildflowers. It was a little piece of heaven. I was glad when I remembered Dobrey offering me this place; it couldn't have been better timing. Ryan had been hovering over me after the attack, but he had to go back to his life, and I needed a lot of time to think. I'd only called him twice since I'd been here. Both times I borrowed someone else's phone and made the calls when I was far away from Gualala. All I wanted him to know was that I was still breathing and was okay. I missed him so badly—mother hen routine and all. He had been my one true friend, but it was time to let him get on with his life.

I had the groceries out of the bags and on the table as I sorted what would go where, when I heard the sound of an approaching vehicle. I never got visitors. My heart picked up speed as I opened my purse and pulled the pistol out and slipped off the safety. Moving to the front door, I watched as a sedan with darkly tinted glass pulled up short behind the Jeep. I froze as I watched who climbed out. I didn't know if I could threaten the one person in this world I loved with such strange desperation. I watched Micah look down the hill at the ocean and then turned and began walking up to the front door.

I couldn't let him inside. I couldn't let him do to me what he did the last time, and I might actually have to shoot him. I certainly wouldn't be shooting to kill, but I couldn't allow him to put a hand on me, not now. I opened the door and gave him my warning as he started to step up on the porch.

"Leese?" he replied in shock, his voice high pitched and strange as he looked at the gun in my hand.

"You taught me to shoot so I don't think it's wise for you to come any closer," I warned.

"I'm not armed," he stated, pulling off the light jacket he wore, and turning around so I could see that he wasn't hiding anything.

"Really? I don't see those hands of yours tied together and they are just as lethal as your guns—at least they were the last time you put them on me."

He swallowed and ran his hand through his hair. I could see his eyes tearing up and the whole time all I kept saying to myself was, 'Don't cave, Leese, don't cave.'

"What I did to you was unforgivable and I can understand why you don't want me to get close, but you've got to believe me, Leese, I swear to you, I wasn't in my right mind that day and I could never do that to you again. I look at you every day and every day I hate myself just a little bit more."

"Well, you can swear all you want; I can't afford to give you another opportunity. We haven't seen each other in months and I know you haven't been following me around all this time, so you haven't seen me every day."

"No, you were pretty tough to find this time, but I have the pictures Ryan gave me."

That made no sense. I doubted Ryan would have anything to do with Micah and he certainly wouldn't have given him pictures of me, "What pictures?"

"The ones he took of you the day after I—I..."

He couldn't say it, but I knew what he meant, "It's called rape, Micah, and if you think it's hard to say then you should try living through it. I didn't let him take pictures."

"I guess then I'm not the only guy who didn't ask for your permission," he said as he reached into the pocket of his jacket and tossed a handful of pictures of me asleep in my bra and underwear onto the porch floor. "But you should at least be proud of the way he delivered them to me." He had an odd sound to his voice, "He showed up with a couple big guys that grabbed and held me while he beat the hell out of me."

My free hand went to my mouth to stifle the gasp.

"I deserved it and he did a good job working me over; fractured four ribs and a cheek bone in the process."

"I'm sorry, Micah. I knew how pissed off he was, but I never dreamed he'd go after you."

"But he also told me a few things, and I needed to see you to get the truth."

My heart jumped in my throat as I prayed that Ryan had kept his promise not to tell what he knew, "What did he say?"

He took a tentative step up onto the porch and bent down to retrieve the photos, and then another step toward the door.

"Please stop, Micah. I can't let you get near me."

The tears had started running down his cheeks. "There is another picture—I—I carry with me," he struggled to say, reaching back into the jacket pocket. He pulled out the picture of us on our wedding day as we stood by the well at the old monastery. "This one is my favorite," he choked on a sob that struggled away from his emotional resolve, "I've got to know, baby. He said you didn't leave me for him. He said someone forced you."

"Was that all he said?" I questioned, an old familiar lump rising in my throat as I tried to steady the gun.

"Yeah—whatever you made him promise, he kept it. You've got to finally tell me. Hasn't it been long enough?"

"I wish I could Micah, but it's too late. I can't change what's happened and if I could have stayed with you, you'd have eventually hated me worse than you do now," I felt the first tear roll down my cheek.

"*Hate you?* I never hated you, baby—mad as hell, sure—but I've never hated you. You were everything I never knew I wanted until I met you. I have to know why you turned my life upside down."

"Threatening to kill me doesn't quite qualify as only 'mad as hell,'" I snapped.

There was no comprehension on his face, "I—I—never threaten to…" he choked up again. "I threatened to kill Ryan, but I would never—"

"I still have the note and the iPod." He looked so confused that I was beginning to wonder if he honestly didn't know what I was talking about, "The one you sent me the day after the final show."

I watched his face grow furiously dark, "I never sent you another iPod, but I did tell someone about sending you the first one. What was on it, Leese?"

"Do you mean to tell me you didn't send me the song 'Breath,' by Breaking Benjamin? You included a note."

"I never sent you anything. I was too ashamed to even approach you at the finale."

All this time I thought he wanted me dead. All this time I had been afraid and hurt. I had a good suspicion I could name the person he told, "Who did you tell, Micah?"

"It doesn't matter. I'll deal with him."

"D'Angelo?" I asked, realizing I was still pointing the gun at him. I lowered it as I watched the strange expression come over his face. "Micah, do you still put stock in your word? If I ask you to swear to God the most honest promise you've ever made, would you do it—and mean it."

The tears were running harder down his face, "I will do *anything* you ask of me—anything other than to leave."

"I'm going to put this gun away, but I want you to swear to me that you won't lay a hand on me. Promise me, Micah, for everything your worth, you *will not* touch me."

"I—I swear, unless you allow it, Leese."

"Sit in a rocker," I told him. "I'll be out in a minute."

He took a rocker and moved it further away from the other and sat down.

I was shaking so bad. I had to go on absolute faith that he meant what he said. If he hurt me again, my life was over.

I put away the gun and grabbed a wine glass and filled it up and walked out cautiously onto the porch. I still couldn't tell him the truth, but I was curious enough now that I did want to talk.

I sat down and took a deep breath, "What have you been doing since I left you? Besides running the country's top new show."

"You're drinking wine?" he asked, ignoring the question.

I could hear an edge to his voice; he didn't approve. "No, it's not wine. I don't drink. This is grape juice. Stemware is the only thing I have in the cottage besides coffee cups."

"Not that I don't believe you, but… I don't believe you—may I?" he asked reaching for my glass.

I sighed and handed it to him. The touch of his hand as he took it was like electricity to my system. He inhaled deeply above the rim, swirled it and then took a tentative sip. His brows raised and he offered me back the glass.

"I'm sorry I doubted you, but Ryan said you were drinking brandy when he took those pictures."

"I—I was in a lot of pain—internally," I shot a look at Micah's face and watched the sorrow hit him. "He told me it would ease it and had me sip down a glassful."

"Did it?"

"Yeah, but I guess he wanted me out for a different reason."

"I'm glad he did it. I didn't realize what I'd done to you."

"How could you not know what you'd done?" I asked incredulously. "I know you'd been drinking, but Micah, you weren't drunk."

"I was—well, for lack of a better term—high."

"What?! Don't tell me you're into drugs?"

He gave an honest laugh, but I didn't find the subject at all funny. "I was on a heavy dose of steroids and amphetamines, they made me—aggressive—I couldn't control my emotions and actions like normal. I drank the alcohol to stop the shakes I had on the way to your place."

"You never told me you took steroids." I was surprised, but, thinking about his muscle mass, the steroids made sense.

"I've never taken them in my life—I don't do drugs—but someone pulled a David on me." He suddenly looked pained as he said it in a term he knew I would quickly understand. "Would you mind if I had a drink with you? I can get it if you—"

"No," I responded quickly. I didn't want him inside the cottage. I didn't trust him, yet. He put out his hand for my glass as I rose up. I handed it to him and went back inside. I glanced at the door several times to make sure he wasn't going to try to follow me in, but he stayed on the porch. I brought out a fresh glass of juice and handed it to him, noticing he had set mine down on the table between us.

He took a sip and then continued, "I honestly didn't know I'd been that rough with you, Leese. I didn't remember much from that day until he showed me the pictures."

"I truly think you could have killed me, maybe not intentionally, but the outcome would have been the same if it had been accidental. But, God has a purpose for everything."

He looked like I'd just hit him with a stun gun, "You—you can't believe that anymore, not after everything that's happened."

"Oh, trust me; I believe it more than ever before."

"Then let me in on the purpose," he said sounding exasperated. "Or better yet just let me in on the reason and then I can figure out the purpose on my own."

"Oh, that," I said, realizing he was talking about why I left him. "I haven't got that one all figured out yet, but God had a purpose for bringing you to me the day you—you raped me."

"I can't stand the sound of that word," he confessed.

I took a long drink and studied the ocean in the distance. "Neither can I, because I wanted you to take me, I just never expected it to be like that."

"Will you tell me why this all happened?"

"I can't—I can't ever tell you." I was trying to force back the tears as I took another sip of my drink.

"Then tell me one thing and, for the moment, I'll be satisfied—is there any way you could still be in love with me?"

That hit me hard. I tried a smile, but the tears were washing it off my face. I couldn't speak.

"I know you'll never forgive me, but I have to know if there is any love left."

"Micah, I've loved you with every single beat of my heart, and I forgave you the moment you were finished with me that day. You still don't know what's going on and I—I'm sure I'm just as responsible for all the rage and anger that day as a dose of drugs."

"Ah, baby, don't say that," he pleaded, but he surprised me as he literally slipped off the rocker and hit his knees in front of me. "I don't deserve forgiveness and I certainly don't deserve your love—I'm just selfish and I want it so bad."

I wanted to reach out and touch him, but I couldn't risk it. I swallowed at the annoying lump in my throat and took another long drink.

"Stop it, Leese—put the glass down—don't drink anymore. I can't do what I came here to do, even if I don't get the answers I need. I can't hurt you, again."

I looked at him for a long moment. His eyes kept going back to my glass. I felt a soft warmness creeping through me and I was instantly alarmed. "*Oh God, Micah, you didn't,*" I stated as terror gripped me. I stood up clutching against my blouse. "Please, please tell me you didn't." I hadn't eaten yet and I knew if I was feeling the effects now, it was in my blood stream. My stomach began to roll as the nausea from the knowledge hit me. I didn't try to stop it as I went to the railing and began to heave.

"I had to know," he said sounding desperate. He got up from the floor and stood behind me, but he kept his word and didn't touch me. "It's the only way I can get you to tell me. I didn't want to do it, but—"

"Micah, you idiot," I snapped, rubbing my temples and turning to face him, "I can't take drugs now—I'm pregnant!"

His face turned the color of ash, "Leese, I had no idea. I'd never hurt a baby, not even Ryan's." Sincerity and regret filled his face. "God forgive me," he said, reaching out to me, but then refraining.

I looked at him. He still didn't understand, "Micah, I've never had sex with Ryan. The only thing I ever did was kiss him."

"But…" he looked more confused than ever.

"This is the purpose God had—this is our baby. It's all I had left of you." I was still growing warmer and knew the drug was in my system. "Oh, God, please," I prayed out loud, "Don't let this hurt the baby." I broke down sobbing and went into his arms. He didn't expect me to do that, but it was too late and he was going to have to get me through this.

"Do I take you to a hospital?" he wept out as he cradled me in his arms.

"There's nothing left inside me. Hold me, Micah, and if I tell you what this is all about you can't change it. You can't stay with me—you can't leave the mob again."

He tipped my face up and kissed me, "I won't hurt you, Leese. I'm just going to take you inside and lay you down."

It didn't matter. Nothing mattered as I grew warmer and weaker. He scooped me up in his arms and my mind started to drift.

I don't remember much of the rest of the evening. I only remember being in his arms, his mouth on mine, and some of what I said. I remember saying D'Angelo's name and Micah's anger, rage, and bitterness, but he was gentle with me. I recalled asking him to take off my clothes and the feel of his mouth against my stomach as he kissed and stroked me tenderly. The only other thing I recall was the constant murmur as he told me how very sorry he was about what he'd done.

Chapter Twenty-Eight

When I woke the next morning, I was nauseous and weak, but the feeling of his arm around me was like finding a lost piece of heaven. I rolled onto my back, my blouse was gone, but my bra was still on me as was my underwear. Micah's shirt was gone, but his jeans were still in place.

"Are you okay?" I heard him whisper.

"I'm still sick to my stomach, but not anything like I was when David did this to me." I didn't even want to discuss it, but I had to know, "How much did you put in my drink?"

"Enough for two; David told me he gave you enough for a half dozen. Leese, I'm sorry I did this to you. I had no idea about the baby. All I knew was that Ryan said someone forced this on you and I had to know. You shouldn't have left. You should have come to me and we would have gotten my family together and figured this out."

"What would you have done, Micah? You would have charged upstairs and someone would have cut you down. I couldn't risk letting him destroy your family or you; my life didn't matter at that point."

I caught the first tear as it flowed down his cheek, "You mean everything to me. Don't ever say your life doesn't matter."

I rose up on my elbow and kissed his lips. I knew we'd kissed last night, but I wanted him to know that, sober, I still loved him so much.

"I don't know how you can even stand to be near me after what happened between us, baby."

"What I couldn't stand was being away from you. Aaah!" I gasped; my hand dropping to the mound where there once was only flat stomach.

I don't think I've ever seen Micah move so quickly from lying down to upright.

"*What's wrong?*" came his panicked reply.

I grabbed his hand and placed it against my stomach and watched the splendid amazement hit him. "I—I can feel the baby moving," he breathed. "Is it okay? I mean have you felt this before?"

"I've felt the sensation, but not this strong. Yes, it's okay—just getting comfortable I think, but help me up. I'm calling my doctor to see if he can get me in. I need to ask him about—Ecstasy."

I called my doctor and told him I had, unintentionally, taken a little Ecstasy last night and I wanted to see him to make sure everything was okay. He paused for a long moment on the phone and I wasn't sure if he was trying to figure out how I'd done it unintentionally or if he was concerned about the effects.

"I'll see you as soon as you get here."

My heart beat grew faster as I thanked him and hung up.

"Do I wait here or—"

"This is your child and I want you with me."

"God, I don't believe it, I—"

"Micah you're the *only* man I've ever slept with," I emphasized, feeling a little hurt at his statement.

"No, it's not that—you know I believe you. It's that, for once in my life, I'm scared to death. I'm shaking," he said, holding out his trembling hands so that I could see.

I rose up and brought my mouth to his for a gentle kiss, "I guess this means I should drive?"

"Yeah, I really think you should."

We didn't say much to each other as we drove along the coastline to the doctor's office. But he kept watching me the entire way. I don't think he ever noticed the cliffs and the beautiful ocean crashing gently against the breath-taking coastline; all he did was stare at me. He finally spoke when we pulled into the medical complex.

"I never thought you could look more beautiful than the day I married you, but I swear you've changed to someone even more spectacular."

I smiled and squeezed his hand, "Let's go."

I wasn't sure how I was going to explain my 'drug use' when Dr. Cray asked me, but Micah spoke before I could open my mouth.

"It's my fault. I didn't know she was pregnant and I—I spiked her drink."

"You know you can go to jail for that," Dr. Cray scowled.

"I know I *should* go to jail for it," Micah confirmed.

Dr. Cray sighed, as he turned back to me, "Leese, if you did this on a regular basis or even just on a recreational basis, we'd be looking at multiple birth defect issues, but since you are in your second trimester and the fact that this is the only time during your pregnancy that you've been…" he shot an annoyed glance at Micah. "…been exposed to it, the baby should be fine. But I do want to get a sonogram, just to make sure everything is normal. Is he the father?"

"Yes," I said, finally finding my smile.

"Good, then he can stay, but don't ever, ever—"

"I swear, never again," Micah spoke up. "I didn't know."

"That part doesn't matter. Never give someone a substance without their knowledge."

"I won't."

The ultrasound machine was brought in, but first he placed a microphone against my stomach to listen to the baby's heartbeat; a rapid pulsing sound filled the room. I'd heard it before, but I watched the smile spread across Micah's face, and then concern.

"It's so fast. Is that normal?"

"Yes," Dr. Cray stated, "babies have much faster rhythms and then they slow down with age. That sounds good to me. What do you think, Leese? Do you want to find out if this is a boy or a girl today?"

I nodded, afraid to speak as the jelly was smeared across my stomach and the ultrasound machine was turned on. Micah gasped as the picture came on the screen of our child. He was squeezing my hand tightly as every detail of the tiny face, arms, body and legs appeared with the three dimensional image. One thing became immediately obvious and I knew it before Dr. Cray could say it.

"It's a—a boy," I stammered. I had a feeling I was carrying a boy, but I didn't know until now.

"Congratulations. Yes, your right, it's a boy."

Micah was a wreck and he dropped down in a nearby chair as the doctor cleaned off the jelly and then helped me sit up.

"All looks fine and—"

"Dr. Cray, what about—about having sex?"

Micah's head shot up as he looked at me, "No, I don't think you're allowed."

Dr. Cray laughed, "I don't get *that* response from too many fathers-to-be. Sex is fine, encouraged even because it has a calming effect, afterwards of course, on your body. As long as you two aren't into anything rough—"

"No," Micah interjected. "Never again."

That earned him another scowl from the doctor, "As I was saying, yes you can. And a lot of women find that it is the most heightened sexual time of their lives because all the senses are extra receptive during pregnancy."

"Thank you," I said, swallowing hard and shaking his hand.

I had never seen anything affect Micah so desperately. I got the opposite reaction on the drive back to the cottage as he stared out the Jeep, head turned hard right as the scenery passed by. I pulled up to the cottage and got out, but he just sat there.

"Come on," I coaxed as I closed my door, but still peering through the open driver's window. "Micah?"

"I don't deserve this," he stated. "I don't deserve you. You should hate me for what I did, and I don't know if I can handle forgiveness. I can't see how this could be anything that God purposed."

I leaned in the door frame, resting my head on my forearms as the brilliant California sunshine warmed my back. "Micah..." I waited for him to look at me. When he turned, I began. "Do you remember the few days we had together, and the conversation about getting me pregnant?"

"Of course I do, but—"

"Do you think that four months after telling me you wanted to wait, you would have changed your mind? I know I wouldn't have."

"You don't want to be pregnant, do you?" he sadly questioned.

"I was okay with letting it happen during those first few times, but I knew it would only be if God planned it." I reached inside the Jeep and grabbed on to his hand, but he looked away. "When I ran away and my period started a week later, I was crushed. I wanted to be carrying your baby so badly because if I couldn't have you, at least I would have had a part of you." I gave his hand a tug to get him to look at me. "I had no clue God had the day of conception already planned—not in a way that either one of us wanted, but it's all a matter of timing. Don't you understand? This baby wouldn't exist if all this didn't happen."

He swallowed as he looked at me with anguished filled eyes, "But—I—hurt—you," he paused on every word to make his point.

"Yeah, you did, like nothing I've ever experienced. But as bad as that was physically, it didn't even come close to the pain of leaving you. Come inside, Micah. We don't have a lot of time together and—"

The expression changed quickly from sorrow to disbelief, "D'Angelo isn't going to keep us apart."

"He said if he finds out that we're back together your family won't last twenty-four hours. I'm not going to let that happen."

"I'm going to kill him," The words were ice cold as a flicker of blankness appeared in his eyes.

"No! You can't go after him. I may not know much about how the mob works, but I know he's your superior and you can't touch him."

"He's used me since I was fourteen to do his dirty work—and I don't mean things that were contracted. When he forced you into this, he stepped over the line and I am going to take his life in payment."

"I want to ask you something, Micah, but, to tell you the truth, I've got to get inside because I still feel a little sick to…" He was out of the Jeep before I could finish the sentence.

I opened the bedroom windows and let the ocean breeze flow into the room and then lay down on the thick comforter, making room for him beside me. He hesitated and then finally joined me.

"D'Angelo told me something that day that's bothered me ever since and I want to know if it's true."

"I'm sure it has something to do with all the people I've killed. I was hoping we'd never get into this, but," he seemed to be steeling himself for my question, "go ahead."

"Not everyone, just the first one." I watched his reaction and knew this was the question he was honestly dreading, "Was it a woman? A woman you slept with?"

"I was fourteen, Leese," he didn't sound like he was offering it as an excuse, but just a sad beginning to a story I knew I'd regret hearing. "My dad determined I was ready to be a soldier for the mob, but D'Angelo was the one who told me I would be different. I should have paid with my life for what he had me do, but we have kept his private work secret from the rest of the family. Believe it or not, the mob values honesty at the highest level. If a superior asks you a question, you'd better be telling the truth. He's had me lying to superiors ever since he had me kill the mob boss's wife."

I knew this wasn't good. If he had been breaking mob rules from the beginning and D'Angelo used it against him… I pulled my body up close to him because I'd begun to shiver in the cool air. He reached over me and pushed the closest window frame shut, to keep the breeze off me.

"D'Angelo told me she was a whore, an unfaithful woman that had wormed her way into a marriage to the head of the clan. He said she didn't deserve a place of honor in the family, but he would give her a chance by testing her loyalty—with me." His breathing was getting shallower and I knew he hated having to tell me this. "D'Angelo said she had a particular weakness for young boys, and, if it was true, and she tried to seduce me, I was to kill her. He said I'd be doing the Boss a favor, but we would never let him know we'd handled it for him." He paused, then asked, "Are you sure you want to hear this?"

"Yes," I shivered, realizing it hadn't been the breeze that was shaking me inside.

"She'd decided to spend a few days in Gulfport gambling and sunning on the beach. It was my first outing as a member of the mob and my parents trusted D'Angelo—they thought I was taking care of a small time hood that had been skimming business and was on the run. They never knew what I was really doing."

"So he took you to where this woman was and—and…"

"I met her out on the beach. I had no idea what to do with a woman. D'Angelo told me to go over and say hello, offer to help her in some way or just hang out near her. He was right, she did like young boys, but particularly well-built young boys and it wasn't long before she had me wrapped around her finger. I spent an afternoon getting to know her; she was beautiful, twenty-one years old and eager to be the first woman I'd ever slept with. I'll never forget her bringing me into her room. I wanted to have sex with her, but the whole time I kept telling myself if we crossed that line, I was supposed to kill her. I didn't want to hurt her; she was fascinating to me."

"He never should have put you in a position like that, Micah. You were too young and—"

"And too stupid," he added. "She took me and I was freaked out by the emotions. I hadn't learned control and, after the first time, she aroused me again, and I knew I had to finish the job. If I didn't, I'd be a failure—most likely D'Angelo would have killed me and returned home and told my parents that the target got me first. I didn't have a gun; he never told me what to do, so I simply turned animal. She seemed to like getting rough, until I got my hands around her throat." His voice caught on the last words. "I killed her with my bare hands and I swore I'd rather shoot someone than to do that again. You know what she went through, Leese. I did the same thing to you when I raped you." The tears were washing down his face. The pain was incredible and intense for him.

"But you didn't kill me, Micah. If you'd been under better control, you'd—"

"I never would have hurt you, Leese, if I could have helped it."

He rolled over and caressed my cheek and then buried his face into my neck as I stroked his hair and tried to quiet his anguish.

"Is that all, Micah?" I had to know if there was anything more to what D'Angelo had done to him. I could feel him shaking his head no, but he didn't seem ready to talk so I simply held him and waited.

When he finally raised his head, he seemed composed and ready to finish telling me what happened. "He was very—very happy with the way I killed her and so, to celebrate, he bought me a whore for the night as a gift for doing what he wanted."

"You were a child, a fourteen year-old child, and he bought you a hooker?" I couldn't keep the ire out of my response.

"Yeah, and if he hadn't been in the same room with me when I… I almost killed her, too. My sexual drive had been linked to murder and I couldn't see how to separate the two. I eventually learned control, but women were nothing to me. They were something to use and walk away from…until I met you."

He rose up on his elbow to look down on me, seemingly wanting to touch me, but was hesitating, "You don't know how different you

315

are. You are so innocent, trusting and naïve, like some kind of creature that never existed in my world. When I met you, I came so close to killing you because you actually frightened me, and that was a new experience. You told me I had to be a gentleman; that was new for me, too. I had control, but I never had that kind of restraint. I couldn't even kiss you. And then when you made the kiss your final request, all I could think was that it would be like going back to the real me—passion and death all over again."

"Then this is what I feel coming from you when I know you're getting near the edge. You're trying not to go back to what he trained into you."

"You can honestly tell? I mean, you can feel me losing control?"

"I see it mostly, usually in your eyes first, but yes I can feel when it's slipping away from you."

"How do you feel right now?"

"Safe, Micah, but…"

The soft smile that had started at the corners of his mouth, quickly faded, "But what?"

"I want you to make love to me, but I'd be lying if I said there was no fear."

"I won't make love to you. I don't deserve—"

"I deserve you, Micah Gavarreen. I didn't marry the monster, I married the man. You aren't the person he trained you to be and someday I pray you'll see that because I know you don't want to be the monster."

"Leese, I annulled our marriage. I have no right to be in your bed."

"You didn't annul my vow and I didn't break my…" A pain hit me hard and I knew he saw it in my face.

"What's wrong, baby," he whispered.

"Micah, it's been eight months and I'm assuming you—you probably didn't keep your…" I couldn't finish the sentence. I couldn't make love to him if he'd been untrue, because I wouldn't put the baby in danger from an experience he might have had.

"I didn't sleep with anyone if that's what you're trying to ask me, Leese."

I didn't mean to seem so surprised, but I was.

"I don't want you to think it was because I didn't try. I don't want to lie to you. Twice I hired someone to—to satisfy me, but each time I couldn't. You don't know how pissed off a hooker gets when she realizes that the man that bought her can't get turned on by her. I was trying to go completely back to my old life, but I just couldn't. I told you you'd ruin me for life for this—you're the only one. Between the lack of sex and sleep, it doesn't surprise me really that the steroids and amps put me over the edge so easily."

"Sleep?" I said, cocking one eyebrow at him, "You couldn't sleep?"

"I told you a long time ago, I can't get comfortable without you in my bed. Why?"

"I couldn't sleep either, I..." Maybe it was not the best idea to tell him how I finally solved the problem. "How did you manage it?" I changed the subject.

"It didn't work quite as well as having you beside me, but I had a lock of your hair that I'd put on the pillow next to me. I'd close my eyes and rest my face against it. It was the only thing that kept me from total sleep deprived insanity."

"Where did you get my hair?"

"The house you stayed at in north Georgia—you threw it in the trash. I loved your long hair and I can't tell you how upset I was that you cut it. But, for the record, you're a beautiful blonde, too. So," he gave a weak smile, "how did you manage without me?"

I was hoping the cringe wasn't totally obvious. "You won't like mine," I tried to say gently.

"Amytal—and you're right, I didn't like it."

I blinked a couple times, "What's Amytal?"

"Leese, please don't lie."

"Micah, I don't know what you're talking about?"

"Five hundred dollars and a stage hand; does that refresh your memory?"

"Is that what that was? I never knew the name and I only took one."

"That's a relief. I had him fired right after Cedric showed me the video. I was afraid you were going to get hooked. That's pretty strong stuff."

"Tell me about it. One pill and I didn't wake for twenty-five hours."

"Why would you do something so dangerous?"

I could tell he was trying not to sound too upset with me, but I was just glad I didn't have to tell him about my real sleep-aid. I should have known better.

"If you only took one," he continued, "and that was four months after you left, then how did you... Leese, I can see it written all over your face. You don't want to tell me. Why?"

"Because you'd probably prefer dope."

"What did you do?"

"Ryan—I mean, I didn't 'do' Ryan—I mean he was the one who—he became your substitute," I winced.

"You said you never slept with—"

"I said I never had sex with him, but I slept with him—a lot." I could see the wheels turning in Micah's head, so I figured I just keep explaining. "After those first several days and he realized I couldn't stay asleep, no matter how exhausted I was, he asked how I slept before. I told him you would hold me with your arm around my waist and we'd stay like that all night. The first time we tried it was our last night in north Georgia and—"

"One bed," he said suddenly sounding relieved instead of angry. "That's why there was only one bed unmade in the house. Gwen and I thought—well, it seemed obvious that you'd been sleeping together—like *sleeping* together."

I hadn't considered the one bed visual we'd left behind. "You're family must really hate me," I whimpered.

"They aren't going to hate you for long because we're getting this whole thing straightened out."

"NO! I told you I can't take a chance of D'Angelo—"

"I won't take any chances, but we will meet with them, even if it's not in Louisiana. They've got to know the truth." But his thoughts quickly returned to the previous conversation, "I am surprised you managed that with—with him. He didn't try to change your mind?"

"Micah, he was a virgin, he didn't even—"

Micah choked on my statement. He sat up tried to catch his breath. I rubbed his back as he gulping air, "You've got to be..." he swallowed another breath, "kidding."

"No, I'm not. He has a girlfriend now, but at the time—"

"I can't believe it. You *must* really love me because I would have thought, especially since you would have been his first, that it would have been a turn on for you. Did you ever kiss in bed?"

"Micah! Can't you just leave it that he is my very best friend and that we didn't have sex?"

"You kissed in bed, and didn't have sex?" He sounded amazed. "It's no wonder he beat the crap out of me. All the frustration of never having you and then I come along and—and take you. I'm surprised he didn't kill me." He could clearly see that I was flustered over his comment, but he added a disclaimer. "You realize I would have forgiven you if you had slept with him, right? The night of the party, all I wanted was you back in my arms, and I was certain you had already slept with him."

"I wouldn't have forgiven myself, Micah. I'm yours, forever." Just as I finished saying what was supposed to be a romantic statement, my stomach growled loudly. I laughed, "Time to feed the baby; he doesn't like it when I skip meals."

"Stay put," he stated, leaning over and kissing my forehead, "I'll fix you something."

I listened to his clatter in the kitchen, the scents and the sounds of breakfast as he prepared it. I was starving, but I rolled to my side and grabbed the pillow he'd used last night and I inhaled with all the power my lungs possessed. Oh, how I missed the smell of Micah Gavarreen.

I dozed off for a little while, but soon he was whispering my name as I rolled over and sat up. He had the breakfast tray prepared for two as he reached over with his free hand and propped the pillows against the headboard.

He scrambled eggs and added ham, fresh mushrooms, onions, and cheese to make an omelet. He filled two wine glasses with orange juice, and found the mammoth cinnamon rolls I bought at the market yesterday. It didn't take long to finish everything off as we leaned together, shoulder to shoulder, and ate. The roll was the last to go. Since they were so large, he only brought one and had cut it in half. It was delicious, and I could have eaten the entire thing, but I peeled it off in half-moon rings feeding a strip to him and then a strip to me until it vanished.

Micah didn't bring a napkin, but he took my sticky, cinnamon bun fingers and placed them slowly, one at a time between is lips and suckled each one clean. It tickled so badly I could barely take it, but it was so unique that I had to do it to him. I took his hand and pulled his index finger across the icing that was left on the plate and then placed his finger in my mouth and slowly clean the sweetness from his skin. He closed his eyes, his breathing becoming faster as I began to repeat the process with his icing-free fingers. He was starting to moan and I knew it wouldn't be long before the tray would be moved and he would have me in those strong arms.

"Drink your juice," he said with a deep quality to his voice as he pulled his hand away.

I did as told and placed the empty glass back on the tray. He was being so slow and purposeful as he sipped his drink.

I took the glass away from him and downed the juice. "Move the tray," I told him as I began to unbutton my blouse.

Instead he rose up, lifting the tray from the bed and left the room. I could hear him in the kitchen rinsing the dishes, but that didn't matter because it gave me enough time to prepare for him to return. When he stepped into the doorway, I had removed my clothes and was laying on top of the comforter and wondering if he found me to still be attractive with the change to my anatomy. One thing was certain, my breasts felt as if pregnancy had double them in size. He wouldn't leave the doorway and I wondered if he disliked my nude appearance. I began to feel unsure under his gaze.

"If you don't like the way I'm—I'm shaped now, I can get under the covers."

"Leese, you're perfect—absolutely stunning pregnant. It's me."

"Please, Micah. Take off your clothes and get in this bed with me. I need you so much."

He sighed and approached me, *"How can you want me?"*

"You've got to stop asking yourself how and start realizing why: I love you. I've loved you since I started falling for you in Pensacola. I loved you in Louisiana and I loved you in Palm Beach. I loved you in Georgia, and Colorado Springs and even in L.A. Why be surprised that I love you here in California?"

I reached up and began undoing his shirt and suddenly he was over me, frightening me to retreat among the pillows.

"But you're afraid of me," he confirmed as he held me in his steady, green gaze.

"Yes, I am. But you're going to change all that right now. I only have one request," I said with a shaky voice as I continued opening his shirt.

"Tell me, baby," he breathed.

"Don't bite me." He used to bite me gently and it felt wonderful, but since the attack the idea of his teeth on my skin terrified me, "You left a couple scars the last time."

"Show me," he whispered.

I rolled my right shoulder forward and showed him the fine pink crescent and then over my left toward the back of the base of my neck resided its twin. He moved to come up behind me as he brought his mouth to cover the spot on my neck. He kissed it so gently and let his tongue roam over the reminder of what had been so violent between us. He kissed and caressed all the way to the mark on the right and repeated it with deliberate slowness. He lowered me back onto the pillows and then stood and finished removing his clothes. He gathered me against himself slowly as I gasped at the warmth of skin on skin.

I never had experienced such deliberation, not even on our wedding night. It was incredible as he stripped away the painful memories of our last encounter and filled me with more desire and need than I knew existed in the human body. The doctor had been right. Every touch, every kiss, the scent of his skin, and the taste of his tongue against mine was magnified to a place beyond my comprehension.

His body joined with mine and took me on the longest building, gradual ascent to climax I'd experienced. I tried to raise my hips to quicken his stroke, but he wouldn't permit it as he brought me there at his intentional pace. I don't know what I was saying by the point I reached the top, but I was loud and breathless as we crested.

What amazed me, as we lay locked in the lover's embrace was that, even lying on me, he never lowered his weight. It was as if he was floating gently at the point of skin to skin contact. The baby moved and I heard Micah's mirth as he felt it against his own stomach. "I think he wants his space back," he snickered against my neck, but then he pulled back slightly and stared into my eyes. "I love you with all my heart, Annalisa," he said, kissing my neck once again and then rising to his feet. "Is your shower big enough for two? I'd love to wash you and then tuck you into bed."

"You have no idea how good that sounds to me, right now." It was mid-afternoon when we finally snuggled into the bed in our favorite position, but this time his arm was across my hip so as not to crowd the baby. We didn't wake until sunrise the following morning. He rolled out and said he was making breakfast, again.

"You're going to spoil me," I teased.

He turned and looked at me very seriously, "I owe you a lifetime of spoiling."

"I accept," I giggled. "Oh, but man, I've got to go pee!"

I came out of the bathroom and heard him on his cell phone as he prepared breakfast.

"...yes, all of you," he was saying. "Do you think I'd ask if it wasn't important? Tomorrow morning at Dad's casino—by ten a.m. Yes, it does and you've got to hear it." He hung up and then turned to me. "Leese, I didn't ask you, but we need to meet with my family. We can fly there in a couple hours, or we can drive there in about eleven, but I'd like to eventually get you back home. I've talked to your mom a couple times and, unless she's as good at hiding things as you are, she doesn't know about the baby."

"No, she doesn't. How long would it take us to drive to Florida?"

"A week at a slow pace, five days if we travel ten to twelve hours a day. Why?"

"I was thinking, after we drive to Vegas, I'd like to drive to Colorado Springs and see Ryan."

His head snapped up from the food he was preparing to look at me, "I need to see him, but I don't know how well it's going to go. Our last meeting wasn't very—friendly. I don't even know if he'll let me in his house."

"I think he'll be willing, if I talk to him first. I've wanted to call him anyway. Do you mind?"

"Of course not."

I took my cell phone and went out on the front porch. The air was crisp enough to make me step back inside to grab my cashmere sweater hanging on a hook by the front door. I sat in the rocker and dialed his number. It was a Tuesday morning in early May and I guessed that Candace might be at school. It was 7 a.m. California time, so that meant it was 8 in Colorado. Perfect timing since she has to be at school by 7:45.

It was going on four rings when he answered the phone and sounded out of breath, "Leese?"

Maybe she wasn't in school.

"Hey, what are you doing? I didn't catch you at a bad time, did I?"

"No, I was in the shower when I heard the cell go off. God, it's great to hear your voice. I've missed you so much. I don't suppose you'd want to tell me where the hell you're at would you?"

"Sure I will. I'm in Gualala, California, and I'm staring at the Pacific Ocean right now."

"Not standing on the edge of a cliff, I hope."

I laughed, "Please stop thinking of me as suicidal. I'm fabulously happy."

The line was silent.

"Ryan?"

"Did you meet someone?"

"Yes, I did and he's very special," I said, my free hand cradling my small bulge.

"Are you sleeping with him?"

Someone else might have found that question too forward, but Ryan had no reason to play coy. "Yes. I don't think I've ever been quite so intimate with someone in my life." Sharing one body was as intimate as it gets, I laughed to myself.

"Sadarius?" he questioned.

"No, you nit wit—that was tabloid trash; you know that. You've—you've never met him before, but you will."

"I will? Like when?"

"How does three or four days sound?"

"You—you mean it? You're coming back to Colorado Springs?" I could hear the elation in his voice.

"Only for a day. We're on a trek back home to Florida."

"Really? But what about... Are you sure you want to go back to Florida?"

"Well, I want Mom to meet him. She's going to be really surprised."

"Damn, it's good to hear you so freaking happy. I told you someday God would make sure you got the happiness you deserve. See you in a few days, baby girl. I love you."

"I love you, too. See you then." And I hung up. Okay, so I didn't tell him about Micah, but my mystery man would be my first line of defense to get him to listen to me.

We cleaned out the cottage and locked it up, and pulled Dobrey's Jeep into the tiny garage. I followed Micah to drop off the rental car and we were off in my Aero. I let Micah drive, because I didn't think I'd be able to sit that still for ten or eleven hours. The scenery on the first part of the trip was spectacular, I'd seen it on the way out here, but my frame of mind had been much different, now I was seeing it with new eyes. Micah seemed to enjoy giving my Aero a chance to stretch out and there were miles of roadway before us.

It was 9 p.m. when we pulled into Las Vegas and drove to the Nuova Immagine hotel and casino. It had been an older building, but Micah explained how his father sank millions into renovations and now the building was elegant and classy, and was turning a steady profit. We made our way through the casino, several men nodding as Micah passed, and I knew this must be a mob hot spot.

"Micah Gavarreen," he stated at the hotel desk. "I called this morning."

"Yes, sir," the young woman responded. "We've been expecting you. Please enjoy your stay," she said as she placed the room keys in his hand.

The elevator doors open and we stepped inside. I clutched Micah's arm as we began moving. He gave me a concerned look.

"I don't trust these things anymore."

"You have no idea how safe you are here," he smiled, kissing my forehead. "You might as well be staying at the White House for all the security we have."

"I'm afraid I haven't developed a 'safety' feeling around the mob yet—at least not with the experiences I've had."

"I don't blame you," he whispered, "but you are safe."

We stopped at the top floor and went down the hallway to our room. He unlocked the door and we stepped into the penthouse.

"Wow, look at the view," I marveled as I approached the wall of glass overlooking the bright lights of Vegas. "Do you come here much? I noticed a lot of people in the casino seemed to recognize you."

"Every once in a while, just to relax and gamble a little."

"Do the people downstairs know D'Angelo?" I didn't want this ending badly.

"D'Angelo doesn't come here. He's much too busy in Louisiana. Besides, these are friends of my dad, and Dad runs with a whole different caliber of people than the likes of D'Angelo."

"I thought—I mean from what you told me—D'Angelo was a friend of your personal family."

"He was at one time, but things changed between them and now they barely speak. You've got to be tired, Leese." He changed the subject. "Do you want me to have some food sent up and then we can go to bed?"

"I'm not tired or hungry, but bed sounds wonderful," I gave him a sexy smile.

He didn't seem to catch my drift at first, but then his eyes lit up.

"Oh… Shower first or second?" Before I could answer he took me in his arms and gave me a long, sensual kiss.

It was so wonderful to be spoiled by him.

Chapter Twenty-Nine

When morning came, we missed sunrise. We were just a little too comfortable to get up and see it. He rolled out of bed a little after eight and disappeared out into the main part of the penthouse, leaving me lounging. I didn't move until I heard a knock at our door. I heard Micah thanking someone and then he appeared in the bedroom doorway with a breakfast cart.

"I figured it was time to feed my baby—both of them."

"I'll come out there and eat at the table; just give me a couple minutes."

We would be meeting his family in a little while and I dressed carefully so that it wasn't immediately obvious we were expecting. I wanted a chance to explain what happened before we gave them the news about the newest member to the Gavarreen family. They had no grandchildren, so this should be a very happy moment for Celeste and Giorgio—that is as soon as they realized I wasn't a lunatic for leaving Micah.

Five minutes before ten, we were on the descent to what Micah called the 'private' floor. It was the floor reserved for Mafia and for his father to conduct business—I was petrified.

When we walked into the small room that looked like any other normal, business conference room, his family was already seated. The reaction as we came through the door holding each other's hand was like when the villain appears on stage in the theater. I could almost hear the boo-hiss roar from this tiny crowd with no more than the look in their eyes.

David was the first to speak, "I knew it. I told you he hooked back up with the little bitch."

I could feel myself recoiling at his angry reaction.

"Shut up, David," Micah stated and then pulled out a chair for me.

Giorgio was the only one who wasn't cutting me asunder with his stare. Celeste and Gwen both held me in utter revulsion by the expressions on their faces, but they said nothing. Gwen decided she wouldn't even look at me anymore as she turned her face and stared out the window.

"Annalisa needs to let you all know the real reason she left when—"

"I saw the reason in Colorado Springs," David snapped. "What's the matter, Angel? Did Ryan finally get some sense and throw you out?"

"Stop it, David," Micah growled.

Giorgio who normally ran the family meetings and kept David in check wasn't holding his sons back this morning.

"I…" But the words were wadding up in my throat as I wondered how he could be so in love with my mother, but not willing to give me a fair chance to defend my actions.

"Well, come on, baby cakes, spill out some good lies!" he snapped, his fist coming down on the conference table so hard that I jumped in fright.

Micah leaned across at lightning speed, latching an iron hold on David's throat with one hand and holding David's dominant hand down on the table with his other. "Don't do that again! She's expecting and I will not have you scare her when all she was doing was saving your ass!"

He had honestly caught David by surprise, but as soon as he turned him loose and righted himself, David let the bitter venom fly.

"Oh, is that what this is all about? She gets knocked up and now you think you're the papa? I wonder what *color* it's going to turn out to be."

I couldn't believe he said that. He was indicating Sadarius as the possible father, but it was the vulgar attitude with which he delivered the words that indicated his racism. Sadarius was a kind, honest and decent person and he didn't deserve to be drug through this, even if it was only by name.

"Micah is the father."

"Sure he is."

"I am," Micah said firmly, "I'm the only one—"

David gave a scathing laugh, "So how far along are you, Leese?"

"A little more than four months," I answered softly. This wasn't the way I wanted the meeting to go. The pregnancy was supposed to be the good news at the end of the bad, but now it was going to be the first battleground to be covered.

"So you mean to tell me," David sneered, turning to Micah, "that four months ago she links up with you after sleeping with who knows who, drops her pants and then vanishes and goes AWOL, again, only to turn up knocked up and ready to be a 'good girl?' You've got to be the stupidest son-of-a-bitch on the planet, Bro."

"She hasn't slept with anyone since she's been gone and she certainly didn't—"

David burst into caustic laughter as Gwen's head finally turned my direction. "That's an out-right lie. Unless you forgot about the bed."

"No, I didn't," Micah tried to state.

David leaned forward and locked his eyes on me, "I've got to admit it, girl, you must have something pretty good between your legs to spread 'em and have him coming running back to you like a—"

"I raped her!" Micah shouted back at his brother.

I didn't realize he brought the photos until they hit the table and I was scrambling to grab them before anyone could see. "NO MICAH!" I cried out as my hands reached, but David was faster. *"Why did you tell them?"* I sobbed. The room was deathly quiet. Even David appeared speechless as he picked up the pictures.

I turned my chair away from the table and buried my face in my hands, my shoulders convulsing from my tears, and feeling the pain of having them know the ugly truth.

Micah was on his knees in front of me telling me he was sorry. His arms wrapped around me, begging me to forgive the insensitive way he blurted it out. "I won't let them think anything less of you, Leese. You don't deserve ridicule for what I did. Can you tell them what happened at the Acqualina, or do you want me to do it?"

"Son," came Giorgio's deep base voice, "did you honestly do this to her?"

I looked at Micah and watched as the pain of having his father know his dirty deed crushed him. He had always been so careful to impress, but now he realized how deeply disappointed the voice from across the table was.

"Yes, Sir. I—"

"It wasn't his fault," I began as I turned the chair to look into their stunned faces.

"Leese," his father spoke, "you seem to always try to take the blame away from—"

"D'Angelo doped him up on steroids," I said quickly. I didn't know if Micah wanted that knowledge shared, but D'Angelo's name was going to come up in the worst possible context in a few moments anyway. They seemed too shocked for words.

"That's still no excuse," Micah began.

"You're right. You should go to jail," Gwen stated as she put the picture she was holding face down, unable to look at it anymore.

"I know that, Gwen," he admitted.

What about Ryan?" she finally asked, looking at me. "The two of you shared one bed in Georgia."

"If you'll give me a second to get myself together, I'll explain everything." Within a few breaths and a chance to dry my eyes, I began the long story of what happened the day I ran away, from the crazy elevator ride to D'Angelo's threats against the family, to flying to Georgia and not being able to sleep without Micah.

"So you see Ryan was only trying to help Micah and me. He knew what was at stake, for all of you, and he felt he had to help. I nearly ruined his life, but God had a plan the whole time. I just never expected it to be this hard."

"What about the steroids?" Giorgio asked.

Micah had been kneeling the whole time, supporting me as I told them what really happened and he finally stood. "He tracked me down at Remake and, the day I was going to try to win her back, we had lunch. I should have known better than to eat and drink what was already prepared, but I had—had other things on my mind. I knew something was wrong by the end of the meeting; my heart was racing and I kept breaking out in cold sweats. I drew some blood, but I didn't have time to have it tested before I chased after her. I never should have tried to see her feeling the way I did, and then when I got to her—I—I lost all sense of control."

For the first time, Celeste moved. She had been like a statue through this whole thing, but now she was up and at my side, "I pray you can forgive me for all the awful things I thought about you, Leese. I should have realized when Micah said something wasn't right in all of this that he knew what he was talking about. Can you forgive me?"

I went into her arms and sobbed my eyes out. I could feel hands resting on my shoulders and back, Giorgio and Gwen were there apologizing and consoling me. David stayed seated.

"We have to discuss what we're going to do about D'Angelo," came David's voice.

"Not with Leese in the room," Micah stated.

"But—" I looked up at him.

"I need to speak to Leese, privately," David interrupted. "Would you all leave us alone for a few minutes?"

Micah shot a worried look my direction, but I told him I would be fine. The family, somewhat reluctantly, left as David closed the door behind them.

He came over and pulled out the chair next to me and sat down, "I wish you'd done things differently, Leese. I know your reasons for not being able to go to Micah that day, and you're right, he would have tried to get to D'Angelo and they would have killed him, but you could have called me."

"I didn't think that was a good idea either," I said, mopping the last of the tears from my cheeks. "Mom's heart would have been broken if anything happened to you."

"I—I don't think I'm ever going to have enough time to tell you how sorry I am. I'm so bull-headed sometimes. Micah and your mom both tried to tell me there had to have been another reason. They both said you wouldn't do what you did without good cause, but I wouldn't listen. Micah was right; he told me you're very different from other people. I guess I just find it hard to believe that someone could be willing to sacrifice everything to save..." his words tangled in his throat and I watched this hard-core hit man's eyes mist over. He gathered the photos and was holding them until he handed them to me. "If you don't let him get his hands on these, your mother will never see them. I really think your mother should *never* see them."

"I'll destroy—"

"Please, forgive me for how I treated you," he interrupted and opened his arms.

I gladly accepted the invitation as he held me securely and then asked me something that blew me away.

"Can I—can I touch..." His eyes dropping to my waist.

I stood up, bringing him with me and then placed his hands on either side of my stomach. The baby was being still, but David was fascinated anyway as he felt the mound.

"Do you know what it is?" he asked.

"A little boy...Uncle David," I said, giving the first tiny laugh since this whole thing started.

He wrapped me in his arms, kissed my temple, and told me we were going to bring the others back in the room.

We'd made our peace.

Micah refused to allow me to remain in the room as his family discussed the D'Angelo issue. I argued for all I was worth, but even his family decided this matter should be between them.

Micah took me back up to the room and told me not to be surprised if this took a long time. He said not to hesitate to call for room service to send up anything I needed, but he would prefer (although he swore I was safe) that I didn't leave the room.

There were no reasons that could make me want to go wandering around with so many mobsters in the building. I was staying put.

Lunchtime came and went, and then suppertime came and went—I was starting to get worried, but I was going to follow directions. I crawled in bed and dozed in and out, thinking about Ryan's shirt that I still carried around with me. It and the awesome Pacific air were the only two things that helped me sleep in my four months of seclusion, but what would Micah think if he came in and found me asleep with it? It was eleven p.m. before I heard the door to the penthouse open. He looked like he'd been wrung completely out, emotionally, physically, and mentally. What had they discussed this long and why did he look so upset?

He crawled into the bed and kissed my forehead. "You should be asleep," he scolded.

"I needed my sleeping pill," I stated and then wrapped my arms around him. "Are you tired?" I whispered.

"Not too exhausted for you," he replied.

He was lying and I knew it.

I sat upright and straddled him, smiling and telling him it was his turn to relax. He was reluctant, but eventually obeyed as I had him roll onto his stomach and began massaging his knotted muscles. He moaned and enjoyed every stroke of my hands from the base of his neck all the way to his calves. Then I turned him over and began with the front. He wasn't expecting what I wanted tonight and at first he refused vehemently, but eventually he gave way to the new experience. He just kept repeating he didn't deserve me, and I kept showing him he did.

Chapter Thirty

Thursday night we pulled into Colorado Springs after a long day in the car. I paid for a year's lease for my house and I still had the key. I told Micah that we might as well stay there tonight and we would go see Ryan on Friday. What I hadn't expected was the reaction we both had when we walked through the living room to get to the bedroom; both of us pausing beside the couch and then looking at each other. The memory of the attack was so vivid for me that I could hear the sound of his hand slapping my face, I felt the painful bites, his grip on my throat, and the sound of his voice when he told Ryan it was 'his turn.' I shuddered without thought as Micah wrapped his arms around me.

"Maybe this was a bad idea," he whispered against my hair. "We could go to a motel tonight."

"No. It's just hard for me. I hate what happened here," my hand motioning to the place on the floor where he eventually took me, "but, I love what happened here," I said, placing his hand on my stomach. "Come on." I pulled him toward the bedroom. We didn't make love, but I fell asleep to the repeated sound of him whispering words of love in my ear.

I called Ryan mid-morning and told him I was in town and on the way over. I was surprised that Micah was anxious to see him, yet I could tell he was worried.

Ryan must have heard my sports car's engine, because he was out the front door as we pulled in. I told Micah to stay in the car until I had a chance to calm him down, because I knew he would be upset. I saw him duck down to look at the driver, but my windows were darkly tinted so he didn't get the first glimpse until I opened my car door.

What came out of his mouth didn't bear repeating in any way, shape, or form.

He was ready to go after Micah right then. I was trying to stop him as he grabbed me to move me out of the way. That was when I heard Micah's door open. All I kept thinking was I wasn't ready for him to get out of the car.

"Please, Ryan."

"Don't touch her," came Micah's warning.

"Get in the car, Micah," I commanded, still holding on to Ryan and blocking his path. "Please, Ryan, calm down. I want you to meet someone—someone else."

That stopped him. He was looking at me like I'd lost my mind as I took his hand and placed it against my soft flowing top. He jerked back like I'd shocked him.

"Ah, don't tell me—he got you—he got you pregnant when he raped you?"

"I have a whole lot to tell you, but I've got to know if you'll listen to me—please, Ryan. I'm going to have Micah leave for a little while so we can talk." He was still staring with angry eyes at Micah when I turned his chin toward me, *"Tell me now if I should leave or if you'll at least hear what I have to say."*

"Don't go," he choked out, "Please, don't go. I'll listen."

"Go back inside. I'll be there in a minute."

Reluctantly he turned and did as I asked. Now I had to get Micah to do the same.

"Go for a drive. I'll call you when he's ready to talk with you." The other reluctant party drove away.

I didn't think it would take quite so long to settle Ryan down, but he eventually began to understand why I was with the one person he felt I should hate instead of love. I explained about D'Angelo and the drugs, how horrible Micah felt about what he'd done, and what he'd learned by Ryan's photos.

"He was so hopped up on anabolic steroids and amphetamines that he barely remembered any of it. I knew I was pregnant several days before I left and I was planning to get away for a while and let you get on with your life, but then a package arrived."

"What kind of package?"

"It was an iPod with a note that appeared to be from Micah. I thought he was coming after me after what I read and what I heard."

"What was on it?"

"'*Breath*' by Breaking Benjamin," I said, watching Ryan's face as he mentally reviewed the words in his head. It was a band he liked and I knew he would remember the song. I saw the anger flush his skin as he understood why I ran. "He didn't send it to me—D'Angelo did to make it look like it was from Micah. He was trying to make sure I took off and the two of us never got back together—it almost worked. I nearly shot Micah when he showed up a few days ago."

His eyebrows went up, "You pulled a gun *on him*?"

"I wasn't going to take a chance of him hurting the baby. We eventually talked and I realized he never wanted to kill me—he was still in love with me."

"But why after all this time of keeping everything secret did you finally tell him the truth about why you left?"

I wasn't ready to blow all the progress he and I made by telling him Micah drugged me. I sighed deeply, "Can you, at least for now, just trust me that there were reasons beyond my control and the truth finally came out—*please, I beg you; don't push it*. Just trust me."

"You should know I trust you, baby girl—I may not trust him for a very long time, but I trust you."

"He wants to talk with you. Can you do that for me without an incident?"

He nodded; I called Micah and told him to return. Candace was due to come home and she actually made it before Micah. When she learned who brought me over, she flipped out worse than Ryan.

I met Micah at the car and told him to stay there for a few minutes.

"I actually wanted to speak to Ryan privately. Just ask him to come out and we'll go for a drive and you can talk with her."

I was trying to read the expression on Micah's face; something was wrong. I was starting to think the whole idea of stopping in Colorado Springs wasn't such a good thing. "Are you *sure* you're okay?" I asked before going back inside to get Ryan. He gave a weak smile and said yes.

Candace didn't want Ryan going anywhere with Micah, but he finally put his foot down and told her to listen to what I had to say and he'd be back in a little while. She watched him from the window as he opened the passenger's door, getting her first peek at Micah. When the door closed and my car literally sped away, she broke down crying.

"If he hurts him," she warned, "I'm gonna kill your husband, ex-husband, or whatever he is!"

"He won't hurt Ryan, I promise you. Please sit down and let me explain."

We talked for a long time and the longer we talked the deeper the conversation went. By the time we'd finished, I was all the way back to when I was hiding out in Pensacola and met Micah for the first time. Then I talked about meeting Ryan for the first time. The conversation went from the end to the beginning and then she wanted to go back through it from beginning to end. Man, that girl was thick headed.

"I just want to know what's taking them so long," she said, biting her nails and glancing constantly to the street.

"When they do return are you going to be able to handle me introducing you to Micah?"

"Yeah, yeah. I kind of want to meet him now, but I just find this whole mafia thing really creepy and I don't know if I'd ever completely trust someone who kills people for a living. I understand what you're saying about him being raised that way, but actually different on the inside, but I don't know," she said with a nervous flutter of her hands, "it's still creepy."

I had always seen Candace as being a very strong-willed, an almost rock-steady type of person, but when it came to Micah, she was a bundle of nerves. I think deep down she was worried because she knew Ryan had beaten the crap out of Micah and she figured he would be the kind of guy to retaliate in some way.

We both breathed a sigh of relief when my Aero pulled in close to 6 p.m. They had been gone nearly five hours. My cell phone rang and it was Ryan's number. He wanted to know if she was calm enough to bring Micah inside.

"Yeah, we're fine. Come on in," I replied.

Candace looked pale. She watched as Micah got out of the car and started for the front door. "Crap, he's big!" she stated. "I can't believe Ryan went after him."

"Andy and Ty helped, I'm sure," I added as they came through the door.

Both of them looked haggard, like they had done much more than talk. Candace went quickly to Ryan's side as I took Micah's hand and turned to her.

"Candace, I'd like you to meet, Micah—someone that I love very much." Reminding her I wanted this to go well.

She reached a trembling hand out and accepted his and then invited us to have a seat.

"Actually," Ryan spoke up, "it's getting kind of late and I know Leese missed lunch coming here so I was thinking we'd go down to the Bistro for a bite to eat."

I was pleasantly surprised and agreed immediately. The remainder of our evening was a little strained, but enjoyable. Candace seemed to be warming up to Micah by the time we finally said goodnight.

"So," Ryan asked, gripping my arm as we walked back to the house, "you're leaving out in the morning to start the trip home?"

"Yeah, Mom knows I'm coming, but I haven't told her all the news," I stated and then stopped walking. "Give me your hand," I said, pulling Ryan's palm toward my stomach. He gave a nervous glance to Micah and then allowed me to place it where the baby was pushing against. I watched the slow grin take over his face.

"That's freaking weird," he stated, "Candace, feel this."

She placed her hand where his had been and she looked kind of squeamish, "What does that feel like—I mean on the inside?"

"Pretty much like it does on the outside," I laughed, "Until he starts pushing on my bladder and then I have to go pee really bad."

Micah just stood by with a very thoughtful expression on his face. I took his hand and resumed the walk as he pulled me tightly to his side and kissed my temple. "I love you," he whispered, but I know Ryan and Candace both heard.

When we were ready to get into my car and leave, Ryan got emotional on me. He wrapped his arms around me and told me he loved me and that he'd always be there for me no matter what, "Be careful on the road and enjoy the trip home."

I kissed his cheek, and told him we would, but then he did something that completely left me speechless. He took my chin in hand and kissed me—on the lips—with Micah and Candace both standing there! Then he raised the car door and held my hand as I slipped mutely into the passenger's seat, "Bye, baby girl."

I looked out the window at Candace's surprised expression and I could tell she was getting ready to slug him as soon as they stepped into the house. Micah didn't even seem fazed as he started the car and pointed it toward my place. I was waiting for him to say something, anything, but he didn't so I finally spoke.

"What took you guys so long?"

"Do you realize how hard it is to convince someone that saw, first hand, what I did to you that I will never, ever do anything like that again?"

Okay, I understood his point, but I still felt he was hiding something and he evidently didn't want to discuss it anymore.

We left my place in Colorado for the last time early the next morning. I hide the key outside and figured, since I had five months left on the lease, I'd tell Ryan where I'd left it and he could offer it to Andy and Ty for the remainder of the time. They were a little wild, but I knew they wouldn't tear the place up. Naomi would get a little break from her boys as a thank you for all the good food she had prepared for Ryan and me.

I called Mom and told her I was coming home with a couple surprises and I would see her in a week or so. Micah said he wanted the return trip home to be slow. He turned the car south and we headed down into New Mexico. The scenery where we were traveling wasn't all that spectacular (except for my view as I stared at Micah), but it contained a lot of open road so we could take advantage of a little unchecked speed. Micah didn't do it much, but I could see the grin working the edges of his lips at one point when he got it up to one-ninety and then backed down.

"How hard have you pushed it?" he asked, the smile getting broader over my responsive little piece of machinery.

"They have a 250 mph club, but I'm not in it," I laughed, watching the big smile on his face. "I stopped at 242, but I was out of runway."

That killed the smile.

"You need to sell the car, Leese," he was suddenly serious.

"I love this car," I defended, "I can kick anybody's—"

"Leese—it's two passenger."

"So? It's perfect for us."

"Where are we going to put the baby seat?"

"My Aston Martin is still sitting in Mom's garage."

"You still need to sell this thing. It's a little too much temptation and you might get hurt or worse."

I rested my hand on his arm, "Micah, I can handle it."

"Not pregnant. Even I shouldn't have done what I just did—not with you in the car. The problem is that it's just too damn enticing to push the pedal down."

"I'm keeping the car," I replied stubbornly, but I didn't want to totally be hard-headed about it. "Maybe it'll sit in the garage and all I'll do is look at it, but I don't want to sell it."

He frowned, but the discussion ended.

He found us a beautiful hotel near Carlsbad with awesome views of the grand vista that stretched before us. We enjoyed a good dinner and a fabulous night together, but he told me we needed some sleep because we were going to get up very early the next morning. Before dawn we drove up to a special place and watched as the millions of bats darken the pre-dawn sky to return to the safety of the caves.

We traveled to San Antonio and he pulled into the Fairmount hotel, where, to my surprise, he had already reserved the Presidential suite for us. He was being sneaky, but this was a good kind of sneaky. He also reserved us a private dining area at Biga on The Banks. I told him if he kept up this kind of romance, I was going to expect it all the time. He smiled softly, gave me a breathless kiss and replied, for the time we had together, I *should* expect this from him.

I liked the idea of constant romance, but I didn't like the way he stated it. It was almost as if he was telling me there was a limit to our time together. That brought up the subject I'd been wanting to discuss, which was what did his family decide to do over the D'Angelo issue? He refused to discuss it with me, and once again he was putting it off. He said there would be a time when it would come up, but for now he simply wanted us to get a little bit of the honeymoon we had been denied so long ago. I couldn't, and wouldn't, argue about that.

The next day he said the drive would be a little bit longer, but he had a surprise for me at the end of the day that he thought I would like extremely well. The problem was the closer we came to the destination the more upset I became. He was driving into Louisiana.

The chances of someone seeing him and reporting to D'Angelo about who he had with him increased a hundred-fold.

Tearfully, I begged for him not to stop the car anywhere in this state unless it was just to fill the tank, and I didn't even want to do that. He promised me D'Angelo would never know we were here. I was unconvinced. We were coming in from the west side of the state so I wasn't familiar with the roads, but eventually he turned down a driveway to the left and I suddenly knew where we were.

"But, you sold it," I said, fresh tears forming in my eyes.

"I bought it back. Mom's been getting it ready for us so we could spend a night or two here." He glanced over at me to watch my reaction as the beautiful plantation style home came into view.

I was hit with so many emotions and absolutely overcome with memories, "Oh, Micah—thank you. I love it, but are you completely sure he won't know we were here?"

He pulled the car around to the back and parked in the exact place he parked the Trans Am so long ago. He leaned over and took me in his arms and said we were totally safe.

The interior had changed a little. Evidently the previous owners didn't keep all his furniture. But his bedroom was the same, as was the guest bedroom. The emotional level when he laid me down in his bed was as high as our wedding night. Sensual overflowed and I had never loved him more than holding him against my body in this house. We stayed for two heart-pounding nights and then, when it was time to restart our journey, he backtracked to get to 51 and headed north, taking a long route around to completely avoid New Orleans. He explained that my car would be enough of a red flag. If word got to D'Angelo that a Shelby Ultimate Aero had come through the city, things would change quickly.

We made our next stop in Pensacola at Bev and Matt's house. I told them they were sworn to secrecy because Mom had no idea about Micah or the baby and that we had to stay out of the press as long as possible. They were ecstatic to see us, but they were concerned over what they heard about our lives since the wedding. I told them we were apart for a little while, but what mattered was we were together again and very happy.

I wasn't sure if I should call Jewels. With everything that had been in the news about me and Ryan, I didn't know if she'd even speak to me. I decided to give it a try and to my pleasant surprise she was thrilled to hear from me. We talked for a long time over the phone about all that had happened in both our lives. She wanted to know how Ryan and I were getting along. I explained that he and I had never been more than good friends, but he finally found someone and was living in Colorado. She said she found someone, too. Brent Rushford, whom she had dated off and on since ninth grade, asked her to marry him. They had only been engaged for a week, but she was already planning the wedding.

We were leaving out in the morning, but I told her I would love to see her, even if it was only for a few minutes.

"How about the school parking lot? That was where we spent most of our time anyway," she giggled.

"All right, but you've got to promise me one thing; no loud music. I don't need Officer Martin to catch us trespassing because I'm trying desperately to stay out of the news."

"Who's with you? Is it that guy from Remake?" she asked with a little squeal.

"You'll see in the morning," I laughed. "Can you get there early, like 7:15? I want to be out of there before all the students start arriving."

"I'll do one better; I'll be there at seven."

Seven a.m. I watched a little white Kia turn into the lot. We had parked just inside the gate and she was drawn like a magnet to the sports car. I was leaning against the hood as she parked.

"OMG! I love your hair! I almost didn't recognize you!"

"That's the idea," I laughed.

"That is a freaking awesome car…" She started to say as she ran to embrace me, but as soon as she threw her arms around me, she discovered my secret.

"Holy crap! You're—you're pregnant?"

The car was suddenly forgotten.

"Would you like to meet the father?" I said, tapping on the driver's window to let Micah know it was okay to step out of his dark hiding place.

He raised the door and started to get out, but she practically knocked him over to hug him.

"I guess this means you approve," Micah laughed, picking her up off the ground as he hugged her back.

"Lord, yes," she blubbered out. She was crying and saying she hoped all along the two of us would end up back together. "You guys were like perfectly matched. When I heard you'd split up, I was *so* pissed at Ryan."

"It wasn't his fault, but the important thing is we're together and our son is due in September."

We spent a few more precious minutes together, but I knew the other cars would be filing in and we didn't need any exposure in Pensacola. We shared a couple more hugs, begged her to keep things quiet, and then we drove away.

Micah wanted to know if I wanted one more hotel stay to break-up the twelve hour drive to Palm Beach, but I was ready to see my family. I called Mom and told her we would see her around eight or nine p.m. The strange thing for me was that Micah's emotional state as we grew closer seemed to lower, almost to the point of depression. I asked him if he was okay, but he just kept saying that Palm Beach held a lot of good and bad memories for him. I knew he was right, and it broke my heart all over again to think about what he went through when I vanished only days after our wedding.

When he and I came through the door, Mom honestly looked like she could faint. Micah was instantly at her side to keep her from hitting the floor. She simply couldn't believe it. Kimmy was happy, but I think she was expecting Micah all along anyway.

After Kimmy went to bed, the three of us sat up and the whole story came out from D'Angelo at the Acqualina to our reunion in California (minus the brutality of the attack and the Ecstasy at the cottage). And as for the baby (which, thank God she was sitting down when we dropped that bomb-shell on her), I just told her he'd come to see me a little more than four months ago and when we parted ways I was pregnant. I told her about what D'Angelo did to make me think Micah had slipped a mental cog, causing me to run again. And, how it all worked out when he found me.

"Well, I hope you are out of the mob again because this marriage has had a rough enough start. Things are going to need to calm down by the time September rolls around and my—I can't believe I'm saying this—my grandson arrives. I don't feel old enough to be a grandmother," she said with a little nervous laugh.

I looked at Micah's face and that same strange expression that had been getting stronger from just before he met with Ryan reappeared. He was starting to worry me, but he insisted he was fine and that I needed to concentrate on the baby and nothing else.

I lay in my own bed that night with him beside me as I babbled on about house hunting and baby names, and how I really wanted a big bowl of hot peach cobbler with lots of vanilla ice cream, and chocolate syrup, and nuts and whip cream and…

He finally started laughing at me.

That was good because I didn't want any more of his serious side to suck away our happiness. "Do you think we can find any place tonight that has peach cobbler?" I asked.

"Baby, it's almost midnight—no, I don't think so. You know you haven't asked me how much I weighed when I was born."

I gave him a funny look, "Why?"

"Because the baby usually follows the father's genes in size."

"So—how much did you weigh?"

"Ten pounds, five ounces," he said, looking at me with a crooked smile, "If you aren't careful, honey, this baby might be as big as I was."

His unpleasant thought was putting a damper on my midnight snack ideas.

Chapter Thirty-One

The next morning, I begged him to go to the store and buy peach cobbler with all the trimmings. I had this insatiable need to eat peaches and it wasn't going to go away until I got what I wanted. He happily agreed, but did ask if I wanted a can of sardines included with my order. I wrinkled my nose and said definitely not.

"But if you can find some good barbecued ribs this time of the morning, I'd like those." I was serious.

He was laughing.

When he came home, he wasn't smiling. He set the bags of groceries on the kitchen counter and then pulled out a magazine and handed it to me.

"It just came out this morning," he said quietly.

The cover was a picture of me with an obvious baby bump, taken apparently at some point when we were either going into or coming out of the restaurant in San Antonio. It was only a shot of me, but surrounding me were three pictures, Micah, Ryan, and Sadarius with question marks over all of them asking "Who's Your Daddy?" That really pissed me off and for once, I was ready to call my attorney and tell him to go after them—they had gone too far.

I read the article and it didn't say specifically I was at the restaurant with Micah, I guess because they wanted to build the suspense for the next issue, but with D'Angelo looking for anything to pop up this could possibly start him investigating. He wouldn't have to go far to get someone in San Antonio to remember the kind of guy that accompanied me to dinner.

I was in tears, but Micah told me he had it under control. We were still safe as far as he was concerned. I wasn't convinced, but he begged me to forget it, at least for today. He baked the frozen cobbler and piled all the items on top, and I finally found my smile as he helped me eat it. He didn't care for the chocolate syrup over the whole thing, but he said it wasn't bad, just different.

He had ribs delivered for lunch and I was in food heaven. It was even better than the cinnamon bun, because he decided to suck the barbeque sauce off my fingers and that took more time than icing. It didn't take long before we were excusing ourselves from lunch and heading for the bedroom. He scooped me up before we reached the door and growled softly as he buried his face into my neck. It was going to be a stellar afternoon.

I didn't come back out for the rest of the evening, but Micah did go downstairs once to bring me another bowl of cobbler. We finished the night with Micah treating me to one of his wonderful, pampering showers and then it was back to bed where he told me, very tearfully, that he thanked God for giving him another opportunity to be with me.

"We've been through hell and back, Annalisa, but it's all been worth it to be right here, right now in your arms. I love you with more strength than I possess in my body," He kissed me with a passion that was different from what he'd ever exposed.

I was trying to come up with an equal response to how I felt about him, when he slid down in the bed and told me he was going to talk to the baby for a little while. I laughed, even though I knew he was serious, but it was still funny to listen to him speaking to my stomach. I had already insisted the baby's first name would be Micah, but Micah senior wasn't quite convinced yet, so he simply called him 'little guy.'

He kissed and caressed my stomach and told our son how very much he loved him and that he wanted only the best for him. "And you've got a great start," he continued, "because you've got the best mother in the whole world. She's smart and beautiful, and sexy and—"

"Micah, I don't think sexy is what we want our son to tell other kids about his mother," I playfully scolded.

"You're right," he said sliding up in the bed and staring into my eyes, "I should be telling you that…but at the moment I think I'd rather show how I feel about you."

What a wonderful experience every night with him could turn out to be. I was exhausted by the time we finally slept and I didn't wake until after nine the next morning. Breakfast was beside the bed, but Micah left a note saying he had to go out.

I carried the tray downstairs and found Mom and Kimmy planning a big shopping adventure for today. They had been bitten by the 'baby bug' and they were going to spend the day putting together a huge layette. Mom wanted to purchase everything from diapers to outfits, to blankets and crib sets.

"I just need to know if you're planning on bottle or breast feeding."

"What is breast feeding?" Kimmy asked.

I looked at Mom and laughed. "I'm going to breast feed the baby, but since you brought it up, you get to explain it," I said, ruffling Kimmy's hair as she followed Mom out the door.

By one o'clock, I was starting to worry about Micah's whereabouts. I tried his cell phone several times, but it kept going to voice mail. I heard a vehicle pulling in around two and I was relieved that he was home, but as I went to the front door and peered out, I realized it wasn't Micah. I hesitated at the open door, wondering if I should close it in case this was a reporter, but when the car door opened I was shocked to see Ryan step out onto the driveway with a large envelope under his arm.

"I don't believe it." I said meeting him halfway and embracing him.

"Hey, baby girl," he held me tightly for a long time.

"Where's Candace?" I asked, pulling away from him and looking around to see if she was in his car.

"Colorado," he answered softly.

"What are you doing here? Just visiting your mom or…" That was when I began to pay attention to his expression. He seemed sad and reserved which could only mean one thing. "What happened? Did you two—did you break up?" I knew he shouldn't have planted that kiss on me with her watching.

"No. Annalisa, we've got to talk. I've got to tell you something and—well, it isn't going to be easy to say. Can we go inside?"

I'd never seen him this way and he was starting to frighten me. I eyed the envelope suspiciously, "Sure, come on in." My heart was starting to flutter over his mysterious reason for showing up at my house. I took him to the living room, talking as I went, "I'm home alone. Mom and Kimmy went shopping and then they're picking up dinner. I hope you can stay and join us." Everything is normal I kept repeating in my head; this is nothing bad. "Micah should be home pretty soon, but to tell you the truth I don't have any idea where he went today. I can't get him to—"

Ryan's expression became pained and his eyes were filling with tears, "Sit down, baby girl, that's why I'm here."

It was like my blood pressure bottomed out when I heard those words. I was suddenly weak and I couldn't stand as he gripped my shoulders and slowed my descent to the couch, "Wha—what do you mean?"

"Micah called me this morning."

"Why would he call you?" My emotions rose mid-throat and locked in place. My tears welled over my lower lids and I knew something terrible was coming, "What's this about? *Ryan, please, please—don't let this be something bad.*"

"Leese, when the two of you came to see me, Micah and I left for a while because he needed my help with something. He told me he was going to call me the day he went after D'Angelo."

"No—no, he didn't—he wouldn't have," I was starting to shake as I began to cry.

"He said he'd let me know when it was almost over," Ryan's tears had started to slide down his cheeks. "I was on the plane here when I got the second call, he's there now."

I covered my face with my hands and wept. The mob wouldn't forgive his actions this time.

"He took me to an attorney's office. He wanted me to be a witness to his will," he said as he removed the envelope from under his arm, "and he wanted me to have his bank account information—for you."

"Shut up, Ryan! You're lying—if he did that then he was planning on... Tell me you're lying," I said, gripping his shirt in a feeble grasp, *"Please... Tell me you're lying."*

"I wish I was, baby girl. He wanted me to be the one to break this to you because he said you'd never let him go if you knew what he was doing. He said I was the only person he would trust to watch over you—and the baby. He doesn't want you leaving Florida and trying to find him."

I was so weak that I swayed as I stood from the couch, "Do you really think you can keep me from going to him?" I threatened.

"Yeah—I'm sorry, but I can."

I started to push my way around him, but the attempt was pitiful. He gripped my shoulders, but he was wide open as I jerked my knee up to try to hit his groin. He must have known I'd try using force because he moved his hips backward as my knee glanced off the front of his jeans.

"Aaah!" I screamed, my hands dropping to my right side. I felt the muscle spasm as soon as I made the rapid movement. My sobbing began as he put me back on the couch.

"Shit, Annalisa, don't do stuff like that! Are you okay? What hurts?"

"My side," I whimpered. It would have been a great ploy to catch him off guard if it hadn't been the truth. I crumbled into his arms. I wasn't going anywhere and I knew it. I had no idea where Micah was at, so flying to Louisiana was a moot point. "They're going to kill him, Ryan. I didn't realize last night would really be my last night with him. Would you pray with me, please? I can't lose him, not now, not like this… *Please help me*," I begged.

He clasped my hands as we bowed our heads and the prayers began going up for Micah Gavarreen.

Chapter Thirty-Two

Micah walked calmly into D'Angelo's office, surprising the young lady at the desk because she hadn't been told that he was coming in.

"Shhh," he whispered with a soft smile, his finger to his lips.

That threw her off for a moment. For one thing, she'd never seen him smile.

He came around the desk beside her as she gathered her wits and tried to get to the intercom button, but he was too fast. The rag was over her face and before the inhaled breath filled her lungs for the scream, she was out cold. Micah laid her down on the floor and then quietly placed her chair underneath the door knob to D'Angelo's conference room. He'd seen the cars in the parking lot and he knew he wasn't alone. He pulled out the real appointment book that he knew was kept inside the desk away from prying eyes, and laid it on top of the fake one that was sitting out.

"Damn it," he whispered.

Two other capos were meeting with D'Angelo. Most likely, they were discussing all the reorganization made necessary when Micah and David brought in the drug lords from South America. That and the people here in the States that needed replacing since he'd had Micah going around privately killing them off.

Micah couldn't kill the other Capos with any justifiable reason, although the mob would see little to no reason for the death of D'Angelo. His family knew what he was doing and they had plans to meet after he finished D'Angelo and approach the Boss, requesting clemency for his actions.

It was a long shot and Micah recalled telling Ryan that he would be lucky if he had a one percent chance of surviving the Bosses judgment. But it was the only option his family agreed he had. They wanted him to go before the Boss without D'Angelo's blood on his hands, but Micah refused. D'Angelo was too vindictive and cunning to remain alive. Micah knew he'd been secretly working with another family and, in the event of possibly escaping before the Boss got to him, he knew D'Angelo would simply change sides; a very bad thing to happen since he knew the inner working of this family so well.

With the door to the conference room secured, he pulled the iPod from his pocket and carefully hooked it into the phone system. There was no other exit from the conference room and for a few terrified moments, D'Angelo would know who and what was waiting for him beyond the door. He hit the button for the music to start and drew his guns.

The sound of electric guitars filled the room as '*Breath*,' by Breaking Benjamin began to pound through the intercom system. Every speaker in the office was pouring out the warning that D'Angelo had sent to Annalisa. He deserved the terror he tried to inflict on the only person Micah would willingly lay down his life for. Annalisa was the only thought on his mind as he watched the door being kicked from the inside as the men worked to break out of the room.

He was ready, and he knew the coward would be the last to come out, hoping the bullets would be spent on the men before him.

Micah smiled.

He was no such amateur. Even if D'Angelo used the other men for a shield, Micah could shoot a fly off a man's head leaving only a part through his hair. D'Angelo was about to pay for everything he'd ever done to make Micah into a monster. Now it was the monster's turn to destroy the man who had been his master.

The door splintered, the chair was knocked away and the shooting gallery opened up. As he guessed, D'Angelo was trying to escape by cowering behind one of the other Capo's, his head and chest well hidden, so Micah simply took him out at the knee. D'Angelo hit the floor cursing and screeching as the other Capos ran from the building.

He normally was so swift that the person never knew what happened, but Micah would delay his bullets for an instant as he stood over D'Angelo. "You hurt the wrong person this time—and now you're going to pay for what you put her through. You want to know the funny thing? Annalisa would have sent mercy. I'm only sending this." It was over in an instant as the Glock went off and D'Angelo went limp.

He pressed the release and let both clips drop to the floor. Micah laid down his guns and dialed his father. "It's done," he breathed. "I don't know if we'll have time for things to go as planned—he was meeting with two other capos and they just ran out of here. No, Sir, I didn't."

He stepped outside with his hands away from his body to make sure anyone who might be waiting could see he was unarmed. He got to his car without incident and drove to where his family was waiting. They were on their way to meet with the Boss, but word had already spread. Giorgio's phone rang within five minutes; the Underboss wanting to know if it was true; had his son killed D'Angelo?

"Yes, and we are on our way to let him plead his case before the Boss. Tell him to expect us within the hour. No, he's not armed—none of us are. Yes, you have my word." The phone was closed and they continued to what would most likely be the end of Micah's life.

Chapter Thirty-Three

When Mom came through the door, she had to do a double take to make sure she was seeing things correctly as I sat curled up in Ryan's arms on the couch.

She asked Kimmy to take the packages for the baby upstairs as I explained to her what was going on. When Kimmy returned, we told her that Micah needed our prayers and we continued our vigil. Exhaustion from crying and praying and hoping hit me hard by ten p.m. Ryan coaxed me into eating a little food, but I just didn't feel like I could consume more than a few bites.

"You need to go lay down. Come on, baby girl, you're going to bed."

Mom showed obvious reluctance to let him take me to my room, but I told her there wasn't anything to worry about and I needed him to stay with me tonight, "It's not what you think, Mom. Micah understood. That's why he sent him."

We lay down in my bed as he begged me to close my eyes and try to rest. He curled his body behind mine and I knew I needed sleep; the baby was restless from all the stress I was under. I willed my eyes shut as Ryan massaged my back, gently rubbed my pulled muscle and kissed my neck.

Somewhere in my pain, I drifted into sleep. As far as I knew, I was safe in Micah's arms and the baby finally settled down.

When I woke it was dawn and I was dreaming that Micah was sitting beside the bed staring at me. Those beautiful green eyes, filled with love and happiness, studied me carefully. I reached out my hand to the dream and felt his steel grip as he took my fingers to his lips and kissed them.

"Micah!" I said sitting up too quickly and curling back down in pain.

"Annalisa, what's wrong?" came his words of deep concern. Suddenly his arm was scooping up under my head lifting me gently to bring me closer to him.

Ryan moaned and rolled away from me.

This was real? They were both here? Suddenly I felt overcome as I tried to wrap my arms around his neck, but the pain in my side wouldn't allow it.

Ryan's eyes must have fluttered open and all I heard him say was, "Freaking Angels!"

"No," I cried out, "but he is to me."

"What's wrong, Annalisa?" Micah repeated.

"I pulled a muscle trying to knee Ryan in the groin," I spilled out. "Thank God, you're alive. We prayed for hours and hours. Are you okay? Is the mob coming after you?"

"No, baby—we're safe."

Ryan was sitting up on the other side of me trying desperately to get the sleepy fog to lift from his brain, "I didn't—we were only—I was just helping her get some rest."

"I know," Micah said with a light laugh, "Thank you for taking care of her. Was she much trouble?"

Ryan's head wobbled, "If she hadn't pulled that muscle, I think she'd of taken me down. So what the hell happened? You otta be fish food by now, dude."

I smacked him and then winced again.

"My family took me before the Boss and I explained my reasons for what I'd done. I told him about the dirty dealings D'Angelo had been up to, and that I had been assisting him." Micah swallowed as the tears rose to the surface. "I told him when I found out what he'd done to you, I realized I didn't have to be his puppet—I had a reason to live, but he would have never let us get back together."

"And the Boss understood?" I said, trying to slowly right myself without jerking the muscle.

"No, I wish. He said if it was up to him he would blow me away himself for all I'd done to undermine the family, but..."

"What? Tell me Micah," I pleaded.

"Someone else thought my deeds should be forgivable. The Boss had a call from someone higher than him, the Capo Dei Capi out of New York, said I was to be left alone. A soldier is considered untouchable unless his capo and Boss agree to take him out, but this time my untouchable status came from a higher authority—and I don't know why." He swallowed as he leaned forward and kissed me softly. "I know leaving you like I did was unforgivable, but I—"

"Micah, you fixed that."

His head cocked slightly sideways.

"The only thing unforgivable would have been for you to not be here right now. I love you, baby—trust me everything is forgiven and I'm praying that your pardon by whoever the big Boss is in New York means no more jobs, no more hits, no more…"

He looked a little upset as I rolled off the list.

"Don't tell me he made you stay in the mob?" I said, back to the verge of tears.

"No, but my Boss said I've got to help clean up the mess I've created with D'Angelo. It's not going to be easy and…" He looked toward Ryan, "A good friend may have to get you through a few rough places, but we'll make it eventually."

"So does this mean I've gotta move back to Palm Beach?" Ryan seemed a little flustered, but the fact that I could tell he was serious warmed my heart.

"You're never more than a few flight hours away. I think it's safe to say you can go back to Candace. And tell her I owe her big time—like payment big time."

"No, no," Ryan stated as he crawled out of the bed. "You two just be happy and safe, and *that* will be payment enough for us. And try," he said looking at Micah, "to give her enough time to have this baby before you call me again 'cause, Dude, she can't kick my ass until she is baby free."

"I think I can handle that request," Micah smiled.

"Four and a half months without danger?" I said raising an eyebrow. "That sounds like a vacation."

Micah pulled me securely into his arms and gave me a breathless kiss.

I knew we wouldn't have an ordinary married life until this was all behind us, but, for right now, it was normal enough to make me happy.

ABOUT THE AUTHOR

Lindsay lives on the west coast of Florida. She is married and has three children. Although she holds a degree in technology, writing full-time (someday) is her dream job. She enjoys dabbling in different genres, but always comes back to writing romance.

Heart of the Diamond – Published
The Substitute (short erotic story) - Published
Kingdom Hill – Coming Soon
Untouchable Trilogy
Untouchable – Book 1 – Published
Unforgivable – Book 2 – Published
Untraceable – Book 3 – Coming Soon

PREVIEW

UNTRACEABLE

Fast Forward

The Aero was moving at tremendous speed, like the wind from a hurricane, as it wove around cars and trucks. No one who lived in the area had any doubts about the beautiful blonde behind the wheel. She was a Palm Beach native and excessively famous. She wore a perpetual smile when she was in the driver's seat of that car, and who could blame her? If you could afford a half million dollar vehicle, you'd be smiling, too.

A stretch of open interstate appeared and the Aero shot forward like its previous speed had been a Sunday drive. The interstate cameras clicked off shots, but the car was moving so fast that it wasn't much more than a blur on the computer screen. The car quickly came up behind the next group of vehicles that appeared to be standing still when approached upon so rapidly. Fast lane, center lane, fast lane, center to far right lane, and back to the fast lane and she was around the grouping with barely a break in speed.

One more vacant stretch of interstate was one more chance to let the car prove that what was under its hood was superior to anything that had ever burned across this driver-cursed, multi-laned menace known as I-95. The radar detector was silent as the speed climbed well into the triple digits.

Suddenly, the driver's front tire exploded into fine shrapnel and the car began its violent tumble through the air; over and over as pieces of it flew hundreds of feet. Seventeen revolutions and it smashed into a stand of trees in the median. Good Samaritans were pulling over and running toward the wreckage, but they would never reach the trapped driver in time as a tremendous explosion went up like a fireball from the splitting of an atom. It was too late to save her and all that was left to do was to watch in horror as the car became an unrecognizable, molten mass.

Photographers and reporters somehow managed to arrive on the scene even before the emergency crews and state troopers. The troopers dispatched someone immediately to her home before the news broke. There was only one Aero in Palm Beach and locating her family wasn't going to be difficult, but telling them about the young, expectant mother's last moments would be.

356

Made in the USA
Lexington, KY
23 August 2012